BETRAYAL OF TRUST

BETRAYAL
OF
TRUST

J. A. JANCE

DOUBLEDAY LARGE PRINT HOME LIBRARY EDITION

WILLIAM MORROW
An Imprint of HarperCollinsPublishers

This Large Print Book carries the
Seal of Approval of N.A.V.H.

For Rebekah Kowalski Ming
and Joan Hoyt
Thank you

BETRAYAL OF TRUST

CHAPTER 1

I was sitting on the window seat of our penthouse unit in Belltown Terrace when Mel came back from her run. Dripping with sweat, she nodded briefly on her way to the shower and left me in peace with my coffee cup and the online version of the *New York Times* crossword. Since it was Monday, I finished it within minutes and turned my attention to the spectacular Olympic Mountains view to the west.

It was June. After months of mostly gray days, summer had come early to western Washington. Often the hot weather holds off until after drowning out the Fourth of July fireworks. Not this year. It was only mid-June, and the on-line weather report said it might get all the way to the mid-eighties by late afternoon.

People in other parts of the country might laugh at the idea of mid-eighties temperatures clocking in as a heat wave, but in Seattle, where the humidity is high and AC units are few, a long June afternoon of sun can be sweltering, especially since the sun doesn't disappear from the sky until close to 10:00 P.M.

I remember those long miserable hot summer nights when I was a kid, when my mother—a single mother—and I lived in a second-story one-bedroom apartment in a blue-collar Seattle neighborhood called Ballard. We didn't have AC and there was a bakery on the floor below us. Having a bakery and all those ovens running was great in the winter, but in the summer not so much. I would lie there on the couch in the living room, sleepless and miserable, hoping for a tiny breath of breeze to waft in through our lace curtains. It wasn't until I was in high school and earning my own money by working as an usher in a local theater that I managed to give my mom a pair of fans for Mother's Day—one for her and one for me. (At least I didn't give her a baseball glove.)

I refilled my coffee cup and poured one for Mel. She grew up as an army brat. Evidently the base housing hot water heaters were often less than optimal. As a result she takes some of the fastest showers known to man. She collected her coffee from the kitchen and was back in the living room before the coffee came close to reaching drinking temperature. Wearing a silky robe that left nothing to the imagination and with a towel wrapped around her wet hair, she curled up at the opposite end of the window seat and joined me in examining the busy shipping traffic crisscrossing Elliott Bay.

A grain ship was slowly pulling away from the massive terminal at the bottom of Queen Anne Hill. Two ferries, one going and one coming, made their lumbering way to and from Bremerton or Bainbridge Island. They were large ships, but from our perch twenty-two stories up, they seemed like tiny toy boats. Over near West Seattle, a collection of barges was being assembled in advance of heading off to Alaska. Nearer at hand, a many-decked cruise ship had docked overnight, spilling a myriad of shopping-intent cruise enthusiasts into our Denny Regrade neighborhood.

"How was your run?" I asked.

"Hot and crowded," Mel said. "Myrtle Edwards Park was teeming with runners off the cruise ships. I don't like running in crowds. That's why I don't do marathons."

I had another reason for not doing marathons—two of them, actually—my knees. Mel runs. I walk, or as she says, I "saunter." Really, it's more limping than anything else. I finally broke down and had surgery to remove my heel spurs, but then my knees went south. It's hell getting old. I talked to Dr. Bliss, my GP, about the situation with my knees.

"Yes," he said, "you'll need knee replacement surgery eventually, but we're not there yet."

Obviously he was using the royal "we," because if it was his knee situation instead of mine, I'm sure "we'd" have had it done by now.

I glanced at my watch. "We need to leave in about twenty, if we're going to make it across the water before traffic stops up."

Since we were sitting looking out at an expanse of water, it would be easy to think that's the water I meant when I spoke to Mel, but it wasn't. In Seattle, that term refers to several different bodies of water, depending on where you are at the time and where you're going. In this case we were looking at Elliott Bay, which happens to be our water view, but we work on the other side of Lake Washington, in this instance, the "traffic" water in question. People who live on Lake Washington or on Lake Sammamish would have an entirely different take on the matter when they used the same two words. Context is everything.

"Okeydokey," Mel said, hopping off the window seat. "Another refill?" she asked.

I gave her my coffee mug. She took it, went to the kitchen, filled it, and came back. She handed me the cup and gave me a quick kiss in the process. "I started a new pot for our travelers," she said, then added, "Back in a flash."

I had showered and dressed while she was out, not that I needed to. There are two full baths as well as a powder room in our unit. When I married Mel, rather than share mine, she took over the guest bath and made it her own, complete with all the mysterious vials of makeup and moisturizers she deems necessary to keep herself presentable. I happen to think Mel is more than presentable without any of that stuff, but I've gathered enough wisdom over the years to realize that my opinion on some subjects is neither requested nor appreciated.

So we split the bathrooms. As long as we share the bed in my room, I don't have a problem with that. Occasionally I find myself wondering about my first marriage to Karen, who is now deceased. Most of the time we were married, we had two bathrooms—one for us and one for the kids. Would our lives have been smoother if Karen and I had been able to have separate bathrooms as well?

No, wait. Denial is a wonderful thing, and I'm going to call myself on it. Despite my pretense to the contrary, the warfare that occurred in Karen's and my bathroom usually had nothing to do with the bathroom itself. Karen was a drama queen and I was a jerk, for starters. Yes, we did battle over changing the toilet paper rolls and leaving the toilet seat up and hanging panty hose on the shower curtain rod and leaving clots of toothpaste in the single sink, but those were merely symptoms of what was really wrong with our marriage—namely, my drinking and my working too much. All the squabbling in our bathroom—the only real private place in the house—was generally about those underlying issues rather than the ones we claimed we were fighting about.

For years, Karen and I never showed up at the kitchen table for breakfast without having spent the better part of an hour railing at each other first. I'm sure those constant verbal battles were very hard on our kids, and I regret them to this day. But I have to tell you that the pleasant calmness that prevails in my life with Mel Soames is nothing short of a dream come true.

Don't let the different last names fool you. Mel is my third wife. She didn't take my name, and I didn't take hers. As for the single day Anne Corley's and my marriage lasted? She didn't take my name, either, so I'm two for one in the wives-keeping-their-own-names department. Karen evidently didn't mind changing names at all—she took mine, and later, when she married Dave Livingston, her second husband, she took his name as well. So much for the high and low points of J. P. Beaumont's checkered romantic past.

When the coffeepot—an engineering marvel straight out of Starbucks—beeped quietly to let me know it was done, I went out to the kitchen and poured most of the pot into our two hefty stainless-steel traveling mugs. This is Seattle. We don't go anywhere or do anything without sufficient amounts of coffee plugged into the system.

I was just tightening the lid on the second one when Mel appeared in the doorway looking blond and wonderful. Maybe the makeup did make a tiny bit of difference, but I can tell you she's a whole lot better-looking than any other homicide cop I ever met.

On our commute, she drives. Fast. It's best for all concerned if I settle back in the passenger seat of my Mercedes S-550, drink my coffee, and do my best to refrain from backseat driving. One of these days Mel is going to get a hefty speeding ticket that she won't be able to talk her way out of. When that happens, I expect it will finally slow her down. Until that time, however, I'm staying out of it.

And don't let all this talk about making coffee fool you. Mel is no wizard in the kitchen, and neither am I. We mostly survive on takeout or by going out to eat. We have several preferred restaurants on our list of morning dining establishments once we get through the potential bottleneck that is the I-90 Bridge.

The people who planned the bridges in Seattle—both the 520 and the I-90—were betting that the traffic patterns of the fifties and sixties would prevail—that people would drive into the city from the suburbs in the mornings and back home at night. So the lanes that were built into the I-90 bridges have express lanes that are westbound in the morning and eastbound in the afternoon. Except there are almost as many people working in the burbs now as there are in the city, and "wrong-way" commuters like Mel and me, on our way to the east side of Lake Washington to the offices of the Attorney General's Special Homicide Investigation Team, pay the commuting price for those long-ago decisions every day.

If we make it through in good order, we can go to the Pancake Corral in Bellevue or to Li'l Jon's in Eastgate for a decent sit-down breakfast. Otherwise we're stuck with Egg McMuffins at our desks. You don't have to guess which of those options I prefer. So we head out a good hour and fifteen minutes earlier than we would need to without stopping for breakfast. Getting across the lake early usually makes for lighter traffic—unless there's an accident. Then all bets are off. A successful outcome is also impacted by weather—too much rain or wind or even too much sun can all prove hazardous to the morning commute.

That Monday morning we were golden—no accidents, no stop-and-go traffic. By the time the sun came peeking up over the Cascades in the distance, we were tucked into a cozy booth in Li'l Jon's ordering breakfast. And more coffee. Because our office is across the freeway and only about six blocks away from the restaurant, we were able to take our time. Mel had pancakes. She's a runner. She can afford the carbs. I had a single egg over easy with one slice of whole-wheat toast.

We arrived at the Special Homicide Investigation Team's east side office at five minutes to nine. We don't have to punch a time clock. When we're on a case, we sometimes work extraordinarily long hours. When we're not on a case, we work on the honor system.

For the record, I do know that the unfortunate acronym for Special Homicide Investigation Team is S.H.I.T., an oversight some bumbling bureaucrat didn't understand until it was too late to do anything about it. In the world of state government—and probably in the federal government as well—once the stationery is printed, no departmental name is going to get changed because the resulting acronym turns out to be bad news. S.L.U.T. (the South Lake Union Transit) is another unfortunate local case in point.

But for all of us who actually work for Special Homicide, the jokes about S.H.I.T. are almost as tired as any little-kid knock-knock joke that comes to mind, and they're equally unwelcome. Yes, we laugh courteously when people think they're really clever by mentioning that we "work for S.H.I.T.," but I can assure you, what we do here at Special Homicide is not a joke. And neither is our boss, Harry Ignatius Ball—Harry I.

Ball, as those of us who know and love him like to call him.

Special Homicide is actually divided into three units. Squad A works out of the state capital down in Olympia. They handle everything from Olympia south to the Oregon border. Squad B, our unit, is in Bellevue, but we work everything from Tacoma north to the Canadian border, while Squad C, based in Spokane, covers most things on the far side of the mountains. These divisions aren't chiseled in granite. We work for Ross Connors. As the Washington State Attorney General, he is the state's chief law enforcement officer. We work at his pleasure and direction. We work where Ross Connors says and when Ross Connors says. He's a tough boss but a good one. When things go haywire, as they sometimes do, he isn't the kind of guy who leaves his people blowing in the wind. That sort of loyalty inspires loyalty, and Ross gives as good as he gets.

That morning Mel and I both managed to survive the terminal boredom of the weekly staff-meeting ritual. After that, we returned to our separate cubicle-size offices, where we were continuing work on cross-referencing the state's many missing persons reports with unidentified homicides in all other jurisdictions. It was cold-case work, long on frustration, short on triumphs, and even more boring most of the time than staff meetings.

When Squad B's secretary/office manager, Barbara Galvin, poked her head into our tiny offices and announced that Mel and I had been summoned to Harry's office, it was a real footrace to see who got there first.

Harry is a Luddite. He has a computer on his desk. He does not use it. Ross Connors has made sure that all his people have the latest and greatest in electronic communications gear, but he doesn't use that, either. It's only in the last few months that he's finally accepted the necessity of carrying a cell phone and actually turning it on. He and Ross Connors are really birds of a feather in that regard—they're both anti-geeks at heart. Occasionally we'll receive an e-mail with Harry's name on it, but that's because he has dictated his message to Barbara, who dutifully types it at the approximate speed of sound and then presses the send button. The same goes for electronic messages that come our way from Ross Connors's e-mail account. His secretary, Katie Dunn, sends out those missives.

In our unit, Barbara Galvin and Harry I. Ball are the ultimate odd couple in terms of working together. Harry is now, and always has been, an exceptional cop who was kicked out of the Bellingham Police Department due to a terminal lack of political correctness that survived several employer-mandated courses in sensitivity training. He would have been stranded without a job if Ross Connors, no PC guy himself, hadn't taken pity on him and hired him as Squad B's supervisor.

Barbara Galvin is easily young enough to be Harry's daughter. Her body shows evidence of plenty of piercings, but she comes to work with a single diamond stud in her left nostril. I suspect that her clothing conceals any number of tattoos, but none of those show at work.

She's a blazingly fast typist who keeps only a single photo of her now ten-year-old son on an otherwise fastidiously clean desk. She manages the office with a cheerful efficiency that is nothing short of astonishing. She prods at Harry when he needs prodding and laughs both with him and at him. When I've had occasion to visit other S.H.I.T. offices, I've also seen how Squads A and C live. With Harry and Barbara in charge, those of us in Squad B have a way better deal.

When Mel and I walked into Harry's office he was studying an e-mail that Barbara had no doubt retrieved from his account, printed, and brought to him.

"Have a chair," he said, stripping off a pair of drugstore reading glasses.

Since there was only one visitor's chair in the room, I let Mel have that one. When Harry looked up and saw I was still standing, he bellowed, "Hey, Barbara. Can you round up another chair? Who the hell keeps stealing mine?"

Without a word, Barbara brought another office chair to the doorway and then rolled it expertly across the room so it came to a stop directly in front of me.

"Sit," Harry ordered, glaring at me.

I sat.

Harry picked up the piece of paper again and returned the reading glasses to the bridge of his nose.

"I don't like this much, you know," he said.

Mel and I exchanged looks. Her single raised eyebrow spoke volumes, as in "What's he talking about?"

"I'm not sure why it is that you're always Ross's go-to guy, but you are," Harry grumbled, sending another glower in my direction. "This time the attorney general wants both of you in Olympia for the next while. It's all very hush-hush. He didn't say what he wants you to do while you're there, or how long he wants you to stay. He says you should 'pack to stay for several days,' and you should 'each bring a vehicle,' which leads me to believe that you won't necessarily be working together. You're booked into the Red Lion there in Olympia."

"I'm assuming from that we probably won't be staying in the honeymoon suite?" I asked.

"I would assume not," Harry agreed glumly. "Now get the hell out of here. Time's a-wastin'."

CHAPTER 2

Since we hadn't packed to go to the office, and since we hadn't brought both cars, we had to go back home to throw some clothing into suitcases and pick up Mel's Porsche Cayman. Driving into Seattle, though, we were able to be a two-person carpool in the right direction for a change. Way to go!

Packing took no time at all. We have no kids at home and no pets, either—not even a goldfish. That meant that all we had to do was turn off the lights and lock the door. Simple. Trouble-free.

Then we headed south, caravanning on I-5 with Mel in the lead.

It's a little over sixty miles from downtown Seattle to downtown Olympia. Driving directions say the trip should take a little over an hour. It actually took an hour and a half due to a semi that jackknifed for no apparent reason on a perfectly dry, straight highway just south of Fort Lewis. Driving alone gave me time to think about what Harry had said about my connection to Ross Connors. He was right. I was and am Ross Connors's "go-to guy" for more reasons than Harry I. Ball knows.

Ross and I have dealt with similar tragedies. Anne Corley, my second wife, chose suicide by cop, although that was long enough ago that the term wasn't in common usage at the time. Ross's wife, Francine, was carrying on a torrid affair with the husband of a friend. In the process she let slip some information on a supposedly protected witness with fatal results for said witness. When Francine realized that the jig was up and we were coming for her, she went out into their backyard with a handgun and blew her brains out.

Ross and I had also had our difficulties with booze before those tragedies struck, and we both had to get a lot worse before we got better. Ralph Ames, who was once Anne Corley's attorney and who is now my friend, helped get me into treatment. When Ross finally came to me for help, I did the same thing for him by personally escorting him into his first AA meeting.

People who venture into AA are given a sponsor—someone you can call in the middle of the night when the temptation to drink is too great and you need a human voice to talk you down out of the trees. My longtime AA sponsor is Lars Jenssen, a retired ninety-something halibut fisherman who became my stepgrandfather by virtue of marrying my widowed grandmother, Beverly Piedmont. He was my sponsor before he married my grandmother and he remains my sponsor to this day, even though, in the aftermath of my grandmother's death, he took up with another widow, Iris Rasmussen, from Queen

Anne Gardens, a Seattle-area retirement home, where the two of them are evidently scandalizing all concerned by openly living in sin.

But I digress. Ross wanted me to be his sponsor. I know from personal experience that having a sponsor who's more than an hour away is a bad idea, so I found him a group and a sponsor in Olympia. That was the part Harry knew nothing about. Mel knew because she had been privy to some of the phone conversations when Ross called me looking for help, and I know for a fact that Mel can be trusted to keep her mouth shut.

Ross must have understood that, too, I theorized, or he wouldn't have asked Harry to send both of us, but I couldn't imagine why. What was going on that Ross couldn't afford to hand the case off to his Squad A home team?

It had to have something to do with politics. Ross is a political animal. He's won reelection to the position of attorney general over and over, usually by wide margins. The last election, after the scandal with Francine, he won again, but that one was a squeaker. He had hinted to me that after this four-year term, he most likely wouldn't run again. Those weren't words that made me feel all warm and fuzzy. S.H.I.T. has Ross's own particular stamp on it, and I couldn't really see myself—or any of us—working for someone else with the same kind of personal loyalty that we all give willingly to Ross Connors.

Whatever this case was, it was also big enough to bring people down.

Harry called while I was still stuck in the traffic jam waiting for the wreckage of the semi to be towed off the freeway.

"Ross says to meet him in the coffee shop of the hotel," Harry said. "What's the matter? Doesn't that 'dreaded Red' have a bar? Or maybe their coffee shop serves booze."

I knew that Ross and Harry had done some drinking together in the old days, but in this instance I played dumb.

"I'm sure you can get anything you want in the coffee shop," I assured him. "Maybe he missed lunch."

"Right," Harry said sarcastically. "Whatever." He hung up.

If you've been in any Red Lion Hotel in the continental United States, you know the drill. There used to be huge wooden carvings on the walls of the lobby and the restaurant. Whenever I saw them, I imagined some crazed woodcarver living off in the woods somewhere, cutting out those gigantic pieces and then warehousing them so there would be a ready supply waiting when it came time to open a new hotel. But things change, and time has taken its toll. Now the Olympia Red Lion lobby is cream and butter-yellow and stone. The crazed carver has probably hung up his chain saw and moved to Palm Springs, where he plays golf every day.

Mel had beaten me to the registration desk. When I walked up to ask for my room key, the desk clerk couldn't help but give me a knowing leer.

"Ms. Soames has already arrived, Mr. Beaumont," he said. "Your room charge is already paid, and she left a credit card to cover incidentals. Would you care to leave a card to cover your own?"

I was wearing my wedding ring, and I'm sure Mel was wearing hers. Her credit card charges and mine were all one account, but I didn't bother explaining that or the last-name situation to the clerk. He was a young guy, somewhere in his late twenties, who seemed astonished by the idea that someone of my advanced age—older than dirt in the clerk's eyes—could possibly be about to get lucky. I wanted to tell him, "Listen up, turkey. I already *am* lucky," but I didn't. Leaving him to arrive at his own erroneous and dirty-minded conclusions, I took my room key and left.

Mel was upstairs in our room and totally unpacked by the time I got there. I told you she drives fast. Like her speedy showers, the unpacking part came from growing up as a military dependent. Every time her family was shipped to a new base, suitcases were unpacked immediately. With clothing in the drawers and closets, it was easier to feel settled faster. She had appropriated the room's only decent chair and was working on her laptop.

"You took long enough," she said.

"Harry called," I told her. "We're supposed to meet up with Ross in the coffee shop right about now."

"I know," Mel said. "I got a call, too, but there's still no hint about what this is all about?"

"None," I said.

"Most likely politics as usual," she said.

"That would be my guess."

Even though I would have been happy to leave my crap in my roll-aboard, I allowed myself to be influenced by peer pressure. I unpacked and put my underwear and socks in an unoccupied dresser drawer. I hung up my extra slacks and clean shirts, still covered with the dry cleaner's plastic wrapping. I'm waiting for the day when someone decides that there has to be an extra charge for putting plastic around your freshly laundered shirts. It hasn't happened so far, probably only because no one has noticed.

"You should check your e-mail," Mel said, peering at her computer screen.

"Why? Something new from Barbara Galvin? Or is that nice Nigerian widow wanting to send me money again?"

My kids, Scott and Kelly, had been pretty much out of my life for years. When their mother died of cancer, we started trying to reconnect, an effort that was helped immeasurably by Dave Livingston, Karen's widowed second husband and my kids' caring stepfather. Kelly, her husband, Jeff Cartwright, and my two grandkids live in Ashland, Oregon. Scott and his wife, Cherisse, live in the Bay Area. For a long time we communicated back and forth by e-mail. Now my generation-X progeny mostly send me text messages or e-mail. Other than work-related messages, most of the other new mail in my e-mail account turns out to be spam.

Mel grinned at me and shook her head. "I was scanning down the junk mail in your spam folder. There's something in there with a subject line that says 'Beaumont, Texas.'"

The room phone rang just then. Mel picked it up. "Okay," she said after a moment's pause. "We'll be right down."

"Ross?" I asked.

She nodded.

"Just move that message to my newmail folder," I told her. "I'll read it later. Right now we'd better go see what the boss has in mind."

"And why he'd rather meet with us here instead of having us stop by his office, which, in my opinion, is a hell of a lot nicer than any hotel coffee shop, and a lot more private, too."

I was glad to know I wasn't the only one who had been wondering about that.

We found Ross in the coffee shop downstairs. It was still early enough that the room was mostly empty. The attorney general, with a cup and saucer in front of him, was seated in a booth in the far corner of the room under a huge oil painting that depicted a salmon heading upstream to a most likely unhappy end. From the morose look on Ross's usually cheerful countenance, the painting seemed like an apt reflection of the AG's current mood.

As a general rule, when I'm in public places I don't like sitting with my back to the door. Neither does Mel. We both want to be able to see who is coming in and going out, just in case. In this

instance, Ross had already appropriated the door-facing seat in the booth.
Mel solved the problem by slipping into
the booth next to our boss and letting
me have the other side of the booth to
myself.

"Your room is all right?" he asked.

"The room's fine," Mel assured him.

A waitress showed up, order pad at
the ready. "They'll have coffee," Ross
said, without bothering to ask our opinion. "Bring us one of those big pots.
When we're ready to order lunch, I'll let
you know."

Nodding, the waitress went away.
She was back a minute or so later with
an insulated carafe of coffee.

"Cream and sugar?" she asked, pouring into the cups in front of us.

"Black," Mel and I answered together.

"Okay," she said, and went away,
leaving us alone.

The moment she was gone, Ross
reached into his pocket. He pulled out
an iPhone, tinkered with it for a moment, and then set it in front of Mel. "I
need you to watch this video *before*

anyone else comes into the dining room," he said.

Mel watched. The sound was turned off. There was no way to tell what was happening on the tiny screen, but from watching the subtle shifts in Mel's features—the tightening of the muscles on her jawbone, the sudden iciness in her eyes, the paleness of her cheeks—I knew whatever it was wasn't good.

When the video ended, she turned on Ross. "Is this real?" she demanded.

He nodded. "I think so."

Without another word, Mel punched what must have been the replay button and pushed the phone over to me. There was a girl on the screen. She looked to be fourteen or fifteen, maybe, straight teeth, dark wavy hair, a blue scarf tied around her neck. She smiled for the camera—a nice smile; a shy smile—as though she was a little nervous about being there. Then two disembodied hands appeared on the screen. Each hand grasped one end of the scarf, and they began to pull. For a moment the girl was docile, as though this was something she expected and might even have welcomed. I had heard of the choking game before. I realized this wasn't a game about the same time the girl did. She began to claw at the scarf and try to loosen its hold on her neck. She surged to her feet, struggling. The camera's focus moved with her, staying on her face, keeping the bodies and faces that belonged to the hands pulling on the scarf safely out of the camera's view.

I watched it all the way to the end. When it was over, I knew the girl was dead. I also understood why Ross hadn't ordered any food. I felt as sick to my stomach as Mel Soames looked.

"Snuff film," I said, unnecessarily. "Who is she?"

Ross shook his head. "No idea who she is or where she's from."

"But there are three people involved in the homicide," Mel said. "Two guys pulling the scarf and one guy running the camera."

"Right," Ross said. "Three."

"So if you don't know who she is or where she's from, how come this is our case?" I asked.

Ross looked uncomfortable as he collected the iPhone and stuffed it back into his pocket.

"Governor Longmire brought it over to my office and dropped it off earlier this morning," he said. "It's the governor's husband's grandson's phone. He's fifteen."

"Do you think he's involved?" Mel asked.

Ross shook his head. "No way of knowing. His name is Josh Deeson. The kid could be one of the hands pulling the ends of the scarf or he could be the guy with the camera. It's also possible that he's entirely innocent. His mother, the governor's stepdaughter, is deceased. From what I can tell, she was pretty much of a loser who overdosed on meth two years ago. The father was declared unfit, and the courts awarded custody to the boy's maternal grandfather, Gerard Willis, who happens to be married to Governor Longmire and who also happens to have undergone quadruple bypass surgery just last week."

"I remember reading something about the governor's husband going in for surgery, but I don't recall anything about his daughter's death being drug-related."

"There are still a few things that aren't fit to print—if you have enough pull, that is," Ross said. "The version of the daughter's death that went out to the media was that she died of an accidental overdose. The custody hearing was conducted behind closed doors, and those documents are sealed. From what I've been able to learn so far, Josh has been living in the governor's mansion since before the custody arrangement was finalized. Sounds like he's got 'issues.'

"Governor Longmire and her husband are giving the kid a roof over his head—a very nice roof, by the way; food to eat; clothing to wear; a cell phone; a computer. In return, he's been giving them fits by ditching school, getting into fights, and sneaking out at night. That's how the phone ended up in Governor Longmire's possession this morning. The governor's security detail saw him letting himself out, using the old rope-ladder trick to climb down from the upper stories. He managed to give them the slip, but they called in a report. Governor Longmire confiscated the rope ladder and was waiting for Josh when he came back to the house early this morning. As punishment, she confiscated his iPhone. Once she turned it on and saw the film, she called me."

With noon approaching, several groups of people had come into the restaurant. For a time the hostess managed to keep our booth separated from other diners. As the place filled, however, that was no longer possible. Two people in the latest group of four nodded in Ross's direction. He was an official with a statewide office and a reputation to go with it. Naturally people recognized him.

He removed the phone from his pocket and handed it to Mel. "You might want to put that in your purse," he told her. Then, to both of us, he said, "No more names, by the way—aliases only when in public. Little Jack Horner is at school today, with one of Old Mother Hubbard's bodyguards along as an enforcer."

"Why school?" Mel asked. "Isn't it summer vacation?"

"Summer school," Ross said. "Supposedly making up classes he flunked. She'd like to see you about two o'clock."

"In her office?"

"At home," Ross said. "You know how to find it?"

"My GPS knows how to find it," Mel said confidently.

"What about the kid's computer?" I asked. "That might have a lot more information than his phone."

Ross nodded. "So I understand," he said. "I told Old Mother that you'd pick it up when you stop by this afternoon. For starters, I'd like you to take it to Todd and let him make a copy of whatever's there."

Todd was Todd Hatcher. He is an electronics wunderkind who also has a Ph.D. in economics. He had come to Ross Connors's attention when he did a study on the high cost of geriatric prison care. Todd's interest in the subject had grown out of his own experience. His father, a convicted bank robber in Arizona, had been sentenced to life in prison. When the father began exhibiting symptoms of Alzheimer's, he was paroled to the care of his wife, a waitress, who exhausted her life savings and her life trying to care for her ailing husband. Todd's doctoral committee at the University of Washington had dismissed Todd's study out of hand. When Ross Connors heard about it, not only had he stepped in to rescue Todd's Ph.D. aspirations, he had also taken Todd on as an occasional consultant whose computer hacking skills went beyond his publicly recognized skills as a forensic economist.

But there was also a subtle warning here for Mel and me. There are some pretty savvy computer experts working for the Washington State Patrol Crime Lab. I couldn't help but wonder why Connors was using a private consultant to examine Josh Deeson's computer. Probably the same reason Mel and I were on the job.

"Search warrants?" Mel asked.

"Got 'em," Ross said. He patted the pocket of his jacket and pulled out a packet of documents, which he handed over to Mel. "That covers Jack Horner's computer, his iPhone, and his room. It's Old Mother Hubbard's house. She bought the computer with her credit card and she's the one who pays for Little Jack Horner's Internet connection. Legally, since she's the one providing his room, she could voluntarily give us access to that and to his computer as well, but just in case the kid is actually involved in a homicide here, we're better off with properly drawn warrants."

"Works for me," I said. "Warrants are always better than no warrants."

"Does Grandfather Time know about any of this?" Mel asked, inventing a suitable alias for Gerard Willis on the spot.

"Not so far," Ross replied. "There's some concern that being given upsetting news right now might interfere with his recovery."

Ross's answer to that question went a long way to explain all the secrecy.

"And why us?" Mel asked. "Why Beau and me?"

"That's easy. Old Mother Hubbard asked for Beau in particular," Ross said, nodding in my direction. "She says the two of you go back a long way."

Mel gave me a quizzical look.

"We were in high school together," I said.

"Oh," Mel responded cheerfully. "That certainly explains it."

There are probably a lot of married men out there who instantly understood that when Mel said that, she meant the exact opposite—that what I had said explained nothing. We would need to have a much more detailed conversation on the subject, but the lack of privacy in the Red Lion coffee shop precluded my providing a detailed explanation of my connections to Governor Old Mother Hubbard.

"Exactly," Ross said, missing the sarcasm entirely. "When she asked for J.P., I told her the two of you were a matched set—that you work well together." He stopped long enough to glance at his watch, a doorknob-size Rolex. I could see the hands from across the table. It was half past noon.

"Are you hungry?" Ross asked. "Your appointment at her house is scheduled for two. If you'd like, there's plenty of time to grab a sandwich before you go. It's on me."

That wasn't entirely true. It wasn't on him nearly as much as it was on his expense account, which meant the tax-payers were the ones paying the freight.

Mel pushed aside her coffee cup, stood up, and then collected her purse. "No, thank you," she said. "After seeing what we saw on that phone, I seem to have lost my appetite."

I stood up, too.

"Same goes for me," I said. "We'll give you a call when we find out more about this oddball collection of nursery rhymes."

CHAPTER 3

Mel and I did not go straight out to the parking lot. Without exchanging a word but by mutual agreement we turned left, got on the elevator, and rode up to our room. It wasn't until the door clicked closed that she asked the question I knew was coming.

"How come I had no idea you knew Governor Longmire?" she asked.

"I didn't," I said. "And I still don't."

"But Ross just said . . ."

"I knew her in high school, Mel," I said. "High school! Do you have any idea how long ago that is? Back then she was Marsha Gray. She was one of the cool kids. I was not. In fact, back in those days, she didn't see fit to give me the time of day. And believe me, other than seeing the woman on the news occasionally, I haven't seen her since, either."

"So you didn't like date or anything?" Mel asked.

"No," I said gruffly. "Not at all!"

Some people recall their high school experiences through an idyllic haze that makes them seem like heaven itself. Not me. Grade school and high school were hell. My mother certainly wasn't the only single mother in the world back then. In the aftermath of World War II, there were plenty of war widows raising kids alone. The problem was, my mother wasn't a widow since she and my father never married in the first place. He was a sailor stationed at Bremerton. They had just gotten engaged when he died in a motorcycle accident on his way back to the base. My mother was pregnant. Her parents were horrified. Her father kicked her out and wouldn't have anything to do with us.

I never knew my father's real name. My mother told me that my last name came from my father's hometown, Beaumont, Texas. I have no idea if she ever made any attempt to contact my father's people. Maybe she did, and maybe given the time and the circumstances, they didn't want to have anything to do with us, either.

I had told Mel that story, and she had asked me why, after my mother's death, I had made no effort to contact them on my own. Mutual disinterest, I suppose. Besides, I couldn't shake the feeling that any attempt on my part to contact them would have been disloyal to my mother's memory. She had fed us and sheltered us with money she earned working as a seamstress. But her sewing was also part of what made my childhood and adolescence difficult. She made most of my shirts, and that embarrassed the hell out of me. I wanted to look like the other kids—the cool kids—the ones with shirts from JCPenney's or Sears or even Frederick & Nelson.

Whenever I think about my mother, I

can't help but be ashamed by how I felt back then. And that's the other reason I've never gone looking for my father's relatives. My father wasn't there for me. My father's family wasn't there for me, either. My mother was. I figure I owe her that much loyalty and respect.

I didn't give Mel the benefit of any of that background information, at least not right then.

I said, "When we were in high school, as far as Marsha and her pals were concerned, I was a joke—a laughing-stock."

"So why did she ask for you now?"

"No idea," I said. "None. In fact, if you get a chance, why don't you ask her?"

While we spoke, Mel had booted up her computer. She sent a copy of the video clip to her iPhone and a second copy of the file to her laptop.

"Ready to watch it again?" she asked.

"Yes," I said. "We'd better."

It's one thing to go to a crime scene after the fact. You view the body. You examine the surroundings. You look for clues. Although this wasn't the first snuff film I had ever seen, this was certainly the youngest victim.

I'm not sure who first coined the expression "choking game" to apply to this monstrosity. Probably the same kind of language experts who invented the words "suicide by cop." Right. That cleans it up. Makes what happens a little more presentable. But, as I said before, this was no game—a game would have ended before the girl was dead. This was straight-up strangulation and cold-blooded murder. The fact that the victim seemed to be a willing participant to begin with made it that much worse. And the fact that the killers had come prepared to film the event made it despicable.

But Mel and I needed to watch it, and we did so, several times, before leaving for the governor's mansion forty-five minutes later. We watched the girl's tentative last smile. We watched for anything about her clothing that might be distinctive. She seemed to be wearing a red sleeveless tank top of some kind. As she lurched to her feet, late in the assault, we caught a glimpse of what

might have been lettering on the shirt—
a logo of some kind—before the camera refocused on her face.

The scarf was blue and made of some
kind of gauzy material—a scarf made
for decoration rather than warmth. We
studied the hands on the ends of
the scarf. They were clearly not a pair.
They were different skin tones, one
whiter and one much darker, but not
black. Hispanic, maybe? And one of
them was definitely wearing a ring of
some kind and the other one was wearing a watch. I knew that a careful com-
puter-aided analysis of the frames containing the ring and the watch might
provide important clues in identifying
our suspects. First, though, we needed
to identify our victim. In order to do that,
we would need some pre-strangulation
"still" photographs that we could send
out to both the media and to other
agencies.

I glanced at my own watch. "It's time,"
I said. "Let's go see Old Mother Hubbard."

Mel was right. The GPS knew exactly
how to get to the governor's mansion.

Lush greenery and immaculately maintained lawns surrounded the stately three-story brick house. With dormers across the top and a spacious balcony opening off the second level, it might have been designed by some of the same people who built the mansions in the Highlands, an upscale development north of Seattle and home to some of the city's most prosperous founding fathers.

As I recalled my Washington State history, the guy who should have been the first person to occupy the Olympia governor's mansion ended up taking sick and dying elsewhere without ever living there. The mansion had fallen on hard times and had been renovated sometime back in the 1970s or '80s. And I seemed to remember their having a recent problem with rats—the four-legged variety, although I imagine plenty of two-legged ones had prowled the premises on occasion, Josh Deeson being a current candidate for Chief Rat-in-Residence.

Mel is a relative newcomer to the Evergreen State. On our way to the governor's mansion I filled in the empty airtime by giving Mel as much background as I could on both the building itself and some of the governors who had inhabited it. This recitation of trivia served two purposes. It kept Mel from asking me more questions about our current governor. It also kept me from jabbering about her, but I realized it was only a stopgap measure. I might have stifled Mel Soames's questions for the time being, but they wouldn't be stopped forever.

We parked out front and walked up to the porch together. We showed our IDs to the uniformed Washington State Patrol officer standing next to the door. He nodded us past, and Mel rang the bell. I expected a maid of some kind would answer the door. Instead, the governor herself stood there. She was dressed casually in a pair of jeans and a purple-and-gold U-Dub sweatshirt. She looked tired and careworn, not at all like her public persona.

Without acknowledging Mel's presence, Marsha Gray Longmire focused all of her attention on me. "Beau?" the governor asked. "Is it really you?"

I nodded. "Yup," I said. "At your service."

She seemed to recognize me on sight, although I couldn't imagine that I still resembled the callow youth I had been in high school. And I saw no sign of the scrawny girl formerly known as Marsha Gray in this formidable but clearly troubled woman.

With a small moan, Marsha Longmire muscled her way around Mel and fell weeping on my shoulder.

"I didn't know what to do," she said in a rush. "I'm so glad you're here. I couldn't bear to talk about this with a complete stranger."

Mel gave me a searching look—one that said, "So what am I, chopped liver?"

Before Mel had a chance to say anything, however, the governor seemed to get a grip. Taking a deep breath, she squared her shoulders, pulled away from me, and turned to Mel.

"Please forgive that outburst," she said, managing to put her public mask on over her private hurt. "You must be Agent Soames. Ross told me about you. Do come in, but if you don't mind, I'll visit with you in my study rather than taking you into the living room. It's more private in there."

I understood what the word "private" meant in that instance. There was a convalescing patient somewhere in the house, and Marsha Longmire didn't want her husband to overhear a word of what we'd be discussing.

After the heat outside, the interior of the house was comfortably cool. Marsha took us into a small office that was just to the left of the front door. Two walls were full of tall bookshelves, loaded with what appeared to be leather-bound volumes—a decorator statement, most likely, rather than books that had ever been read. There was a magnificent but apparently little-used desk at the base of one wall of shelves. There was a seating area in front of the desk made up of four worn leather chairs around a coffee table. Depending on the season, the focus of the seating area could be either a gracious window that overlooked the front of the manicured grounds or a gas-log fireplace on the opposite wall. Currently the window was in vogue.

Marsha directed us to the seating area. Before taking a seat herself, she plucked a box of tissues from the corner of the desk and placed it on the coffee table in front of her.

"Have you seen it?" she asked.

Mel and I didn't have to ask what "it" meant. We both knew.

"Yes," I said. "We've both watched the clip several times."

Marsha Longmire's eyes looked haunted. "I've never seen anything like it," she said. "At first I thought it was just a game, but it's not. It wasn't."

"No, ma'am," Mel agreed. "It wasn't a game."

"And the girl is really dead?"

"So it would appear," Mel replied. "We can't be certain, of course."

Tears welled up again. Marsha took a ragged breath. "She had such a nice smile. I'm going to be seeing that smile in nightmares for the rest of my life. You have to find out who did this, even if . . ." She stopped cold because she was thinking the unthinkable—that somehow one of the hands pulling the deadly scarf tight around an unsuspecting little girl's neck belonged to her husband's beloved grandson.

Marsha seemed to focus on Mel now rather than on me. "How do you do it?" Marsha asked. "How can you stand to deal with all those dead people?"

"Someone has to," Mel answered. "Someone has to look out for the victims. Sometimes we're all they have."

Marsha nodded. "That's what Ross said, too, but I can't believe that Josh would be involved in something like this. The idea that he'd even have the image—" She broke off and then shivered. "It's chilling. I can't take it in. But if he wasn't involved somehow, why would someone send it to him?"

There's a time for brusque questions, and there's a time for gentle conversation. This was the latter, and Mel is better at doing that than anyone I know.

"First off, Madam Governor—" she began.

"Please, call me Marsha," the governor interrupted. "I'm not feeling very much like a governor today."

"First off, Marsha," Mel began again, "there's no way to tell how old the film is. We may discover that it's something that has been out there on the Internet for a long time."

"You mean like on YouTube or something? Do they have sites like that?"

"Unfortunately, yes," Mel answered. "Lots of them. More than you can imagine."

"So maybe it didn't happen here—in Washington, I mean," she said.

That was a bit of light in a very dark tunnel. Marsha Longmire grabbed at that straw for all it was worth.

"That's what we'll hope," Mel said. "What time does your grandson come home from school?"

"My husband's grandson," Marsha said.

Marsha had obviously been shocked and shaken by what she had seen on the iPhone, and she was suffering because of it. Up to that moment, the one when she deftly distanced herself from her grandson, I had let myself be carried along by a wave of sympathy for her. Just then, though, I caught a glimpse of the teenager who, along with her fat-cat pals, had found it so easy to torment a gawky poor kid from downtown Ballard who had the unmitigated nerve to inhabit the same universe. And behind the gleeful expression on the mocking teenager's face from long ago and the pained one on this woman's face, I could see Marsha Longmire for what she was—a tough-minded politician. Josh Deeson might live in her home, but if he was involved in some kind of sordid mess that might dim Governor Longmire's chances for reelection, the kid was about to be thrown under the bus.

As they say, blood is thicker than water, and Josh's connection to Marsha Longmire had apparently just turned into H_2O. I wondered if he would have been treated the same way if he were an actual blood relation. In fact, given the public scandal that was bound to ensue, I wasn't so sure Gerard Willis, the First Husband himself, would manage to make the cut.

Strike one for Governor Longmire. In her book being a politician came first; wife and mother were a distant second.

When I turned back to the conversation at hand, I found that Mel had continued the interview without me.

"But you didn't recognize the girl when you saw her."

Governor Longmire shook her head. "No, I didn't."

"And as far as you know, she's not one of Josh's friends or acquaintances."

"Josh doesn't have any friends," Marsha said. "Or at least not many. That's one of his problems."

In my book, that constituted strike two for the governor. When you're a friendless, parentless kid, you're stuck in a cruel universe that is not of your own making. I had never met Josh Deeson, but I was already in his corner.

"Does Josh wear any jewelry, like a watch or a ring?" Mel asked.

"Josh has the Seiko watch Gerry gave him for eighth-grade graduation. At least I think he still has it. Although, now that you mention it, I don't think he's been wearing it much lately."

Strike three. Governor Longmire was clearly far too important to notice what the kid she's supposed to be looking after might be wearing. Believe me, I know teenagers can be annoying as hell. And I have some experience with being a less than exemplary parent, but I had also read about some of Marsha Longmire's stump speeches where she waxed eloquent on a return to "traditional family values" and talked about how loving parenting was needed to bring at-risk kids back from the brink, as long as said at-risk kids weren't part of her own extended family. How do you spell hypocrite?

Mel glanced at her watch and closed her notebook. "Since you'd like us to complete the search of Josh's room before he gets home from school, we should probably get started. We won't be disturbing your husband, will we?"

"No. Gerry is in a hospital bed in what used to be the maid's quarters on this floor. Before the surgery, going up and down the stairs was just too much for him. Josh's room is on the third floor."

"I understand he was using ropes to get in and out?"

Marsha nodded. "Rope ladders, really," she said. "This is an old building with old wiring and lots of wood. For safety's sake we keep a rope ladder in each upstairs room to serve as emergency exits in case of fire. Josh used two of them—one to lower himself out his window and onto the balcony over the front portico. He used a second ladder to go from the balcony to the ground.

"One of the guys on my security detail called to report seeing someone exiting the building. Whoever it was managed to get away, but they were pretty sure it was Josh. I went to his room to check. He was gone, but his window was open and the upstairs ladder was tied to the headboard of his bed. I told the security guys that I'd handle things from there, and I did. I left the ropes where they were. When Josh came scrambling back into his room a little after sunrise, guess who was lying in wait? He was quite surprised to see me."

"I'll bet he was," I said. "Is that where Josh's computer is, on his desk?"

She nodded. "I tried accessing it, but it's password-protected now with his password instead of mine."

Somehow I doubted a fifteen-year-old's idea of an unbreakable password would be much of a barrier to a computer-savvy guy like Todd Hatcher.

"What about your husband?" Mel asked. "Might he know the password?"

"He might, but please don't ask him. As I said, Gerry is ill. If I can be trusted to handle the governing of Washington State, I can certainly handle a recalcitrant fifteen-year-old. I told Josh that, because he broke curfew, he was losing all his privileges, including his cell phone and his computer. He knew I wasn't bluffing, and he handed over the cell phone. The computer is up in his room. I made sure he didn't delete anything before he left for school."

"I'm assuming you didn't mention anything to Mr. Willis about what you found on the phone."

"Absolutely not," she declared. "I saw no reason to upset him. It was bad enough that I was upset."

Mel stood up and collected her purse. "Let's go upstairs and execute that search warrant," she said. "We don't have much time."

CHAPTER 4

Marsha Longmire led us through the house and up two sets of stairways, all the while giving us a running commentary about who the mansion's builders were, how much it had cost to build it, how much it had cost to renovate, and how much it had cost to rehab the place after it had been allowed to deteriorate almost to the point of demolition.

It was like listening to one of those canned recordings that you can carry around in a museum to give yourself a guided tour. I'm sure the governor had conducted that kind of tour countless times. I had been to a charity auction or two where a guided tour of the mansion had been on the auction block. No doubt this was the first time two homicide investigators had been given the full meal deal tour treatment.

Clearly the house was more a public edifice than it was a private home. The framed oil paintings on the walls were official portraits of notable folks in Washington State's history rather than anything that might have come from the governor's own family. The oriental rugs in the hallways and on the stairs were no doubt expensive, but they were also worn. By the time we reached the top floor—Josh's floor—they were downright shabby. Apparently the mansion renovation budget didn't stretch all the way to the top floor. I also noticed that the wooden steps creaked noisily under our weight. That probably explained why Josh had found it necessary to use the emergency rope ladders to go in and out.

In the third-floor hallway, Marsha stopped in front of a closed door and pushed it open. Before stepping inside,

Mel removed the search warrant from her purse. "Don't you want to take a look at this?"

Governor Longmire shook her head. "Ross Connors's office drew it up. I'm sure it's in order."

Her cell phone rang. She pulled it out of her pocket, glanced at it, and then put it back.

"You're welcome to be here while we do the search."

Marsha shook her head. "That was my husband on the phone. He needs some help. You'll give me receipts for anything you take, including the computer, right?"

"Right," Mel answered.

"Fine," Marsha said. "No need for me to hang around then. I'd just be in the way."

She left in what struck me as a big hurry. Yes, her husband was ill and yes, he maybe needed her, but there was a real urgency in the way Marsha almost sprinted back down the stairs.

Once she was gone, Mel handed me a pair of latex gloves and then pushed open the bedroom door. She stepped inside and I followed. The hallway out-side the room had been totally imper-sonal. This was the opposite. Every inch of available wall space had been cov-ered with drawings—both in pencil as well as in pen and ink—from a troubled kid who was suffering the agonies of the damned.

These were not pretty pictures. All of them unframed, they were stuck to the wall by tacks and Scotch tape that would no doubt damage the wall finish.

Mel and I studied the pictures in si-lence for some time, moving from one image to the next as though we were walking through an art gallery special-izing in the art of the macabre. Several appeared to be devoted to various com-plicated implements that could have been instruments of torture used in the Spanish Inquisition. The instruments themselves were carefully rendered in every mechanical detail, but the faces of the suffering victims appeared to be chillingly modern. I suspected that if we examined Josh Deeson's high school yearbook, some of those faces might be readily identifiable.

In the pictures there were people being savaged by medieval weapons—swords in some cases, or iron maces. Others were being mowed down in hails of bullets. In each of those, the spray of blood, created one dot at a time with pointillist precision, probably would have done a crime scene blood-spatter expert proud. There were gaping wounds. There was suffering. And for some odd reason, those bloody wounds were all the more chilling for having been artistically and painstakingly crafted in pen and ink.

Mel broke the long silence with a single word. "Whoa!" she said, reaching up to take down one of the drawings. "No wonder Marsha's next call was to Ross Connors."

I nodded in agreement and then added, "What do you want to bet that it's been a long time since either the governor or the First Husband have set foot in this room?"

"Absolutely," Mel agreed. "If they had, they might have blown the whistle on this budding Columbine kid a long time earlier than just today. First I'll photograph and number these, then I'll collect them," she added. "You look at everything else."

Mel carries a tiny digital camera in her purse for just this kind of occasion. She dredged it out of her purse, turned it on, and put it to use photographing all of Josh Deeson's pictures in situ.

She had told me to handle everything else. At first glance, there didn't appear to be a whole lot of "everything else." There was a small flat-screen TV set on the dresser. When I switched it on, it came up on the Playboy Channel. That was pretty predictable. I switched it back off.

Lots of boys have mountains of sports stuff scattered around their rooms. Not this one. If Josh Deeson was interested in any wholesome sports, there was nothing here to prove it. A freestanding bookshelf stood next to the desk. It was mostly bare. There were no photos of any kind and no knickknacks, either. The second shelf down held only four books. One was a combination biography and collected works of Sylvia Plath. One was a history of the Spanish Inquisition, complete with a section of shiny pages that contained photographs of some of the equipment we had already seen depicted in Josh's drawings on the wall. One was a biography of Kurt Cobain. One was a King James version of the Bible with the name "Elizabeth Desiree Willis" printed in gold on the leather-bound front cover.

I still have the Bible that was given to me in my early teens after I had gone through confirmation classes. It was imprinted with my name in gold leaf the same way this one was. Clearly the Bible had belonged to Josh Deeson's mother, not that it had done her much good. It made me wonder if anyone had ever cared enough about Josh to point him in the direction of church attendance. If so, I doubted if anything he had learned there had taken root. Judging from the books he kept, Josh was twice as interested in suicide as he was in (a) the Spanish Inquisition or (b) his immortal soul; take your pick.

The room itself was neat and clean, spookily so. Emphatically so. I looked through all the dresser drawers, top to bottom. There were socks—carefully paired socks—in the sock drawer, folded briefs in another, folded under-shirts in a third, and a selection of folded T-shirts in a fourth. I checked the bot-toms of each drawer to see if anything was hidden there, but I found nothing.

For a teenager, Josh's closet was atypical. All the clothing was carefully hung on hangers, with pants, slacks and even jeans at one end of the closet, while shirts, carefully divided into long sleeves and short sleeves, hung at the other end. There were several pairs of shoes—also neatly arranged—on the floor of the closet. There was a clothes hamper in one corner, half filled with dirty clothes. The only thing stored on the top shelf was an extra blanket.

As an adult, my son, Scott, gives ev-ery appearance of being neat and well organized, but I remember his stepfa-ther, Dave Livingston, telling me how when Scott was fifteen his room was such a mess that Dave and Karen had found mushrooms growing in his closet. That was certainly not the case here. For a kid with very little parental involvement, I had the sense that the compulsive cleanliness of the room was Josh's doing and nobody else's.

It didn't seem likely to me that a housekeeper working for the governor would have ventured all the way up here to the third floor to spend time in this unwanted child's room doing cleaning. Any right-thinking housekeeper in the universe would have taken one look at the disturbing subject matter in those pictures and freaked. Most likely she would have gone straight downstairs and ratted out Josh Deeson either to the governor or to the First Husband.

The old-fashioned en-suite bath was also scrupulously clean. His medicine cabinet contained a carefully arranged collection of toothpaste, men's cologne, and deodorant; nail clippers, comb, brush, and a bottle of styling gel. The only visible medication there was a nearly empty prescription tube containing what was evidently a topical treatment for acne. But there was no dust on the glass shelves. There was no grime, and no film of dead toothpaste in the sink. No garbage in the trash can.

To top it all off, the toilet seat was definitely down. That was the capper on
the jug. Even if I'd never seen the pictures on the wall, I would have said from
studying the bedroom and its attached
bath that Josh Deeson wasn't normal—
not at all.

When I came back out of the bathroom, Mel was finished with the photos
and had started removing the artwork.
Where they had once been I could see
tracks of tape and tacks. Once Josh
moved out of this room it would have to
be spackled, sanded, and painted, floor
to ceiling.

"Anything?" Mel asked.

"Nothing. The whole room is neat as
a pin."

"Scary, isn't it," Mel said. And I had
to agree.

The rope ladder had been fastened
to the bed frame and headboard, and
the bed had then been pushed up
against the window. I disconnected the
rope ladder from the bed and dropped
it into my evidence box. If we ever had
an actual crime scene, distinctive fibers
from that ladder or the one on the sec-

ond-floor balcony might very well be important.

I put the rope in the Bankers Box I had brought up from the car to use in gathering evidence. Then I looked at the bed. It wasn't made, but I guessed that was an unusual occurrence. What appeared to be a bedspread was neatly folded on the floor. I wanted to look under the bed, so I picked up the mattress and box spring and peered down at the floor through the bed frame. Nothing. Not even a respectable collection of dust bunnies on the hardwood floor underneath.

Then, as I was putting the mattress and box spring back in place, I happened to think to look between them. What I saw hidden there was enough to make me feel sick at heart. It was a scarf, a blue silk scarf I was pretty sure I had seen before—wrapped around the throat of an unidentified dying girl in an iPhone video.

"Uh-oh," I said, leaving the mattress crooked enough that the scarf still showed. "Bad news. You'd better bring that camera over here."

Mel turned away from the wall. "What?" she asked.

"Come take a look."

Mel retrieved her camera and came over to where I was standing. As soon as she saw the scarf she raised the camera and began photographing the bed.

"Give me your keys," I said.

"Why?"

"By the time we pack up the computer and the artwork, we're going to need that spare evidence box you've been carrying around in the back of the Cayman."

I managed to limp down the two flights of stairs, but on my way back up, my knees were screaming at me. When I finally reached the top floor, I had broken out in a cold sweat. I paused in the hallway outside Josh's bedroom door long enough to wipe the moisture off my forehead with the sleeve of my jacket. I had told Dr. Bliss about how bad my knees were, but somehow I hadn't mentioned it to Mel.

Back in the room I discovered that Mel had finished taking pictures of the scarf and had returned to collecting the drawings. I began dismantling Josh's computer system—a PC laptop and a tiny printer—into the Bankers Box I had dragged up from the car. Each time I added an item to the box I noted it on the evidence inventory form waiting there. Once I tore the two-page form apart, I'd have an original as well as a copy.

One at a time, I went through every drawer—every exceptionally neat drawer—in the desk. I expected to find some kind of camera or video equipment there, but I didn't.

We were almost finished when I heard footsteps on the stairs. Mel and I both turned to the door, expecting to have our first glimpse of Josh Deeson. Instead, Marsha Longmire stood in the doorway. She looked at the scarred and empty walls and shook her head.

"I wanted to let you know that class is getting out. He'll be here soon," she said.

I walked over to where she was standing. "Until this morning, you had no idea, did you?"

She shook her head. "None at all."

I took her arm and led her over to the desk where the Bankers Box was still sitting open. "You need to prepare yourself," I warned. "This is bad."

I reached into the box and pulled out the clear bag in which we had placed the now-folded scarf. Worried about preserving trace evidence, we had handled it as little as possible. Through the plastic it was apparent that the bag contained a swatch of material of some kind—light blue material. Marsha knew what it was without a moment's hesitation.

She gasped and sank almost to the floor and knelt there with her face buried in her hands. "It's the scarf," she murmured. "It's the damned scarf!"

I reached out to help her up, but she waved aside my hand and rose from her kneeling position without any help from me. Preoccupied with Marsha, neither of us heard the sound of other feet on the stairs or on the worn rug in the hallway.

"Who are you and what are you doing in my room?" Josh Deeson demanded from the doorway. "And what have you done with my artwork? Those pictures are mine. Give them back."

He was a tall, scrawny, blond blue-eyed kid with spiked hair and a terminal case of acne. He looked more like a geek than a Goth. No black clothing. No visible piercings. His pants—ordinary jeans—were belted around his waist, not worn gangbanger style, riding down somewhere near the bottom of the butt. He wasn't wearing an oversize hoodie or sweatshirt as some kids do regardless of the weather. He wore a light blue short-sleeved buttoned shirt; ready-made and most likely from somewhere like Nordy's. It was exactly the kind of shirt I had always lusted after back when my mother was making mine.

He wore no jewelry of any kind, including that Seiko his grandfather had given him.

With his hands outstretched, he lunged toward Mel, probably intent on grabbing the artwork out of her hand. I leaped forward and cut him off.

"We're police officers," I told him. "We have a search warrant."

Bristling with anger, he stopped a foot or so away from me and gave me a cold stare. He was tall enough that he nearly looked me in the eye. For a moment he glanced around the room, looking first at the bed with its displaced mattress and then at the desk.

"Where's my computer?" he wanted to know. "Where's my printer?"

"They're in an evidence box," I explained. "You'll have a receipt for everything we take with us. As I said, we have a search warrant as well as your grandmother's permission. That document applies to your room here as well as to both your computer and your cell phone."

"She's not my grandmother!" Josh Deeson said. He spat out the words with enough venom that it was instantly clear there was no love lost between him and the governor, not in either direction.

Marsha seemed to have recovered her equilibrium. "These are police officers, Josh. They're investigating a homicide. You need to let them continue searching your room. Come downstairs with me. I'll call an attorney."

"I'm not going downstairs," Josh declared. "And I don't need an attorney."

"Yes, you do," Marsha insisted. "You can't stay in the same room with these people, Josh. You mustn't talk to them."

"Sure," Josh said. "Like I can't talk to them without an attorney present, the way they say on TV. Give me a break."

I waited to see if he would crack and do as he was told. If he played to type, I knew for sure his teenage resentment and arrogance would work against him just as it would work in our favor. For the space of almost a minute no one moved in the room and no one spoke.

Marsha was the one who finally broke the long silence. "Are you coming or not?"

"Not," he said.

"Very well," she said. "I'm going to have to go tell your grandfather what's going on."

"Right," Josh said. "Go ahead. Tell him. What's he going to do about it?

Come dragging his sorry ass all the way up here in his wheelchair? Like that's gonna happen!"

"Josh," Marsha said, "I order you—"

"You can't give me orders. I don't work for you." He sneered. "I'm not one of your so-called civil servants. I don't have to jump just because Governor Longmire tells me to."

Ever since Josh entered the room, Marsha had been holding the evidence bag with the scarf in it. Tightening her lips and handing me the bag, she started to say something, then stopped. When she did speak it was with the forced calmness of someone who has carefully stifled a sharp remark.

"You don't understand," she said. "This is a homicide investigation. Whatever you say can be used against you."

"I get it," Josh replied, mocking her. "One of those Miranda warnings. Big deal."

"All right," Marsha said. "Suit yourself."

Closing the door with what I considered to be remarkable restraint, she left the room.

"She's right, you know," I told Josh. "You probably shouldn't talk to us."

"I don't care," he said. "That witch doesn't give a damn about me. I'll talk to you if I want to."

There are times in this business when teenage rebellion and bravado can be very good things. Apparently this was one of those times.

If Josh Deeson chose to be stupid rather than smart, it was his problem, not ours.

CHAPTER 5

Out of the corner of my eye, I saw a movement from Mel's part of the room. She put the stack of loose drawings down on Josh's now-empty desk and then groped for something inside her purse.

There are lots of addictions in this world. Mel Soames is a self-admitted "purse slut." She loves purses, all kinds of purses, but especially expensive purses. I had been with her, carrying the Amex card in my pocket, when she picked out this particular version for her last year's Christmas present. I had learned by bitter experience that choosing a purse for her wasn't something I should attempt on my own. For instance, left to my own devices, I never would have bought this huge alligator-skin monstrosity that cost more than I paid for my first VW Bug.

I never cease to be amazed by all the stuff she carries in it, some of which—like the digital camera—often turns out to be exceedingly useful, especially since I don't have to carry it.

I'm sure some of the guys who knew me back in the day would spit their coffee or beer out through their noses to hear those words coming from me. When I first landed at Seattle PD, the departmental culture was pretty much this: Never hire a man whose wife works and never, ever hire a woman.

In other words, there were no purses in my professional life for a very long time. Now there are, and I was happy to see what Mel pulled out of hers—a tiny cassette recorder. She switched it on and set it down on the desk, on top of the stack of drawings.

"You have the right to remain silent . . ." she began.

"Yeah, yeah, yeah," he said. "Don't
bother."

But Mel did bother. She recited the
whole Miranda warning from beginning
to end without having to resort to a
cheat sheet. Josh was in the room, but
he wasn't paying attention. He was a
kid who had no idea that his whole future was hanging in the balance.

He looked at her with complete contempt. "What do you want to know?"

In the world of homicide interviews
the guy the suspect thinks is stupid is
the one who should ask the questions,
even if the "guy" in question isn't a guy.

"Who's the girl?" Mel asked.

"What girl?"

"The one on the video."

"What video?"

"We're not stupid," Mel said. "The
video on your cell phone. We saw it. So
did your grandmother."

"She's not my—"

Mel cut short his objection. "So did
the governor."

"I don't know what video you're talking about."

"Maybe this will remind you." I had inventoried the cell phone and placed it in the Bankers Box along with the computer equipment. Mel extracted it now, turned it on, and scrolled through to the video until she found the file in question. She set the file playing and held it close enough for Josh to see the images on the tiny screen. Mel and I watched Josh while he watched the screen.

At first he acted nonchalant, as though the drama playing out in the video had nothing to do with him. Then his eyes got bigger. He took a step backward. His face went pale. This was the first time Josh Deeson was seeing those images, no question.

"So who is she?" Mel asked. "Who's the dead girl?"

Shaking his head and covering his mouth with his hand, Josh staggered far enough back across the room until he sat down hard on the misplaced mattress.

"I don't know who she is," he said.

"I've never seen that video before, I swear."

Josh was a kid. His not-quite-changed voice cracked with emotion when he spoke.

Mel didn't let up. She read off a phone number. "Whose number is that?"

"I don't know that, either."

"So you expect us to believe that someone you don't know sent this file to you and you have no idea who it is?"

"I've seen the number before, but I don't know whose it is," he said doggedly. "And I don't know why someone would send this to me."

Mel shrugged. "It doesn't matter if you don't recognize the number. We have a warrant. It'll take time, but the phone company will be able to trace the call. We'll find out who sent it."

Josh swallowed hard. "Is she like, you know, really dead?"

Mel was deep in her role of bad cop. "What do you think?"

Josh didn't answer.

Mel reached into the evidence box and pulled out the scarf. "Whose is this?" she asked.

Josh looked at it blankly without seeming to register what was in the bag. "I found it in my locker at school. I don't know who put it there."

"You don't know who put it in your locker?" Mel asked.

Josh shook his head.

"Who do you suppose put it under your mattress?"

"I did," he said. "But that's not . . ." He paused and took a shaky breath. "I mean, is that what killed her?" Again his voice cracked when he spoke.

"That's what we think," Mel said. "What do you think?"

She sounded like such a hard-nosed bitch that I couldn't help but be grateful that I wasn't her suspect. But I also understood her urgency. The animosity between Josh and Governor Longmire might well be enough to call Marsha's consent to our search into question. It might even be enough to void the search warrants Ross Connors had obtained. If the First Husband had any idea what was really going on in this room, I wouldn't have been surprised if he had risen from his deathbed, Lazarus-style, and crawled up the stairs to put a stop to it. I'm sure Mel suspected, as did I, that an attorney would show up momentarily. When he or she did, this conversation would be over. If the warrants were thrown out, what we got from Josh now might be all we had. Period.

"Where were you last night?" Mel asked.

"Around," he said.

That was a one-word weasel answer if I've ever heard one. It's exactly the kind of answer suspects give when they know they don't have an alibi that will hold up to any kind of careful scrutiny.

"Are you kidding me?" Mel replied. "You went to all the trouble of climbing down two rope ladders to get out of the house and that's the best you can do—around? Who were you with?"

"Nobody," Josh insisted. "I was by myself."

I thought he had been telling the truth about not recognizing the girl and maybe even about not knowing how the scarf had magically appeared in his locker. All I had to do was look at his face to see he was lying about being by himself. He had definitely been with somebody, and once we went through his phone and scrutinized his text messages, we'd probably have a name and a phone number. I didn't call him on it, though, and neither did Mel. Instead, she favored me with a meaningful look that said it was time for the good cop to come to Josh's rescue.

"Leave him alone," I said to Mel. "He's had a shock, and I don't blame him for being upset." I turned to Josh, putting on the charm and doing my best to sound sympathetic.

"Come on, Josh," I wheedled. "Let us help you. This is the time. If you had nothing to do with what happened to the girl, you don't have anything to worry about. Just tell us who she is and who did it. That's all we want to know—who and maybe where. Somebody killed that poor girl, and it's our job to find out who those people are. We don't really care what's on your phone or on your computer. We need to find out who killed her. Help us do that. Tell us what you know."

Lying to suspects in interviews is

standard operating procedure. I don't
like doing it, but sometimes telling a few
little white lies is the only way to make
any progress in the investigation.

"I already told you. I don't know who
she is. I don't know who killed her."

"Where's your watch?" Mel asked.

"What watch?"

"The Seiko your grandfather gave you
for eighth-grade graduation."

"I don't know where it is," Josh said.
"I lost it."

"When?" Mel asked. "Where?"

"If I knew where I was when I lost it,
then it wouldn't be lost, now would it?"

Josh tried to reassume his devil-may-
care attitude, but it didn't quite work.
Once again his cracking voice gave him
away.

"How long ago did you lose it?"

He shrugged his shoulders. "I don't
know. It was a while ago. Maybe a
couple of weeks."

"Who else comes in this room?"

"Nobody," Josh said. "I'm the only
one."

"No maids?" I asked. "No house-
keepers?"

"I already told you," Josh said. "Nobody comes here but me. I'm up here all by myself, like the Prisoner of Zenda or something."

I was more than a little surprised that he even knew the words "Prisoner of Zenda." I wondered if he'd actually read the book.

Mel didn't allow herself to be deflected.

"Tell me about the scarf," she said.

Josh crossed his arms. "I already told you. I don't know anything about the scarf," he insisted. "I found it in my locker."

"Why'd you hide it under your mattress? If the scarf turns out to be our murder weapon, that's going to put you at the top of our suspect list."

"Maybe it's not the same scarf," Josh said.

Mel shook her head. "Guess again, Charm Boy. We found the scarf concealed here in this room where you, by your own admission, are the only person coming and going. A video file showing what appears to be the same scarf being used to strangle someone shows up on your phone, and you expect us to believe that you don't know anything about it? Give me a break. This isn't my first day, you know."

Josh said nothing.

Far below us I heard the sound of a ringing doorbell. Whatever reinforcements Governor Longmire had summoned—probably one of her fat-cat major contributors—was riding to Josh's rescue. That meant our chance to interview Josh Deeson was almost over.

"Look," I said quickly. "We know you didn't kill her. I get that; Ms. Soames here gets that, but I'm guessing you do know who's responsible. You need to tell us who she was and who did this to her. You need to name names. Let us help you put this terrible mess behind you. This is your last chance to make that deal work, Josh. We'll go to the prosecutor. We'll tell him you helped us. That'll be a big mark in your favor with everybody, including that poor girl's parents. Their daughter is dead. They need to know what happened to her."

Josh's facade cracked a little right along with his voice. "Sure," he said, "like being a snitch is going to make my life better? But I already told you. I don't know who did this. I've never seen that girl before just now. I don't know who she is or what happened to her."

"You do know what happened to her," Mel shot back. "You saw it on that video. Someone strangled her before your very eyes."

Switching topics, Mel tapped a scarlet-tipped fingernail on the stack of drawings. "You are a kid who likes thinking about dead people, aren't you," she said. "You must think torturing people is cool somehow. Who are the people in these pictures, Josh? Are they people you know from school, maybe people you don't like very much?"

"It's art," Josh said. "It's what I do in my spare time. It doesn't mean anything. Art isn't against the law. Isn't there something called freedom of speech in this country?"

"These drawings speak to the type of person you are," Mel said. "They tell us the kinds of hobbies and interests you have as well as the kinds of things you'd like to do to other people if you ever have the chance."

We were running out of time. Mel and I knew it; so did Josh. All three of us heard the sound of heavy footsteps pounding up the second flight of stairs. Josh crossed his arms, shook his head, and said nothing.

The bedroom door slammed open hard enough that it bounced off the wall behind us.

A burly man in a well-cut suit charged into the room.

"I'm Mr. Deeson's attorney," he said. "I demand to know what's going on here! Who are you? What are you doing here?"

Mel stepped forward to meet him, holding up her badge in one hand and the search warrant in another.

"My name is Melissa Soames," she said. "This is my partner, J. P. Beaumont. We're with the attorney general's Special Homicide Investigation Team. We're executing a properly issued search warrant of this young man's room. I don't believe I caught your name."

"Garvin McCarthy," he growled, snatching the search warrant from Mel's hands. "Let me see that."

The gesture would have been more effective if McCarthy hadn't had to dig a pair of reading glasses out of the jacket of his designer suit in order to read what was written on the documents. Before he began reading, however, he shot a venomous look in Josh's direction.

"Not another word from you, young man. Understand?"

I half expected Josh to balk at this unmistakable order from someone he didn't know, but I think our questions had scared the crap out of him. He knew he was in trouble. He knew he needed help even if that help was unappreciated and coming from his "not" grandmother. He nodded and kept quiet.

While McCarthy read the warrant through, line by line, Mel quietly switched off the recorder and stowed it in her purse. Finished reading, he handed the warrant back to Mel.

"What's this all about?" he demanded. "Why Special Homicide?"

"Ask your client," she said.

"Who's dead?"

"Ask your client."

"What are you, a one-trick pony?"

Mel smiled at him and handed him a business card. That was her only answer. Then she picked up one of the Bankers Boxes and turned to me.

"We're done here," she said casually. "Let's go. We can stop by and see Mr. Willis on our way out."

That comment got a rise out of Garvin McCarthy and out of Josh Deeson as well.

"No," they said, speaking in inadvertent unison.

The lawyer turned his ire on Josh. "I told you to be quiet and I meant it," he said, shaking an admonishing finger in the kid's direction. "Not another word." He turned to Mel. "Receipts," he said. "I want receipts for everything in those two boxes."

"Talk to my partner," Mel said sweetly. "He's the one in charge of paperwork."

I gave him a lowly carbon copy of the

receipt form. I knew in advance that it wasn't especially legible. McCarthy looked at the paper, then at me.

"You expect me to read this?" he demanded.

"Sorry about that," I said with a shrug. "Old technology and all that. I can copy the originals and fax them to you later if you like."

McCarthy didn't say yes or no to that. "Is my client under arrest?" he asked.

"Not so far," I told him cheerfully. "Right now he's merely a person of interest. With any kind of luck on our part, however, he'll be a full-fledged suspect under suspicion and under arrest in no time at all."

Scowling, McCarthy gave me a business card with his name and a whole collection of phone numbers embossed on what looked and felt like expensive paper. I dropped the card in my jacket pocket. I offered him my hand. He ignored it. I love it when attorneys can't bring themselves to be collegial, to say nothing of polite. In my book, that was strike one against Garvin McCarthy.

I took my box and followed Mel out

into the hall. On the second floor I made my way to the balcony and picked up the coil of rope ladder that was still lying in the far corner of the balcony where Josh had left it. Once that was in my Bankers Box, I finally stripped off my latex gloves and dropped them into my pocket.

Back in the hallway I heard raised voices coming from the landing at the bottom of the stairs. I recognized the governor's voice. Hers was followed by a man's voice, an angry man's voice. The First Husband had evidently emerged unexpectedly from his hospital bed in the maid's quarters. It sounded as though he wasn't happy to discover that any number of things had transpired behind his back.

"What the hell is going on up there?" he demanded. "Who are all these people coming and going?"

"Some police officers stopped by," Marsha responded pleadingly. "Please, Gerry. It's just a little problem with Josh. I'm taking care of it. It's handled."

"It's not a little problem," Mel said, stepping briskly into the argument as well as into the lion's den. "My name is Agent Melissa Soames. I'm with the attorney general's Special Homicide Investigation Team, Mr. Willis. My partner, J. P. Beaumont, and I are here executing a search warrant of your grandson's room."

"A search warrant?" Gerry Willis repeated. "What kind of search warrant? Why? What's going on? Is Josh in some kind of trouble? And what team again?"

I came down the last flight of stairs in time to answer that one.

"Special Homicide," I told him. "We found some troubling images on your grandson's cell phone."

"What do you mean, 'troubling'?"

At the bottom of the stairs Mel and Marsha Longmire stood on either side of an angry older gentleman in a wheelchair. Since the man was seated, it was difficult to tell how big he was, but he struck me as a large man, with a fringe of iron-gray hair around a balding pate. Knowing Gerry Willis had recently undergone bypass surgery, I expected him to look wan and sickly. He did not.

His coloring was great, and from the fit he was pitching, there was nothing at all the matter with his vital signs or mental faculties.

"Snuff film," Mel said in answer to his question.

"Snuff film," Gerry repeated. "As in somebody died?"

Mel nodded. "Apparently," she said.

Gerry Willis's hardened eyes flashed in his wife's direction. "You knew about all of this and didn't tell me?"

"The doctor says you need to take it easy. I didn't want to worry you."

"Screw the doctor! My grandson is under suspicion in a homicide and you didn't want to *worry* me?" he demanded. "What's the matter with you, woman? Are you nuts?"

In that moment, Governor Marsha Longmire crashed to earth. She was an ordinary human being caught in the everyday turmoil of living in a blended family, loving her husband and wanting to protect him from his progeny's folly. It was the old blood-and-water routine all over again, only this time Marsha was on the wrong side of the equation, the water side.

"Ms. Soames and Mr. Beaumont are just leaving," Marsha said. "Once they've gone, I'll be glad to tell you everything."

"No," the First Husband responded. "If this has something to do with Josh, you'll tell me everything about it right now, all three of you."

Governor Longmire shook her head in frustration. She'd had every intention of smuggling Mel and me into the house and out of it again without raising any alarms as far as her ailing husband was concerned. That was why she had hustled us first into the study across from the front door and why she had then unceremoniously herded us on upstairs. We were unwelcome but necessary visitors, and she had wanted to steer us clear of the first floor as much as possible.

Unfortunately for her, that plan had just come to grief.

"As you wish," she said to her husband.

She watched as Gerry Willis rolled his wheelchair away from the landing and through an arched doorway into what was evidently the mansion's formal living room.

With a resigned sigh, Marsha Longmire turned to us. "After you," she said.

CHAPTER 6

For years, the Rainier Club was the last bastion of male privilege and exclusivity in downtown Seattle. It was built in that separate but equal era when "men were men." For social interaction, women were expected to toddle off to the Women's University Club, for example, and not make a fuss about it.

All those male-only rules are changed now, and the Rainier Club's lobby has changed, too. The living room in the governor's mansion was reminiscent of all those bad old days, and it hadn't changed a bit. It was fully stocked with reupholstered period furniture that was long on looks and short on comfort. I hoped that somewhere upstairs there was another living room with furniture that was actually comfortable.

Unwilling to let the evidence boxes out of our direct control, Mel and I carried them into the living room. Gerry Willis rolled his chair to a place of prominence in front of an immense fireplace while the rest of us arranged ourselves around him as best we could. Mel and I sat side by side on a sofa that had been built without taking the vagaries of the human shape into consideration.

"Well?" Gerry demanded abruptly. "What's going on?"

His barked question could have been answered by any of us, but Mel and I stayed quiet, leaving the field open for Marsha to respond.

She did so, giving her husband an abbreviated version of Josh's overnight adventures. She told about his being spotted making his rope-ladder exit and how, upon his return, she had confiscated his iPhone in punishment. She ended by relating her discovery of the appalling video and making the fateful call to Ross Connors.

"I had to do that," she said. "I couldn't just ignore it."

"No," he said. "You couldn't. Show me the film. I need to see it."

"Gerry, it's really rough. Are you sure?"

"Show me," he insisted.

Glancing in Mel's direction, Marsha nodded. Without a word, Mel donned a pair of gloves. Then she opened the box, retrieved the phone, turned it on, and held it up for Gerry Willis's viewing pleasure while she played the vile video in question.

I was more than a little surprised by Gerry's response or, rather, by the lack thereof. He watched the film from beginning to end without comment and without blanching. It made me wonder what Mr. Gerard Willis had done before he became "First Spouse."

The video ended. Mel switched off Josh's iPhone and returned it to the box.

"That doesn't mean anything," Willis said. "Just because that video turned up on his phone doesn't mean Josh is involved in what happened."

Parental denial is pretty much standard the world over. "Whatever it was, my kid (or grandkid) didn't do it. Couldn't *possibly* have done it!"

Next Mel retrieved the bag containing the scarf and handed it over.

"We found the scarf in his bedroom," Mel said quietly. "It was concealed between Josh's mattress and the box spring. Josh claims it was placed inside his locker at school without his knowledge."

"That isn't necessarily the same scarf," Gerry argued, handing it back.

Mel smiled at him before returning the scarf to the box. "Believe me, Mr. Willis," she said. "We're going to make every effort to determine if this is the same scarf."

"Where's Josh now?" Gerry asked.

"He's upstairs with his attorney, Mr. McCarthy," Mel said. "Your wife saw fit to—"

Gerry turned a disbelieving eye on Marsha. "Does that mean you've hired Garvin to be Josh's defense attorney?"

"He's good," Marsha said quickly. "He's very good."

"He's also very expensive."

Marsha nodded. "He is that, but you need to go back to bed now, Gerry. It's four o'clock. It's time for your medication—the one you're supposed to take with food."

"I'm not going back to bed," Gerry said determinedly. "I need to think. If you'll bring the meds, I'll take them here."

Looking depleted, Marsha Longmire stood up. Right that minute she was a long way from being Governor Longmire.

"I'll go make some sandwiches for everyone, then," she said. She turned to Mel and me. "Is tuna on whole wheat okay?"

I remembered then that we hadn't had lunch.

"Sure," I said. "Tuna would be great."

I should have thought that the governor would have a cook at her beck and call. There's a good reason I don't play poker. Most of the time the expressions on my face are a dead giveaway. That's what happened this time, too.

"Today is the chef's day off, and we've had to cut back on her helper's hours. So on Mondays Gerry usually cooks. Not at the moment, however, so you'll have to settle for what he likes to call my burnt offerings."

For the first time I saw a look of genuine affection pass between the governor and the First Husband.

"You're not such a terrible cook," Gerry said. "I don't think anyone is going to starve."

Marsha smiled gamely. Since we had been turned into inadvertent guests who were evidently going to be there for a while, she must have decided that a bit of hospitality was in order.

"What would you like to drink?"

"It's summer," I said. "Iced tea if you've got it."

Marsha turned to Mel. "And for you?"

"Iced tea would be great."

As Marsha walked past her husband's wheelchair, she gave Gerry a breezy buss on the top of his balding head. Once she disappeared through an open

doorway that led into an immense dining room, Gerry Willis immediately
turned to us.

"How much do you know about my
grandson?" he asked.

Whenever possible, it's always a good
idea to let the subjects of interviews ask
and answer their own questions. A lot
of times they'll blurt out exactly what
you need to know. Or, by carefully avoiding a topic, they'll still give themselves
away.

"Not much," I admitted with a shrug.

"This is a second marriage for Marsha and me," Gerry explained. "We met
at a party for lobbyists while Marsha
was still in the state legislature. My wife
died years ago in a car accident in eastern Washington. Marsha was divorced,
amicably so. Sid, her ex, works as a
lobbyist for the Master Builders Association. He and Marsha have a joint
custody agreement that has gone surprisingly smoothly. It turns out their relationship was a lot better after they
were divorced than while they were
married.

"Marsha and I got married within a

matter of months before she started campaigning for governor the first time. Lucy, my first wife, and I married young. Marsha married much later. Her two daughters, Giselle and Zoe, are only a couple of years older than my grandson."

As Gerry related the story, some of the details were beginning to come back to me, although I have to admit the idea of lobbyists marrying politicians doesn't exactly leave me feeling all warm and fuzzy. Gerry looked to be somewhere in his early seventies. Since Marsha was my age, if she had kids who were still that young, she probably hadn't gotten around to doing the parenting thing until very late in the game, when her biological clock was ticking in overtime.

"When my first wife died," Gerry continued, "my daughter, Desiree, was still in high school. We were both grieving. She needed more from me than I was able to give her. Long story short, I blew it. I let her down. She ended up falling in with the wrong crowd and went completely haywire. She dropped out of school and made a complete mess of her life. I tried to help her over the years, but there was really nothing I could do. She ended up getting involved in drugs. She married a jerk, a guy who went to prison and is still in prison for drug dealing. Desiree died of an overdose in a meth lab out in the woods down by Long Beach a little over three years ago."

The regret in his voice over his fatherly shortcomings was heartbreaking, especially when I knew firsthand how fatherly failures stick with you and your kids pretty much forever.

Gerry paused for a moment and then went on.

"Since you're cops, I suppose you've seen meth labs?"

Mel and I both nodded.

"By the time Marsha and I married, I had completely lost track of my daughter," Gerry continued. "It was just too painful to see what she was doing to herself. I didn't even know Josh existed until he was nine. That was six years ago, right after Marsha and I got married. When I found out about the squalor he was living in, I tried to get him out of it. Marsha was willing to adopt him, and for a time Desiree was willing, but then, when the father refused to sign away his parental rights, she backed out, too.

"A year later, when Josh ended up in foster care, I tried suing for custody. Desiree found herself a lawyer who managed to make it sound like her Big Bad Powerbroker Daddy and his wife, the Governor, were trying to run all over poor little her. I'll say that much for Desiree. She was a very capable liar. The social workers at CPS seem to have or at least had a real bias toward keeping families intact."

"They gave him back to her," Mel said.

Gerry nodded. "We finally got custody three years later when Desiree died, but I'm afraid it was too late. Josh was twelve by then, and the damage was done. He came straight from foster care. He had the clothes on his back. Everything else was in a single grocery bag."

I've seen kids come out of homes

where the parents abuse drugs—crack, cocaine, meth, it doesn't matter which one. The parents care far more about their next high than they do about their offspring. The kids are lucky to have clothes to wear or food to eat. As for going to school? That doesn't happen, and once they get into "the system," that often makes bad situations worse. A lot of foster parents do good work, but there are also some bad apples out there pretending to be do-gooders when they're not.

The story Gerry Willis related was sad and all too familiar. I found myself feeling sorry for the First Husband and for Josh Deeson, too. I was also feeling a tiny bit sorry for Governor Longmire. Yes, she was beyond exasperation with the kid now, but once upon a time she had been willing to adopt him. When you try to do a good deed, it's not nice when it comes back years later and bites you in the butt.

Gerry continued. "Josh can read. He taught himself. Used it as a mental escape hatch when he was living in terrible circumstances, but when it came to academics? Forget it. Giselle and Zoe were both in Olympia Prep when he came to live with us. Josh was so far behind his grade level, there was no way he could cut that, so we sent him to a public school. That's why he's taking classes this summer—trying to catch up. At least he was supposed to be catching up."

So Zoe and Giselle went to a private school while Josh was relegated to public. I love it when politicians put their kids in private schools. A little bit of the feeling-sorry stuff for Governor Longmire went away.

"We tried to make him feel like a member of the family," Gerry went on. "We offered him a room on the second floor just like everybody else. At the time he came to live with us, the girls—Zoe and Giselle—were willing to share a bedroom so he could have one of his own, but Josh wasn't having any of that. He's the one who decided he wanted to live up in the damned attic."

Okay, so now I learned that Josh's supposed Prisoner of Zenda plight was entirely self-imposed. Two points for

Zoe and Giselle. Take one away from Josh. This was like an emotional tennis match, and I was having a hard time keeping score.

"But Josh didn't want to have a family," Gerry said. He paused and then asked, "Do you ever read Dean Koontz?"

As far as I was concerned, this was a question from way out in left field. I shook my head. "Doesn't he write horror stuff, sort of like Stephen King?"

In high school, my son, Scott, was a huge Stephen King fan. Me, not so much. I was a homicide cop. I didn't need to read about horror. I saw too much of it every day.

"Similar but different," Gerry said. "One of Koontz's books is called *Watchers.* It's about a DNA experiment gone horribly awry. Two things come out of the experiment and they are the exact opposite. One is this incredibly intelligent golden retriever named Einstein. The other is a terrible monster. They turn out to be Good and Evil personified. And the scene that got to me in that book—"

"I know," Mel interrupted. "The scene

in the cave—the monster's carefully made bed and his treasured Disney toys."

"That's it exactly," Gerry Willis said.

Then he buried his face in his hands and sobbed. It took some time for him to get himself back under control and dry his eyes. In the meantime I was left thinking about how much more than a purse Mel Soames had brought with us to this interview.

"We noticed the book on the Spanish Inquisition," I said when Gerry finally had regained his equanimity enough that he could once again answer questions. "Where did that come from?"

"I ordered it for him from Powell's down in Portland," Gerry said.

In terms of bookstores, Powell's is a Pacific Northwest institution. They sell new books, of course, but they also have a huge reputation and a well-oiled system for tracking down old books, some of which are quite valuable.

"It's an old college textbook," Gerry continued. "As far as I know, it's considered to be one of the definitive books on the Spanish Inquisition, and it's been out of print for years. Josh was doing a history report and ended up being fascinated by the subject. That's why I bought it for him."

"You've seen his drawings, then?" I asked.

Gerry gave me a hollow look and nodded. "Until today I honestly thought they were just drawings," he said.

"The girl in the video," Mel said. "Did you recognize her?"

"No."

"Is there a chance that she's a friend of your grandson's?"

"I doubt it," Gerry said. "As far as Marsha and I can tell, Josh doesn't have many friends, at least none who ever come here to visit."

I surmised that the rope-ladder routine meant Josh did have friends somewhere, just ones he couldn't or didn't want to bring back to the house.

The governor chose that moment to return from what must have been a fairly distant kitchen. When Marsha walked into the living room she was carrying a tray stacked with sandwiches. A slim blond girl wearing short shorts and an even shorter tank top followed her. The girl carried a second tray loaded with glasses, spoons, various sweeteners, and a pitcher of iced tea. The hair, the skin, the vivid blue eyes indelibly marked this sweet young thing as her mother's daughter.

"Zoe, this is Mr. Beaumont and Ms. Soames," Marsha said. "These are the people I was telling you about. This is Zoe, my younger daughter. Would you please go get Gerry's prescription bottle off the counter in his bathroom? It's the one he's supposed to take every four hours."

Zoe gave us a quick smile, then dashed off to do as bidden while Marsha handed out paper napkins. Mel took the tray of sandwiches and passed it around while Marsha poured the iced tea. Then she settled on a straight-backed chair and pulled it close to Gerry's.

"I suppose you've told them the whole sordid mess?"

Gerry nodded. "Yes," he said. "I have."

Zoe returned to the room with a pill bottle. She handed that to her stepfather, grabbed two sandwiches from the stack, and then raced off in the direction of the stairs.

"Zoe," Marsha commanded. "Remember your manners."

Zoe slid to a stop on the hardwood floor on the landing. "Nice meeting you," she said over her shoulder. "Bye." Then she disappeared up the stairs.

The truth is, Governor Longmire wasn't much of a cook. The iced tea was okay, but the tuna sandwiches were just that—tuna. There was butter on the bread, but that was it. No mayo. No seasoning of any kind. If this was Marsha's idea of feeding folks, the whole family must have dreaded the cook's day off.

Once Zoe was gone, Marsha reached out and gave Gerry's knee a comforting pat.

"I'm sorry I didn't tell you," she said. "When I found out he'd been sneaking in and out of the house, I just went ballistic. I couldn't believe he'd pull a stunt like that with you so sick. I thought that taking away his electronic equipment was the only punishment that would have any kind of impact, but then when I saw the video . . ."

"I know," her husband said. "I'm sure you did the right thing. That goes for calling in Garvin as well. But if Josh really did do this terrible thing"—Gerry paused for a moment, gathering himself—"then I should pack up and move the two of us out of here right now. None of this has leaked into the public yet, has it?"

That question was directed at Mel and me. We both shook our heads.

"That's a blessing," Gerry said. "But it's a reprieve that won't last long. Even if these folks don't do it, someone will leak word to the press. Once that happens, the opposition will be calling for your head on a platter. The party will drop you like a hot potato. Just you wait, the next time you're up for reelection, the party bigwigs will be backing someone else in the primary. If Josh and I leave now, before this all hits the fan, we might be able to do some damage control."

"You're not leaving," Marsha said firmly. "Neither one of you is leaving."

There were steps on the stairs—heavy steps—that were definitely not Zoe's.

Garvin McCarthy poked his head around the end of the archway. "You shouldn't be talking to these people," he said curtly, addressing the governor. "You shouldn't, and neither should your husband."

I didn't like it that he spoke about the First Husband rather than to the First Husband when Gerry Willis was right there in the room. Subtract two points from Mr. McCarthy, although, being a criminal defense lawyer, in my book he was already in negative territory to begin with.

"Call me at the office," McCarthy added. "Or on my cell. You have them both."

Marsha nodded.

"Don't bother showing me out," he added gruffly. "I know the way."

"He's an arrogant bastard, but he's

also the best money can buy," Marsha said, turning to Gerry. "He'll do what needs to be done."

This time Gerry was the one who nodded. For the first time, he looked ill. His skin color had faded. Obviously Marsha was right and this was too much for him.

"I think I need to go back to bed for a while," he said.

Marsha jumped to her feet. "Are you okay? Should I call the doctor?"

"No," he said. "Don't call the doctor, and you don't need to come with me. I just need to lie down for a while. I believe I overdid it."

He rolled himself out of the room while Marsha subsided onto her chair. She waited until Gerry was out of earshot, then she turned to Mel and me.

"Just you wait," she said. "If this kills him, I'll strangle that little shit with my own two hands, and you may quote me on that."

CHAPTER 7

Before leaving the governor's mansion, we each gave Marsha Longmire our business cards loaded with the full collection of contact information. She looked at the cards and nodded. "I'll be keeping a very close eye on Josh," she said. "He won't be going anywhere or doing anything without my knowing about it."

What was it my mother used to say? Something about locking the barn door after the horse was already gone. I decided against passing that bit of folk wisdom along to the governor.

"Good idea," I said.

Once outside, I loaded the evidence boxes into the backseat of Mel's Cayman. "Next stop Todd Hatcher?" she asked.

I nodded.

"Do you have an address?"

"I'll call Ross's office and get it."

While we had been in the governor's mansion, we'd had our phones turned off. Two of the missed calls on my phone were from Katie Dunn, Ross's secretary. One of the missed calls on Mel's phone was also from there.

"You wanted to talk to us?" I said when Katie came on the phone.

"Mr. Connors would like to see you both," she said. "He's in a meeting right now and has another one early this evening. He was wondering if you'd mind stopping by his house later this evening, sometime around eight."

"We'll be there," I said. "Meantime, we need the physical address for Todd Hatcher. I know where he used to live, but I understand he's moved."

Katie gave me the necessary information, a rural address outside Oakville, half an hour away. I relayed the message and the information to Mel. While she set off in what constitutes rush-hour traffic in Olympia to get us there, I sat back to enjoy the ride. When Mel is making like a Formula One driver behind the wheel, I often find it helpful to think about other things. In this case, I thought about Todd Hatcher.

Call me a hopeless romantic. I love happy endings, or, rather, happy beginnings.

Todd Hatcher is a very smart guy with a Ph.D. in economics, a couple of books to his credit, and a natural flair for computers. In the olden days, he might have been a prospector out wandering in the wilderness during the California gold rush. These days he's a geek who specializes in data mining. As I understand it, that's what his latest book is all about—data mining for fun and profit.

But Todd is a most unlikely-looking geek, not at all the buttoned-down type. He wears cowboy boots and cowboy hats—not the rhinestone-cowboy variety, but the scuzzy down-at-the-heels boots that have seen years of wear in all kinds of terrain and all kinds of weather. He's tall, skinny, and bow-legged from too many hours in the saddle. That's how he supported himself through college—working as a ranch hand in southeastern Arizona.

When I first met Todd several years ago, it took some time for me to realize that Ross Connors had stumbled on a diamond in the rough. Back then, Todd was barely making ends meet. He lived in a studio apartment, got where he needed to go by using a bus pass, and existed on a diet that consisted mostly of Top Ramen noodles. He was a kid from a small town in the desert stranded in the big-city wet of western Washington where it really does rain, even though tourists who come through the state in the summer are convinced that it never does.

The work Todd did and still does for Ross Connors helped put him on a more stable financial footing. Getting his doctorate and having his first book published didn't hurt. Both of those professional accomplishments led to his doing consulting work for other states. Within a matter of months his life had turned around: he was still living in western Washington and it was still raining, but instead of using a bus pass to get around, he was driving a new dual-cab Ford pickup truck. To ward off a bad case of homesickness he started following the local rodeo circuit, sometimes participating, sometimes as a spectator.

That was what had taken him to the Kitsap County Fairgrounds out on the Kitsap Peninsula the previous summer. Each year during the Kitsap County Fair and Rodeo, one of the rodeo's evening performances benefits the breast cancer foundation Susan G. Komen for the Cure. At that performance, everyone is supposed to wear pink, and a local organization donates money to the foundation for everyone who wears pink and wins one of that night's events.

As Todd told me shortly afterward, "It takes balls for a cowboy to wear pink."

On the evening in question, he had screwed his courage to the sticking place, dressed himself in a brand-new pink Western shirt, and showed up. Sometimes the fates are with you and that's all you have to do—just show up. Sometime during the rodeo he was introduced to Julie Dodge, who was the winner of the evening's barrel-racing contest and who was also wearing pink.

As a fund-raiser at the rodeo, people are able to show their support by purchasing pink balloons that are released all at once in a moving ceremony at the end of the evening's performance. When it came time to let go of his balloon, Todd Hatcher found himself standing next to Julie Dodge, and the rest is history.

It turned out to be a match made in heaven. Julie had inherited her father's horse farm, where her divorced father had raised her along with plenty of prizewinning quarter horses. She had grown up helping him run the farm. After his death, she ran it solo, hiring help only as needed. It was also after her father's death that she managed to reconnect with her mother. Julie's mom had bailed when she discovered she wasn't cut out for ranch life or motherhood. She died of breast cancer only a few months after being reconciled with her daughter.

I think standing there side by side, holding those stupid pink balloons, caught Todd and Julie with their customary defenses down. Todd had been through a lot with his own parents' stormy relationship. He and Julie let go of their pink balloons, went to the nearest Denny's, and spent the rest of the night, well into the wee hours, talking. They got married a few short weeks later—saying their vows before a justice of the peace in Gray's Harbor County with the two of them dressed in boots, jeans, and matching pink cowboy shirts. At the ceremony, Ross Connors stood up for Todd. Julie's best friend from high school stood up for her. Mel and I were invited along to serve as witnesses.

So now Ross's consultant-in-chief lives on his wife's horse farm out in the boonies, where he has a top-of-the-line Internet connection and plenty of real manure to shovel whenever he gets tired of shoveling the politically motivated, man-made, virtual variety. From the looks of it, he and Julie are partners in every sense of the word.

It was five-thirty in the afternoon when we pulled up in front of a picturesque farmhouse set back several hundred feet from the banks of the Black River. The house, boasting a relatively recent coat of white paint, looked as though it had been plucked off a farm in Iowa or else from a movie set and dropped unscathed in the wilds of western Washington. The barn, gleaming with an equally new coat of bright red paint, could have come from the same source.

Todd emerged through the screen door on the front porch and then bounded down the steps to meet us. He was in his favorite duds—worn jeans, worn boots, worn shirt. He waved and greeted us with a lopsided welcoming grin.

"Come on in," he said, grabbing Mel's hand and half dragging her out of the driver's seat of the Cayman. "Julie's inside making supper. She's dying to see you."

Supper, I noted, *not dinner.*

"It's a pork roast, homemade apple-sauce, and early corn fresh from the garden, picked just this afternoon. We've got plenty. She said to tell you she's already put extra plates on the table and you are not allowed to say no."

I got the feeling from being around Julie Hatcher that she didn't believe in anyone telling her no, which probably also explained why she and Todd were married. Besides, my single half of one of Governor Longmire's tuna sand-wiches was long gone. I have to admit that the idea of eating a real home-cooked meal had a lot of appeal.

"Sounds good to me," I said.

"What have you got?" he asked.

Mel stepped out of the car, opened the door, and showed him the evidence box with the computer in it. "Here it is," she said. "Help yourself."

He picked up the box, hefted it, rat-tling, onto his shoulder, and led the way into the house.

I have been in farmhouses occasion-ally in my life, and some of those oc-casions have been during summer months—hot summer months. So make that miserably hot farmhouses. As I walked across the front porch, I was happy to note that on a concrete pad beside the porch sat a huge Trane AC unit quietly humming away. Julie and Todd's house was not going to be miserable. In fact, once we got inside, compared to the summer heat outside, it was practically chilly.

Todd led us through both the living room and dining room and into a spacious country kitchen, where a round oak table held four place settings. Julie, smiling in greeting, was carrying a platter full of corn on the cob to the table. The pork roast was already there.

"Everything you see here is homegrown," Todd said proudly. "The corn is from our garden. Even the peaches in the cobbler for dessert come from our own fruit trees—last year's crop. Not the pork, though. That comes from a guy who raises pigs down in Lewis County."

"A friend of my dad's," Julie explained. "And we buy sides of beef from a guy in Toledo."

I know enough about Washington geography to understand she didn't mean Toledo, Ohio. Mel was smart enough not to ask.

The pitcher of iced tea on the table was fruit-flavored and presweetened, which was fine with me. Mel drank hers without complaint, and we both dug into the food, which was utterly delicious. All during dinner we chatted about this and that, making sure we made no reference to the purpose of our visit in front of Julie. If Todd saw fit to confide in her after we left, that was his business, but Mel and I didn't mention it.

Finally, when Julie got up to clear away plates and serve the peach cobbler, she looked at Todd and said, "Well, are you going to tell them or am I?"

"We're expecting," Todd announced with a proud but sheepish grin. "We confirmed it just this week. She's almost two months along."

Mel and I both offered enthusiastic congratulations, although mine were tempered by thinking about Gerard Willis's rocky venture into fatherhood, not to mention my own. That's the thing with having kids. You can never tell what's going to happen or how they'll turn out.

The peach cobbler arrived still warm from the oven and topped with a generous dollop of store-bought vanilla ice cream. I did my best not to clean my dessert plate, but I didn't succeed. Once dessert was over, Julie shooed all of us out of the kitchen so we could work while she cleaned up.

"Okay," Todd said. "What have we got?"

He led us to a room that, in another era, had probably once been the farmhouse's master bedroom. Now it was a fully functional office space, complete with multiple computers, copiers, printers, and scanners. On the way to the office I picked up the Bankers Box containing Josh Deeson's electronics equipment. Once in the office, I set the box down on Todd's desk. Without a word of consultation, we donned latex gloves. We all knew that the less the computer and phone were handled, the better. We also understood that we needed to access the information from the devices as soon as possible. I was worried that Garvin McCarthy would make some effort to erase the contents of both the phone and the computer remotely before anyone else had a chance to see what was there.

Todd directed Mel and me to chairs. Then, whistling under his breath, he set about examining everything we had brought along. "Great," he said. "I've got a power supply for this right here." Moments later he busied himself copying the laptop's hard drive as well as the information on Josh Deeson's phone.

"Once I have the information off the computer, I'll be able to analyze it," Todd said as he waited for the hard drive to finish copying. "Before I can do that, though, I need to know what I'm looking for and what you're hoping I'll be able to find."

"One of the last files sent to this phone is the video of what appears to be a snuff film, the murder of a juvenile female," Mel told him. "Are you okay with that?"

Todd gave her a bemused look, but then he nodded. "I guess," he said. "I've never seen a snuff film, but I've butchered cattle, if that's what you mean."

"All right then," Mel said. "We need to know who sent that video and when. We also need to try to isolate the girl's face in a benign enough manner that we can use the image in an attempt to locate her next of kin. We may also be able to match the photo with an unsolved missing persons case."

"Of course," Todd said. "You can't very well go around showing copies of the original video to the victim's possible relatives."

"When you look at the film," Mel continued, "you'll see that the murder weapon is most likely a scarf, a blue silk scarf. We believe we now have the scarf in our possession, and we'll be taking that to the crime lab in hopes of finding DNA evidence."

Looking at the cell phone, Todd frowned. "You do understand that, for any of this to be legal, I need a search warrant."

Without a word, Mel reached into her

purse, pulled out the search warrant, and handed it over. "And now you have one," she said. "Ross expects you to follow up on all of Josh Deeson's text and e-mail messages—who they came from and where and when they went. Working with phone company records and cell phone towers, we're hoping you'll be able to triangulate and tell us where Josh Deeson was physically when he sent and received those text messages."

"Josh Deeson being the suspect," Todd confirmed.

"Yes."

"But why us?" Todd asked. "Why bring all of this stuff to an outside consultant and not to the Washington State Crime Lab? They've got plenty of computer-savvy folks there."

"Yes, they do," I told him. "And plenty of potential media leaks, too. Ross wants to be as far ahead of the game as possible before any of this hits the media."

"How come?" Todd asked.

"Because Josh's grandfather and guardian is a man named Gerard Willis—Gerry Willis—who happens to be married to Marsha Longmire, who is Josh's other guardian."

Todd's eyes widened. "You mean Governor Longmire?"

"One and the same," I told him.

"Okay," Todd said. "I get it, and I'll get right on it. I'll work on extracting the photo first. I'll let you know first thing in the morning if I've made any progress."

"Great," I said. "Ross says to bill it at your usual rate."

We sat and watched for some time while Todd made his copies. By the time I glanced surreptitiously at my watch, it was almost seven-thirty. From here it would take us a good half hour to get back to Ross Connors's place in Olympia. If we didn't get under way soon, we were going to be late for our meeting with him.

"Sorry to eat and run," I said. "But we need to go."

Todd nodded. "And from the sound of things, I need to go to work."

We gathered up the computer and the iPhone and returned them to the Bankers Box. In the interim Julie had finished cleaning the kitchen. We found her sitting in the living room, curled into a comfortable ball on a big easy chair, thumbing through a glossy magazine called *Your Baby and You.* We thanked her for the wonderful dinner, then Todd carried the evidence box back out to the car and loaded it for us.

"Stay in touch," Mel called as we headed out.

Todd nodded and waved, but I could tell from the preoccupied look on his face he was already busy, mentally turning the problems at hand over in his head.

In Washington in June, the sun doesn't set completely until around ten at night. Once we turned east on U.S. Highway 12, the sun was still fairly high in the sky. We were happy to have the sun to our backs, although it was probably blinding to the traffic coming toward us.

"Todd and Julie will make great parents," Mel said. "And that farm! What a wonderful place to raise kids."

"I hope so," I said.

I'm sure I sounded more morose than

I intended, and Mel gave me a quizzical look.

"If you ask me, that sounded pretty pessimistic," she said.

"Why wouldn't it be? Given everything we heard from Gerry Willis this afternoon, parenthood isn't exactly a walk in the park, not even under the best of circumstances."

"You're right," Mel said. "I don't suppose it is."

"And speaking of Gerry Willis," I added, "you never met the man before today, right?"

"Right."

"Then how is it possible that as soon as he mentioned that book . . . ?"

I paused, unable to remember the title in question.

"*Watchers,*" she supplied.

"Right. *Watchers.* How come you knew immediately which scene he was talking about?"

"It's the most important scene in the book," Mel answered. "The pivotal scene. The whole time you're reading the story, you're enchanted by this incredibly brainy golden retriever named

Einstein, but you're also aware of this terrible force out chasing down victims, hoping to destroy everything good, including the dog. Without ever seeing the monster, you end up hating him, hoping the good guys will get rid of it before it destroys them. And then, in that one scene, you see how lonely and lost and isolated the poor monster must be. In spite of yourself, you find yourself feeling sorry for him as well."

"You end up empathizing with the monster?"

"Exactly," Mel said.

I thought about Josh Deeson, coming to the governor's mansion with only a grocery sack of possessions. And in that flimsy bag, along with whatever clothing he had carried, he had brought with him his mother's worn Bible. Somehow it had been meaningful enough for him to keep. Was it just a memento, the only thing he had to remember his mother by? Or had it been more than that? Had he hoped that inside that Bible his mother might have found her salvation and his? If so, it was also a symbol of dashed hopes and dreams.

"Sort of like how, by the time Gerry Willis finished telling us Josh's story this afternoon, we ended up feeling sorry for the poor kid."

"Yes," Mel agreed. "Just like."

"Crap," I said, and meant it.

CHAPTER 8

Ross Alan Connors may have gone on a two-and-a-half-year-long bender after his wife committed suicide in their backyard, but that doesn't mean he's stupid. Drunks can be smart about a lot of things, even when they're terminally dim about booze.

Once Francine was dead, Ross no longer took any pleasure in his palatial brick home with its slate roof and oddball turret. Yes, he still had a view of Capitol Lake, but he couldn't bring himself to face being in the yard. So he did two things. First he redesigned the yard and put in an in-ground pool and spa. Then he sold the place for top dollar just before the real estate bubble burst. And when that happened, he was ready, too. With prices suddenly lowered, he went shopping in a newly completed condo high-rise, purchased two two-bedroom units high up in the building for almost pennies on the dollar and converted them into a single enormous unit with three bedrooms and an office.

This was, as Ross had confided to me, his "toes-up" house. He planned to stay there, with someone else doing the yard work and maintenance, until he was ready to be hauled out, toes up, on a stretcher. His unit came with a visitor-parking place. It was five to eight when Mel tucked her Cayman into that and we headed upstairs. He hadn't specifically asked us to bring the evidence boxes in with us, but we did anyway, just in case.

Upstairs, the door was opened by Ross's longtime live-in retainer, Iris O'Malley. As far as I knew, Iris had worked for the Connors family for a very long time. It appeared to me that Iris was your basic toes-up employee as well. She would stay on until Ross croaked out or else until she did, depending on who gave up the ghost first.

Apparently Iris O'Malley carries a lot more weight in the Connors household than simply serving as chief cook and bottle washer. She was the one who called me and alerted me to the fact that Ross had been in bed drunk for the better part of three days. I'm not sure how she knew I was in AA, but she did. She ran up the flag, and I came straight to Olympia to see what, if anything, could be done. On that occasion Ross's reaction to my showing up beside his bed of pain had been to tell me to get the hell out in no uncertain terms. It was another three months before he finally picked up the phone himself and called to ask for help.

Note to people with loved ones on that thorny path: You can't make them be ready to ask for help, and there are no high bottoms. Low bottoms are what it takes for people to decide they want to get better.

"Top of the evening to you, Mr. and Mrs. Beaumont," Iris said.

I wasn't sure about Iris's age, but she was evidently from a generation that didn't hold with women hanging on to either their maiden or their previously married names. Mel raised an eyebrow at that but let it pass.

"Right this way," Iris added. "Himself is in his office."

Lars Jenssen, my grandmother's widower, a retired Alaskan halibut fisherman, speaks with a Norwegian accent that is thicker on the phone than it is anywhere else, except when he's in the company of other retired Norwegian halibut fishermen. Then he's barely understandable.

As Iris led us to Ross's home office, I couldn't help wondering about her Irish brogue. Was it real or was it something she cultivated and put on occasionally, when it suited her, along with the gray uniform and dainty white apron?

She motioned us into the room. I was glad to see that the old teacher's desk that had once graced Ross's turret office in the Water Street house had made the transition from one place to another, most likely with an interior designer dying a thousand deaths in the process.

Ross stood up and shook our hands in greeting. "Have you eaten?" he asked. "If you're hungry, Mrs. O'Malley here whipped up her standard lemon-and-vanilla Irish curd cakes earlier this afternoon."

"Thanks," I said, "but Julie Hatcher made sure we didn't go away hungry."

He smiled and shook his head. "I'll say one thing for that girl, she sure can cook. Something to drink then?"

Between the governor's mansion and Todd Hatcher's place, I'd had enough iced tea to float a battleship. Mel must have been in the same condition.

"No, thanks," she said. "We're good."

"All right then, Mrs. O'Malley," Ross said. "That's all. Thank you, and good night."

Mrs. O'Malley tottered off, and Ross gestured us into a pair of high-backed leather chairs. Unlike the desk, the derelict recliner from his old office hadn't survived the move, so the interior designer had won at least one round.

"I'm assuming those are the evidence boxes?" he asked as I placed them on the desk.

"Yes," I said. "We thought you'd want to see what we picked up."

Once again we donned gloves. Once again we removed what was in the boxes and went through it item by item.

"Todd made copies of everything on his computer's hard drive," Mel explained when we got to the laptop. "There might have been other files on an external drive or online storage, but we didn't find any evidence of an additional drive."

"And he's working on the phone records?" Ross asked.

"He'll be working on extracting a photo from the video first," I said. "The phone records will be second. The way Todd works, I expect we'll have a photo in hand first thing tomorrow morning."

"Good," Ross said. "That's the first step—identifying the victim."

There was no need for a comment from either Mel or me. We were both in full agreement. In a homicide investigation, once you have the name of the victim and/or a crime scene, everything else grows out of that.

"So what's your read on the situation?" Ross asked. "With the governor's grandson, that is."

Ross hadn't been around to hear all the spoken and unspoken commentary about Josh Deeson's relationship to Washington's first family, and it didn't seem necessary to fill in all those details right then. Besides, the attorney general wasn't asking for a solution that would hold up in court. He was asking for an opinion from two experienced homicide cops in the middle of an investigation.

"Whoever the victim is, she wasn't killed last night," Mel ventured. "From what Governor Longmire told us, she intercepted Josh when he came back in and didn't let him out of her sight until he left for school. That means he would have had no time to conceal the scarf under the mattress if he brought it home last night because we were there before he arrived home this afternoon. So on the one hand, just because he had the video doesn't mean he did it, but the scarf would suggest that he did—and that he kept the scarf as a trophy."

Ross looked at me.

"I agree about the murder not happening last night," I said. "But it didn't happen very long ago, either, because the file was sent to Josh's phone this morning at one twenty-three A.M. People don't waste their time sitting up at night sending out old videos. They send out new videos."

"Garvin McCarthy has quite a reputation as a defense attorney," Ross said. "And he's going to do everything in his power to get the search warrant thrown out. If that happens we also lose the scarf. We need to come up with a whole lot more. Did you search anywhere else in the house?"

"The warrant was specifically limited to his room."

Ross nodded thoughtfully. "He may have had something else squirreled away in another part of the house."

"That's true," I said. "It's a big house."

"Josh knows he's under scrutiny," Ross said. "I know how kids like that operate. If he's got incriminating evidence hidden in the house, he's going to try to ditch it without arousing further suspicion."

Ross stopped talking, reached in his pocket, and pulled out a quarter. "I guess it's time to flip a coin," he said. "Call it."

"For what?" I asked.

"Call it," he said again.

"All right," I said. "Heads."

And heads it was.

"What's this for?"

"Too bad, Beau. You're the one on permanent trash duty."

"For what?"

"To go through the governor's garbage. Once the cans are hauled down to the street, what's inside them is fair game. That's true for everyone's garbage, even the governor's. No warrant is necessary."

"What about Squad A?" I asked hopefully. "Couldn't one of those guys—"

"I brought you and Mel in on this because I don't want to involve the home team," Ross interrupted. "The fewer people who are in the know, the better.

And if anyone asks what you're up to, we're looking into allegations of bullying—school bullying. There's to be no mention of a homicide investigation until we confirm it *is* a homicide investigation."

"What about the crime lab?" Mel questioned. "Our evidence boxes have Josh Deeson's name and address right on them. Once the guys at the crime lab in Seattle see the address on the labels, what are the chances one of them will recognize it and know we're talking about the governor's mansion?"

"The guys down here or the ones in Seattle might recognize it, but they won't be seeing the evidence boxes." Ross had been idly shuffling through the stack of Josh Deeson's drawings. Now he returned the pictures to the boxes, along with the other items we had collected. Then he picked up the lids, patted them into place, and secured them with clear packing tape.

"Once you sign and date these, I'll be taking charge of them," Ross said. "It so happens that I have a meeting with Squad C first thing tomorrow morning.

I'll drop your boxes off at the satellite crime lab in Spokane while I'm there. I think it's unlikely that someone working in the Spokane lab will put two and two together. Josh Deeson's name isn't the governor's name, and the address here is a simple street address that most likely won't raise any red flags east of the mountains."

It crossed my mind that Ross was playing a dangerous game. Once Josh Deeson turned into a real suspect, all hell was bound to break loose. In the old days the media had refrained from printing the names of juveniles who were part of a criminal investigation. Some journalists still pay lip service to that quaint tradition, but when the juvenile happens to be a relative of a politician, all bets are off.

That's the problem with politics and politicians. If, like Marsha Longmire, you're lucky enough to scramble to the top of the electoral heap, you can bet there are all kinds of people on both sides of the aisle hoping to knock you off your perch. And if they have an opportunity to use said politician's kids, grandkids, and other assorted relatives as weapons in that process, they do so, without a moment's hesitation.

That was my opinion, but it's never a good idea to tell your boss that you think he's off in the weeds somewhere, not if you're interested in continuing to work for the man. It's just not done.

"Okay," I said. "You take charge of the evidence boxes, but what do you expect of us? If you want me to sort garbage, where am I supposed to do it? Right this minute, Mel and I are checked into the local Red Lion. I can't drag the governor's garbage cans into the lobby or the parking lot so I can go through them. What days does the garbage get picked up? And what's Mel supposed to be doing in the meantime while I'm sorting through crap?"

"Trash, not crap," Ross corrected with a smile. "You mustn't take all this S.H.I.T. stuff so personally."

The three of us had a good laugh about that, but Ross Connors stopped laughing before anyone else did.

"Excuse me while I make a phone call."

He picked up a desk phone and dialed a number. "I need to know what days trash is picked up at the governor's mansion," he said.

Ross never bothered introducing himself, so whoever was on the other end of the line knew his voice well enough to recognize it. The attorney general waited for a several minutes, ignoring us and idly tapping the top of his desk with a fountain pen, a distinctive Mont Blanc Thomas Mann model. Finally, the person he was waiting for came back on the phone. He listened for a time, nodding.

"All right," he said finally. "To the winners go the spoils." He put down the phone and then looked at me.

"Bad news," he said. "The governor's trash is picked up every day, recycling and garbage both. So I'll need to work on how to manage the pickup as well as where you'll do the sorting. I'll have it handled before I leave town in the morning. As for you, Mel, once you have that photo in hand, I want you to go to work on the missing persons end of this."

Mel nodded.

"How old do you think the victim is?"

"Maybe junior high," Mel said. "More likely a high school freshman would be my guess."

That was my assessment, too. Ross nodded in agreement.

"I thought so, too," he said. "As soon as Governor Longmire showed me the video, I did some preliminary checking. In the past four months, we've had four teenage deaths in western Washington that are in line with that demographic. A drive-by shooting in Kent, a single-vehicle rollover car wreck in Kelso, a drug overdose in Raymond, and an alcohol-related head-on accident on I-90 near North Bend. In each of those incidents, the victim was a high-school-age Caucasian female with brown hair. But those cases also had full autopsies. None of them shows any sign of strangulation."

"Which means the body of our victim is still out there somewhere," Mel said. "Hence the missing persons files."

"And not just from Washington, either," Ross said. "The girl who was shot in Kent was from Portland and was visiting her grandmother over the summer. The girl in the head-on collision was from Coeur d'Alene, Idaho. These days kids have driver's licenses and cars. The girl in the video could be from Canada for all we know. Mel, I know you've worked with agencies in other states in the U.S. as well as in Canada. I want you to do it again."

"Yes, sir," Mel said. "Will do."

"You showed the video to Josh?" Ross asked.

"We did."

"What kind of reaction?"

"Shock," Mel said. "He claimed he hadn't seen it before, and I think he was telling the truth about that, but I'm not so sure he was being truthful when he said he didn't know her."

Ross nodded. "Right," he said. "So where do kids meet other kids?"

"School, the mall, the movies," I suggested.

"Okay," Ross said. "So here's the deal. Todd is a hard worker. I'm assuming that by the time you finish sorting your first batch of trash, he'll have come up with the photo. Then I want you to hit the bricks. We'll start with secondary schools within a fifty-mile radius or so. I'll have Katie put together a list of school principals along with their contact information. Someone out there knows who this girl is.

"Again, when you talk to the principals, your cover story is that we're investigating a possible case of bullying. School bullying is a big deal these days, the media flavor of the month. People will be a lot more likely to help if they think that's all it is. They'll turn skittish if they know it's a homicide.

"And speaking of skittish. You're going to need to talk to the governor's daughters. They may not be best pals with Josh, but kids always know what other kids in the family are up to. When we were kids, my older sisters all thought I was a regular pain in the butt, but they would have died first before ratting me out to our parents. And I felt the same way about them. Someone needs to interview the girls."

I was already shaking my head in objection. "Ross, I already know that isn't going to happen. Marsha Longmire isn't going to let us within arm's reach of Zoe and Giselle Longmire. Neither is Garvin McCarthy."

"You're right," Ross said. "I'm sure Garvin has seen to it that you've been declared persona non grata as far as the governor's mansion is concerned, but this may help."

He slid a piece of paper across the desk. On it was a Lacey address I didn't recognize. Lacey is a suburb just north of Olympia.

"What's this?" I asked, picking it up.

Ross smiled. "That would be the address of Sid Longmire, the governor's ex, and the ex's new wife, Monica. They live in a gated community on a golf course in Lacey, and they share custody of the two daughters, Zoe and Giselle. Actually, now that Giselle is eighteen, officially they share custody of the younger daughter only. Considering the way ex-wives and new wives usually interact, I have a feeling you'll have a lot more luck interviewing Zoe at her father's house than you will at the governor's mansion."

I folded up the address and put it in

my wallet. Ross Connors is a wily old bastard. He's a good guy to have in your corner, but I think it would be a bad idea to piss him off.

"Is that all?" I asked.

He nodded. "For right now."

"Okay, then," I said, standing up and offering my hand. "If you've got an early-morning plane to catch, we'd better be going."

Mel followed suit.

"You'll keep me apprised of any and all progress?" Ross asked.

"Absolutely," Mel said.

We left the office and started for the front door, expecting to make it there on our own. Ross had told Mrs. O'Malley good night sometime earlier, but she was nonetheless hovering somewhere in the background.

"Right this way," she said, appearing out of nowhere. She was still in her uniform; still in her apron.

She led us to the door, opened it, and shooed us into the hall.

"May the saints preserve you," she said.

Since I was riding back to the hotel

with Mel at the wheel, that wasn't such a strange wish.

"Thank you," I said. "And the same to you."

CHAPTER 9

We went back to the hotel. It wasn't that late, but it had been a long day, and my knees were killing me. I took some Aleve and went to bed. Mel was still at the desk in the corner checking her e-mail when I drifted off to never-never land, thinking about Gerry Willis's grandson, Josh Deeson.

Mel is more of a night owl than I am. That doesn't mean she's a slugabed in the morning, because she's able to function on far less sleep than I do. I went to bed early, she went to bed late, and we both got up at the same time.

Don't try to tell me that God doesn't have a sense of humor, because S/He does. Just the morning before I had been pondering the joys of having separate bathrooms. The next day dawned with us ensconced in the Olympia Red Lion with only a single bathroom in sight. And, in the world of bathroom use, men and women are definitely not created equal. Women win; men lose.

The bathroom had a single washbasin and what would have been an adequate countertop had Mel been there alone. I found a place in among her bottles and potions to put my shaving kit on a temporary basis. I'd had the good sense to shower while Mel was out on her morning run and had my shaving kit safely back in my luggage when she came back. Once she disappeared into the bathroom to shower and do her makeup, when a need arose, I had to take myself down to the lobby and make use of a men's room down there.

I was back in the room, seated at the desk, and had just booted up my computer when she emerged from the bathroom looking like a million bucks. Not so long ago, her appearing like that within touching distance would have caused me to whisper sweet nothings in her ear and try talking her out of the clothing she had just put on.

Not on this particular morning. I believe I may have mentioned that I hate having bad knees. They interfere with far more important activities than just going up and down stairs.

"Did you check your e-mail yet?" She asked the question while slipping on a fetchingly dangly pair of earrings.

Like purses, earrings are something else that must be chosen by the person who will wear them rather than by the person purchasing them. At this late date I have finally concluded that bringing Mel along on the shopping trips is a foolproof way of making sure all her birthday and Christmas presents are perfect.

On that morning in Olympia, what floored me was that she performed this tricky operation—putting what looked like chandeliers into tiny holes in her earlobes—without having to look in a mirror, even though one of those was there on the wall right next to her. And please do not ask me to explain why someone who has been shot more than once would turn squeamish at the idea of putting on a pair of pierced earrings. All I can say is I'm glad the earrings were destined for Mel's ears and not for mine.

As for e-mail? Yes, we're on the same account, so we can both see the list of each other's new mail. But it's like using the bathroom together. It's just not done. I don't read hers and she doesn't read mine.

I scrolled through my list of new mail, including any number of male enhancement messages, until I found the one with the subject line of Beaumont. I opened it and read the following:

Dear Mr. Beaumont,

My name is Sally Mathers. I believe you are my cousin, my mother's brother's son. I hope you'll forgive me for writing to

you like this, but time is of the essence.

My mother, Hannah Greenwald, is in her eighties now and not doing very well. I am her only child. At her insistence, I've been sorting out the house here in Beaumont, Texas, where she has lived all her life. The house originally belonged to her parents, my grandparents, Frederick and Hilda Mencken, and my grandmother lived there with my parents after Grandpa Mencken died in the early sixties.

I knew from stories I heard as a girl that my mother had a brother named Hank. His full name was Henry Russo Mencken. Russo was my grandmother's maiden name. From what I gathered over the years, Hank joined the navy in World War II, went away, and never came home. He died in a motorcycle accident before being shipped overseas.

There were a lot of men who didn't come home after the war.

I had a number of girlfriends whose fathers either didn't come home at all or who came home as decorated heroes. From what I could gather around the dinner table, Hank wasn't one of those. He was a bit of a scalawag—sort of the black sheep of the family—who was given a choice between joining the service and going to jail. Compared to jail, the U.S. Navy must have seemed like a reasonable option.

As I said, according to my mother, Hank was a bit of a wild thing. By the time he joined the service, he had been in enough trouble that my grandparents, and especially Grandpa Mencken, pretty much washed their hands of him. You probably can't imagine a parent doing something like that to his own child. Most people can't, but Grandpa Mencken wasn't an easy person to get along with.

Actually, in that regard he and my grandmother were a matched pair. My father always said of Grandma Mencken that she was "as mean as a snake," but he only said it when he was well out of earshot. I think it's a miracle that, growing up the way she did, my mother turned out to be such a nice person. You can believe me when I tell you that she and my dad made a lot of sacrifices over the years in looking out for Grandma when other people probably would have walked away, but Mother was Hilda's only surviving child. There wasn't anyone else to do it.

I had to stop reading just then because my eyes had misted over. Unfortunately, I could very well imagine a parent washing his hands of his own child. It was the same thing my mother's father, my other grandfather, had done to his own daughter when he learned she was pregnant with me.

"What is it?" Mel asked. "Is something wrong?"

She was seated in the chair directly behind me, the so-called comfortable one, with her own computer open on her lap. I'm sure she saw me mop my eyes, and she must have wondered what was happening.

"Just a minute," I said. "Let me finish reading this."

I returned to the text of the e-mail:

Grandma Mencken lived with us the whole time I was growing up. She was over a hundred when she died. With her it's the opposite of the good dying young. Somehow I don't think Mother will make it that long, probably because she used up so many of her good years in looking after Grandma.

At any rate, Mother and Hank were close growing up. They were brother and sister, but they were also good friends. As far as I can tell, after he joined the service, she was the only member of the family who wrote to him regularly. There may have

been other letters, but I only found the ones he sent to her. In them he mentioned receiving her letters and told her how much he appreciated hearing from home. He never mentioned letters from anyone else.

Mother said she kept all his letters, tied together with a ribbon. Shortly after the war ended, the packet disappeared. My mother mourned losing those letters; she always blamed herself for being so careless. It turns out they weren't lost at all. I found them up in the attic, hidden away in the back of one of the drawers in Grandma Mencken's pedal sewing machine when I took it to the local historical society.

I already mentioned that my grandmother was mean. She once lay down on the floor and pretended to be dead because my mother didn't buy the kind of cookies she liked. It was only AFTER Mother called 911 and the ambulance was on its way that Grandma got up off the floor and told her, "See there? I fooled you." I'll say!!!

But I think hiding Hank's letters tops that trick. The truth is, my mother never lost Hank's letters. Grandma Mencken took them. Big difference. Once I found them, I read through them all, one by one. Hank wrote to Mother about a wonderful girl he had met in Seattle. He said that her name was Carol Ann Piedmont, although in his letters Hank always refers to her as Kelly. He told Mother that he was in love, that he had bought Kelly a ring, and that he hoped, after they got married, that she'd come back home with him and live right here in Beaumont. The letters stopped because he died in a motorcycle accident.

After he died, my grandparents refused to get in touch with the girl. Mother was still living at home at the time and couldn't bring herself to go against their wishes. By the time she was ready to do something about it on her own, the letters had disappeared—until I found them a few months ago.

I didn't mention finding them to Mother because I didn't want to get her hopes up that we'd be able to locate Hank's long-lost Kelly. I used the Internet and searched the available records for your mother's name. I was surprised to learn that she had never married. It made me sad when I found her obituary, like that was the end of it right there, but that's when I discovered she had a son.

When I saw your name there in her obituary I had goose bumps. Suddenly it seemed possible that you might be Hank's son and that your mother had given you at least that much of your father's history, his hometown, because, I'm sad to say, she had nothing else of his to give you.

Please don't think I'm a stalker, but I managed to track down your high school photo. I put it side by side with Hank's senior photo the year he graduated from Beaumont High School. The two of you could have been brothers or even twins. I can scan the photo and send you a copy if you like.

If you're still reading this, you probably see my writing to you now, after so many years of silence, as an unwelcome invasion of your privacy. I can hardly blame you for that, and if you choose not to answer, I'll certainly understand. After all, my family betrayed both of you. For your mother, struggling to raise a child on her own in the aftermath of World War II couldn't have been easy.

It's possible that my grandparents didn't know you existed. I hope that's true, but I'm prob-

ably being too charitable. Otherwise, how could they have turned
their backs on your mother when
I'm sure she could have used
their help, to say nothing of their
considerable   financial   resources, to raise their only
grandson? That's what you are,
by the way—their only grandson.
I have two granddaughters and
a grandson, but that makes him
a great-grandson. You were then
and still are their only grandson.

So here comes the asking part
of the letter—the one you've
been dreading and the thing this
whole exercise has been leading
up to. I'm hoping I'll be able to
convince you to come to Beaumont to see Mother while there's
still time.

This would be at no cost to
you, of course. I'd be happy to
pay your way. If you're married,
I'll pay your wife's way, too. I
hope you'll consider it. Mother
loved your father so very much,
and being able to lay eyes on

you would be a gift beyond anything I could ever give her. It
would fill an empty spot in her
heart that has been there ever
since she lost her beloved
brother Hank.

I'm putting my contact information at the bottom of this
page so you can be in touch if
you so choose. Again, I understand that you have every right
to be angry with my family, but
please don't take it out on
Mother. What happened be-
tween Grandpa and Grandma
Mencken and Hank was their
fault, not hers.

Sincerely,
Sally Mathers

For a long time after I finished reading, I didn't move. Couldn't move. At my
age, it was astonishing to me to hear
someone—a stranger—refer to my
mother by her given name. Once my
grandmother died, there was no one
left in my life to do that. Carol Ann—
Kelly—Piedmont was always just Mother

to me, and of course that's where my daughter's name comes from—my mother's name.

It seemed astonishing to me that Kelly Piedmont had gone out in the world and found a man whose parents were as difficult and as judgmental as her own. Of course, maybe that was part of the attraction. She and Hank both knew what it was like to try to live their own lives with parents who regarded their children as puppets and who stayed just out of sight, offstage somewhere, pulling their kids' strings for all they were worth. No wonder Hank Russo Mencken and Carol Ann Piedmont had bonded. And if Frederick Mencken and Jonas Piedmont had ever had occasion to meet, they probably would have gotten along like gangbusters. After all, birds of a feather do flock together.

"Beau," Mel said. She spoke from behind me, her voice full of concern. "Did you hear me? Are you all right? What is it—someone claiming to be a long-lost relative and trying to put the bite on you?"

"No," I said quietly. "It seems like exactly the opposite."

I passed her my open computer and waited while she read Sally's letter. "Wow!" she said finally, when she finished. "That's an amazing story. Do you think any of it is true?"

Mel is a cop. Her first instinct is always to question—to wonder if someone is lying, and if so, why. But I knew as soon as I read the words that this was all true, every bit of it. Everything Sally Mathers had said in her letter corroborated what my own mother had told me. J. P. Beaumont wasn't an orphan. I still had an aunt, one I had never met. I still had a cousin, a cousin who was reaching out to me, and some grandnieces and a grandnephew, too.

"What do you think she wants?" Mel asked. "Maybe she's figured out that you have money and she's looking for a handout."

"That's not what she said," I responded. "She claims that the only thing she wants is for me to come visit a dying woman she believes to be my aunt, a woman who's supposedly my father's sister. But don't forget, she also offered to pay my way there. If she had any idea that I had money, she wouldn't have done that."

"All the same," Mel said, "before you go hopping on the first plane to Beaumont . . . Now that you mention it, where the hell is Beaumont, Texas?"

"Near Houston," I said.

When my mother told me my name had come from a city, I had looked Beaumont, Texas, up on a map. As a kid I spent years wondering what it was like and how it would be to live there.

"So," Mel continued, "before you go hopping on the next plane to Houston, how about if we have Ralph Ames make some inquiries for us and find out if this woman is on the level?"

I probably would have argued with her right then, but the phone rang. Caller ID was blocked, but I answered it anyway. At first all I could hear was sobbing—a woman sobbing.

"Hello," I said. "This is J. P. Beaumont. Who's calling, please? Is something wrong? If this is an emergency, hang up and dial 911."

"It's Marsha," she managed. "Marsha Longmire. The cops are here and the ambulance, but he's gone. Oh my God. He's dead!"

I had visions of Gerry Willis's heart giving out from the strain of everything that had gone on the day before. And I couldn't help but remember that one of the last things Marsha had said to Mel and me before we left the house—that if anything happened to Gerry because of Josh's misbehavior she would murder the kid herself. I hadn't taken the threat seriously then, and I didn't now. It's the kind of empty threat parents make from time to time—a variation on a theme of "ain't it awful."

So I have to admit that my first thought was about Josh. At age fifteen the poor kid had already been abandoned time and again, by his no-good parents and by a child protective services organization that had let him go back to a horrible situation. Now he was being robbed of a grandfather who was, as far as I knew, Josh's only surviving blood relation. Marsha Longmire had taken on the guardianship more as a duty than as an act of love. From what I had seen of her, she had been less than enamored of the boy to begin with. Now, if she saw Josh as the proximate cause of Gerry Willis's untimely death, I could well imagine the kind of anger she'd feel toward the kid, to say nothing of the kind of guilt she'd dish out.

"How's Josh taking it?" I asked.

Marsha practically screamed at me. "Haven't you been listening to a word I said? Josh is dead. I found him just a little while ago, hanging from the closet door in his room. He had strung together a bunch of Gerry's old neckties. Then he tied it to the doorknob on one side of the door, threw the rope of ties over the top of it. He stood on a chair, put the noose around his neck, and then kicked the chair out from under him. He's dead, and I can't believe it happened! Damn! Damn! Damn!"

"Who's there?" I asked. "Who responded?"

"I called 911. Olympia PD showed up with the ambulance, but since it's the governor's mansion, they weren't sure about jurisdiction. They said someone should probably call the Washington State Patrol and I've notified my security detail, but after yesterday, I decided to call you as well."

"Thank you, Marsha," I said. "Good thinking."

Mel was already out of the chair and slipping on her shoes.

"What happened?" she asked.

"Come on," I said. "We've gotta go. It's Josh Deeson. He may have committed suicide last night. Olympia PD is responding, but since it's the governor's mansion, they're deferring to the Washington State Patrol. Governor Longmire decided to call us in as well. It'll be a horse race to see who gets there first."

CHAPTER 10

We took the Cayman. Mel drove and I called Ross Connors's cell phone. That's one of the things I like about him. His people, even the grunts out in the field, have access to the big guy, and I was able to get right through. But with the blue bubble on top of Mel's car, we got to the governor's mansion in no time, sooner than I was able to finish explaining to Ross what was going on.

"No!" the AG gasped when I related my bad news.

"The local cop shop is citing jurisdictional issues and has stepped down in favor of the Washington State Patrol."

"I'll call the head of the WSP and tell them we'll be working on this with them. It's a good thing Governor Longmire called you," Ross said. "Give me a minute. I'll get back to you."

Ross ended the call. I got out of the Cayman and followed Mel up the paved brick driveway that led to the governor's mansion. There were a couple of city cop cars parked out front and a WSP command car as well. If an ambulance had been summoned, it had already come and gone. In its place was a van with an insignia that said "Thurston County Medical Examiner."

A baby-faced kid decked out in an Olympia PD uniform, who looked far too young to be on the job, opened the door. Mel showed him her badge.

"Oh," he said. "You're the ones the governor wants to see. She's in her office."

He gestured toward the study. When we knocked on the door frame, the governor motioned us in through the open door.

Between her tearful phone call a few minutes earlier and now, Marsha Longmire had managed to compose herself. She had donned her official look, in both clothing and expression, that announced to all comers: "I am the governor and I am in charge." That maybe impressed the unsophisticated kid manning the front door, but I wasn't as awed by the surroundings as he was. Besides, I glimpsed the gratitude on Marsha's starkly pale face when Mel and I first walked into the room.

I caught the look and I read the message: Governor Longmire didn't want *any* cops in her home, but she had decided we were okay—the best of a bad bargain.

"Thank you for coming," she said.

Since Ross had ordered us onto the case, doing anything less would have been dereliction of duty, but I didn't tell her that.

"I'm so sorry," I said. "What happened? Who found him?"

"Zoe," Marsha answered. "When he didn't come down for breakfast, I sent her up to get him. And there he was.

The way she screamed . . ." Marsha paused and shook her head. "It was terrible. I've never heard a sound like that. She's in shock. I called our family doctor. He's going to come by and give her something."

"He hasn't yet?"

"No," Marsha said. "He's on his way, but as far as I know he hasn't arrived.

"Is there anyone else here besides Zoe?"

"No, it's just the three of us. Giselle spent the night at her dad's place."

Mel stood up. "Where's Zoe right now?"

"She's up in her room on the second floor," Marsha began, "but I'd rather you didn't—"

"We need to talk to her now," I explained, interrupting her objection. "If the doctor gives her something to settle her down, it may also remove some important detail from her memory of the scene."

"All right," Marsha said reluctantly. "Turn right when you get off the stairs. It's the room at the end of the hall."

As Mel left the room, my phone rang.

It was Ross. "I need to take this," I told Marsha. "It's the AG."

She nodded and waved, but I'm not sure she was really paying attention.

"Are you at the mansion?" Ross asked.

"Yes," I said.

"Please give the governor my condolences," he said.

I held the phone away from my ear. "Mr. Connors says he's sorry for your loss."

Marsha nodded, but again she didn't seem connected to my words.

"Here's how this is going to go down," Ross continued. "S.H.I.T. will handle the investigation, but we'll be using state patrol crime scene investigators. It'll be a joint case."

It was also going to be a big case. I understood Ross's thinking. It was better to spread the responsibility around. If the case turned into a blame game somewhere along the line, that could be spread around as well.

"Where did it happen?" Ross asked.

"Upstairs in his room. It's on the third floor."

"Is there anyone there right now?" Ross asked. I relayed the question to Marsha Longmire.

She sighed. "I believe the M.E. got here a few minutes ago."

"Did you hear that?" I asked Ross.

"Yes, I did," he replied. "The Thurston County M.E. isn't one of my favorite people. If that yahoo is on the scene, you'd better get your butt there, too."

I excused myself to the governor and then, bad knees or not, I ran all the way up the stairs to the top floor, to Josh Deeson's floor.

M.E.s and cops are supposedly on the same side, but we're not necessarily on the same page. Medical examiners want to know how someone died. Homicide cops want to know who did it and why. Medical examiners are concerned with bodies. They're not concerned with preserving crime scene evidence. Cases often turn on the smallest particles of trace evidence. For that reason, crime scenes have to be treated with great reverence and care. The items found under those circumstances need to be handled like fine, fragile antiques.

Some M.E.s are great, but some end up being the proverbial bulls in a china shop.

Unfortunately the Thurston County M.E., Larry Mowat, falls in the latter category. And since Olympia is both the state capital and the Thurston County seat, Ross Connors most likely had had enough dealings with Mowat to know whereof he spoke. I had met Mowat at various conferences, but I knew him primarily by reputation, which wasn't necessarily a good thing.

I stopped outside the door long enough to slip on a pair of crime scene booties and a pair of latex gloves. Mel and I keep a ready supply of them in our vehicles so we can slip them into our pockets at a moment's notice. I found Dr. Mowat sitting on the edge of Josh's bed—his carefully made bed. The M.E. wore neither booties nor gloves. He was staring down at the dead boy, who lay on the floor between the open closet door and the closet itself.

As Marsha had already explained, a makeshift rope had been manufactured by stringing together a whole set of out-of-date neckties. They had been tied with knots that would have done an Eagle Scout proud. It wasn't surprising that a kid obsessed with instruments of torture and death would be able to fashion an impressive noose for himself, one that had done the job for which it was intended.

Josh was clearly dead, but his stiffly spiked hair remained perfectly intact. I had a feeling someone—his grandfather, most likely—would come along and flatten out those spikes before Josh Deeson was laid in his final resting place.

I noticed something else, too. He was wearing a wristwatch—a good-quality wristwatch with a stainless-steel band. I would have had to turn Josh's hand over to see if it was his graduation-present Seiko, but I didn't. Until the crime scene photos had been taken, I didn't want to touch anything at all.

I recognized Dr. Larry Mowat. He didn't recognize me.

"You crime scene?" he asked. "I called for my guys a while ago. I've got no idea what's taking them so long. They should have been here by now."

I knew exactly what was taking so long. His guys weren't coming. Ross Connors had sent word down from on high. As a result Thurston County had called off their forensics people because Ross was sending in CSIs from the Washington State Patrol. The fact that no one had bothered to let Dr. Mowat know told me he was almost as popular with his fellow Thurston County employees as he was with the attorney general.

"I'm with Special Homicide," I told Mowat. "I understand we'll be handling this case from here on out."

"Special Homicide? You mean that S.H.I.T. outfit that works for the AG?" Mowat asked derisively. "Somebody needs to tell Ross Connors to get over himself. This is a suicide, not a homicide. I know Ross holds me in pretty low regard, but it doesn't take a whole lot of brainpower to see that this kid offed himself. He even left us a note."

"What note?" I asked. This was the first I had heard of any note.

"On the desk over there. It says, 'I can't take it anymore.' What a joke. Take what? Like living in the governor's mansion is some kind of hardship?"

For Dr. Larry Mowat, this qualified as wit.

I went over to the desk and looked down at the note. I didn't touch it and I hoped Mowat hadn't touched it either as I read it myself, aloud. It was, as they say, short but brief:

"I can't take it anymore." The initials J.D. were scrawled underneath those stark five words.

I noticed right away that there was a grammatical problem with that sentence. It was a case of what my high school English teacher, Mrs. Reeder, would have called "faulty pronoun reference." In fact, if she'd still been alive and had seen the note, I'm sure those are the very words she would have written on Josh's suicide note in bright red-colored pencil: FAULTY PRONOUN REFERENCE!!! She always wrote her remarks in capital letters with plenty of exclamation marks after them.

As I remember her long-winded harangues on the subject, pronouns are used in place of nouns, more specifically nouns that precede the pronouns in question—the pronouns' antecedents. Mrs. Reeder was a holy terror, by the way, and spending a year in her class was tantamount to being brainwashed. After all these years, how else would I even remember the word "antecedent," to say nothing of what it means?

In the case of Josh's note, the pronoun "it" had no antecedent, but it told me there had been something terribly wrong in his life. Josh was a kid who had already suffered some pretty hard knocks. As a homicide cop, I leaned toward the idea that Josh's mysterious "it" referred to his involvement with the girl in the video clip and to the part he had played in her death.

I've seen that happen over and over. Josh wouldn't be the first suspected murderer to choose to exit on his own rather than deal with the legal consequences of his actions. Still, I couldn't help wishing the kid had spelled "it" out for us in more detail so we'd be able to give his grieving relatives some real answers.

Dr. Mowat had looked at the note and immediately assumed that what was written there had something to do with ordinary teenage angst. I looked at it with the dubious benefit of having information Dr. Mowat wasn't privy to. (I won't even mention Mrs. Reeder's opinion about ending sentences with prepositions!) What I saw in my mind's eye were those two hands, pulling inexorably on the ends of that blue scarf, choking the life out of our still-unidentified victim.

Out in the world of criminal justice, a fair amount of attention is given to so-called deathbed confessions. This was neither—not a confession and not a denial.

I looked up from the note and found Dr. Mowat was still sitting on the bed, watching me speculatively.

"Maybe he killed himself because his folks wouldn't let him have a computer,"

Mowat said with a nonchalant shrug. "What teenager these days can get along without a computer? Isn't not letting your kid have a computer considered to be a form of child abuse?"

I happened to know that Josh Deeson did have a computer. At that very moment it was off in Spokane and being analyzed by a branch of the Washington State Patrol crime lab.

Rather than comment on the computer issue, I changed the subject.

"Who cut him down from the door?" I asked.

The M.E. shrugged. "Probably the EMTs," he said. "It sure as hell wasn't me," he added. "I've had my ass chewed a couple of times for doing just that. And take a look at this. Just before he killed himself, the kid was reading his Bible. Get a load of the verse he underlined."

I saw the book then, hidden behind Dr. Mowat's considerable bulk. He stood up when I walked over to the bed. The Bible lay open on the bedspread that probably hadn't been rumpled before Mowat sat on it. A red roller-ball pen marked the page. The book was open to the Gospel According to Saint John. John 14, Verse 2, was underlined in red ink.

"In my Father's house are many mansions; if it were not so, I would have told you. I go to prepare a place for you."

It tugged at my heart that in the last hours and minutes before taking his own life, Josh Deeson had been reading his Bible—his mother's Bible.

"Still think this is some kind of homicide instead of a suicide?" Mowat asked. "That looks like a suicide note, too, right there in black and white. Red and white, actually," he corrected himself.

"I think," I said truthfully, "suicide or not, there may be more going on here than meets the eye."

I heard a doorbell, followed instantly by the now-familiar sound of footsteps ascending the creaking stairs. Whoever was coming paused outside the door of the room, no doubt doing the same thing I had done—putting on booties, putting on gloves.

"The CSI guys are here," I said. "You

should probably go wait somewhere else until they finish up."

Mowat balked. "Go wait somewhere else? Are you kidding? You're kicking me out of my own crime scene? You can't do that. This is Thurston County."

The bedroom door opened. I looked up expecting a group of CSI folks to enter. Instead, Mel Soames, wearing her own booties and latex gloves, slipped quietly into the room, closing the door behind her and leaving a trio of CSI techs stuck on the far side of it.

She looked at Mowat and gave him a thin smile. Not a nice smile, an icy smile. If she had given me that look, it would have shriveled my balls.

"Yes, he can," she said to him. "You need to go."

Mowat leered back at her.

"Hey," he said. "I remember you. I thought you were some kind of detective, but I guess you got kicked back to the gang and now you're one of the crime scene dolts."

"Actually, I'm not a crime scene dolt," she replied, giving the last three words an emphasis I recognized as nothing short of menacing. "I'm still a detective, and I work for S.H.I.T., too, right along with Mr. Beaumont here. If you know what's good for you, you'll get the hell out. There's a captain with the Washington State Patrol downstairs talking to the governor. Her name is Joan Hoyt. Give her your information. When we're ready for you to come pick up the remains, we'll have Captain Hoyt give you a call."

Had I said the very same words, the results might have been quite different, but since the orders seemed to come from an entirely unexpected quarter, they threw Mowat for a loss. He didn't know quite how to react. He looked uncertainly from Mel to me and then back at Mel again.

"You can't talk to me that way," he complained. "It's disrespectful."

"Sorry," she said with a shrug.

Mel said the word "sorry," but with her, tone of voice is everything. I understood exactly what she meant, as in, "Too bad. I just did talk to you that way." She wasn't sorry in the least.

Mowat stalked across the room and

wrenched open the door. The three CSI guys were still waiting in the hall. From the way they were chuckling among themselves, there could be little doubt that they had heard the whole exchange. What's more, they had evidently loved every word of it.

"Weren't you a little tough on the poor guy?" I asked Mel in an undertone once Mowat was gone.

"Are you kidding?" she said. "When I was down here in Olympia working on a special project, that guy tried to put the make on me."

"In that case," I replied, "you weren't nearly tough enough."

The Washington State Patrol crime scene team entered stage left. It was made up of three guys—three experienced guys. They may have come into the room laughing at Dr. Mowat's expense, but they got over it in a hurry and went to work. Someone higher up the food chain had given them marching orders. This was the governor's mansion. The dead boy was the governor's stepgrandson. The team had been told to do what they had to do, process the scene, take their photos, be respectful, and get the hell out.

I noticed they took particular care in untying the end of the necktie rope from the doorknob. One of the CSI techs coiled it as gently as possible and then stowed it in a waiting evidence bag.

People assume that you have to have a hard surface to collect fingerprints, and they did check every hard surface, but that's yesterday's technology. I knew from past experience that it might well be possible to collect usable fingerprints from the silk ties, too. More important, however, there was almost certain to be DNA evidence caught on the material. The problem was, in addition to trace evidence from Josh and from whoever might have worn the ties long in the past, there was probably also DNA evidence from the EMT who had cut down the body.

One of the techs was in charge of taking photos. Every time he snapped a picture, Mel used her little digital camera to photograph the same item. She took the photos while I took notes that would explain each of the photos for easy reference. The WSP crime scene photos would be the official ones—the ones that would be part of any legal proceeding. They would be available to us in good time, which is to say eventually or whenever the state patrol got around to giving them to us. Mel's photos would fill in the gap and give us working copies we could use in the meantime.

As far as I was concerned, the watch was possibly the most important piece of evidence in the room. I was dying to see if it was the supposedly missing graduation Seiko. I didn't make a fuss about it because I didn't want to give away our prior involvement. Instead, I waited patiently while the photographer finished with his pictures of the body.

Since someone had cut Josh down, we all understood that the pictures of the body in situ probably weren't all that important. Still, everybody played along and went through the entire protocol charade all the same.

"Okay," the photographer said at last. "I'm done. You can call the M.E. back anytime."

"First I need to see the watch," I said.

Obligingly one of the techs turned Josh's wrist over so the face of the watch was visible. My distance vision is fine. It's up close where I need reading glasses, and I was able to read the logo with no difficulty—Seiko. Just yesterday, Josh Deeson had told us that the watch he'd been given for graduation was lost. Now, inexplicably, it was back.

On pieces of property, especially watches and cameras, sales receipts and serial number information can often be verified if you go to the trouble of digging far enough. If this really was the supposedly missing watch, then where had it been while it had been among the missing, and how had it been returned?

The crime scene photographer leaned in and took a close-up photo of the watch with his camera. As soon as he moved out of the way, Mel did the same thing with hers.

The crime scene guys were packing up to go when the door swung open again. I was amazed to see Gerry Willis standing in the hallway. His face looked gray. He had abandoned his wheelchair on the ground floor. He was panting and leaning heavily on a walker. It had taken tremendous effort on the First Husband's part to make it all the way up to the third floor. I doubted Governor Longmire had any idea of where he was or what he was doing.

He stood there in the open doorway staring at Josh's bare feet. That was all that was visible from behind the half-open closet door.

Of all the people in the room, Mel was the one who came to her senses first. She didn't tell Gerry he shouldn't have come all the way upstairs. And she didn't deny him entrance to the room, although, since it was still an active crime scene, she most certainly could have. Instead, she hurried to the door, took Gerry by the arm, and gently escorted him over to the bed.

"You should probably sit down and catch your breath," she said.

Gerry Willis nodded gratefully, but before he took a seat, he reached out and smoothed the part of Josh's bedspread that Larry Mowat had left rumpled. Only when the bed was perfectly smooth again, as Josh must certainly have left it, did Gerry turn his walker around and ease himself down onto the mattress.

From that perspective, I knew that Josh's body was completely exposed. In another minute or so, the CSI guys would have covered the corpse with something, but right at that moment, they hadn't.

Gerry looked at the body for a moment, then he looked away, shaking his head sadly as tears spilled out of his eyes and dripped off his cheeks.

"Josh was meant to be a good boy," he said hopelessly. "I failed him, just like I failed his mother."

Far too often in my life I've been the one to bring parents—many times unsuspecting parents—the dreadful news that their beloved children are dead—that they've been murdered by some known or unknown assailant. Most of the time, the grief they feel rises up like a huge ocean wave—an emotional tsunami—that wipes out everything in its path. Losing a child to murder is awful.

And, having lost a wife to suicide, I can tell you that the anguish I felt after losing Anne Corley was worse than anything that ever happened to me. Nothing before and nothing since has ever come close.

But this was different. This was the suicide of a child, and Gerry Willis had been charged with the care and keeping of that lost child. The poor man's understandable anguish seemed to suck the air out of the room. I didn't say I understood how he felt, because I didn't. Besides, saying something like that would have diminished us both. Mel got that, too.

"I'm so sorry," she said softly. "Is there anything we can do?"

Gerry didn't answer her for a long time. Instead, he sat there staring at his grandson's still body and let tears flow unchecked. Finally he wiped his eyes and straightened his shoulders. I thought he was going to stand up. Instead, a puzzled frown crossed his face.

"I wonder where he found it," he said. "He hadn't worn it for several weeks. He told me he lost it, and I was pissed off about it because I paid good money for that watch. I expected him to take better care of it, but then last night, when he came to dinner, there it was on his wrist. I meant to ask him about it, but as you can imagine, last night's dinner wasn't a time for casual conversation."

Mel and I exchanged glances. We had both been in this very room earlier that afternoon and had heard Josh tell us the watch was lost. How was it possible that it turned up so soon after that discussion? And where had it been in the meantime?

I looked around the room, where everything was neat as a pin—where absolutely nothing was out of place. Josh Deeson had come to this house with next to nothing. He hadn't lost his mother's Bible. It didn't make sense that in all this excessive neatness he had somehow misplaced a relatively expensive watch that had to have counted as one of his prized possessions. Then again, since it came from his grandfather, maybe Josh hadn't prized it all that much after all.

"Can I have it?" Gerry asked. "If you don't mind, I'd really like to keep it."

Just then all those years of being a homicide cop kicked into overdrive. "I'm sorry, but you can't have it right now," I said. "It's still part of the crime scene. We were about to bag it and take it into evidence, but I'll make sure it gets back to you."

"Promise?" Gerry asked.

"Yes," I said. "I promise."

The CSI guys were still in the room and they had been taking in every word of the conversation. Without being asked, one of the techs obligingly slipped the watch off Josh's wrist. He placed the Seiko in a glassine bag and then passed it along to the guy who was keeping the evidence log.

Gerry looked back at Josh's still body. "What happens next?" he asked.

"The M.E. will have to come collect the body," I told him.

"And then an autopsy?" Gerry's voice cracked over that last word. Josh's voice had cracked because he was a boy becoming a man. His grandfather's voice broke because now that transformation would never happen.

"Yes," Mel said gently. "Under the circumstances, an autopsy is required by law."

Gerry shuddered. "I see," he said.

Then, heaving a sigh, he grabbed hold of the handles on the walker and pulled himself upright. "I'd better be going," he said. "Before Marsha figures out I'm gone."

Suspicions confirmed. Governor Longmire had no idea that Gerry had made the long pilgrimage up to the third floor, to the attic, as he had once called it.

"If you'll give us a couple more minutes to finish packing up, Mr. Willis," one of the CSIs said, "we can give you a hand getting back down the stairs. And then I'll let Captain Hoyt know to send the M.E. and his guys back upstairs."

"Thank you," Gerry said. "That would be a big help. I think getting back down the stairs on my own might be more than I can handle."

So much for the guys the medical examiner had scathingly referred to as the CSI "dolts." I'd take one of them over Dr. Larry Mowat any day of the week.

Once they took Gerry with them and

headed downstairs, Mel and I were left alone for the first time in the better part of an hour.

"What do you think about the note?" I asked.

"He was planning on dying," Mel said. "If he did this because he was involved in the strangulation of that girl, it seems to me that he would have stepped up and accepted responsibility instead of denying it. On the other hand, if he didn't do it, why commit suicide? What was it he couldn't stand anymore?"

It was gratifying to know that Mel and I were on the same wavelength.

"Did you talk to Zoe?" I asked.

Mel shook her head. "The doctor got there too soon. He said he was giving her a sedative and wouldn't let me hang around. I did talk to Todd, though. He says he has a photo for us. He sent a jpeg with pretty reasonable resolution to my computer. I used my air card to send it to Katie Dunn. I asked her to run us off a couple hundred copies. I have a feeling we're going to need them. But what's the deal with the watch?"

"The watch was missing for a period

of time. If someone else had it while it was MIA," I said, "what's the best way to carry a watch?"

"On your wrist," Mel answered.

"So maybe whoever had the watch made that same mistake? I'm sure the crime lab will find Josh's DNA stuck between the links. With any kind of luck, someone else's DNA will be stuck there, too."

"But these are kids," Mel objected. "What are the chances that their DNA will be in any of the databases?"

"What are the chances that we'll find the same DNA and/or fingerprints on that blue scarf?"

"Got it," Mel said with a smile. "Because one of the people pulling on that scarf was also wearing the watch, but if the kid's prints aren't in the system, that still won't help us."

That's what happens in investigations—you take two steps back for each step forward.

Dr. Mowat turned up about then carrying a body bag and bringing with him two beefy assistants.

"It's about time," he grumbled. "I've

had my guys waiting downstairs for damned ever."

We stayed long enough to see the body zipped into the bag and loaded onto a gurney. I didn't envy the two assistants the job of taking a loaded gurney back down the stairs. I also didn't envy their having to work for Mowat.

Mowat started to follow the gurney down the hallway. When my cell phone rang he stopped, waiting, I suppose, to see if the call had anything to do with him.

"How's it going?" Ross Connors wanted to know.

"They're just now picking up the body."

"So that jerk Mowat is there?" he asked.

"At the moment," I answered.

"And it's definitely suicide?"

"Sure looks like it."

"I got off the phone with Katie a few moments ago," Ross continued. "Tell Mel that the copies of that photo she asked for are ready."

"Do you want us to stop by and pick them up?"

"No," Ross said. "I don't want either one of you anywhere near the office down there. Since the WSP crime lab people were on the premises, people will most likely assume they're handling the investigation. I want to leave it that way for the time being. Of course, that's counting on some discretion from Larry Mowat, which is probably leaning on a bent reed.

"Anyway, I told Katie to put the photos in an envelope and leave them for you at the desk at the Red Lion. And as for the garbage . . ."

I had been so tied up with the crime scene investigation that I had somehow assumed that my garbage-sorting detail had gotten lost in the shuffle. Not so.

"I had one of my friends empty the garbage cans in question into a pair of tarps. He's taken them to one of those self-storage unit places just off the freeway down in Tumwater." He started to dictate the name and address.

"Wait a minute," I said. "Let me write this down."

Once I had pen in hand, he gave me the information.

"Go in, ask to speak to the manager on duty. That'll be Rebekah Ming." It was an unusual name, and he had to spell it out for me. "Show her your ID, tell her Ross sent you," he continued. "She'll give you the key."

"Great," I said. "That's exactly how I wanted to spend the rest of my day." I didn't say "sorting garbage" aloud because Dr. Mowat was right there, listening to every word.

"Right," Ross said cheerfully. "That's why I pay you the big bucks."

"Not enough," I grumbled. "Maybe it's time I asked for a raise."

"Just be sure you get to the storage unit before five," Ross said. "That's when Rebekah goes off duty, and she's my guy, if you will. She also knows about what's being dropped off there. When you finish going through the stuff, she'd like you to drag everything that's left out to their Dumpsters and get rid of it. With it being summer and all, they don't want that stuff left inside overnight attracting vermin."

"Yes," I said. "I understand. I'll get right on it first thing this afternoon."

I also understood all too well that it was going to be a dirty, smelly job.

Mel waited until I ended the call. "Okay," she said for Dr. Mowat's benefit and again without mentioning the word "garbage." "Let's go downstairs and see if we can interview members of the family."

The situation on the ground floor of the governor's mansion had changed remarkably in the length of time—close to two hours—since Mel and I had gone upstairs. Time flies when you're having fun. Earlier, except for a couple of cop cars and Dr. Mowat's van, the driveway had been empty. Now it was packed with people—media people—with a full contingent of reporters equipped with camera crews and microphones. Mel's Cayman was stuck right in the middle of a traffic jam of media vans. The only way we were going to extract her vehicle was by using a winch and a crane.

Captain Hoyt of the Washington State Patrol met us at the bottom of the stairs. "The reporters are waiting for a statement," she said, nodding toward the crowd milling outside. "Are you going to do the press conference or should I?"

"Go ahead," I said. "By all means."

Besides, I knew Ross Connors would have my head if I put my mug in front of a television camera.

Captain Hoyt turned to Mel as if for verification.

"Please," Mel said. "We need to talk to the family."

"All right," Captain Hoyt said dubiously. "But don't say I didn't give you first dibs."

Mel and I let her go with cheery good wishes. Once Captain Hoyt has a few bad media experiences to her credit, she might see giving a press conference in the same kind of light Mel and I do—which is right up there with going to the dentist for a root canal.

I looked toward the study. Inside I counted at least four visitors in the room in addition to Marsha Longmire. That count made for two more occupants than the room could comfortably hold. Mel and I were standing there trying to decide what to do when Gerry Willis appeared in the doorway of the dining room, two rooms away. He was still using the walker, but he looked somewhat better. Like the governor, he seemed to have gathered his resources, composed himself, and put on his "company" face. He motioned for us to come to him. I think he was still tired from his long trip up and down the stairs.

"We were hoping to conduct some family interviews," I ventured.

"Marsha is busy with some of her big donors, Zoe's still sleeping, and Giselle is at her dad's place," Gerry said. "That leaves only me. Come have some lunch."

Mel and I had missed breakfast, and we had both missed lunch. The last food that had passed my lips had been the peach cobbler and ice cream at Julie and Todd Hatcher's place the night before. As hungry as I was right then, even one of Marsha Longmire's unadulterated tuna sandwiches would have been welcome. Once I caught sight of the chow laid out buffet style on the dining room table, however, I realized that it was Tuesday. A miracle had occurred. The governor's cook was back from her day off, and she had whipped up a spread that would have done most church potlucks proud.

"We expect people will start stopping by once word gets out," Gerry said. "Help yourselves."

And so we did. I picked up a small china plate from a stack on the buffet along with a tiny cloth napkin. Yesterday's sandwiches had been served on paper napkins. Today was different— real dishes and real napkins. The cook evidently made the food and washed the dishes.

I loaded my plate with a couple of deviled eggs, some slices of ham and cheese, some grapes from a tray heaped high with fruit, and a freshly baked biscuit still hot from the oven. On a sideboard sat a coffee urn flanked by rows of china cups and saucers. There were also rows of glassware clustered around pitchers filled with various kinds of fruit juices and iced tea. Apparently an army of friends was expected rather than just a few, but at that point Mel, Gerry, and I were the only people in the dining room.

We hadn't attempted to interview Gerry upstairs in Josh's room. For one thing, the CSI techs had been there. For another, the poor man had been too overcome with emotion. It seemed likely that this would be one of our last chances to see him alone. Once crowds of well-wishers descended on the governor's mansion, that wouldn't be possible. I set my loaded plate on one corner of the dining room table. Then I sat down and pulled out my notebook. As soon as I did so, Mel reached in her purse. I didn't have to ask. I knew she was switching on her powerful cassette recorder.

"What can you tell us about Josh's state of mind last night?" I asked.

"Nothing, really," Gerry said. "I've been going over and over it all day long, wondering if there was something out of kilter that I should have noticed, but there wasn't. He went out for a run late in the afternoon."

"By himself?" I asked.

"I wasn't in any condition to go with him."

"But no one else went along?"

"He came by my room and asked if it was okay. I admit going for a run seemed a little out of character for Josh, but Marsha was too busy with other things by then for me to ask her about it and at least he asked permission. I told him fine as long as he was back in time for dinner. He was."

"Other than his going for a jog, did anything else strike you as unusual?" Mel asked.

"Other than the obvious? No. Josh knew he was in trouble for sneaking out the night before, so maybe he was a little quieter than usual—contrite."

"What happened next?" Mel asked.

"Nobody felt like cooking, so we ordered a pizza and had it delivered. When the pizza got here, Zoe went upstairs and told Josh it was time for dinner. He told her he wasn't hungry and didn't want any. I started to go upstairs to talk to him, but Marsha went instead. She told him when things get tough, families are supposed to stick together. She also told him that he couldn't hide out in his room forever and that he needed to come down and eat with the rest of us.

"So he did. He came to the table and ate a couple of pieces of pizza. Pepperoni is his favorite." Gerry paused, squeezed his eyes shut, and said, "Pepperoni *was* his favorite. When dinner was over, he said he was tired and went back upstairs. He even excused himself before he went. I guess if there was anything unusual besides his going for a jog, being polite like that would be it. I believed the part about his being tired. After all, he was evidently out most of the previous night and then he was in school all day. That's the last time I saw him—when he went upstairs after dinner."

"He didn't seem angry or upset?" Mel asked.

Gerry shook his head. "Not really. As I said already, he was subdued."

"Tell us about the watch he was wearing," Mel urged. "You seemed surprised to see it today."

"I was. As I told you earlier, as far as I knew, the watch had been missing for weeks. At least that's what Josh told me. He must have had it all along and just stopped wearing it."

"And he was wearing it when he came down to dinner?"

Gerry nodded. "Yes," he declared, "he was."

"Did Josh have any visitors last night, either before dinner or after?"

"Not that we know of," Gerry said. "I mean, no one came to the front door and rang the bell, if that's what you mean, but how would we know for sure? We didn't know he was getting out overnight, which he had probably been doing for months before Marsha finally caught him at it. If he's been going in and out without our knowing it, then there's a good chance other people have been coming in without our knowledge, too.

"But in view of what happened the previous night, he shouldn't have been able to sneak someone in. Marsha asked the security detail to make sure that the guards that patrol the capitol campus would stop by here overnight as well. I don't know how often they came by, but no one reported seeing any rope ladders going up or down the side of the building. If they had been there, I think someone would have noticed."

"How did Josh get along with the governor's girls?" Mel asked.

"With Gizzy and Zoe?" Gerry asked.

I nodded.

"Okay, I guess," Gerry said. "I'd say it wasn't like a real blended family—more like a blended family once removed. Even though Josh and the two girls are fairly close in age, he was my grandson, not my son. When he first got here, there was some jockeying for position and so forth, but that's just kids. I think we made the right decision when we sent him to public school rather than Olympia Prep. With the other girls ahead of him in school, there would have been undue expectations from some of the faculty members. Josh had holes in his academic background that meant he never would have measured up. Regular high school was tough enough. Olympia Prep would have been impossible."

"Someone mentioned that he'd been getting in fights," I said.

"I'm not sure how it happened, but some of the kids evidently learned about what happened to his mother. They teased him about it. He was a good-looking kid, but not as good-looking as he could have been. He should have had braces to straighten his teeth, but his mother never had the money or the inclination to do that. By the time I offered to take him to an orthodontist, he didn't want to go. He said he was too old for braces. As I understand it, the fights came out of teasing at school. One boy asked him if his teeth were crooked because he had meth mouth like his mother."

"Kids can be such mean bastards," Mel said.

Gerry looked at her, smiled, and nodded sadly. "That's the only instance I know about for sure," he said. "There were probably plenty of others. I should have protected him from all that, but I didn't."

Gerry Willis was back to blaming himself, not for the first time and doubtless not for the last. As far as I was concerned, he was right to do so. Josh had lived in the Willis/Longmire household for more than three years. Somebody should have stood up for him.

"You couldn't protect him," Mel said kindly. "No matter how much parents want to, they can't save their kids from all the little creeps in the world. Kids have to go out there and sink or swim on their own."

Gerry swallowed hard. "And Josh sank," he said bleakly.

I had barely touched the food on my plate, but I no longer wanted it. Ross Connors had decreed that our cover story had to do with Mel and me investigating a phony case of school bullying. Now, with the meth-mouth comment, it seemed our cover story had turned all too real and at least two kids were dead.

"Can you give us the names of any of Josh's friends?" Mel asked after a pause.

"Not really."

"Outside interests? Extracurricular activities?"

"He wasn't an athlete, if that's what you mean. That was why the jogging surprised me. He was interested in chess, though. There's a chess club at the high school. I met the adviser, a Mr. Dysart, briefly at an end-of-school pizza party, but I didn't know any of the other kids. I know it sounds strange that we can't tell you more about him, but he was a pretty self-contained kid."

"Given his background, maybe he had to be," I said.

"Thank you for saying that," Gerry said.

Just then the doorbell rang. A group of people came into the house. They stopped briefly in the entryway. The door to the governor's study opened. The people who had been closeted in there with Marsha Longmire filed out and milled around with the newcomers, talking and shaking hands. When they all started toward the living room, Mel and I decided it was time to take our leave.

"It would probably be better if we weren't here when your guests arrive," I said. "Is there a way we could leave without causing a disruption of some kind?"

"Sure," he said, pointing. "You could go out through the kitchen."

And that's exactly what we did. The cook may have been a little surprised when we came through and asked to be let out the back way, but she was evidently used to off-the-wall requests. When we came around from the back of the building we were relieved to see that most of the media presence was gone. Captain Hoyt had done an admirable job of getting rid of them.

There were new cars scattered around the driveway, but Mel was able to squeeze the Cayman out between a bright blue Jaguar and a red Volvo station wagon without denting any of them.

We didn't speak until we were back on the street and headed for the hotel. "So what's the truth about Josh Deeson?" Mel demanded. "Is he a killer or a victim?"

"Maybe a little of both," I suggested.

"Maybe the girl was one of his tormentors," Mel said after a pause. "Maybe the killing was all about revenge, and he just couldn't deal with the consequences."

That seemed plausible enough. We drove the rest of the way back to the hotel in silence while I considered what Mel had just said. Unfortunately, it was all too true. When Josh Deeson came to live at the governor's mansion, he had been dirt poor and years behind his peers in terms of academic achievement. Those separate ingredients had combined into a fateful mix that had made him ripe to become a target for mindless bullies. As a friendless loner he had most likely been the butt of countless ugly jokes. Now he was also dead.

All of that left me wondering about just one thing: Whatever happened to Josh Deeson's civil rights and the civil rights of the unidentified girl who had been strangled with the blue scarf?

I knew that both Governor Longmire and Gerard Willis cared about what had happened to the poor kid, but Mel Soames and I were the ones who were actually charged with finding out the whys and wherefores behind Josh Deeson's death, and the unknown girl's death, too.

I was determined that we would do just that, come hell or high water.

CHAPTER 12

Once back at the Red Lion, we stopped by the front desk long enough to pick up the envelope of photos of the video clip's dead Jane Doe. Riding up in the elevator, we pulled one out of the envelope. Todd Hatcher had done an excellent job of extracting a usable head-shot photo from the video. His enhanced image showed an average-looking brown-haired girl with a tentative smile—the smile Marsha Longmire had said would haunt her for the rest of her life.

"You know what?" I said. "From that

photo, I'd say she was a willing participant, at least initially."

"Yes," Mel muttered, sliding the offending photo back into the envelope.
"The old 'choking game.' Some game!"

Up in our room, while Mel sat down
at the desk and booted up her computer, I studied the clothing I had brought
along in my suitcase.

"What's wrong?" Mel asked.

"I seem to have brought along nothing but work clothes. When I packed I
had no idea that garbage was going to
be part of the work agenda."

"Try Goodwill," Mel said. "You should
be able to buy stuff you can throw away
after you use it."

"Good thinking," I said. "Where's the
nearest Goodwill?"

I was fully capable of looking it up on
my own, but Mel already had her computer open and at the ready. She gave
me the address.

"What are you going to do while I'm
off on garbage detail?" I asked.

"See if Todd can enhance the images
of the arms pulling the scarf."

I knew what she meant. She wanted

to know if the watch in the picture was Josh Deeson's watch. So did I. I left her to it and set off on my own. With help from the GPS, I pulled into the Goodwill parking lot in a matter of minutes.

The irony wasn't lost on me. I arrived at the thrift store to buy cheapo clothing while driving a very expensive Mercedes. Since I had no idea of how many days of garbage duty I was in for, I went wild and stocked up. I came out of the place fifteen minutes later feeling like I had scored and carrying a plastic bag that contained three pairs of shorts, three T-shirts, and a pair of flip-flops—all for under fifteen bucks. I loaded my bag of purchases into the trunk of the Mercedes and sped off.

The storage unit was a multilevel affair. To my amazement and relief, it was also air-conditioned. Who knew? I found the front desk, asked for Rebekah, and gave her my name.

"Unit D-335," she said. "Take the elevator to the third floor."

As she handed me the key, she gave me that singularly disapproving one-raised-eyebrow look all women seem to use on occasion. In the old days I wouldn't have had a clue about what that look meant, but being married to Mel has made me almost fluent in non-verbal female-centric lingo.

Rebekah thought I was overdressed for the job at hand. So did I.

I held up my bag of thrift-store duds. "I'm planning on changing," I said.

Without a word Rebekah handed me a second key. This one was on a ring that also contained a large wooden paddle that was too big to slip into a pocket. Written on the paddle was the word RESTROOM.

"Good," she said. "The restrooms are just beyond the elevators on the right."

I changed clothes there. Then, carrying my good clothes in the bag, I located unit D-335. Even with the AC going, a pungent odor assailed my nostrils the moment I opened the rolling door. There were two separate and bulging tarps on the floor of the unit. The first one, the recycling bin, was easily disposed of. It consisted primarily of soda cans and clear plastic water bottles. There was also a whole bale of shredded paper, along with an impressive stack of print newspapers. Obviously Governor Longmire preferred to get her news in dead-tree fashion rather than over the Internet.

Keeping the recycling safely contained, I tied that tarp shut and dragged it out into the hallway. The second tarp was a bit more problematic. In last-in-first-out fashion, the garbage heap was topped with yesterday morning's coffee grounds. It was possible to trace the previous day's events in chronological order, ending with a pizza box that no doubt dated from last night's dinner. Somewhere in the middle I found the flurry of paper napkins that had accompanied our unadorned tuna sandwiches—several of which had been tossed into the garbage along with the napkins.

Let me say right now that I was very grateful Washington's First Family had no pets. That would have made a tough job even tougher. It was clear, however, that these folks were big on fresh fruit. There were apple cores, orange peels, and banana peels in abundance. What happens to dead apple cores and banana peels overnight in the heat of summer isn't pretty, but it's nothing compared to witnessing any given autopsy, so I soldiered on, trying to do so with a cheerful heart.

I sifted through the garbage as best I could and found nothing that looked remotely related to what we were doing. I found a newspaper page with a completed Sudoku puzzle that had made it into the garbage instead of the recycling. Nowhere did I find any wadded-up sheets of notebook paper with cryptic phone numbers or coded messages. This was garbage—plain and simple garbage.

I spent forty-five minutes on the thankless task, then I tied up the tarp of garbage and dragged both that and the recycling downstairs. I emptied the tarps, folded them as best I could, and then took them back up to the storage unit so they could be reused. Josh Deeson might be dead, but I had a feeling that Ross Connors's interest in Governor Longmire's garbage wasn't going to end anytime soon.

I locked up and returned the keys to Rebekah. I drove back to the Red Lion feeling conflicted. I felt virtuous because it was a dirty job and I had done it. I felt frustrated because I had found nothing.

Mel wasn't in the room when I got back. There was a piece of hotel note-paper sitting on top of her closed computer. There was only one word written on it: AUTOPSY.

That surprised me. Mowat had picked up the body a relatively short time ago. Usually there was a little more wait time built into the system, but I chalked it up to Josh's being related to Governor Longmire. That probably greased the skids and made things happen faster than they would otherwise.

I headed for the shower with the slightest bit of guilt added to the mix. Sorting garbage wasn't my first choice of afternoon activity, but it beat the hell out of spending the afternoon with Dr. Larry Mowat.

I threw away the first set of Goodwill clothing and wore the second one. Yes, Ross Connors expects his agents to go out in public properly dressed in business attire. For men that means slacks, dress shirts, jackets and ties, even in the dead of summer. As long as I was working in the privacy of my hotel room, there was no reason not to be comfortable.

I turned on my computer and booted it up. There were several new e-mails listed. I cleared those out one at a time. Among them I found three from Todd Hatcher and one from Ross, which meant that one really came from Katie Dunn. There was also a copy of the e-mail Mel had sent to Ross giving him an overview of what had gone on earlier in the day. The next message after that, the one I'd saved as new, was the one from Sally Mathers—the one marked "Beaumont." I owed her a response, but I wasn't ready to deal with all of that, at least not yet.

I avoided the issue by hiding out in work and opened Todd's first message instead. That one contained two attachments—a copy of the snuff video and a copy of the Jane Doe jpeg. The second contained a short note and two jpeg attachments. I read the note first.

> **Look at both jpegs. I'll have to go somewhere else to do a more detailed enhancement to see if we can identify the watch. Back to you when I can.**

I opened the attachments. Each one contained a photo of an individual hand and arm, with the hand knotted into a tight fist around the end of the scarf. I squinted at the watch in the one photo. I wished I had a magnifying glass on me to help make out the details, but I didn't. In the other photo, the top of the thumb was clearly visible. Todd was online, so I sent him an instant message.

> **Is that nail polish on that thumb? Does that mean one of the assailants is a girl?**

He wrote back almost immediately.

> **You're out of the loop, J.P. These days boys wear nail polish, too.**

Not this boy, I thought.

The door opened and Mel came in looking surprisingly grim. More than a little surprised, I glanced at my watch.

"You're done already?" I asked. "That has to be one of the fastest autopsies in history."

"As far as I know, the autopsy has yet to start."

She came over and sank down on the bed. That's when I noticed she was holding a bag of ice against her right hand.

"What happened?" I asked.

"I punched him," she said. "Right in the kisser. If I'd made better contact, I would have broken his nose, but he ducked back out of the way. With any kind of luck, though, I loosened his front tooth. I know for sure he's got a split lip."

"Who ducked?" I asked. "Whose front tooth?"

"Who do you think?" Mel asked irritably. "Dr. Mowat, that's who. He listened in on your conversation with Ross earlier and figured out that you'd be tied up doing something else this afternoon.

That's why he claimed he had moved up the Deeson autopsy. He thought getting me alone was a good idea. Turns out it wasn't."

"You punched him?"

I admit there should have been a little more husbandly concern in the question and a lot less admiration, but I doubted Mel had been the only target of Larry Mowat's inappropriate attentions. Most likely the creep had deserved having his lights punched out for a long time. Of course, if he ended up filing an official complaint against Mel, that might have all kinds of long-term repercussions.

Right that minute, however, neither Mel nor I was thinking long-term.

"I sure as hell did!" she declared.

"Let me take a look at it." I scrambled up out of the desk chair, hurried to the bed, and lifted the ice pack off her knuckle. There was a neat cut across one of them where one of Mowat's front teeth had broken the skin. The whole back of her fist was already discolored and swollen. I could tell from looking at it that her hand probably hurt like hell. I also knew she'd bite her tongue off before she'd admit it. Without being asked, I went straight to my shaving kit and got her a couple of Aleves. I came back from the bathroom with the pills and a glass of water.

"He's probably filing a complaint even as we speak," she said once she had swallowed the tablets.

"Were there any witnesses?" I asked.

"Are you kidding?" she scoffed. "Jerks like that always make sure there are no witnesses."

"Did you write up a report the last time he hassled you?"

"I did," Mel said. "It's in the file. There's evidently been some bad blood between Mowat and Ross. At the time Ross told me he'd appreciate it if I'd leave it at that. And I did. Now all bets are off. If he files a complaint, I'll file a countercomplaint."

"Do you want me to go over to the morgue, finish witnessing the autopsy, and clean Mowat's clock while I'm at it?"

She gave me a sheepish grin. "Thanks for the offer of being my Sir Galahad, but don't bother. I already did a reasonable job of cleaning his clock myself. As for that autopsy? It turns out that wasn't really scheduled for today after all. That was just a ruse to get me over to the morgue."

"A phony autopsy as opposed to phony etchings," I muttered. "Classy."

Mel's phone rang. Because she would have had to put down the ice pack to answer it, I plucked it out of her pocket and answered it for her.

"Mel Soames's line," I said.

"She punched him?" Ross Connors roared into my ear. "She flat-out punched him?"

"No," I said. "I think it was more of a balled-fist situation than something flat-out."

"Don't be cute, Beau," Ross said. "Mowat just called my office and raised all kinds of hell with Katie Dunn. I'm pretty sure he didn't get a whole lot of sympathy from that quarter. Katie doesn't like him any more than I do. How's Mel?"

"She'd talk on the phone herself, but she's holding an ice pack on her knuckles," I told him. "She can't do both at the same time."

"Put me on speaker, then," he said. "I need to talk to both of you."

With some difficulty I managed to punch the appropriate numbers to activate the speaker function. It seems to me that there should be some standard operations that go from one kind of cell phone to another. That's not the case, though. The controls on Mel's phone differ enough from mine that I'm always baffled when I have to do anything with her phone.

"Are you there, Mel?" Ross asked.

"I'm here," she answered.

"Good. Are you okay?"

"My knuckles are a little swollen, but I'm fine. Why?"

"I've had people monitoring new missing persons cases from all over the state in hopes of identifying the Jane Doe on Josh Deeson's phone. A promising lead just turned up with the Lewis County Sheriff's Department. The girl's name is Rachel Camber. She's fifteen years old, Anglo, and she's been missing since Sunday. Her folks, who probably won't qualify for any Parents of the Year Award, woke up this morning and figured out that their teenage daughter wasn't home and hadn't been home for several days."

"Any other info on the girl?" Mel asked.

"Only that this isn't the first time she's run away. More like number three or four."

"Where did she go the other times?"

"If the deputy found out during his initial contact with the parents, I don't have that information at this time."

"What about a photo?" I asked. "Does Lewis County have one and can they send us a copy?"

"As I understand it, the deputy who took the report picked up a copy of last year's school photo while he was there at the house. He's bringing it with him, and he's on his way from Packwood to Chehalis right now. It's about an hour and a half from Packwood to Chehalis. He's probably another hour out at least. Between Olympia and there it's right around half an hour. If Mel is up to it, I'd like you to be waiting for him at the sheriff's department in Chehalis when he gets there."

"I'm up to it," Mel said determinedly.

"Keep ice on that hand and let Beau do the driving," Ross advised her. "You know where the Lewis County Sheriff's Department is located?"

That question was evidently directed at me. I knew how to get there all too well. Once, years ago, I'd been hauled into the Lewis County Jail by an overly enthusiastic deputy. It wasn't one of my best moments, and it wasn't something I had ever mentioned to Mel, or to Ross Connors, either. Some things are better left unsaid.

"Don't worry," I told them both. "I can find it."

"As for Larry Mowat," Ross continued, "don't you worry about him for a moment, Mel. If he tries to make any kind of fuss about what happened between you, I'll squash him flat like the bug he is."

"Thank you," Mel said.

I was all for squashing Dr. Larry Mowat. I would have told Ross Connors thank you, too, but it was Mel's deal, not mine, and it wasn't my place.

"I'm at the airport getting ready to fly out of Spokane," Ross continued. "I have a few minutes before the plane is due to board. You probably don't need to leave for Chehalis for another half hour, so how about bringing me up to date on what went on at the governor's mansion. I've been out of the loop."

Before Mel left for Larry Mowat's faux autopsy, she had sent Ross a fairly detailed report about what had gone on at the Josh Deeson crime scene. Ross hadn't seen it because he refuses to use his damned computer.

I had half a mind to pull Mel's report up on the computer and simply read it to him word for word, but I didn't. Instead we told him about our time at the governor's mansion. We touched on everything we could remember off the top of our heads, including the part about Josh having been bullied by the kids at school as well as Mel's and my reading of his supposed suicide note.

"It sounds like you don't think he killed the girl," Ross said.

"I think it's possible he didn't kill her," Mel corrected, "but we're going to have to prove it one way or the other."

Mel has a way of saying things that allows for cover later on if that should prove necessary. She'd make an excellent politician, if she didn't occasionally feel obliged to punch someone in the mouth.

"The watch sounds important," Ross continued. "I'll contact the crime lab and get them working on collecting DNA from the watchband. I told the guys in Spokane to do the same thing on the scarf. Once we have DNA profiles, all we'll need is a couple of suspects so we can match them up. Case solved."

That was my idea, too.

"What about the garbage detail?" he asked. "Did you find anything?"

"Nothing."

"Too bad," Ross said. "I was hoping you'd find something that would help us."

"So was I," I said.

I could hear a public address system talking in the background.

"Oops," Ross said. "They just called my flight. I need to go."

He hung up. I stripped off my shorts, T-shirt, and flip-flops in favor of something a little more official-looking. If Mel and I were going to drive to Packwood that night to tell some poor unsuspecting parents that their precious daughter had most likely been murdered, then I wanted to look the part. That difficult assignment requires a certain amount of gravitas. In my book, it also requires a sports jacket and a tie, no exceptions. For those kinds of occasions, Mel favors a tailored suit and low heels. It's what we do.

Once we were both properly put together, we refreshed Mel's ice pack and rode down to the car. Mel insisted on bringing along our computers and our air cards in case we had any waiting time on our hands later.

I happen to know that Packwood is in the far reaches of Lewis County, within ten miles or so of Mount Rainier and right up against the edge of the Gifford Pinchot National Forest. I thought the likelihood of our having an Internet connection from way out there was slim to none, but I packed up the computers without a word of complaint and carted them down to the car.

Mel is one of those women who are capable of and usually prefer to open and close doors all by themselves. This time she kept the ice on her hand and made no remark about my dashing around the car and playing the role of gentleman. And once we were belted in and headed toward the freeway, she did absolutely zero backseat driving. None.

It occurred to me, somewhere along the way between Olympia and Chehalis, that her taking a swing that had connected with Dr. Larry Mowat's front tooth might turn out to be an excellent thing in terms of our own personal domestic tranquillity.

CHAPTER 13

Ross Connors, the Washington State Attorney general, weighs in as a state-wide elected official. That makes those of us who have the privilege of working for him employees of a statewide elected official. Over the years I've learned that some places are a lot more welcoming to people who work for Special Homicide than others.

It turned out that, as far as the Lewis County Sheriff's Department was concerned, Ross Connors was golden. Since Mel and I worked for him, so were we. We arrived in Chehalis well after five, but Sheriff Louis Tyler was waiting for us with the light on and the welcome mat out. He asked for the nurse practitioner from the Lewis County Jail to come over and take a look at Mel's injured hand. Then we all settled in to wait for Deputy David Timmons to arrive from Packwood.

But there was more to Sheriff Tyler's hospitality than just good manners. "You're Special Homicide," he said. "So what's your interest in a fifteen-year-old runaway from my jurisdiction?"

It was a reasonable question that merited a straight answer.

"We think there's a good possibility that Rachel is dead," I said. "And we have reason to believe that her death might be related to the possible suicide of a boy in Olympia, a kid named Josh Deeson, one of whose guardians happens to be Governor Marsha Longmire."

Sheriff Tyler thought about that for a long moment before he nodded. "Hold on," he said, "I'll be right back."

He returned a few minutes later carrying a stack of paper folders.

"This is the third time Rachel Camber

has run away. If you look at these, they may give you some idea of why."

He shoved the file folders across his desk. Mel took one off the stack. I took another. I ended up with the mother's file—Ardith Louise Haskell Camber Mills Stapleton. Unfortunately there was a mug shot. Think of any frowsy blonde you've ever seen in one of the domestic-violence clips on *Cops*—several missing teeth, stringy hair, and a nose that showed evidence of having been broken numerous times. Not an American beauty. The birth date listed made her thirty-two, although she looked decades older than that. And if she had a whole series of ex-husbands and a fifteen-year-old runaway daughter in the background, it was simple to do the math. Babies having babies is seldom a good idea, although Kelly and Jeremy, my daughter and son-in-law, seem to be exceptions to that rule.

I thumbed through the file. Ardith had arrests and convictions for DUI, domestic violence, drunk and disorderly, and disturbing the peace. She had been charged with child neglect, but there was no conviction on that one.

"And the men are?" Mel asked.

"Husbands and ex-husbands," Tyler said. "She marries them, they beat her up, they leave her with a kid or two, and then she gets a divorce and moves on."

"How many kids?" Mel asked.

"Six, I believe, but don't quote me," Tyler said.

"How does she support them all?" Mel asked.

"Let's say she doesn't get much child support from her exes," Tyler said. "She works as a bartender in a low-life bar in Randle. She also may get some government help. The current man in her life is Ken Broward, who signed on after her last arrest. Kenny used to make a decent living driving log trucks. He's been off work for months. They called him and wanted him to come back today. He couldn't on account of not being able to locate Rachel. He needed her to look after the younger kids. He's the one who turned in the missing persons report."

"Not the mother," Mel said.

"No," Sheriff Tyler said. "Not the mother."

Mel and I traded glances and folders. I gave her the thick one on Ardith, and she gave me the ones that dealt with the parade of lowlifes in Ardith's life. I thumbed through them.

"Nothing on Ken Broward?" I asked.

"Not so far as I know," Sheriff Tyler said. "From what I've been able to learn about him, Ken's a straight arrow. Ardith's lucky to have him, and Ardith's kids are even luckier."

"Except for Rachel," Mel said. "Rachel's definitely not better off. Maybe we should show Sheriff Tyler that video. He should know what we're up against. He'll know if there have been any other cases of that around here."

Mel had loaded the clip onto her iPhone. She started it playing and then handed the phone to Sheriff Tyler. He watched it through with no comment other than a tightening of the muscles along his jawline. When the clip finished, he handed the phone back to Mel.

"Choking game," he said quietly. "We've had a few instances of that around here, mostly with junior high school kids. By the time kids are Rachel's age, they find other ways to get high, like stealing their parents' prescription drugs or raiding their parents' liquor cabinets."

"Any deaths?" I asked.

He grimaced. "What do you call landing in a vegetative state at age twelve? Close but no cigar? Her name is Kim Hope from Pe Ell. Hope—that's a hell of a name for a kid like that because, as near as I can tell, she doesn't have any. She's on a ventilator and a feeding tube and stuck in a nursing home for the rest of her life because her parents don't believe in pulling the plug no matter what. But I'm guessing there are times in the middle of the night when her parents find themselves wishing she had been found and cut down a few minutes later, when it was all over. The other choking game victim, Richey Kincaid from Toledo, was lucky. He came away with nothing but rope burns around his neck. His mother heard him making a strange noise and came to check on him. Kim's mother heard a noise, too, but she was doing something else and didn't pay attention until it was too late."

"No one else was implicated in either case?" I asked.

Tyler shook his head. "No one. Both Richey and Kim were alone in their rooms when it happened."

"Is there a chance all these kids—Kim Hope, Richey Kincaid, and now Rachel Camber—knew one another?" Mel asked.

Sheriff Tyler shrugged. "With the Internet, I suppose anything is possible, with all that Facebook junk that's going around, and Tweetie."

Clearly Sheriff Tyler didn't have a whole lot of familiarity with what Mel and I sometimes laughingly refer to as the iPhone generation.

"You mean Twitter," Mel corrected.

"Whatever you want to call it," Tyler replied. "It doesn't make a lick of sense to me, but back to your question. Toledo's a little burg just off I-5 about twenty miles from here on Highway 12. Packwood is about an hour and a half east of there, also on Highway 12. Pe Ell is on Highway 6, about twenty-five miles west of here in the opposite direction from Packwood. Physically that puts Rachel and Kim Hope a good two and a half hours apart. All three of them are small-town kids. Richey and Kim come from what I'd call solid families. Not so with Rachel. They're all too young to drive, so if they're connected it is probably through the Internet."

"How big is Lewis County?" Mel asked.

Mel Soames is a relative newcomer to Washington State. She lived in Texas briefly when she was growing up, but as an adult she spent several years living, working, and driving back east. I think the distances out here surprise her occasionally. For instance, it still confounds her that you can drive for six hours to get from Seattle to Spokane and still be in Washington. Try explaining that to someone who hails from, say, Delaware or New Hampshire.

There was a light tap on Sheriff Tyler's closed door.

"Come in," he called.

The door opened to reveal a young uniformed officer standing outside. He was all spit-and-polish. I didn't know if it was the beginning of his shift or the end of it, but his uniform looked like it was fresh from the laundry. The creases in his pants were still sharp.

"Sorry to disturb you, sir," he apologized. "But Dispatch told me you wanted to see me right away."

"Have a seat, Deputy Timmons," Sheriff Tyler said. "These two officers, Mel Soames and J. P. Beaumont, are agents from the attorney general's Special Homicide unit. They're here to speak to you about Rachel Camber."

I appreciated his avoiding the term S.H.I.T., and clearly Deputy Timmons was duly impressed.

"Yes, sir," Timmons said. He edged his way into the room and took a seat on the only remaining chair. Not a seat so much as a perch. He sat fully upright, as though he were still standing at attention.

Ex military, I told myself, *maybe the Marines.*

"Did you bring that photo with you?" Sheriff Tyler asked.

"Yes, sir," Deputy Timmons said.

He reached into his shirt pocket and pulled out a notebook. Opening that, he removed a piece of paper that had been folded to the exact dimensions of the notebook. He unfolded the paper and handed it to Sheriff Tyler. The sheriff studied it silently for a moment and then passed it to Mel, who eventually handed it to me. It was a school photo with the same shy, tentative smile we had seen at the beginning of the video.

Looking at the photo made my heart hurt. If the two girls weren't one and the same, then they would have to be identical twins.

Deputy Timmons seemed to find the silence in the room unnerving. "I'm sorry, sir," he said, "but did I understand you to say homicide? Does that mean Rachel Camber has been murdered?"

"It's possible," Sheriff Tyler said noncommittally. "How about if you bring us up to speed with what you learned in Packwood."

Timmons's notebook, which had been properly stowed in his shirt pocket, came back out. He opened it and began reading through his notes.

"According to Kenny—"

"Kenny?" Sheriff Tyler repeated. "You mean Kenneth Broward, Ardith's most recent husband?"

"And Rachel's stepfather then," Mel supplied.

Deputy Timmons nodded and returned to his notes. "Kenny said that the last time he saw Rachel was Sunday afternoon. She told him she was going to see a friend and that she planned to spend the night."

"Does this friend have a name?" Mel asked.

"Janie," Kenny said. "Ken assumed Janie was someone from school, but Conrad Philips, the high school principal, is an old personal friend of mine. I gave him a call when I was on my way back from Packwood. He knows every kid in his school on a first-name basis. He says there isn't a Jane or Janie in the bunch."

"Is there a chance that Mr. Broward was mistaken about the name?" Mel asked.

"I suppose," Timmons said with a frown, "but I doubt it."

"So according to Mr. Broward, the last he saw of Rachel was Sunday, when she left on her own."

"Yes," Deputy Timmons said. "That's correct."

I knew where Mel was going. There's a lot to support the idea that stepfather/stepdaughter relationships can be fraught with peril, so when she asked her next question, I wasn't at all surprised.

"Have you considered the possibility that Mr. Broward might have something to do with Rachel's disappearance?"

The genuinely shocked expression on Deputy Timmons's young face made his verbal answer unnecessary.

"So you don't think there was something inappropriate going on between Mr. Broward and his stepdaughter . . ."

"No, ma'am!" Timmons said decisively. "I never gave that possibility any thought at all. I've known Kenny Broward all my life. If there was ever a truly upright guy, he's it, although how he could get mixed up with someone like Ardith Haskell is more than I can understand."

I glanced back at Ardith's mug shot. Haskell was the first name listed there, a maiden name, as it were. People from your hometown are usually the only ones who stick to those first names, so it occurred to me that Deputy Timmons had known Ardith all his life as well.

"I've heard what Ardith's place was like before," Timmons went on. "Before Kenny was in the picture. You'd be amazed, Sheriff Tyler. Now the place is clean as a whistle. He cut down all the weeds in the backyard and put together one of those wooden swing things out there so the kids would have something to play on. When I got there, they were outside having fun like normal kids. If you ask me, Kenny's more of a father to that bunch than all those other guys put together."

"Okay," I said. "Let me understand this. Rachel went off with this supposed friend named Janie on Sunday."

"Yes," Timmons said. "She left Sunday afternoon about four, just after her mother left for work."

"How did she leave?" I asked. "Did she walk? Did she ride?"

"She rode. Somebody picked her up, somebody driving an older-model pickup truck. Green. Chevrolet, Silverado. Kenny didn't see the license, so that doesn't help us much. There are lots of old Chevys in Packwood."

"Okay," Mel said. "She left on Sunday. Why did she leave after her mother went to work?"

"According to Kenny, Ardith and Rachel fight a lot. If Rachel had asked for permission, there probably would have been a big argument."

"When was she reported missing?"

"This afternoon," Deputy Timmons said. "Kenny called it in after Ardith left for work, for the same reason. He didn't want to start another argument. I think I may have mentioned that Ardith isn't exactly a nice person, a reasonable person."

"Don't you think it's odd that Rachel's stepfather is the one who turned in the report and not Rachel's own mother?"

Deputy Timmons sighed. "He told me what she said."

"What who said?" I asked.

"What Ardith said about Rachel's running off," Timmons said.

"What was that?" Sheriff Tyler asked.

"She said, 'Good riddance. One less mouth to feed.'"

On the face of it, Kenny Broward sounded too good to be true, and Ardith Haskell was just the opposite—too bad to be real. Either way, the situation at the home in Packwood had been bad news for Rachel, and it had sent her running pell-mell into something much worse.

"Do you know where Ardith is right now?" I asked.

"Sure thing," he said. "Tending bar at the Bike Inn bar in Randle. It's a pretty rough crowd, but Ardith has worked there for years. She fits right in and can hold her own with the best of them—or the worst," Deputy Timmons added. "Take your pick."

I stood up. "We should probably go have a talk with her," I said. "And maybe with Mr. Broward as well."

Sheriff Tyler nodded. "Good idea," he said. "But if I were you, I'd let Deputy Timmons take you there. You can drive your own car, of course. I wouldn't expect you to go there in a squad car, but I caught a glimpse of your wheels when you got here. If you drive up to the Bike Inn by yourselves in that pretty little Mercedes of yours, those guys are likely to clean your clocks." He grinned at Mel. "I have it on good authority that you're fully capable of handling yourself in a pinch, but let me ask you this. If you were going out on an African safari, would you head off on your own, or would you pick up a local guide before you took off?"

"Local guide," Mel said.

"Exactly right," Sheriff Tyler said. "And this is the same thing. As far as the outside world is concerned, Randle and Packwood are a little like the back of the beyond. When Deputy Timmons came back home from his tour of duty in Iraq, I hired him to work that eastern sector of the county because he grew up there. He knows those logging roads like the back of his hand. He knows the people, the good ones and the bad ones.

"And why did I do that? Because,

when I sent deputies from other parts of the county to Morton or Packwood or Randle and the like, asking questions, they never seemed to get to first base. If you go there on your own, it's likely the same thing will happen to you. You can ask questions until you're blue in the face. You're not going to get any answers."

What Sheriff Tyler was saying made sense. Mel stood up and turned one of her classic smiles on poor unsuspecting Deputy Timmons. I wasn't the least bit surprised. When it comes to bringing unsuspecting young guys to heel, she's a killer. I've seen her do it before, and it works like magic every single time.

"If you have time to take us there, Mr. Timmons," she purred, "we'd be ever so grateful."

Timmons blushed from the top of his collar to the roots of his hair. A few short minutes earlier, Mel had been the one voicing the suggestion that there might be some kind of unsavory connection between Timmons's boyhood pal Kenneth Broward and Rachel Camber. In the face of Mel's radiant smile, however, all remembrance of her unpleasant suggestion was zapped right out of Deputy Timmons's random-access memory.

"Yes, ma'am," he said, grinning back at her. "I'd be happy to."

If I had tried pulling that coy-smile bit, it wouldn't have done a thing for Deputy Timmons, and it wouldn't have done much for us, either.

"Would you mind going now?" she asked.

I believe Mel could have asked Deputy Timmons to march straight into hell about then, and he would have done it without question.

"Not at all, ma'am," he replied. "Whenever you're ready, I'm ready."

And off to Randle we went.

CHAPTER 14

I've never been to the Ozarks. Mel tells me they're beautiful and that I'd love it there. The closest I've ever come was reading my mother's well-loved collection of books written by Harold Bell Wright. *The Shepherd of the Hills* and *The Winning of Barbara Worth* are the ones I remember reading myself, but my mother had a whole shelf filled with them. Those were books she read over and over when she was growing up, and they were books I read to her aloud when she was in the hospital dying. I think she had whole passages of them memorized.

I wouldn't be surprised, however, if the Ozarks aren't a whole lot like the far-eastern stretches of backwoods Lewis County—Morton, Randle, and Packwood included. U.S. Highway 12 is made up of miles of tree-lined blacktop punctuated occasionally by tiny towns and isolated houses, where elk and deer and the occasional bear wander across the roadways.

As we drove, it was easy to imagine that we were time-traveling back to a simpler, quieter era, but that was an illusion because bad things happen everywhere. Some of the towns and houses we passed were decidedly worse for wear. The downturn in the housing market had hit the logging industry hard. People who were just barely making it before were a lot worse off now.

Mel had used her considerable charm to bring Deputy Timmons to heel, but in the privacy of our own vehicle she was not amused at the idea of being led into the wilds of Lewis County by a local scout.

"I don't care what Deputy Timmons has to say about his sainted friend, Kenneth Broward," Mel said. "They're pals, meaning he can't possibly be objective about the guy. I have no intention of believing Rachel's stepfather is in the clear until I see proof of it with my own eyes. And no mother in her right mind would say 'Good riddance' about a fifteen-year-old runaway."

We drove into Randle through the lingering late-afternoon sunlight that is typical of Washington in the summer. We knew Mount Rainier was a huge snow-topped presence lurking only a few miles away, but the mountain was mostly out of sight behind the wall of trees that lined the road. Driving through the woods at that time of day means watching out for wildlife. We saw several deer grazing along the highway. As Mel was noting how beautiful they were, a fawn spooked for some reason and leaped across the road directly in front of us. Mel and I were both grateful for the Mercedes's top-notch braking system. The unscathed deer, springing off into the forest, should have been grateful, too.

We'd already had some hints that the Bike Inn wouldn't be a quaint country hotel catering primarily to bicycle riders in their bright Gore-Tex outfits. Denizens of the bar were of another species altogether. We're talking Harleys and leathers here, not Trek and Spandex.

The building itself was a disreputable ramshackle kind of place with several Harleys angle-parked out front. In among the collection of Harleys were hidden a couple of Honda Goldwings and even, I was surprised to see, a fully restored Indian Chief. The Indian was an original that dated from the early forties, not a reproduction like those currently being built in North Carolina. There may have been shiny new leather on the seat, but this one came complete with the old-fashioned suicide shifter. When it comes to Indians, I'm something of a purist.

It was almost eight o'clock when we stopped the car in front of the row of cycles. We exited the climate-controlled comfort of the car and landed in surprising heat that was unsurprisingly muggy.

The building stood alone. Rather than having a sidewalk out front, it sported a worn wooden walkway that creaked when we stepped up onto it. There were still a few vestiges of color on the outside walls that indicated the building had once boasted a coat of blue paint, but now there was far more mold than paint showing. Off to the side of the building sat a relatively new AC unit that probably cost more than the building itself, but I welcomed its low-throated roar. In the baking heat, the prospect that the Bike Inn was air-conditioned was a welcome surprise.

Deputy Timmons stood waiting for us on the boardwalk. Once we joined him, he pushed open the door and ushered us inside. I had never been in this particular bar before, but I've spent enough time in disreputable places over the years that this was an entirely familiar "ambience." The first thing to hit me was the smell. Cigarette smoking inside bars and restaurants may be prohibited

in Washington State now, but genera-
tions of smokers had left behind clouds
of smoke that had absorbed into the
Bike Inn's very core. In this case, I suspected the dark paneling on the interior
walls and the upholstered booths were
most likely the main smoke-sink cul-
prits. The bare plank flooring had
sopped up plenty of spilled beer over
the years. The olfactory residue of that
lingered, blending with the stink of
burned grease from a kitchen that probably wasn't any too clean, either.

From the invisible dollar signs on the
two-wheeled rides parked outside, I
could tell most of these guys could have
afforded to hang out in a better place,
but for some reason they didn't. They
preferred this one.

After the bright sunlight outside, the
room was gloomily dark. Most of the
light came from fixtures that dangled
over two fully occupied pool tables. The
light over the bar was a lot dimmer than
the light over the pool tables. There
were four guys playing pool, two men
and two leather-clad women sitting in
two separate booths along the far wall,

and three guys at the bar—two on one end and a solo at the other end near the kitchen. One of the pool players wore a handgun—one that looked like a .38—in a holster on his hip, but I assumed that wasn't the only weapon in the room.

A woman wearing a tank top stood behind the bar with one tattooed arm raised while she pulled draft beer into a glass. After viewing all those mug shots, I recognized Rachel Camber's mother the moment I saw her. In the flesh, I saw that her mug shot wasn't an exact likeness, but that's hardly surprising. Even movie stars look like crap in mug shots—just ask Charlie Sheen or Nick Nolte.

As the door opened, I had heard the sound of someone whacking the cue ball into a newly racked triangle of pool balls. We stepped into the room while the balls were still skittering across the felt-lined table. One of them dropped into a side pocket, but before that happened, complete silence fell on the room. I've been in bad-news bars before, and that kind of ominous silence makes me wary as hell. Right then I busied myself with a head count—nine men and three women—against the three of us. If Mel had been at the top of her game, the odds might not have been too bad, especially since Timmons was a trained Marine. Still . . .

The silence was broken when Ardith slammed the beer glass down on the bar hard enough that half of it slopped out onto the counter.

"Who the hell is this, Davy?" she demanded sharply of Deputy Timmons as we walked past the pool players and took possession of three unoccupied bar stools. "Whaddya think you're doin' bringin' folks like this into my bar?"

I noticed right off that she didn't call him Deputy Timmons or even David— as his name badge clearly stated—but Davy. It sounded like she was using a nickname that was most likely a carry-over from childhood and predated Timmons's time in the Marines as well as his time as deputy. Ardith's use of "Davy" was similar to the deputy's calling Ardith by her maiden name. In some cases, turnabout really is fair play.

"They're cops, Ardith," he said, stating the obvious. "They need to talk to you."

Timmons was the only one wearing a uniform, but everyone in the bar had recognized Mel and me as cops the moment we had stepped across the threshold.

"I don't talk to cops," Ardith replied. She topped off the beer to replace what she had spilled and then slid the glass down the bar to the solo sitting next to the kitchen.

"No kind of cops," she added, "unless my lawyer is present, which, if you'll look around the room, you'll see he ain't."

I heard a slight guffaw from somewhere behind me, most likely from one of the pool players. I waited, hoping for the sound of a cue ball striking something else, but the games were currently halted while every eye and ear focused on us, the unwelcome interlopers.

"It's not about you, Ms. Broward," Mel said quietly. "It's about your daughter."

"Oh," Ardith said. "So it's Rachel

again, is it? Well, whatever she's done this time, I've got nothin' to do with it."

"If we could speak to you in private—" I suggested.

She cut off my words with a hoot of laughter. "Private?" she repeated. "The only thing private around here is the ladies, and that's only if there's still toilet paper filling the peephole somebody drilled through the wall from the gents. And what's supposed to happen to my bar while you and me have this cozy little chat? I can't exactly call in a pinch hitter and ask 'em to substitute for me, now can I!"

"It's about your daughter," Mel said again.

Ardith's jaw slammed shut. That's when I realized what was different about her. Someone had gone to the trouble and expense of helping her get her teeth fixed. The front teeth that had been missing in her mug shot were no longer missing.

The lone wolf at the far end of the counter was a leather-clad giant of a man with a headful of frizzy reddish hair pulled back into a ponytail that ended near his waist. He stood up, sauntered down the bar, and stopped in front of Ardith.

"You go take care of whatever you've gotta take care of, Ardy," he said. "I'll mind the bar and the till."

He wasn't the kind of guy I would have trusted to take over my cash register or my bar in my absence, but Ardith nodded her agreement, then turned and walked away. With the three of us trailing behind, she left the bar and turned down the hall marked RESTROOMS. She walked past them and let herself out a back door marked EMERGENCY EXIT ONLY, although no alarm sounded when she opened it and led us outside. By the time she stopped next to a stinking garbage Dumpster, she had a cigarette in her mouth and was lighting it.

"Okay," she said. "What's Rachel done now?"

"I take it you've been having problems with your daughter?" Mel asked.

"I'll say." Ardith blew a cloud of smoke into the air. "I told her the last time she run off not to bother comin' back if she did it again. People laugh at me for havin' so many men in my life, but I've married every one of them. That's the God's truth. I sure as hell don't do it for the money, and I won't have a slut who puts out like that livin' under my roof and bein' a bad influence on the little ones."

"Wait a minute," Mel said. "Did I understand you to say that you think Rachel has been involved in prostitution?"

"I don't *think*," Ardith responded. "I *know!* I wasn't born yesterday. When I found four hundred bucks in crisp new one-hundred-dollar bills hidden in her underwear drawer, I didn't figure her fairy godmother dropped it off just for the hell of it. She was whoring for it, plain and simple. Where else is a plain-looking girl like that gonna come up with that kind of money?"

"Do you know the names of any of the people she might be involved with?" Mel asked.

"Are you kidding? I'm Rachel's mother. She's not likely to tell me anything."

"Are there friends from school who might know the names of some of her associates?"

"Associates?" Ardith scoffed. "You make it sound like a lawyer's office or something. No, I don't know her friends. If she's got 'em, she doesn't talk about 'em, leastways not to me. You can ask Kenny, my husband. He's been laid off for months, so he's around home a whole lot more than I am. He keeps telling me that I'm too hard on Rachel. He got called back to work. Today was supposed to be his first day back on the job. Rachel promised she'd be here to look after the younger kids. I suppose you can guess how well that turned out! She probably got herself a better offer than babysitting for free so she could have a roof over her head and food on the table."

"Ms. Broward," Mel said softly, "I'm sorry to have to tell you this, but we have reason to believe your daughter is dead. That's the real reason Rachel didn't come home today."

Ardith dropped her half-smoked cigarette and ground it into the dirt.

"Dead?" she repeated in disbelief. "You're saying Rachel is dead?"

Mel and I both nodded.

"Where?" Ardith demanded.

"That's the thing," I said. "We don't know where. That's what we're trying to figure out."

"If you don't know where Rachel is, how do you know she's dead?" Ardith asked.

"There's a video clip," Mel said.

"What do you mean, a clip, like on *America's Funniest Videos* or something?"

"Yes," Mel said. "It's like one of those film clips, but it's not funny."

"You mean someone took pictures while they were doing it, while they were killing her?"

Mel nodded.

Stricken, Ardith staggered backward until she banged into the side of the Dumpster. The blow sent a cloud of flies bursting skyward from the top of the garbage heap. The woman's ruddy face had gone pale.

"Show me," she said.

"Really, Ms. Broward, I'm not sure . . ."

"Show me!" Ardith exclaimed. "I'm not going to believe Rachel's dead until I see it with my own eyes."

Mel pulled out one of the photos Todd had made. "This photo was taken from the clip. Does this look like your daughter?"

Ardith barely glanced at the photo. "I want to see the video," she insisted.

Mel shot me a questioning look. The clip was a terrible thing to show to the victim's mother.

"Really, Ms. Broward," I began. "It's really not a good idea . . ."

"Show me!"

With a resigned sigh, Mel reached into her pocket and removed her iPhone. I had every reason to believe that we were somewhere in that supposed five percent of the country where AT&T doesn't reach, but Mel had loaded the clip onto her phone. No connection was needed. Mel messed around with the screen for a moment or two. Then, once the clip began playing, she held it up for Ardith to see.

Had it been in bright sunlight, the tiny images might have been a little hazy, but it was close enough to dusk now that they were clear. As Ardith watched in apparent shock and horror, one of her hands went helplessly to her own throat as if in the vain hope of loosening the scarf's deadly hold on her daughter's neck. When the clip was over, Ardith squeezed her eyes shut. Her body slid down alongside the Dumpster as though her legs had lost the ability to hold her upright. She came to a stop only when she was seated flat on the ground with her legs splayed out in front of her.

"Oh, no," she said. "No, no, no. I had no idea that's what was happening. I mean, I saw the bruises—"

"What bruises?" Mel asked sharply

"On Rachel's neck," Ardith said. "The second time she ran away. When she came back home, she kept wearing this one black turtleneck sweater over and over. Then, one night, I came into the kitchen when she was doing the dishes and wearing a regular top. That's when I saw the bruising on her neck. I asked her about it. She said it happened at school during gym when some of the kids were playing around."

"Kids may call it playing," I explained. "It's sometimes called the choking

game. Kids do it because they're operating under the mistaken impression
that if they do it long enough that they
pass out, they'll get high."

"Does Kenny know?" Ardith asked.

Mel shook her head. "We came to tell
you first."

Ardith dried her eyes on the hem of
her tank top and then struggled to get
up. Deputy Timmons and I each grabbed
a hand and levered her back to her feet.

"I'll go close up," she said. "It may
take me a few minutes to throw these
guys out, but then we've got to go tell
Kenny. It'll break his heart. He loved
that girl like she was his own."

Mel cut me a look that said "Yeah,
right," but she didn't say it aloud.

"Do you want us to wait for you, or
do you want us to go on ahead?" I
asked.

"Wait for me," she said. "I should be
the one to tell him and the other kids,
not you."

And so we waited. And it didn't take
long for the guys inside to spill out onto
the wooden walkway, where they stood
around in a subdued group, talking qui-

etly among themselves. The last customer to emerge was the big guy who
had taken over bartending duties while
Ardith went outside with us.

Last of all came Ardith. She emerged
clad head to toe in leather and carrying
a helmet. She climbed onto one of the
Goldwings, started it up and headed
out, with Deputy Timmons and Mel and
me trailing after her.

"I didn't think she'd ride a motorcycle,
too," Mel said.

"I didn't, either," I agreed. "That
woman is full of surprises."

CHAPTER 15

It was verging on twilight when we trailed Ardith Broward's Goldwing into the yard of a house that could have been a carbon copy of others we had seen along Highway 12, with one major difference. This one had been recently painted. Someone had taken a Weed Eater and mowed down the grass and weeds around the house. Partially visible behind the house was a redwood kids' play structure, complete with a canvas cover. I don't know how much those things cost in dollars and cents, but I helped my son-in-law put one together a couple of years ago. Believe me, when they say, "Some assembly required," they mean it.

A shirtless guy in greasy jeans was crouched, wrench in hand, next to another Goldwing. The idea that Kenneth Broward was a shade-tree mechanic gave him a leg up in my book. Behind him in a rutted driveway stood a beaten-up Toyota minivan that they probably used when they were hauling kids or groceries around, but with the price of gasoline, I suspected using the Gold-wings was as much a cost-saving strategy as it was a philosophical statement.

Despite an evening full of circling mosquitoes, four towheaded kids clambered down from the play structure. Barefoot and carefree, they came bounding across the yard to greet their mother, yelling, "Mom's home. Mom's home."

A pair of spotted mongrel dogs galloped happily after the kids, barking like crazy.

Ardith Broward may not have won any Mother of the Year awards, but her kids and dogs seemed happy enough to see her. Ditto for Kenny. He stood up and wiped his greasy hands on his already greasy pant legs. He started toward her, smiling, until he saw first Deputy Timmons's patrol car and then ours pulling into the yard behind Ardith's Goldwing. The smile disappeared. He stopped, turned around, picked up a rag of some kind, and then came back again, still wiping his hands.

Ardith parked her bike next to his. She leaped off it, tossed her helmet on the ground beside it, and then threw herself into Kenny's arms with enough force that she almost knocked him off his feet. It wasn't how we would have delivered the bad news. Ardith did the job her way, leaving us nothing to do but watch.

Ardith was not a small woman—five eleven or so. Kenny was a good head taller than she was. He was broad-shouldered. As far as I could see and unlike his wife, he had no tattoos at all. He and Deputy Timmons were probably a good five years younger than Ardith. For a moment I found myself wondering what Kenny saw in her. Then I remembered Mel and started wondering what she saw in me. Sometimes you're better off just not going there.

Still holding Ardith, he said something to the circling kids. Without a word of argument, the oldest one, a boy of about eleven, herded the younger ones into the house, taking the dogs with them. Ken helped Ardith, still sobbing, over to the edge of the porch and eased her down onto it. Then he turned to Deputy Timmons.

"Who's that?" he asked, nodding in our direction.

"They're homicide cops," Deputy Timmons said. "They work for the attorney general."

Kenny took my badge wallet, examined it for a moment, and then handed it back. "So it's true then, what Ardith just said? Rachel is dead?"

"Yes," I answered. "That's what we believe. She appears to have fallen victim to what kids call the choking game. They tie a rope or something around their necks long enough to cut off the supply of oxygen to their brains in the mistaken belief that it's some kind of high. Unfortunately, some kids die of it."

"What's this she's saying about a video? There's a video? Somebody filmed this?"

Mel was already reaching for her iPhone. Ken Broward stood absolutely still the whole time the video was playing. By the time it was over, his face was ashen. He turned away and bolted around the side of the house, where we heard him puking his guts out.

I don't suppose puking would hold up in a court of law as a declaration of innocence, but it was pretty damned convincing as far as I was concerned. Kenny's face was still ghostly white when he came back to the front of the house. He sat down next to Ardith, put a hand on her shoulder, and pulled her close.

"Who the hell would do such a thing?" he demanded, more angry than grief-stricken. "Who?"

"That's what we were hoping you could tell us," Mel said smoothly. "You told Deputy Timmons that Rachel left the house on Sunday afternoon. That she rode off with a friend and was planning to spend the night."

"Yes," Ken said. "That's right. She told me her name was Janie. That she knew her from school."

"Last name?"

Ken just shook his head. "You know how kids are. They never mention last names, ever." He paused, shook his head, and wiped his eyes. "I should have asked. She just told me she was leaving, going to Janie's house, and that was it."

Ardith reached over and patted his knee with a small comforting gesture that reminded me of the way Governor Longmire had patted Gerard Willis's knee for much the same reason.

"What did she take with her?" I asked.

"Just her backpack," Kenny answered. "I don't really know what was in it. Overnight stuff, I guess."

"Did she seem upset about anything? Was she angry?"

Kenny shook his head. "Not at all. She said she'd be home on Monday to look after the younger kids so I could go to work on Tuesday. Harlan's eleven,"

Kenny said. "We don't mind leaving him in charge of the little ones for a couple of hours, but for all day . . ."

Mel aimed a questioning look in Ardith's direction.

"I got the chance to pull a couple of double shifts," Ardith said with a shrug. "We need the money real bad."

"But you didn't report her missing when she didn't come home on Monday."

"We had a fight about it," Ardith said. "Kenny thought somethin' was wrong. I thought she was just actin' up or actin' stupid. I told him she was just askin' for trouble, but I didn't mean . . ."

Ardith swallowed hard and looked like she wished she could take back not only the words but also the thought.

"Of course not," Mel said kindly.

I thought it was a good idea to change the focus a little.

"Do you ever remember her mentioning having a friend or acquaintance named Josh?" I asked. "He's from Olympia."

Ken and Ardith Broward shook their heads in definitive unison.

"Rachel doesn't have any friends in Olympia," Ken declared. "How would she? And who's Josh?"

"A boy from Olympia," I answered. "That's where we found the video—on Josh's cell phone."

"Ask him about it, then," Ken said. "He should know where he got it."

"We can't," Mel said.

"Why not?"

"Because he's dead. He committed suicide last night."

"So there you are," Ken said. "The cowardly little creep did this to Rachel and then committed suicide to keep from having to face the consequences."

"He actually said he didn't do it," Mel said. "At least, that's what his suicide note led us to believe."

"How?" Ken asked.

"How what?"

"How did he kill himself?"

"With a rope," Mel said. "He knotted some of his grandfather's ties together and hanged himself on the closet door in his room."

"Was that part of this same choking-game garbage?" Ken asked. "Maybe he didn't intend to die, either."

I had seen the kicked-over chair and the knotted ties that had been tied together in a fashion that meant they wouldn't give way. And I had seen the expertly crafted noose. No, Josh's death hadn't been an inadvertent consequence of the choking game. But suddenly I was seeing the scarf again. The scarf around Rachel's neck had been inexpertly knotted.

When I tuned back into the conversation, Mel had her notebook out and was making a list that included the names of as many of Rachel's friends as her mother and stepfather were able to provide. There was no question of using Rachel's cell phone directory or history to reconstruct Rachel's social network because Rachel didn't have a cell phone. Neither did either one of her parents. The Broward household was evidently one of the last of the breed when it came to having only landline telephone service.

By the time Mel finished writing and closed her notebook, Ardith was staring at her. "What are we supposed to do now?" she asked.

"What do you mean?"

"She's dead," Ardith said huskily. "You know that, and we know that, but only because we saw it happen on the video; but if there's no body, how do we have a funeral? What do we tell the other kids? What do we tell our friends? I don't want to have to tell them about it. I don't want them to see it."

Ardith had aimed her questions toward Mel, and I was happy to have that particular ball dropped in her court.

"That's up to you," Mel answered finally, "but if Rachel were mine I believe I'd say that she ran away, that she's missing and presumed dead. You don't have to say anything more than that. You don't owe people detailed explanations about what's happened."

"Missing and presumed dead." Ardith repeated the words slowly, as if trying them out on her lips and on her heart. "I'm not sure I can say that."

Then she dissolved into tears once more. Surprisingly enough, the belligerent bartender from the Bike Inn didn't seem nearly as belligerent now, not to us and not to Kenny Broward, either.

"We'll have to try, honey bun," Ken said, holding her close. "We'll just have to try."

After we gleaned all the information we could from Ken and Ardith, Ken summoned Rachel's younger brother, eleven-year-old Harlan, to see if he was able to add anything to what the parents had already told us. He wasn't. Or, if he knew something about Rachel's mysterious friend, Janie, he wasn't ready to spill the beans. When we finally left to head back into town, we had Deputy Timmons lead the way to the home of Conrad Philips, the high school principal.

There were only three hundred or so students in White Pass's combination junior and senior high school. Conrad Philips knew them all. According to him, Rachel had been far more trouble in junior high than she was now as a high school sophomore. He chalked her behavioral turnaround to Ken Broward's arrival on the scene. He didn't have

much good to say about Ardith, but he
had a lot of good to say about Kenny.

Unlike Rachel Camber's parental
units, Conrad Philips was able to provide not only last names for the kids at
his school but also phone numbers and
addresses. He also gave us a rundown
of the various cliques at the school. It
was late by the time we finished talking
to him, but we came away with an arm-
load of information about Rachel and
her friends, none of which could be
tracked down until Wednesday morning. We thanked Deputy Timmons for
his help, told him good-bye, and headed
for the barn in Olympia.

Mel was uncharacteristically quiet as
we drove back down Highway 12 toward
I-5. I was busy watching for stray wildlife crossing the road. She was evidently
mulling over our Lewis County interviews.

"I guess I was wrong about Kenny
Broward," she said finally. "I was so
ready to believe that the stepfather
would be a bad guy."

It's odd to be involved with and married to a woman who will come right

out and admit it when she's wrong—
odd, and more than a little refreshing.

"Does that make you guilty of sexual
profiling?" I asked.

"Yup," she said. "Now, what's there
to eat around here? I'm starving."

We ended up with Subway sandwiches from a combination gas station/
restaurant at an exit south of Chehalis.
Over our sandwiches and coffee, we
strategized.

"There has to be some connection
between Josh and Rachel," I told Mel.
"Once we find that, we'll be close to
pulling the whole thing together."

"Right," she agreed. "We need to go
at it from both ends. How about if I
come back to Packwood tomorrow and
start working my way through the girls
whose names Conrad Philips gave us.
You can work the Olympia end."

Talking to Josh's fellow summer-
school students was the place to start,
but I didn't expect to find a bunch of
exemplary students enrolled there.

"Right," I said. "You get the regular
kids from Packwood while I'm stuck

with the juvenile-delinquent types who are about to flunk out of school."

"Want to trade?" Mel asked.

"No," I said. "That was just pro forma grumbling. You'll do better with the girls and I'll do better with the rough and tough boys."

"I wonder if Todd's made any progress on tracking down the source of that file," Mel said.

We both looked at our watches. It was long past midnight. Even though we knew Todd worked all hours, it wasn't fair to call in the middle of the night and risk waking Julie.

"We'll check with him in the morning," I said. "Let's go."

We made it back to the Dreaded Red Lion, as Mel and Harry I. Ball both call it, without incident. We rode up in the elevator. I stripped off my clothing and fell into bed. Two cups of late-night coffee had absolutely no impact on my ability to fall asleep. I took a pair of Aleves and was out cold before Mel ever emerged from the bathroom. I probably could have slept for several more hours, but the jangling landline telephone in our room jarred me awake minutes after 6:00 A.M.

"Just had a call from Sheriff Tyler down in Lewis County," Ross Connors said without preamble. "They're in the process of recovering a body from a water-retention pond north of Centralia. Looks to be a young female."

"Rachel Camber," I said.

"That would be my guess," Ross said. "I want you and Mel there on the double."

"What?" Mel asked sleepily.

"It looks like Ardith Broward is going to get her wish and have a body to bury after all."

Mel sat up in bed. "They found her? Where?"

"The Lewis County Sheriff's Department is in the process of dredging the body of a young female out of a retention pond north of Centralia. Sheriff Tyler thinks it's probably Rachel. Ross wants both of us there ASAP, so give me first crack at the bathroom. I'll take my car; you take yours."

The term "on the double" is more applicable in terms of my getting up and out than it is to Mel. Fortunately, the ice-pack treatment we had applied to her hand had helped enough that she'd be able to drive herself once she was ready to go. I was back on the freeway and headed south with a cardboard cup of hotel-lobby coffee in hand less than fifteen minutes after Ross rousted me from a dead sleep.

Just north of the Harrison exit in Centralia lies an unnamed body of mostly muddy water that supposedly keeps pollutants from a nearby abandoned gravel quarry from getting into the water table. As I came around the long freeway curve at Ford's Prairie, I caught sight of a clutch of emergency vehicles gathered at the far north end of the pond. I exited I-5 and made my way there as best I could with the GPS bleating plaintively, claiming that I was "off road" and in an area where "turn by turn directions" were not possible.

Once on the scene, I found several Lewis County Sheriff's vehicles along with an ambulance and a Lewis County coroner's meat wagon. A guy still wearing a dripping wet suit was in the process of helping two other people load a zippered body bag onto a gurney. There was a parking place next to the coroner's van. I guess it's simply the nature of the beast, but relations between the attorney general's office and the Lewis County coroner haven't always been any more cordial than relations with Larry Mowat, the coroner's counterpart up in Thurston County. When I saw Sheriff Tyler standing outside one of his patrol cars, I approached him instead of going to the coroner directly.

"How's it going?" I asked.

"Not well," Tyler said. "We've got ourselves another dead girl. This one looks a lot like Rachel Camber, but I doubt it's her. Mid-teens, brown hair. Sounds like the same MO."

"Bruising on her neck?"

Tyler nodded. "And dead before she went into the water. We located a spot about a hundred yards south of here where we think she was rolled out of a vehicle and dumped."

"So she wasn't killed here?"

"No sign of it."

"How long has she been dead?"

Tyler shrugged. "So far we don't have an exact time of death, but the coroner's initial estimate is that this victim has been dead for less than twelve hours. That means she was still alive yesterday afternoon when you were in my office showing me the video of Rachel being strangled."

Sheriff Tyler continued. "Same age, same victimology, and same MO, but this has to be a different girl unless Bonnie's way off about the time of death."

"Bonnie?" I asked.

"That'll be Bonnie Epstein, the new Lewis County coroner," Sheriff Tyler said. "Dr. Bonnie Epstein."

Tyler's emphasis on the doctor part was designed to get my attention.

"Do you think she'd mind if I take a look before they haul the body away?" I asked.

Tyler shrugged. "Suit yourself," he said. "But you should know that Dr. Epstein doesn't take kindly to having people looking over her shoulder."

"In other words, do so at my own

risk. Does Dr. Epstein realize Special Homicide is involved?"

"If she does, it's not because I've told her," Tyler said. "And I also failed to mention that this incident might well be related to Josh Deeson's death up in Olympia, which, in case you're interested, is front-page news all over the state this morning."

The suicide of the governor's grandson was bound to be big news. It also meant that Mel's and my ability to conduct our operation under the radar was about to come to a screeching halt.

I looked back toward the coroner's van and saw they were getting ready to load the gurney into the back of the vehicle.

"I guess I'll go try my luck."

Tyler smiled and shook his head. "You do that," he said. "Just don't say I didn't warn you."

CHAPTER 16

With Sheriff Tyler's words of caution in mind, I approached Dr. Bonnie Epstein with my ID wallet in hand and my missile defense system fully operational.

"Excuse me, Dr. Epstein," I said. "If you could give me a moment."

She whirled around. She was nearly as tall as I am and wore her long dark hair in a frizzy style Mel and I refer to as the light-socket wave. She was dressed in a kind of orange jumpsuit with the word CORONER stenciled across the back. Unfortunately, in other jurisdictions, that same jumpsuit with slightly different stenciling probably works very well as jail inmate attire.

When we were face-to-face, I saw that the zipper on the front of the jump-suit wasn't zipped up far enough to cover completely some very impressive scenery. Bonnie Epstein had the kind of cleavage that encourages men to gaze longingly in that direction. I'm old enough to understand how entrapment works and smart enough to disregard the bait. Instead, I looked directly into Dr. Ep-stein's glacially blue eyes.

Turning away from the loading pro-cess, she favored me with an apprais-ing glance. "And you are?" she asked.

The question was asked in full push-back fashion. As soon as she opened her mouth, I knew she was from New York City. Other people with more East Coast experience could probably hear those three words and be able to iden-tify the speaker's exact borough, by be-ing able to differentiate between the ac-cent of someone from the Bronx, for example, or from Queens. All I could tell was NYC somewhere. That knowl-edge told me a lot about the culture

clash between Sheriff Tyler and the coroner. It also made me glad that I had
looked into her eyes and nowhere else.

"My name's J. P. Beaumont," I said,
handing her my identification wallet. "I
work for the attorney general's Special
Homicide Investigation Team."

She studied my information and then
handed it back. "It says here you work
for S.H.I.T."

I tried to take the long view of the
situation. She was probably relatively
new to the state. I had no idea how she
had come to be in rural western Washington, which seems like the exact antithesis of New York City. I wondered if
she had come here on purpose, or had
she arrived unwillingly? It was possible
that she had been dumped in Washington at the end of a marriage that hadn't
worked out to anyone's satisfaction, but
she was here now, and she needed to
learn to play by western Washington
rules.

The longer I work for Special Homicide, the less patience I have with that
tired old S.H.I.T. joke. This morning in
particular, without having had enough

sleep, breakfast, or even my morning dose of Aleve, I was in no mood for joking around.

"I'd like to get a look at the victim before you haul her out of here."

"And I'd like to win the grand prize on *American Idol*," she said. "But you know how it goes—wish in one hand, crap in the other, and see which hand gets full first."

"I'm with the attorney general's office," I said. "I'm here at his request. This case may be connected to a related homicide."

"This is a Lewis County homicide . . ." she began.

"It's a Washington State homicide," I corrected. "Ross Connors is the chief law enforcement officer in the state of Washington. He's also my boss."

Mel chose that moment to arrive. I don't know how she got dressed and ready that fast, but she did.

"What did I miss?" she asked.

"Who's this?" Dr. Epstein asked.

"My partner," I said. "Melissa Soames. She works for the same guy I work for."

"Is there a problem?" Mel wanted to know.

"Yes, there's a problem," Bonnie Epstein said. "This is my jurisdiction and my case. I don't appreciate having people I don't know come horning in on what I'm doing and second-guessing my every move. Now, if you'll excuse me, we'll go ahead and transport the victim to my morgue. Once I've completed the autopsy, I'll be more than happy to give you and your boss the results. In the meantime you, your partner, and your boss will all have to take a number and wait."

While the coroner was delivering this speech, Mel was reaching into her purse. As Dr. Epstein ended her tirade, Mel extracted one of the photos of Rachel Camber and passed it in front of the good doctor's nose. Bonnie Epstein was quick, but not quite quick enough to cover the jolt of recognition that instantly passed across her face. Sheriff Tyler had noted the similarities between this new victim and Rachel, but the disparity in the timing of the two deaths had caused him to discount the connection. Dr. Epstein instantly assumed that the girl in the photo and the girl on her gurney were one and the same. Now so did we.

"If you know who she is, you have to tell me," Epstein said, reaching for the photo. "As the coroner, it's my job to identify the victim and notify the family."

By then Mel had already slipped the photo back into her purse. "I'm sorry," she said. "I understood you weren't interested in working with Special Homicide on this. Cooperation is a two-way street."

"But you're interfering in the investigation of a homicide."

"Yes," Mel said. "There's apparently a lot of that going around this morning. But I regret to inform you, Dr. Epstein, that before my partner and I can provide any information regarding the victim's identity, you'll need to go through official channels, too."

"Give me the attorney general's name and number," Dr. Epstein said. "I'll give him a call."

Shaking her head, Mel dug in her

purse. I knew exactly where this was going and how it was going to turn out.

"Unfortunately," Mel said, "there aren't any shortcuts. Before you can talk to the AG, you'll need to speak with our immediate supervisor. Here's his name and number." Mel handed Dr. Epstein a business card.

"Come on, Beau," Mel said. "We've got places to go and things to do."

We were almost back to our separate cars before Dr. Epstein looked down at the card in her hand. I saw her lips move as she read the words printed there. "Harry I. Ball." She looked up and glared at us. "Is this some kind of joke?" she yelled.

"No," Mel called back. "It's not a joke."

But of course it was—a very old S.H.I.T. squad joke, and being able to turn it loose on Dr. Epstein made the whole morning seem a little brighter. I realized that old jokes are just fine as long as you personally aren't the butt of them.

When we reached our vehicles, I was going to tell Mel thank you, but she was already on the phone with Barbara Galvin back at the Squad B office in Bellevue.

"That's right," she was saying. "Her name is Dr. Epstein. She's a royal pain in the butt. She's going to want to talk to Harry about our helping her identify her homicide victim. The longer you can stall her, the better."

There was a pause. "What are we going to do in the meantime?" Mel looked at me and grinned. "With any kind of luck, Mr. Beaumont here is going to buy his partner some breakfast."

We drove back to the Harrison exit and ate a farmer's breakfast at the Country Cousin, one of I-5's longtime roadhouse destinations. My only regret was that it was breakfast time—far too early for the Country Cousin's signature fried chicken. I had to make do with chicken-fried steak instead.

School was out everywhere, so the main dining room was crowded with vacationers traveling with hordes of noisy ankle-biters, none of whom, it seemed, were ever required to stay in their seats during mealtimes. By begging, we managed to be seated in an otherwise empty section of the restaurant. Not only was it quieter, I felt we could discuss the complexities of our two co-joined cases without someone at a nearby table listening to our every word.

In the old days, we would have come up with a couple of quarters and dragged a single copy of some dead-tree newspaper into the restaurant with us. Instead, we brought in our computers, fired up our air cards, and read online versions, both of us scanning quickly to see how much of the Josh Deeson story was now common knowledge.

Finished reading, Mel closed her computer, sipped her coffee, and looked thoughtful. "If Rachel Camber didn't die until twelve hours ago, the snuff film was a fake," she said at last.

"So it would appear," I said. "And an effective one at that. The first time someone made it *look* like someone had killed Rachel Camber. The second time they really did kill her, and not here, either," I added. "Sheriff Tyler's pretty sure she was murdered elsewhere and then dumped in the retention pond."

"Yes," Mel said. "And the 'here' in question happens to be partway between Olympia and Packwood, but why would someone pull a stunt like pretending to kill someone?" Mel asked. "And what does any of it have to do with Josh Deeson?"

"Our first order of business," I said, "is making the connection between Josh and Rachel. But let me ask you this: Did you notice what happened when you showed Rachel's photo to Dr. Epstein?"

Mel shrugged. "Yes, the minute she saw it, she knew who it was. I could see in her face that she recognized her—that the girl in the photo was the same person the diver had just dragged out of the mud puddle."

"Exactly," I said. "That's my opinion, too. Now think back to when we showed Josh Deeson that video when we were up in his room. Do you remember his reaction?"

"Sure," Mel said. "He was shocked

by what he was seeing, just like everyone else who sees it is shocked."

"What else?"

"He claimed he didn't know the dead
girl—that he had no idea who she was."

"Do you think he was telling the
truth?"

While the waitress brought our plat-
ters of food and poured more coffee,
Mel considered the question.

"Yes, I do," she said finally.

"So do I, as a matter of fact," I agreed
once the waitress left us alone. "Josh
was just a kid. If he had known who the
dead girl was at the time we showed
him the video, we would have seen
some sign of recognition on his face,
just as we both did on Dr. Epstein's face
a little while ago. Doctors are trained to
keep from revealing their thoughts and
feelings. Josh had no such training. If
he had known who Rachel was, he
would have ratted himself out."

"But I still don't understand what
we're dealing with here," Mel said. "If
Josh had no idea who the girl was, what
was the point of sending him that video?
Shock value, maybe, or some kind of

joke? Maybe whoever's behind it was hoping that someone at school, like a teacher or an administrator, would find the offending video on Josh's phone. That would probably have been enough to land him in all kinds of hot water. He might even have been expelled. Imagine how the media would have jumped on that. The only fly in that ointment is that Governor Longmire was the one who found the video, not someone from school. And instead of being expelled from school, now Josh is dead."

Nodding, I picked up my phone. I scanned through my call history until I found Todd Hatcher's number. When I dialed it, Julie answered.

"You missed him," she told me. "He had an early-morning breakfast meeting in Olympia today. He said if you called I should tell you that he's tracking on the ISPs and that he expects to have some additional information for you by the end of the day."

There was a click on my phone that meant a new call was coming in. I checked, saw that the caller was Harry, and let that one go to voice mail.

"Okay," I said to Julie. "Just tell him we're waiting to hear from him."

By then Mel's phone was ringing. "Hi, Harry," she said. "What's up?" She glanced at me, smiled, bit off a mouthful of toast, and then chewed while Harry gave her an ear-splitting blast.

"Yes," Mel said finally when she could get a word in edgewise. "She struck us that way, too. Pushy."

Harry went off on another rant. Mel calmly bit off another hunk of toast. "Absolutely," she said finally. "That's the impression we got from Sheriff Tyler— that the murder happened elsewhere. This is just a dump site."

There was another long pause during which Mel listened to Harry while sipping her coffee and pouring herself another cup from the carafe the waitress had left on the table. I couldn't help noticing that the knuckles on the back of her hand provided an interesting study in bar-brawl-worthy bruises.

"Yes," Mel said brightly, nodding in my direction, as though expecting my wholehearted agreement. "Of course. We'll be glad to give her the message.

Sure thing, and we'll keep you posted, too."

Mel ended the call.

"What message?" I asked. "For whom?"

"For Dr. Epstein," Mel said. "Who else? This case now involves three separate jurisdictions. Dr. Epstein called and gave Harry a ration, so Harry called Ross to pass it on, and Ross called Sheriff Tyler. Upshot is, what goes around comes around. Special Homicide is now in charge of this investigation. You and I are primary."

"What are we supposed to do, spend the whole day sitting around Chehalis with our hands in our pockets waiting for Dr. Epstein to get around to doing an autopsy so we can witness same?"

"No," Mel said with a grin. "It's much better than that. Ross is faxing Sheriff Tyler an order expressly forbidding Dr. Epstein from performing the autopsy and remanding the custody of the Centralia victim to the King County medical examiner's office in Seattle. You and I are expected to drive to Packwood, give Rachel's folks the bad news, and then bring them to Chehalis, where we'll ask them to identify the remains as is and before the body is transported to Seattle."

"As is?" I asked. "You mean without cleaning her up at all?"

Mel nodded. "As is," she confirmed.

"That'll be hard on them," I said.

"Yes, it will be, but Ross believes it's the only way we can be confident that all potential trace evidence is properly preserved. He's heard some things about sloppy workmanship and corner cutting in Dr. Epstein's morgue, and this case is too important to risk bumbling it. Once the ID is complete, King County will send someone down to take charge of the body. They'll transport it, examine it for evidence, and perform the autopsy. The fax should be in Sheriff Tyler's hands sometime in the next twenty minutes. Dr. Epstein will not be pleased."

Mel's deadpan comment caught me with a mouthful of not-quite-swallowed coffee. "Pleased!" I sputtered. "The woman is going to have a cow!"

"Yes, she will," Mel agreed with a

grin. "And I'm only too happy to help facilitate the delivery."

"So we wait for the fax."

Mel nodded again. "In addition to that, Ross is making arrangements with a Lewis County judge to issue a search warrant for the Browards' place in Packwood, as well as their telephone records."

"Do we need a warrant?" I asked. "Once they know Rachel is dead, chances are they'll give us permission to search her room anyway."

"That's true," Mel said. "You and I don't think the Browards are involved in what happened, but Ross wants to cover that base just in case. He'd rather we go there armed with a warrant than without one."

Mel and I left the restaurant in both cars. That made for a slight detour in our plan for the day, but overall we were working the same program. First Mel and I would take the Mercedes to Packwood, where we would give Ardith and Kenny Broward the bad news and bring them to Chehalis for the official ID ordeal.

With four people in the car, my Mercedes was a better choice for that part of the trip than Mel's Cayman, and the two hours going and coming would provide ample opportunity for us to do a long informal interview. After the ID, I would drive the Browards back home to Packwood, and Mel would drive herself there in the Cayman. That would leave her free to execute the search warrant and then spend the remainder of the day backtracking on Rachel's Packwood friends while I drove to Olympia to start the same process with friends, acquaintances, and classmates of Josh Deeson.

At the Lewis County Sheriff's Department we waited in a small lobby just outside Sheriff Tyler's office while he finished up with what his secretary told us was an important phone call. When he finally emerged, he was carrying several pages of faxed documents and grinning from ear to ear.

"You two really know how to make my day," he said, handing the paperwork over to Mel. "It's about time someone put that woman in her place. Call me after you finish IDing the victim. If it turns out to be Rachel, Judge Andrews will sign off on the search warrant and you'll be able to take that back to Packwood with you."

"Will do," Mel said.

I thought we'd be able to walk from the sheriff's office to the morgue. No such luck. The morgue was nowhere near the rest of the Lewis County government complex. Instead, it was up a steep hill and in the basement of a local hospital. We used both cars for the drive there as well.

Standing in the hospital parking lot and looking out over downtown Chehalis, I realized that it wasn't nearly as hot as it had been the previous two days. A low-pressure system had blown in off the ocean the night before. Instead of clear blue skies overhead, there was a pleasant cover of gray with a hint of moisture in the air. My favorite kind of Seattle summer day—gray and cool and damp with no rain.

Mel got out of the Cayman armed with her paperwork. We both knew what was written there would send Dr. Epstein into a spasm. I'm sorry to admit it, but I was actually looking forward to this confrontation.

Mel must have caught the slight grin on my face. "What's so funny?" she asked.

"I hate to think about how many guys in Homicide used to sit around talking and dreaming about leaving Seattle PD behind and finding themselves a nice little job in some quiet burg where they'd be immune from politics. But that's what this whole thing is with Dr. Epstein—a lesson in small-town politics."

"Yes," Mel said. "And if you ask me, small-town politics are worse. They're more personal because everybody knows everybody else."

Two minutes later we were ushered into Dr. Epstein's office. She wasn't happy to see us.

"We haven't started yet," she said brusquely. "I told you I'd call when I had the autopsy results."

Mel smiled and put the fax down on Dr. Epstein's shiny wooden desk. "No," she said. "I'm afraid we'll be the ones calling you."

Mel seldom gets mad at me, and it's a good thing. When she's mad, she can be a ring-tailed bitch. Dr. Bonnie Epstein had done the unforgivable and had made Mel Soames mad.

As Dr. Epstein read through the fax, her cheeks flushed deep red.

"Ross Connors can't do this!" she declared at last, spinning the papers away from her. They fluttered off the edge of her desk and landed on the floor. I reached down, collected them, reassembled them, and turned them into a neat stack.

"Yes, I'm afraid he can," Mel said. "I believe we mentioned that to you earlier this morning. He's the chief law enforcement officer in this state. What he says goes."

"Who's his boss, then?" Dr. Epstein wanted to know. "The governor? I'll call her next."

"Go right ahead," Mel said. "But I have a feeling the governor is a little busy this morning. I doubt she'll be taking calls from anyone, let alone you."

"But—"

Mel continued as if Dr. Epstein hadn't

opened her mouth. "Mr. Beaumont and I are on our way to Packwood to pick up Rachel's parents so they can come and do the official ID. You're to instruct your people to unzip the bag for them, or you can do it yourself, but that's it. You're to do nothing else with the remains, especially no cleaning. The M.E. in Seattle will be responsible for collecting and processing all evidence."

"Rachel?" Dr. Epstein asked, plucking that single word out of what Mel had said. "That's her name, Rachel?"

"Yes," Mel said. "That's most likely our victim's name—Rachel Camber of Packwood."

Our victim, I noted. With those two words she laid out the ground rules and took possession of the case.

Dr. Epstein didn't go down without a fight. "It's my job to notify the victim's family," she objected. "What was that name again, Camber? How do you spell that?"

"C-A-M-B-E-R," Mel said, carefully calling out the letters one by one.

About then, I found myself feeling a little sorry for Dr. Epstein. She wrote the letters down quickly, without any idea that Mel Soames was cheerfully handing her a dead-end deal.

Given the circumstances, it seemed likely that Dr. Epstein might try to beat us to the punch and contact Rachel's parents before Mel and I had a chance to do so.

We both knew that wasn't going to happen. Ardith Broward hadn't been Ardith Camber for a very long time.

CHAPTER 17

Dr. Epstein was in the process of attempting to call Governor Longmire when Mel and I left her office. On the way out of town, we stopped at a drugstore and stocked up on batteries for the cassette recorder Mel keeps in her purse. Fortunately she keeps a supply of extra cassettes tucked in there as well.

The trip to Packwood was still the same distance as it had been the day before, but somehow knowing where we were going made it seem shorter.

"We must have done all right with the

locals yesterday," I said. "At least it wasn't necessary to send Deputy Timmons along to look after us."

"Are you going to tell Kenny and Ardith, or will I?" Mel asked.

"We could always draw straws," I suggested.

"No," Mel said. "We'll play it by ear."

As we drove through Randle we noticed that there were no motorcycles parked in front of the Bike Inn, and a red-and-black CLOSED sign hung on the door. I had no idea who owned the bar. As far as I knew, Ardith was an employee. It struck me as a kind gesture on the owner's part to have closed the place down for the day in honor of the tragedy playing out in Kenny and Ardith Broward's lives. Once we arrived in Packwood, however, I was downright impressed.

Kenny and Ardith's yard was full of motorcycles—two dozen or more, along with a collection of woebegone minivans and pickup trucks. People milled around on the porch, where a washtub full of ice, beer, and sodas was the center of attention. Out in the front yard, someone was lighting up an old-fashioned charcoal grill.

You could tell the motorcycle guys from the loggers by the way they were dressed, leathers as opposed to overalls and flannel shirts. A collection of kids dressed in shorts, some of them barefoot, clambered over the play structure. And even without stepping inside the house, I knew that it was full of neighboring women who had probably covered every available flat surface with a collection of casseroles and potluckworthy hot dishes. Packwood was a small town, and the folks had gathered there together to show their respect and offer their condolences in time-honored small-town fashion.

In a way, this was surprisingly similar to the people who had come to the governor's mansion once news of Josh's death had leaked out. Friends had gathered there, too, offering sympathy and support, but that had been a far better dressed crowd; the vehicles involved had been more expensive; and to my knowledge, none of the guests had come to the governor's mansion with a covered-dish casserole in hand.

Everyone paused and watched with interest as I squeezed into one of the last available parking spots. When Mel and I stepped out of the vehicle, Conrad Philips—the high school principal and the only visible black man in attendance—extricated himself from the group around the charcoal grill.

"Did you find her?" he asked.

I nodded. He understood the implications. What we had to say wouldn't be good news.

"Wait here," he said. "I'll go get them."

Philips disappeared into the house and returned a few moments later with Kenny and Ardith in tow. Mel and I had agreed we'd play this one by ear, but I don't think either of us had anticipated that we'd be speaking to the Browards in front of this kind of audience. The silence in the yard was absolute—like the silence in the Bike Inn the day before—only bigger, much bigger, and far more attentive.

As Conrad Philips led the bereaved parents through the throng of people, I was struck by how they looked—broken, red-eyed, and hopeless. They had tried to prepare themselves for the bad news. Now they faced it together.

"You found her?" Kenny asked.

"Yes," I said. "We believe so. The body of a young woman was found floating in a retention pond north of Centralia early this morning."

Ardith swayed slightly on her feet and then buried her face in her hands. Kenny reached out to steady her, holding her upright, while somewhere in the nearby trees a bird of some kind began to sing. That's what I'll always remember about the scene—Ardith Broward weeping, the bird singing in the background, and everyone else waiting and watching in utter silence.

When Ardith quieted, Mel stepped forward and took one of Ardith's hands in hers.

"The body has been taken to the morgue in Chehalis," she said quietly. "If you and Mr. Broward don't mind, Mr. Beaumont and I would like to drive you there to see if you can identify the remains. And, of course, we'll bring you back."

Ardith looked up at Kenny as if for guidance. "Right now?" he asked.

"Yes."

"We can take our van," he offered.

"No," Mel told him. "That won't be necessary."

"All right then."

We helped them into the back of the Mercedes. While I started the engine and backed out of the parking place, Mel removed her recorder from her purse, switched it on, and placed it on the seat beside her.

As we started back down Highway 12, Mel told them some of what we knew or suspected, but she left out a few important details—like the possibility that Rachel had been dead for only a few hours when she was found in the pond. We explained how the identification process would work. We tried to prepare them for the shock of what they would see and apologized in advance for the fact that their daughter's body would still be in the same condition in which it had been found.

"Why is that?" Ken asked. "Why couldn't you clean her up?"

"Because we might lose evidence in the process," Mel said. "Evidence that could help us convict her killer later."

"Oh," Ken said. "All right then."

I was content to do the driving and let Mel carry on the conversation. Somewhere along the way, Mel began explaining about the search warrant that would include both their home and their telephone.

"That reminds me," Ken said. "I don't know what else you'll find, but Ardy and I went through Rachel's room last night. We found this hidden in her jewelry case."

He handed Mel a small business card. She looked at it and passed it to me. The design on the card showed a simple peaked roof with several stick figures gathered beneath it. The words JANIE'S HOUSE were written on the card, along with a phone number with a 360 area code. There was nothing else there, not on the front or the back.

"What's this?" Mel asked.

"I have no idea," Ken said. "But that's

what Rachel told me on Sunday—that she was going to Janie's house!"

Mel took out her iPhone and began surfing the net. "It's a drop-in shelter in Olympia," she said. "In other words, it's not a place where people stay, but they serve as a centralized source of needed services for homeless youth. It's named after a girl named Janie Goodson, who was murdered in 1985 while living in a homeless camp outside of Olympia. Janie's grandmother started it. It supplies showers, laundry facilities, meals, tutoring, and a place to hang out."

"But why would Rachel even go there?" Ardith demanded from the backseat. "She had a home. She had us."

I knew there weren't any easy answers to that question. I had asked myself the same kinds of things years ago when my own daughter, Kelly, had taken off. In her case, the answer had to do with a boy named Jeremy. Maybe the answer for Rachel was something similar, but with a far more tragic outcome. A few years down the road, Kenny and Ardith wouldn't end up with a couple of cute little grandkids to show for all their heartache. No, the best they could hope for was having a chance to lay their daughter to rest. On the other hand, that's more than far too many parents of runaway kids ever have a chance to do.

In any case, I knew that as soon as the identification was out of the way and the Browards were safely home in Packwood, Janie's House in Olympia would be my next destination.

"Can you get me a street address on that shelter?" I asked.

"Can do," Mel said. "I'm working on it right now."

The ID session was every bit as bad as we had expected. That was due in large part to the condition of the body. But it also had something to do with Dr. Epstein, who made her displeasure known by being disdainful and conde-scending to the point of being rude. It was fine for her to be mad at Mel and me. We deserved it. In fact, we had gone out of our way to provoke her. In-stead, she took it out on the Browards, slamming the gurney with the body bag on it into the middle of the room and then jerking down the zipper to reveal the ghastly, still mud-covered face.

"Is that her?"

"Yes," Kenny whispered while Ardith nodded wordlessly.

"All right then," Dr. Epstein said. "We're done here."

As in "Here's your hat. What's your hurry?" If that was Dr. Epstein's idea of bedside manner, she had done the world of medical science a huge favor by becoming a coroner rather than working with living, breathing patients. Maybe that was the path of least resistance if you don't want to deal with customers who actually talk back. Ditto for Dr. Larry Mowat, the Thurston County M.E., although in terms of status, serving as Lewis County coroner was most likely a big step down from a position where you got to put the words "medical examiner" behind your name.

On the way into town, I think Ardith had clung to the faint hope that the body they were going to see wouldn't be Rachel's. On the way back to Packwood, knowing the worst, she seemed intent on starting to put together a plan for finding a coffin and holding services.

"You won't be able to do that right away," I cautioned. "King County will most likely send someone to pick up the body today, but the autopsy won't be until tomorrow at the very earliest. You won't be able to make plans for a funeral until after the M.E. releases the body."

"So by the beginning of the week, then?" Ardith asked.

"I can't say for sure," I said. "I know it's tough to be stuck in limbo like that, but that's the way it is."

For the trip back, with Mel driving her own vehicle, Kenny had taken my front passenger seat while Ardith rode in the back. After that exchange about funeral arrangements, Ardith fell silent. Eventually Kenny glanced back at her.

"She's asleep," he said. "Neither one of us slept last night—at all. Ardy blames herself, you know, for being too hard on Rachel and driving her away. That's probably true."

"What do you mean?"

Kenny shrugged. "I think Ardy looked

at Rachel and saw too much of herself when she was that age. She didn't want her daughter to make the same mistakes she had, but the more Ardy tried to rein Rachel in, the wilder she got."

"What about you?" I asked. "What did you think about Rachel?"

"I didn't grow up the way Ardy did," he said. "It seemed to me that Rachel was just a regular kid. I kept trying to tell Ardy that you catch more flies with honey than with vinegar."

"That's why you let her go on that overnight on Sunday?" I asked.

He nodded bleakly. "It was just supposed to be that one night." He fell silent, too, and spent the next twenty minutes weeping silently. I gave the guy credit for doing his crying when his wife was asleep. I also understood the real reason for his tears. Yes, Rachel was dead, but that was only part of it. Ardith may have been blaming herself for her daughter's fate, but Kenny Broward was doing the same thing—drowning in blame.

I understood exactly how it had all come about. He and Ardith had been playing good cop/bad cop with Rachel Camber. Unfortunately for all concerned, in this case both cops had lost.

Kenny finally managed to get it together and decided to tell me the rest of the story. "Ardy found money hidden in Rachel's drawer along with that business card, and it wasn't the first time, either. That first time she left it there so Rachel wouldn't know we were snooping.

"How much money?" I asked.

"Eight hundred dollars," Kenny said.

"That's a lot of money for a kid to have stowed away." *Especially for a kid without a regular job,* I thought.

Ken nodded miserably in agreement.

"Rachel wanted to go to cheerleader camp next month. One week costs a thousand bucks. We told her we didn't have that kind of money lying around. We're making ends meet, but just barely. I think she was saving up for that."

That meant that Rachel had amassed an additional four hundred bucks to go with the four hundred Ardith had already mentioned. "But a total of eight hundred dollars?" I asked. "Where do you suppose she would get that kind of money?"

Kenny shrugged. "Ardy seemed to think Rachel was putting out, like a prostitute or something."

"What about you?"

He shrugged hopelessly. "Drug dealing, maybe? That would make sense, but if she was really running away, why didn't she take the money with her?"

"Probably a lack of trust," I suggested. "I'd say Rachel knew the people she was going to be with on Sunday afternoon, and she was worried they might steal whatever she brought along with her."

There was a long period of silence after that while ten miles or so of blacktop unwound itself between opposing banks of towering evergreens.

"Will we get her stuff back?" Kenny asked finally.

"What stuff?" I asked.

"Nothing valuable," he said. "I was hoping we'd be able to give her a class ring next year. That's not going to happen, but she did have a bracelet."

When he first said it, what popped

into my head was a charm-bracelet kind of thing—gold or silver with lots of little dangly thingies on it. My daughter, Kelly, had one of those once, but Kenny Broward soon disabused me of that notion.

"It's an elephant-hair bracelet," he said. "It looks a lot like the wire we used to hang my dad's dropped ceiling. It has a little sliding fastener on it so you can make it bigger or smaller."

"Elephant hair?" I repeated.

"An exchange student from South Africa came to school here last year," Kenny explained. "Her name was Estelle. She and Rachel became good friends. At the end of the year, when it was time for Estelle to go back home, she gave Rachel a bracelet made out of elephant hair and made her promise to wear it every day. She did, too."

I had an idea that the elephant-hair bracelet in question was now lying somewhere on the muddy bottom of the retention pond, but I didn't say as much to Kenny.

"Anything that was found with the body will be inventoried and returned to the family unless it's considered to be evidence of some kind."

"All right," he said. Then he shook his head again. "I guess I need to try to let Estelle know."

"She probably has e-mail," I said. "Try asking Conrad Philips. He'll know how to get in touch with her."

Ardith was awake again by the time we got to their house in Packwood. The yard was still parked full with people waiting to hear the bad news and to help the Browards cope with it. I knew Mel was right behind me. She'd execute the search warrant, then interview all these folks to see if anyone knew anything. In the meantime, I dropped off my passengers and headed right back out.

I pulled off the freeway in Centralia because I needed to buy gas. By the time I finished filling the tank, it was lunchtime and the call of that Country Cousin fried chicken was more than I could resist. I went inside and drew the same waitress who had served Mel's and my breakfasts.

The chicken comes with a fresh salad,

a dollop of mashed potatoes, and a stack of green beans. The salad includes a layer of tiny cubes of steamed beets. Back when I was growing up, my mother had to threaten me with bodily harm to get me to eat steamed beets. She'd be astonished if she knew I now eat them voluntarily.

The drawback on Country Cousin fried chicken is that it takes time to cook—a full half hour. I occupied my time by opening my computer, logging on, and checking my e-mail. The first e-mail on the list was the one from Beaumont, Texas—the one from my presumed cousin, the one I hadn't replied to yet. I scrolled past that one. At the bottom of a long string of Viagra ads was one from Dr. Mowat, or, rather, LWMowatME, according to his e-mail address. The message itself was short if not sweet.

Deeson autopsy completed. As per the attorney general's instructions, I gave the autopsy results and a certified copy of the death certificate to Captain

Hoyt of the Washington State Patrol. Let me say for the record, Ross Connors is a jackass.

It did my heart good to know that Ross Connors's dislike of Larry Mowat wasn't the least bit unrequited. It's sort of a waste when one person hates another one's guts and the first guy doesn't get it.

As far as I was concerned, I had my own opinions about good old Larry. In fact, I was so happy to avoid talking to him about the Deeson autopsy that I spent twenty minutes of my chicken-waiting half hour tracking down Captain Hoyt's telephone number. I wondered what kind of approach I'd need to make in order to glean any usable information. Those concerns turned out to be unfounded.

"I've been expecting your call," she said. "Ross Connors told me you'd be in touch. What do you need?"

"To know everything you know about Josh Deeson's autopsy."

"I don't have the official report," she said. "All I have right now is what Mowat told me. Cause of death is plain old as-phyxiation," she said. "Definitely sui-cide. No initial sign of drug use of any kind, which is fairly unusual in these cases. Kids who decide to end it all of-ten turn out to be the ones who've al-ready screwed up their bodies and their futures with some pretty obvious sub-stance abuse."

"What about personal effects?" I asked.

"Nothing much. The M.E. found only one item on the body—a gold chain with some kind of skeleton key on it. The crime scene team inventoried a Seiko watch. That's already been sent along to the lab."

I knew about the watch. The key was a surprise.

"A key?" I asked. "What's it to?"

"Beats me. His room, maybe?" Joan replied. "It seems to me that the rooms on that top floor of the governor's man-sion all have old-fashioned keyhole door locks, but as far as I know the door wasn't locked."

"You're right," I said definitively. "And since the door wasn't locked, that means the key is to something other than the door to his room."

"How do you know that?"

"Think about it. Josh was about to commit suicide. That's a hell of a lot worse than, say, thumbing through back issues of *Playboy* or *Penthouse.* If he'd had a key to the door of his room, he would have used it."

"Yes," Captain Hoyt said. "I see what you mean. I'll have my people do some checking and see if we can figure out where the key is from."

My chicken showed up. It smelled wonderful, but I could tell from the steam that it was still too hot to eat.

"All right then," I said, poking a hole in the crispy skin to allow some of the heat to dissipate. "I'll let you go."

"One more thing," she said. "I spent some time with Gerard Willis. You can't help but feel sorry for the man. He's really broken up about Josh."

"I know."

"So even though it's not my case, I have to ask. Yes, I know Josh killed himself. I saw the room. There was no one else in there with him who could

have been responsible, but do you re~
think he killed that girl, too?"

"No," I told her, "he didn't, but ~
two cases are connected someh~
and I'm going to do my damnedes†
figure out whatever that connec†
might be."

CHAPTER 18

I had ended the call with Captain Hoyt and taken one very hot taste of chicken when the phone rang again.

"Hey," Ross Connors said. "Where are you?"

"Centralia," I said. "On my way back to Olympia." I didn't mention that I had stopped off for lunch. That was on a need-to-know basis only.

"I just got a call from the crime lab in Spokane. It took a while for them to figure out Josh's computer password so they could access his files. I passed that along to Todd."

I would have been surprised if Todd Hatcher hadn't already found his own access to the data he had lifted from Josh's hard drive, but I let that pass without comment.

"The kid played chess," Ross continued. "He had a half-dozen Internet chess games going at any one time, but what's more interesting is that this really is a case of bullying—cyber bullying. Josh kept a file called *My Life* on his computer that contained copies of all his text messages, even after he deleted them from his cell phone. Spokane sent a copy of the file to Todd and one to me. Katie just printed it out. Some of the messages call Josh MM for Meth Mouth. Let's see, here's a brief sample: 'You're too stupid to live.' 'Go back to where you came from.' 'How does it feel to be brain damaged?' 'Protect the gene pool—always wear a condom,' along with the usual teenage crap saying he's a queer. All told, there must be hundreds of derogatory comments."

It was clear that the text messages mirrored the kind of taunting that had provoked the fights Josh had been cited for at school.

Call waiting buzzed. A glance at caller ID told me that Todd Hatcher was on the line. "Gotta go," I told Ross Connors. "It's Todd."

Ross hung up before I had a chance to do so first.

"Hey, Todd," I said. "What have you got?"

"Some information on the source of that video. It was sent to Josh Deeson from a computer located in Olympia. I've got a physical address for you," he added. "Ready?"

I'm not one of those people who can talk on the cell phone and get it to take messages at the same time. The waitress had dropped off my check, so I grabbed that and wrote on the back of it.

"Shoot," I said.

He read off an address on Seventeenth Avenue Southeast in Olympia. "It seems to be a kind of rec center or a shelter or something, sort of like a boys' and girls' club, only different."

"It wouldn't happen to be called Janie's House, would it?" I asked.

"Just a minute."

I heard him typing and then waiting. "Yup," he said at last. "You got it. That's what it's called—Janie's House. How did you know that?"

"I'm a detective, remember? What about the text messages sent to Josh Deeson?" I asked.

"Ross sent me a copy of those a little while ago. I didn't tell him that I was already working on them. They're certainly ugly enough. They all come from phones on the same cell phone account, one that leads back to Janie's House. I ran a preliminary analysis on the texts. Based on language-usage profiles I'd say they were written by several different people—four or five at least—all of them ganging up on the same kid."

"Do we have any record of him responding?"

"Josh saved copies of the texts that were sent to him. If he made responses, he didn't save those. However, we may be able to get those from the receiving cell phone accounts. That'll require another set of search warrants."

"Let Ross know, so he can go to work on getting what we need."

"What are you doing in the meantime?" Todd asked.

"I believe I'm going to pay a visit to Janie's House. Before I go, I need two things."

"What?"

"Send a copy of the video from Josh's phone to my cell. Mel has a copy of it on her cell phone, but I need one, too. The other thing I need is a photo of Josh Deeson, preferably a jpeg. I know there was one on the *Olympia Daily News* Web site today, but I want to have one available that doesn't show any connection to the news story. When I show up at Janie's House, I want to be prepared with my own version of shock and awe."

"It might take a while," Todd cautioned.

"Don't worry," I said. "I'm going to sit right here and do my homework on Janie's House."

I Googled Janie's House and ended

up reading the same information Mel had recounted to me earlier when I wasn't paying attention. Now I was.

Felina Jane Goodson was fifteen years old when she went to war with her parents, who refused to let her apply for a learner's permit until her grades improved. Janie Goodson had responded by running away from home. Two weeks later, while staying in a homeless camp near Tenino, she had been raped and bludgeoned to death in a crime that remained unsolved until 2007, when a Washington State Patrol cold-case squad got around to retesting old DNA evidence found at the scene, evidence that in 1985 had meant nothing. The new test linked the resulting DNA profile to a fifty-seven-year-old man serving life without parole in Walla Walla after being convicted in three other cases in which victims had been raped and killed.

The identification and subsequent conviction of Jane Goodson's killer came twenty years too late for Deborah Magruder, Janie's maternal grandmother. Deborah came from an old

Washington family, one that had made a fortune in the timber industry. Deborah had spent the last years of her life and a good portion of her remaining wealth trying to help "troubled youth." Her goal had been to create a "safe haven" where distressed young people could access a smorgasbord of needed services—counseling, food, and clothing, as well as educational help and direction.

The result was Janie's House, a facility made up of three former residential homes that had been cobbled together to form a single unit. I was copying down the phone number when my phone buzzed, announcing an incoming message. The video was there along with a jpeg file of Josh Deeson's most recent yearbook photo.

Then, with all my ducks very nearly in a row, I did something smart. I called Mel. That's one of the first rules out of Police Academy 101—don't go chasing bad guys all by your lonesome. That's why God created partners—so you can have backup. But calling Mel made sense for more than one reason: I knew for sure she'd be royally ripped at me if I didn't.

"How are things in Packwood?" I asked casually.

"One dead end after another," she grumbled. "I executed the search warrant. Other than the eight hundred dollars, I found nothing of interest. So far I've talked to half a dozen of Rachel's friends and none of them knows anything, either. Or, if they do, they're not saying. Why?"

"We may have just caught a big break. Todd Hatcher tells me the snuff video was sent to Josh's computer from one located at Janie's House—that homeless shelter in Olympia."

"The same shelter that was on that business card found in Rachel's room?"

"The very one," I said. "I'm planning on going there, but it occurred to me that if I want to go on living, I'd better give you a chance to go along."

Mel laughed. "You've got that right."

"Also, the crime lab in Spokane broke into the files on Josh's computer. Along with a group of ongoing chess games, they also found a collection of ugly text messages that were sent to Josh. It turns out those texts came from cell phones that are billed to Janie's House as well."

"Sounds like your basic full-service shelter," Mel said. "I'm on my way now. I'll be there as soon as I can."

"Do not speed," I cautioned. "I promise, I won't go anywhere near the place until you're with me."

Telling her not to speed was really wasting my breath. I had no doubt the blue bubble light was already firmly affixed to the Cayman's roof and her lead foot was on the gas pedal.

"And don't bother stopping for lunch," I added. "I'll bring the rest of my chicken to you in a doggy bag."

"Do you mean to tell me that after that huge breakfast you went back to the Country Cousin for lunch?"

"Guilty as charged," I said. "And I'm not apologizing for it, either. Wait until you try it."

She laughed. "I'm glad you saved some for me," she said. "Where should we meet?"

"At the hotel," I suggested. "In the

meantime, I'm going to drop by the high school and see if the principal there knows as much about his students as Conrad Philips knows about his."

"If I were you," Mel said, "I wouldn't hold my breath on that score."

Outside in the parking lot, I keyed the Olympia High School campus into my GPS. When I got there I soon found that Mel's assessment was correct. The name of the principal was Annette Tompkins. She and Conrad Philips were both secondary-school principals. That meant they probably had similar schooling and credentials. Since Ms. Tompkins's school was far larger than the one in Randle, I'm sure she brought home higher wages than he did. If I'd been writing their paychecks, that situation would have been reversed.

For one thing, once she knew I was there to discuss Josh Deeson, she was very reluctant to talk to me. She said she was sorry one of her students had died; she claimed no personal knowledge of Josh Deeson's history or difficulties, to say nothing of his friends or enemies. It was only by taking Ross

Connors's name in vain that I finally got Ms. Tompkins to cough up the names and phone numbers of Josh's summer-school teachers, both of whom were still in classes and currently unavailable for interviews. She also furnished the name and phone number for the chess club adviser, a guy named Samuel Dysart, who volunteered his services with the chess club, although he didn't serve on the faculty in any other capacity. I tried his number, but when his phone went to voice mail, I hung up. This was something that required a live conversation, not a message left on someone's answering machine.

Rather than wait around for classes to be dismissed, I headed back to the hotel. I figured I had about half an hour before Mel was due to arrive—long enough to stretch out on the bed and maybe grab a nap. It had been a short night and it was stacking up to be a long day.

I had been asleep for about fifteen minutes when Mel showed up. We're a good pair. I didn't ask her about how fast she had driven, and she downed my leftover chicken with no wry comments about that, either.

Ten minutes later we parked at the curb outside Janie's House on Seventeenth Avenue Southeast. The three houses involved were all older homes in good repair. The lawns were mowed. The edges were trimmed. The exterior paint jobs were relatively new. From the article I had read I knew that the middle building, the one with the word OFFICE stenciled on the wall next to the doorbell, had once belonged to the shelter's founder, Deborah Magruder.

Mel and I were standing on the front porch, preparing to ring the doorbell, when the front door was opened by a middle-aged woman with aggressively orange-and-purple hair and enough piercings to belie her age. "May I help you?" she asked.

There are times when those four words constitute a real offer of help. There are other times when they mean "Get lost." This was an example of the latter.

Mel presented her badge and ID. "We're with Special Homicide," she said. "We'd like to speak to you about someone who is possibly one of your clients."

"We don't discuss our clients with anyone," the woman said. "We're here to help them. We're not here to make it easy for cops to hassle them. Believe me, by the time the kids get to us, they've usually had a bellyful of people like you."

"Homicide investigators?" Mel asked sweetly. "Some of your clients have been suspects in murder investigations?"

"I mean cops in general," the woman said.

"And you are?" Mel persisted.

"My name is Meribeth Duncan. I'm the executive director of Janie's House. I have nothing to say to you."

Meribeth attempted to turn and go back inside, but somehow Mel managed to insert herself between the executive director and the front door.

"Does the name Rachel Camber mean anything to you?" she asked.

"No," Meribeth said. "And I wouldn't tell you if it did. The kids who come here do so with the understanding that the services we provide are confidential. Most of them are homeless or come from homes that are so horrendous that they'd be better off homeless. They come here needing a place to hang out where they can be safe and clean. Do you have any idea how hard it is to stay warm or dry or clean when you're on the streets? We have showers here. We have clothes washers and dryers along with a supply of donated clothing."

"What about beds?" I asked.

"Our mission is to serve as a drop-in center only," Meribeth replied.

"What does that mean?"

"We provide counseling, educational support like homework help and computer access. We don't allow for overnight accommodations. Our liability insurance specifically precludes us from doing so."

That made me wonder. Rachel had told Kenny she'd be staying with "Janie." That wasn't true, but clearly she had stayed somewhere between the time she left home on Sunday and the time she turned up dead. We needed to know where she had stayed during that time, and if she had stayed there because she wanted to, or had she been held somewhere against her will?

"If you don't know Rachel Camber," Mel said, "what about Josh Deeson?"

Meribeth's eyes narrowed. "The name sounds familiar, but . . ."

"You may have heard it on the news this morning," Mel said. "He's Governor Longmire's stepgrandson."

"The kid who committed suicide?" Meribeth asked.

Anticipating that there would most likely be a female gatekeeper at Janie's House, Mel and I had decided on a plan of action. Mel would do the talking. I would be in charge of show-and-tell. About the time the woman was saying she didn't know Josh, I pulled out his photo and held it out to her.

"That's him?" Meribeth asked. "That's Josh?"

I nodded.

Meribeth shook her head. "He's definitely not one of our clients. I've never seen him before. Besides, if he lived at the governor's mansion, Josh Deeson was a long way from needing our kinds of services."

"And this is Rachel," I said. "Rachel Camber from Packwood, Washington. She was found dead, murdered, in a water-retention pond in Centralia early this morning. Her parents just went back home after identifying her body."

This time Meribeth winced. It was a tiny gesture, but a telling one. Meribeth knew Rachel, and she didn't try to deny it.

"Her name is Amber, not Rachel," Meribeth said. "At least that's the name she went by when she was here." She sighed and then looked up and down the street. "I suppose you should come inside," she added reluctantly. "We need to talk."

She led us into the house—through a foyer, past a reception desk, and into a small office that had been carved out of what must once have been a spacious living room. She sat down behind a cluttered wooden desk and motioned Mel and me into chairs in front of it. We might have gotten off to a rocky start, but the mention of Rachel's murder had broken down some of the barriers.

"What about the dead boy?" Meribeth asked. "Is he a suspect in her death?"

"Josh probably would have been," Mel said, "but he died a good twenty-four hours before Rachel Camber was killed. That means he's dead, but he's also in the clear. You're sure you've never seen him before?"

"Never!"

Meribeth's answer was forceful. As far as I could tell, it was also truthful.

"So how does this work?" Mel asked, gesturing at the Janie's House surroundings. "Kids can come here and stay for free for as long as they like?"

"No," Meribeth answered. "As I said earlier, we're not a group home facility. No one sleeps over. The shelter opens at seven in the morning and closes at ten at night. Drop-ins only. Generally boys hang out in the house west of here and girls on the other side. This building is the only one that's truly coed. We have a library here as well as the computer lab. The other houses have TVs and VCRs, showers, kitchens, and laundry facilities. Here we try to maintain a kind of study hall atmosphere. During the school year we concentrate on academics. There's some of that during the summer as well. A lot of our kids need remedial help, but during the summer months the emphasis is on having fun."

"Supervision?" I asked.

"We have volunteer houseparents who manage each building," she said. "Those are often former clients who've gone on to make better lives for themselves. And don't think what we do here is free. We don't charge money for our services, but the kids who come here are expected to help out. They do chores—dusting, sweeping, painting, loading dishwashers, yard work—just like kids are supposed to do at home."

"You make computers and cell phones available to your clients?" Mel asked.

"Of course. Social networking is vital these days. Kids who are too poor to have access to e-mail or texting are marginalized or even ostracized. We do what we can to rectify that. There's a cell phone in each building that's for client use, and we have a total of ten computers."

"Do you keep track of Internet usage?"

"We keep track of who uses the computers, but we certainly don't monitor what they do on them, and we don't censor them, either," Meribeth said.

"What about attendance?" I asked. "Do you keep track of who comes and goes, check photo IDs, anything like that?"

Meribeth shook her head. "No. We're a support system and we're privately funded. We don't have to keep attendance records to justify our existence."

"What about those chores?" I asked. "Are there sign-up sheets for those?"

"Yes," she said. "The houseparents handle those. They're in closer contact with the kids than I am, but this is all done on a first-name basis only. Or at least what they claim to be their first names. And we don't keep track of those, either. We work on an honor system. I assume you know what that is."

The first-name-only ploy was just

that—a ploy to protect Janie's House clients from people like Mel and me. I didn't much like Meribeth's snide "honor system" dig, either, but I didn't push back right then because I saw Mel was reaching into her purse and retrieving her phone. That meant she was about to deliver some serious push-back of her own.

"Do you happen to offer any drama classes here?" Mel asked. "Or filmmaking?"

"We don't offer any official classes as such," Meribeth said. "We have a staff of volunteer tutors that comes in to help out as needed. That's not to say that some of our clients aren't involved in those kinds of classes, however. We actively encourage those pursuits. Through the years we've found that creative arts activities can be very therapeutic."

"I'm sure," Mel said agreeably. "And I can tell you for sure that some of your clients have a real flair for the dramatic. If you don't mind, I'd like to show you something."

"What?"

"It's a film clip that we believe may have originated here. At least it was sent out as a file first from one of the computers in this building and then from one of your cell phones. You'll probably find it to be graphic, offensive, and quite shocking. We did, too. You do know what a snuff film is, don't you?"

"A snuff film?" Meribeth repeated. "You mean one of those movies where someone is actually killed on-screen? If that's what you're about to show me, I'm not interested," she declared. "I will not watch such a thing. I won't allow you to show it to me. You need to leave now. If you don't, I'll call the police."

"We are the police," Mel reminded her. "And you don't need to worry. It turns out that although this film is very convincing, it's also make-believe. We now know that the young woman who is supposedly being murdered in this video, the girl you said was Amber, was still alive for a period of time after the film was made."

Without saying anything further, Mel activated the clip. Despite Meribeth's protestations, there was absolute silence in the room as the clip played. By the time it finished playing, Meribeth Duncan's face was ashen.

"Are you sure she wasn't really dead?" Meribeth asked. "It looked so real."

"Yes, it did look real," Mel agreed, "but according to the medical examiner, she didn't die until sometime later."

"And you think one of my clients is behind this . . . this . . ."

Unable to find a strong enough word to express her horror, Meribeth left the sentence unfinished.

"The clip was downloaded onto one of your computers here, probably from a thumb drive," Mel explained. "Next it was uploaded to one of your cell phones. From there it went to Josh Deeson's phone. That's where it was found early Monday morning. We believe your cell phones were also used to send Josh any number of ugly text messages."

"Josh—the boy who committed suicide?"

"Yes," Mel said. "That happened yesterday morning. Rachel Camber's body was found early this morning, but the coroner estimates that she was killed only a few hours before she was found."

"What do you need from me?" Meribeth asked.

"We're in the process of getting a search warrant so we can access your phone and Internet records. I'm expecting it to show up any minute."

"You won't need a warrant," Meribeth said. "As far as I'm concerned, you have my full cooperation."

CHAPTER 19

Meribeth Duncan may have been a raging bleeding heart with a knee-jerk contempt for the police, but once she reached her tipping point, she was all in. It turned out a number of folks in the neighborhood had been waging a land-use war with her for years, trying to shut Janie's House down completely.

"Once this gets out, that might give them enough ammunition to go to the city council," she said. "So how do we fix it? And how do we do it without letting the other kids know what's up? Some of them might not come back at all if they find out the cops have been here."

My concerns tended to go in the opposite direction. I was afraid the troublemakers would do their best to delete any offending files from the computer system as well as from the phones. I had a good deal of faith in Todd Hatcher's ability to recover any missing data, but still the idea of avoiding an obvious police presence at Janie's House seemed like a good one. And certainly my Mercedes, parked on the street in front of the office, gave no hint of being a cop car.

Finally, at my suggestion and citing a bogus plumbing emergency, Meribeth went from building to building, dismissing the houseparents who were on duty and shooing out any kids who had settled in for the day. Once they were gone, she posted a notice on each of the front and back doors saying that Janie's House would reopen at 7:00 A.M. on Thursday.

When Todd Hatcher arrived, properly drawn search warrant in hand, he came to the party in a mud-spattered pickup truck that didn't look any more like a copmobile than my S-550. Nothing about our vehicles gave any kind of hint that Janie's House, currently off-limits to its teenage clients, was dealing with anything other than a plumbing problem, or that the place was currently being scrutinized by members of Ross Connors's Special Homicide Investigation Team.

One whole wall of the director's office was lined with four-drawer file cabinets. It turned out that Meribeth knew a lot more about the clients Janie's House served than she had let on initially. She may not have kept official "attendance records," but each client had a file, a paper file, with both first and last names attached, kept under lock and key in that collection of file cabinets.

During three separate visits to Janie's House, Rachel Camber had operated under the alias of Amber Wilson. Meribeth plucked the file with Amber's name on it out of a drawer, opened it, and perused the papers she saw there for the better part of a minute. Then she closed the file and handed it to me.

"When clients come here, they fill out that first page. If they want to give us an alias, we respect that. This is our needs assessment page. It's designed to tell us something about where the kids are, especially if there's any area of study that's giving them trouble. We also want to find out what it is they're hoping to accomplish. One of our jobs is to do what we can to help them meet their goals, no matter how mundane or how lofty. If you look at Amber's goals statement, you'll see she wanted to attend a cheerleading camp."

"I know," I said, studying the information on the page. "Her stepfather told us about that. He said they couldn't afford it."

"Right," Meribeth agreed. "Those can be prohibitively expensive. One of my people was working on locating scholarship money that would have enabled her to attend a cheerleading camp later this summer. We expected to hear back on that any day now. That, of course, she would have attended under her real name."

"So you have both."

Meribeth nodded. "Usually," she said.

I took another look at Meribeth Duncan. With her orange-and-purple hair and her iconoclastic manner of dress—army fatigues and scuzzy boots—I doubted she had ever had any yearnings to be a cheerleader. A lot of folks in her position might have tried to steer her charges into things more to their own liking. The fact that she had supported Amber/Rachel's ambition rather than denigrated it made me revise some of my initial thinking about Meribeth.

"So did she come here this week?" I asked.

Meribeth shook her head. "Not that I know of, but it's possible she was here without my seeing her. We can check with the houseparents who have been on duty this week."

I made a note to do just that while Meribeth turned to another file cabinet. "I'll give you a list of names and phone numbers," she said. "These four drawers contain information on all of our volunteers. Some of them do nothing but fund-raising. Some specialize in finding sources of appropriate scholarships. You'll find files on all our houseparents, past and present, in here, as well as all our tutors. Some of those are retired teachers and businesspeople, although most of our tutors come from nearby high schools and colleges."

"Kids teaching kids?" I asked. "How does that work?"

"You'd be surprised," Meribeth said. "With kids who have a natural aversion to authority figures, peer-to-peer tutoring works surprisingly well."

By then Todd, working in a carrel-lined study, had located the offending computer—the one that had been used to upload the film clip to one of the shelter's cell phones.

In a matter of minutes he hit pay dirt. "Hey," Todd said. "Come take a look at this."

I have a bad reaction to standing beside someone's chair and trying to look at a computer screen. I guess it reminds me too much of standing next to a teacher's desk to have a paper corrected.

"Just tell us," I said.

Todd looked at Meribeth. "Let me guess. This whole computer system was donated, right?"

She nodded.

"Whoever did that was interested in helping you, but they must also have had some concerns that their donated system might be put to some kind of nefarious use," Todd explained. "There's a hidden file in this computer that functions as a virtual logbook—an invisible virtual logbook. The same program is probably on the other computers as well. Before new users can access the system, they have to create profiles that include their names—or at least whatever aliases they employ here—as well as their user names. After that, the logbook maintains a record of each time that user logs in or out as well as which computer was used."

This all sounded good as far as Mel and I were concerned. Meribeth Duncan was outraged. "You mean we've

been spying on the kids' computer usage all this time?"

Todd laughed. "You could have been,
if you had known the file was there. But
here's our guy. We know the film clip
was sent to Josh's phone at one twenty-
three Monday morning. And it was sent
to the Janie's House cell phone from
this computer at nine thirty-five on Sunday night."

"But how could that happen?" Meribeth asked. "The cell phone, I mean.
We're not even open at one twenty-
three in the morning."

"Janie's House may not have been
open," Todd said, "but the Janie's House
cell phones were alive and well somewhere."

"Can you find out where it was and
who was using it?"

"Eventually," Todd said. "Right now
the logbook tells us that a guy named
Hammer was online on this computer
at the time the file was sent to the cell
phone."

"Who's Hammer ?" Meribeth asked.

Todd did a cross-check with the user

profiles. "Hammer," he said, "aka Greg Alexander."

"No!" Meribeth exclaimed, shaking her head in dismay the moment she heard the name. "That can't be. It's not possible for him to be mixed up in something like this."

"Why not?" Mel asked.

"Because Greg is one of our best kids—the last person I would have expected to go off the rails like this."

That reminded me of something my mother used to say, about finding things in the very last place she looked. No doubt the answers we needed were also lurking somewhere in that wall of file cabinets, although we had no clue about the first place to look, to say nothing of the last.

"Sorry," Todd said. "According to this, Greg is the one who was online on this computer at the time the film clip file was uploaded."

Resigned, Meribeth nodded. "Okay," she said. "I'll go pull his file."

Once she left the room, I turned back to Todd. "Is the original file there, too?" I asked.

"No, they probably used a thumb drive to load it onto this computer and then deleted it as soon as it was uploaded to the phone. But these are kids. They think that once they punch the delete button, everything goes away completely, but they're wrong. The data may be de-indexed, but the deleted file sits there on the hard drive for a period of time, waiting to be overwritten. The file was sent out Sunday night. There hasn't been that much activity on this computer since then."

"You think it's still in there?" Mel asked.

"Yes," Todd said, "and you can bet money I'll be able to find it."

Meribeth returned carrying another file. Unlike Amber's, this one had more than one sheet of paper in it. I was mildly interested in the fact that, despite all the computer power sitting around, Meribeth Duncan put her faith in paper files stacked in metal cabinets.

"Greg works part-time in the produce department at the Safeway store in Tumwater. He's due to graduate from high school next spring. Greg's family is a mess. Both his parents and his older brother have been in trouble with the law. They buy junk from garage sales and private parties and try to resell it to metal recyclers. That's the business they claim to be in. Their trash heap is on the far side of Tumwater.

"Greg lives in a moldy, wrecked motor home that doesn't even have running water. He comes here to shower and wash his clothes. When he filled out his needs assessment he said that his long-term goal is to graduate from high school and join the military. I was hoping we could help him rise above his family's bad karma. I even helped set up a meeting for him with an Air Force recruiter." Meribeth shook her head sadly. "He was all excited about it, but if he's mixed up in this mess, his getting into the service probably isn't going to happen."

"Do you have a street address on their place?" Mel asked.

Meribeth nodded and read it off. "I don't recommend going there, though," she said. "I'd try finding him at the grocery store first. I took him home one night when his car broke down. Their place isn't officially a junkyard, but it comes complete with a full assortment of junkyard dogs. They were pretty scary."

Meribeth sounded disheartened, and I didn't blame her. She had invested years of her life, her time, and her effort on behalf of a ragtag bunch of kids nobody else seemed to give a damn about. Now one of those investments had most likely betrayed everything the poor woman stood for or hoped to accomplish.

It was clear to me that Greg "Hammer" Alexander and his pals were using the safe haven offered by Janie's House for a lot more than just "hanging out" and doing their laundry. It was also clear that if word got out that the shelter was under any kind of law enforcement scrutiny, the kids involved in what had happened to Josh Deeson and Rachel Camber would disappear like puffs of smoke.

"You said Greg has a vehicle of some kind?" Mel asked.

"An old Toyota, I think," Meribeth said. "Don't quote me on that."

When Mel and I left a few minutes later, Meribeth was watching as Todd copied data from the computers' hard drives so he could analyze them at his leisure. Once we were in the car, I took over the driving while Mel found the only Tumwater, Washington, Safeway store and had the GPS guide us there— to no avail. This happened to be Greg's day off.

"That's all right," Mel said. "I love going to scary places that have guard dogs."

She put the Alexanders' home address into the GPS and we headed there next. On the way to and through Tumwater, Mel checked with Records for rap sheet details on Greg's family. His father, Demetri; his mother, Barbara Jane; and their older son, Matthew, weren't exactly what you could call stellar. Matthew was a twenty-one-year-old guy currently out on bail on a weapons charge. Demetri had an extensive criminal background that included drug dealing and grand theft auto. Barbara had two DUI arrests and had spent six months in Purdy on possession of stolen goods.

All that information was enough to make me glad both Mel and I were armed and wearing vests. We weren't really expecting to be shot at, but people who end up having repeated run-ins with the law aren't the kind of folks who make sensible decisions. Their first response to having a cop show up on their doorstep might well be a hail of gunfire.

When we arrived at the address, we could see that what might have been a legitimate auto junkyard at one time had devolved into little more than a privately owned dump. I was surprised the county hadn't shut it down. Maybe the planning and zoning folks weren't any fonder of guard dogs than Mel and I were.

A closed chain-link front gate, complete with a hand-painted BEWARE OF DOG sign, barred our way. As if to prove the sign was telling the truth, a chorus of dogs let us have it from the far side of the gate, barking, snapping, and snarling. A smaller sign with an arrow said

RING BELL. Taking the dogs into consideration, we rang the bell—several times.

Eventually a man emerged from a collection of moss-covered motor homes that stood to one side of a tangle of rusted-out vehicles. They were circled end to end, like a wagon train, and they must have leaked like sieves because they were all draped with tarps aimed at helping keep the no-doubt moldy interiors partially dry. Living in one of those during Washington's cold, wet winters couldn't be fun.

The man, presumably Greg's father, Demetri, was broad-shouldered and heavyset. Everything about him was gray—his hair, his skin, his clothing. In all that monochromatic grime it wasn't easy to determine his exact age. He could have been fifty; he could have been seventy. As Demetri moved toward us, he brought with him the unmistakable odor of unwashed flesh. I remembered what Meribeth had told us about Greg's place of residence having no running water.

Demetri approached us with a newly lit cigarette in hand, but the smoke from that was just a layer of cover to disguise the reek of recently smoked weed.

"Whaddya want?" he demanded.

No gunfire was in evidence, but Demetri wasn't exactly rolling out the welcome mat, either.

"We're looking for Greg Alexander," I said, showing him my badge. "Are you his father?"

"That's right. I'm Demetri, but Greg's not here. Whaddya want him for?"

A 1988 Toyota with a collection of mix-and-match bodywork was parked just inside the gate. I was pretty sure that was Greg's ride, and that meant he was most likely home.

"That's his vehicle, isn't it?" I asked.

The old man started giving us a song and dance, but before he got very far a young man emerged from inside a different one of the circle of wrecked motor homes, one that was much smaller than the old man's.

"What is it, Dad?" he asked.

"Nothin'," Demetri said. "Go back inside."

"Are you Greg?" Mel asked.

"I am," he said. "What's this all about?"

"We're police officers. We have a few questions we'd like to ask you about Janie's House," Mel said. "It won't take long. Just a couple of minutes."

"It's okay, Dad," Greg said to this father. "I'll handle it."

Shaking his head in disgust, Demetri went back the way he had come. Greg, moving the pack of barking dogs to one side, made his way out through the gate to where we were standing.

I showed him my badge.

"You're cops?" he asked. "Is something wrong?"

Despite Greg's rudimentary living arrangements, he was neatly dressed. Thanks to the services available to him at Janie's House, Greg was clean and so were his clothes.

"You're Hammer, right?" Mel asked.

"Excuse me?"

"That's your online name—your user name on the computer system at Janie's House—Hammer?"

"Oh, that," he said with a laugh. "Yeah. I was going to use 'Saw' for my user name, but that was too short. You have to have at least six letters, so I chose Hammer instead."

There was almost no resemblance between Greg and his father. Demetri looked like an Eastern European thug. Greg looked like an all-American kid—a clean-cut nice kid—who, right at that moment, seemed to be in the process of breaking Meribeth Duncan's heart.

"What can you tell us about Josh Deeson?"

Greg shook his head. "I've never heard of him. Who is he?"

"His name has been in the papers a lot the last couple of days," Mel said.

Greg gestured back toward the Alexanders' unsightly pile of trash. "My parents aren't big on newspapers," he said. "And I don't have time to read them online."

"What about Rachel Camber?" Mel asked.

"Who?"

"You might have known her under her other name, Amber Wilson."

"Sure," Greg said without a hint of hesitation. "I know Amber. I met her a couple of times at Janie's House when she showed up there. Nice girl. We watched TV and loaded dishwashers together a few times. Why? What about her?"

His answers were open, direct, and seemingly guileless. Greg Alexander was either one hell of a liar or he was absolutely innocent of any wrongdoing.

"Where were you Sunday evening?" Mel asked. "Say, seven to ten."

"This past Sunday? I was at work. School is out. Everybody wants to head out on vacation. I've been picking up extra shifts right and left."

"So we can check with your supervisor to find out if you were at work?"

"Sure," he said. "You can also check my time card. We have to punch a time clock every time we come on shift and every time we go off."

"And you have coworkers who will be able to say you were there?"

"Absolutely," he said confidently. "But you still haven't told what this is all about? Is something wrong?"

"Did you go to Janie's House on Sunday?"

"Sure. Sunday afternoon. I was there just long enough to shower and clean up before I had to go to work."

"What time?"

"What time did I go there?"

I nodded.

"Sometime around four, I guess," he answered. "I was due to go on shift at six. Got off at midnight."

"Did you happen to see Amber there?"

"No."

"What about last night?" I asked. "Were you at work then, too?"

The previously open look on his face abruptly slammed shut. "I don't have to tell you where I was," he said. "Not until I know why you're asking all these questions. And if I'm a suspect, don't you have to read me my rights?"

That's what I love about kids these days. That's the only thing most of them seem to know about the law—that police officers are supposed to read them their rights.

"Show him the file, Mel," I said. "That'll give him a better idea of why we're here."

"What file?" Greg wanted to know.

"Sunday night, someone using your user name uploaded a file from one of the Janie's House computers to a Janie's House cell phone," Mel explained. "That file was eventually sent to Josh Deeson's cell phone."

"I already told you I don't know Josh Deeson."

Mel located the file in her cell phone, cued it up, and then handed the phone to Greg. He glanced at it. "That's Amber," he announced when the clip started playing. "I already told you I know Amber."

"Keep watching," Mel said.

He did. Gradually, Greg's eyes widened. I didn't have to see the screen to realize that, as Amber's apparently lifeless body stopped struggling and fell face forward onto a table, all color abruptly faded from Greg's cheeks.

"Oh my God!" he exclaimed, stepping away from the phone and leaning hard against the gate. "Did they really kill her right then? Really?"

In terms of Greg Alexander's future, those were the right questions for him to be asking. And his questions turned out to be the correct answer to any number of potential questions Mel and I might have asked. Unlike Greg, Mel and I both knew that the snuff film was faked. If Greg believed that he had just seen Amber Wilson murdered on the little screen before it was sent to Josh, then he hadn't been involved in either the filming or in dumping Rachel's lifeless body into the retention pond once she really was dead.

It was several moments before Greg was able to speak. "Why did they do that?" he asked finally, wiping his eyes. "She seemed like a nice girl to me. She wanted to become a cheerleader."

Yes, I thought. *Greg Alexander did know Rachel Camber.*

"How could they gang up on her like that? It had to be at least three to one. What's fair about that?"

I had to remind myself that Greg was young. He still thought life was supposed to be fair.

"Do you know of anyone who had some kind of beef with Amber?"

"No. Not at all, and she was only

there a couple of times. I think she was from somewhere out of town."

On the far side of the gate, the door opened on the same moss-covered motor home into which Greg's father had disappeared. An immense woman stepped out. She was wearing flip-flops and a tie-dyed muumuu that would have been totally at home at a Grateful Dead concert. She tottered down the steps and came walking purposefully toward us.

"Greg," she yelled as she walked. "You get back inside here right now! Dad says these people are cops. We don't want you talking to no cops."

"It's okay, Mom," Greg said reassuringly. "It's no big deal."

I changed the subject by gesturing toward the Toyota. "Is that your ride?"

He nodded. "It's a piece of crap. I keep it running with junked parts. Once I graduate, I want to join the Air Force and learn how to be an airplane mechanic so I can afford a better car."

"You still haven't told us where you were last night," Mel said.

Asking the same question over and

over works on occasion, and this was one of those times. With Greg's mother bearing down on us, Mel must have looked like the lesser of two evils.

"I've got a girlfriend," he admitted. "She's older—a lot older than me—and divorced. I met her at work. I was with her last night, at her house."

"What time?" I asked.

"We both got off at seven. I went to her place after that and didn't leave until sometime after midnight."

"Can we check with her?"

"Sure, as long as you don't tell my folks."

"Why not?" Mel asked. "What's wrong with her?"

"Nothing's wrong with her. She's Indian—like from India. My parents are . . . well . . . let's just say they're a little prejudiced."

"Greg!" Barbara Jane Alexander demanded. "Did you hear me?"

By then Greg's mother was not only within earshot, she was also within smelling distance. I was pretty sure that she, like her husband, had been smoking dope in the privacy of their moss-covered abode. She looked like one tough broad, and I wouldn't have been the least surprised if she had reached over the fence, grabbed her son by the scruff of the neck, and dragged him bodily back inside.

"How about if you let us buy you a late lunch or an early dinner?" Mel suggested.

I understood exactly why Mel was inviting him to dinner. Readily verifiable alibis made him less attractive as a suspect, but as a source of information he could prove invaluable. He was a regular Janie's House client, and his take on the people there would be far different from what we'd learn from someone in an official capacity like Meribeth Duncan, for example, or one of the houseparents.

"Am I under arrest?" Greg asked.

"No, not at all," Mel assured him. "We'll buy you lunch, ask you a few questions, verify your alibis, and bring you right back here."

Making up his mind, Greg turned and waved at his mother. "See you, Mom," he said. Then he hustled into the backseat of our car before she had a chance to tell him otherwise.

"Where do you want to go?" I asked.

"I'd love a Grand Slam, and there's a Denny's not far from here."

"You've got it," I said.

CHAPTER 20

My grandmother, Beverly Piedmont Jenssen, always used to quote that old saying about the quickest way to a man's heart being through his stomach. The same holds true for starving teen-agers when you're looking for answers to thorny questions.

Greg's Grand Slam came on a man-size platter. While he devoured the food, Mel and I drank coffee, asked ques-tions, and took notes.

It turned out that Greg went to Janie's House almost every day, usually in the afternoons. That meant he knew most of the people who went there, Amber Wilson included, in a manner not open to someone like Meribeth Duncan. She knew the kids by name and by what they wrote on their needs assessment. Greg knew them up close and personal.

"Tell me about the computer lab in the administrative building," Mel said. "Do you use it much?"

"Sure," Greg said, between shoveling forkfuls of hash browns and scrambled eggs into his mouth. "I use the computer lab almost every day. I don't have a computer at home, and even if I had one, I couldn't get on the Internet with it because we don't have landline phone service. My parents can't afford it."

"What about a cell phone?" I asked.

Greg shook his head. "We don't have one of those either. I use the ones from Janie's House occasionally, and Nadia's, too, when she isn't low on minutes."

His parents can afford weed, I thought, *but they can't afford a telephone.*

"Tell us about yesterday," Mel said.

"What's there to tell? I worked eleven

to seven—a full eight-hour shift. After work, I went to Nadia's."

"Nadia?" I asked.

"Nadia Patel," he said. "My girlfriend. She lives with her kids here in Olympia. She has a computer. She let me log on and check my e-mail last night."

"What if I told you that your user name, Hammer, was logged on to the Janie's House computer network for four hours on Sunday evening?" Mel asked. "Some of that time was spent uploading the video that was sent to Josh Deeson. The remainder of the time was spent visiting porn sites."

"It wasn't me," Greg insisted, sounding peeved. "I already told you I wasn't there Sunday night. I was at work. My manager's name is Mr. Newton, James Newton, and here's his number." Greg reeled off a 360 number. "Go ahead. Call him. Ask Mr. Newton to check my time cards. He'll be able to tell you exactly what time I came on duty and what time I got off, all week long—Sunday, Monday, and Tuesday. I think I used the Janie's House computers for a while on Monday, but that's the only time I've been on them this week."

"Should I call him right now?" Mel asked.

"Sure," Greg said. "Go ahead. Why not? I've got nothing to hide."

Mel made the call, spoke to Mr. Newton, and got an immediate verification of Greg's work schedule for all three days.

"Now tell us about what you did after work last night," Mel said.

"I already told you that, too," Greg said. "I was at Nadia's. We went there after we both got off work. Her kids are with their dad this week. She made us some curry for dinner."

"And what time did you leave?"

"Sometime after midnight." Greg paused and gave Mel a shrewd look. "I suppose you need to check that, too."

Mel nodded. "Yes, we do."

With an exasperated sigh Greg gave Mel another phone number. "You won't be able to call her until after six. That's when she gets off tonight."

He was quiet for a minute, then asked, "So this is all because someone was using Janie's House computers to surf the net and visit porn sites?"

"That's part of it," I said, stepping into the fray. "We believe the person doing the surfing is also the person who sent the video you saw to Josh Deeson. We need to know who that person is."

"Why don't you ask Josh, then?" Greg asked.

"We can't," I said, "because he's dead, just like Amber Wilson."

Greg paled and put down his fork. "You mean someone did the same thing to him?"

"Not exactly," Mel said. "Amber was murdered. Josh committed suicide. We believe the two cases are related, but so far we haven't found any connection between Josh and Amber."

"Do you think this Josh guy killed her?" Greg asked.

Mel didn't say yes and she didn't say no. She let her shoulders rise and fall and left Greg to draw his own conclusions.

"Is Josh from here?" Greg asked. "From Olympia?"

"Yes," Mel said.

"What school?"

"Olympia High," Mel answered.

Greg shook his head. "I thought maybe he might be one of the tutors, but I don't recognize that name."

We had already asked Meribeth Duncan if Josh had been involved in Janie's House. According to her, there was no record of Josh Deeson visiting Janie's House for any reason, not years earlier as a client when he was living in the care of his troubled mother and not as a volunteer since moving in with the First Family in the governor's mansion.

"Tell us about the tutors," I said.

Greg shrugged. "They come from several different schools. Olympia Prep requires that every student perform so many hours of community service. They also have an official 'mentoring' connection with Janie's house. Sort of like that city in Japan—I forget the name—that's Olympia's sister city."

"You're saying that a lot of the kids from OP serve as tutors?"

Greg nodded. "Lots of them. They

even have a school bus, a van really, that drops them off at Janie's House."

Now I was starting to see what had happened. Somewhere out in the adult PC world, a brainiac had decided that, in the name of diversity, it would be a great idea to mix things up between the sons and daughters of the rich and powerful—the kids at Olympia Prep—and the offspring of the local poverty-stricken church mice—the denizens of Janie's House.

Talk about a culture clash. Maybe it sounded good on paper, but the road to hell really is paved with good intentions. Two kids were dead, one demonstrably rich and the other poor. If that supposedly good idea had somehow gone tragically awry, what were the chances that the death toll would continue to rise?

"So are the tutors okay?" Mel asked.

Greg shrugged. "Some of them are great; some of them are jerks. You know, since they're 'volunteering . . .'" He used his hands to draw quotation marks around the word. "A few of them are really stuck on themselves and seem to think we're supposed to kiss their asses or something. Others are nice. Like Zoe, for example. She's just this really neat girl. She's not stuck up; she's not mean. You'd never know from talking to her that she's the governor's daughter."

Greg's offhand mention of Zoe Longmire's name was the first hint of a connection between the governor's mansion and the other people involved. The realization arced between Mel and me like an electrical spark. I'm surprised Greg didn't notice. Or maybe he did.

"Wait a minute," I said. "Wait, wait, wait. You're telling us that Zoe Longmire volunteers at Janie's House?"

"Sure," Greg answered. "So did her older sister, Giselle."

Mel went on asking questions about the other kids at Janie's House—kids on both sides of the poverty line, while I went wandering off on a tangent of my own. I tried to square what Greg had said about that good-as-gold Zoe Longmire with what I knew about Zoe's mother.

In Ballard High School, Marsha Gray had been an unmitigated snob. Her parents had money. The Grays were part of the top strata of Seattle society. Marsha had loved rubbing it in and lording it over all the less fortunate, all those negligible "little people," of which yours truly was definitely one.

The bullying text messages that had been sent to Josh had been not only mean-spirited but entirely personal—like mother, like daughter, maybe?

When I focused on Greg once more, he was definitely slowing down in terms of eating. The only things left on his plate were the half-eaten remains of two pancakes. I suspected he was a kid who had actually suffered from being hungry due to parental neglect. That made him too poor not to clean his plate. That could be part of why he wanted to go into the service, the prospect of having three squares a day for the duration.

When I came back to the conversation, Mel was trying to determine if Greg had given his user name to anyone else.

"I don't ever remember doing that," Greg said. "But I suppose it's possible."

I changed the subject. "Did Zoe Longmire ever complain to you about quarreling with anyone in her family?" I asked.

"Not to me," Greg said. "But I didn't work with her that much. She tutors things like American history and English. I need help in stuff like physics, chemistry, and AP math."

"Is there a volunteer who looks after the computer lab?" Mel asked.

Greg nodded. "Mr. Saxton. He's a retired software designer. He's not there all the time, but if the computers crash or something, he comes right over and gets them restarted."

I wondered if Mr. Saxton was the reason the Janie House computers had that complicated user log. He was someone we'd most likely need to talk to, right along with Zoe Longmire.

Right that minute, Mel was focused on equipment more than on people.

"Tell me about the Janie House cell phones," she said. "How do those work?"

"There's one in each building," Greg said. "It's in a little room like one of those old phone booths with a place where you can sit to use it and close the door for privacy. The phone is attached to the wall by one of those little security gizmos like they use on equipment at Best Buy so people don't just steal them."

That meant that whoever had called Josh Deeson's phone to send the file had done so from inside Janie's House. I wondered if there was a security camera somewhere on the premises that would tell us what we needed to know.

"So there are three phones altogether?" I asked casually.

"One of the cell phone companies donates the equipment and the minutes," Greg replied. "I don't know how many phones are on the system altogether. There are just those three that are available for kids to use."

"Is there any kind of a sign-up or sign-on process for those?"

Greg shook his head. "You just like take turns."

Saying that, he pushed his empty plate away, looked down at his watch, and then squirmed uneasily. It was almost six.

"Is something wrong?" Mel asked.

"Nadia's about to get off work," Greg said apologetically. "Would you mind dropping me off at the store? That way you can meet her and ask her whatever you want about last night."

Greg's real motives were so transparent as to be almost laughable. His parents were off in a marijuana-induced never-never land. If he went home, there was a good possibility that Mr. and Mrs. Demetri Alexander would be so paranoid about his having gone off with us that they wouldn't let Greg out of their sight for the remainder of the night.

"Sure thing," I said easily. "We'll be glad to drop you off."

I signaled the waitress to bring me the check. When I got out my wallet, I handed him a business card with my collection of contact numbers listed on it.

"If you think of anything else Agent Soames and I might be interested in knowing, give us a call."

Greg nodded and slipped the card

into his pocket. "I hope you catch who-ever did it."

"We do, too."

I thought about telling him that the snuff film was a fake—that Amber hadn't actually died in the filmed sequence he had seen—but I decided not to. I was sure Greg was going to go out and talk to everyone about what had happened—about what he had seen and what he'd been asked.

From Mel's and my points of view, it was good to leave a little misinformation out there. If Rachel's killers thought they were off the hook because we were focused on Josh Deeson as the doer, then we had a better chance of their making a mistake of some kind. An overly confident crook is a stupid crook. An overly confident teenage crook is even more so.

I paid the bill. We got in the car and drove to Safeway, where Greg managed to bound out of the Mercedes and in-tercept a pretty dark-haired young woman as she headed for the parking lot. He called her over to our car and introduced us.

"Tell them about last night," he said.

"Why?" she wanted to know.

"Just tell them."

Nadia shrugged. "What's to tell? We got off work, he came to the house, we had dinner, and he went home."

"What did you have for dinner?" Mel asked.

"Curry."

"What time did he leave?"

"I don't know," she said. "It was pretty late."

From the time we started talking to Greg until we started talking to Nadia, he'd had no chance to warn her about us or our questions. So either their stories were straight because they had set that up well in advance or else they were straight because they were both telling the truth.

They left the parking lot together, with Nadia behind the wheel of a battered Ford Focus.

"She's got to be thirty if she's a day," Mel said. There was a certain hint of disapproving umbrage in her voice.

"Oh," I said. "Sort of like the difference in age between you and me?"

You could say that was the end of *that* sauce-for-the-goose discussion.

"What now?" I asked, changing the subject again.

Josh Deeson's only extracurricular activity had been the chess club, so we made it our business to track down the chess club sponsor's address. Samuel Dysart lived in an old-fashioned but neat little bungalow in Olympia proper only a few blocks away from Janie's House. He wasn't home. The curtains were drawn and the blinds were closed. It looked like he might be on vacation. Considering the fact that school was out, he could very well be.

"Okay," Mel said as we left Samuel Dysart's front porch and walked back to the car, "what next?"

"Josh's bullying messages came from Janie's House, which is also the source for the phony snuff film. At the moment Zoe Longmire is the only person we know of with a foot in both worlds—in the governor's mansion and in Janie's House. Let's go talk to her."

"And now that we know those are stationary cell phones," Mel said, "while you drive us there, I'll get on the phone with Todd or Meribeth Duncan and find out if Janie's House has any working security cameras. Given Meribeth's horror at the idea of spying on the kids' Internet usage, I'm not very hopeful about that."

It was a little over a mile from Sam Dysart's house back to the governor's mansion. Stopping the car, I was struck by the stark contrast between the carefully manicured lawns surrounding the governor's digs and the Alexanders' run-down moss-ridden campers.

Somewhere in between those two extremes stood Janie's House, an experiment in cultural diversity—a fragile beaker in which elements from both ends of the social spectrum had been thrown together in what should have been a win-win situation. Except it hadn't been win-win for Rachel Camber or for Josh Deeson.

When we got there, Mel was on hold waiting to talk to Meribeth.

"Look at this place," I said to Mel, waving at our surroundings. "How does a kid with Josh's neglected upbringing figure out where he fits in when he lands in a place like this? It seems to me that he would have had a lot more in common with the charity-case clients at Janie's House than with his new family."

"Are you implying that maybe Cinderella really didn't live happily ever after?" Mel asked.

"Probably not."

As I started out of the car, Todd came on the line. While Mel talked to him, I walked on up to the front door. It seemed odd that I could walk up to the front door of the governor's mansion and ring the bell. I know there are crazies out there, and I was relieved when once again a youthful but uniformed Washington State Patrol officer emerged from the shadows. They may not have paid enough attention when Josh was going in and out and up and down ladders, but they were paying attention now.

"Governor Longmire and Mr. Willis aren't here at the moment," he told me when I showed him my credentials.

"What about the daughters?"

"Zoe is here," he said. He was young;

she was a tempting dish. Of course he knew she was there.

Thanking him, I rang the doorbell. To my way of thinking, a uniformed maid would have answered the door. Instead, Zoe Longmire herself threw it open.

"Oh, hi," she said, recognizing me. "Mom and Gerry went to the mortuary. You know, to make the arrangements."

Finding her alone was a gift. Asking her questions while she was alone was probably going to cause a lot of trouble. Governor Longmire would not be amused, but it seemed likely that talking to her alone would be a lot more effective than talking to her with some watchdog like Garvin McCarthy hanging on our every word. Marsha had summoned him when she thought Josh was in some kind of legal jeopardy. She would certainly do the same if her own daughter was being questioned.

"They probably won't be gone much longer," Zoe told me. "Would you like to come in and wait for them?"

"If you wouldn't mind. My partner's on the phone right now. When she finishes, maybe we could ask you a few questions."

"About Josh, right?" she asked. "That's all anyone can talk about—Josh. I mean, I'm sorry he's dead. And Gerry's really sorry he's dead, but it isn't like Josh was a regular part of our family. He was part of Gerry's family, but he wasn't—" She stopped talking suddenly and blushed. "You think I'm terrible, don't you."

"There's an old saying about how you can choose your friends but not your relatives," I said. "Maybe you could tell us a little about Josh. It would help if we knew something about his interests and his friends. Who better to ask than you?"

"You mean like asking his stupid little not-sister?"

Then, in a surprising move, Zoe suddenly glued herself to my shoulder and burst into tears. That's how things stood when Mel came in through the front door. I was holding Zoe Longmire close to my chest while the poor kid cried her heart out, with me realizing for the first time that Zoe had been younger than

Josh. More sophisticated, perhaps, and certainly more polished, but younger.

Mel reached into her miracle purse and produced a packet of tissues. With each of us taking one of Zoe's arms, we walked her into the living room and sat her down between us on the couch.

"I'll never forget what he looked like, just hanging there. I never saw anyone dead before. It was awful. And why did he do it?" Zoe wailed through her sobs. "I mean, weren't we good enough? Why couldn't he just be happy living here with us? Are we so horrible that being dead was better than being with us?"

Those are always the essential questions after a suicide, when the survivors are left to deal with a lifetime of self-doubt. What's wrong with me? Why wasn't I good enough? For the people left behind, suicide is the ultimate rejection and an irrecoverable loss.

"You loved him, didn't you," Mel said.

Zoe nodded wordlessly, emphatically.

She was in the throes of so much pain that I couldn't help but be a little pissed at Marsha Longmire and Gerry Willis. How was it they could be so caught up in their own processes and in "making arrangements" that they had gone off and left Zoe alone to deal with her part of this family tragedy?

"Tell us about Josh," Mel urged. "Please."

Zoe drew a long ragged breath and blinked back tears. "Gerry told us about Josh when he and Mom first tried to get custody. That was before Josh's mother died. You know about that?"

Mel and I nodded in unison.

"When we found out he was going to come live with us, I was so excited. I mean, I've always had a big sister—I've always had Giselle—but I always wanted a brother, too. And that's what I thought Josh would be—a big brother. Even though Gizzy treats me like a pest sometimes, we were willing to share a room so Josh could have a room on the second floor along with everyone else, but he wanted to live upstairs, like a hermit or something. And he told me he didn't need a sister—any sister, but especially not a 'little sister.' Especially not me."

Mel took Zoe's hand and held it. "It's

tough when you offer to be someone's friend and they just walk away."

Zoe nodded her head and then blew her nose into one of the tissues Mel had given her.

"I think it's possible that there were a lot of things going on with Josh that no one knew about," Mel continued. "For instance, did he ever complain to you about people sending him text messages?"

Zoe shook her head. "He didn't talk to me about anything. He treated me like I was invisible or something."

"What about his friends?" Mel asked.

"What friends?" Zoe asked.

"He must have had friends of some kind," I said. "After all, when he was sneaking in and out of the house overnight, he must have been going somewhere or visiting someone."

"That's another thing," Zoe said. "That's my fault, too. I'm the one who told Josh about the rope ladders and how to time it so the patrols wouldn't catch you. Gizzy told me and I told him. And that's what started this whole mess, when Mom caught him sneaking back into the house."

That wasn't exactly true. Regardless of who taught Josh to let himself in and out of the house at will, it had been the film clip found on Josh's phone that had sent everything into a tailspin. There had already been enough wrong in Josh's unfortunate life that, when Marsha Longmire found the offending video, it had been the capper on the jug or the straw that broke the camel's back or any other cliché you care to use that means one thing too many. Josh had committed suicide because he couldn't take the possibility of any more abuse. Rachel Camber was dead because she had been a participant—an initially willing participant—in an ugly game called "let's all torment Josh Deeson."

I suspected that might be the real reason Rachel was dead. She had known who was targeting Josh Deeson because she had been part of it. What I didn't understand was *why* she was part of it.

"Tell us about Janie's House," Mel said.

"It's a cool place," Zoe said. "It's a way of helping the less fortunate. Most of the kids who go there are, like, really poor, and we get to help them with schoolwork and stuff."

"Did Josh ever go there?"

"Not that I know of."

"Did he know any of the people there?"

"Besides Gizzy and me? He could have, I suppose," Zoe said. "I mean, some of the kids that go there, as volunteers and as clients, come from the other high schools around town, his included. So I guess he might know some of them from school. But most of the tutors come from OPHS because Olympia Prep has more advanced placement classes than any other school in town. The smarter kids tend to go there, if their parents can afford it."

Zoe's parents certainly could afford it, and they could have sent Josh there, too, if everyone around him hadn't deemed him too stupid. When Zoe made that comment, she was just offering what was probably the Olympia Prep party line—that the school was the home of the superachieving/super-intelligent future leaders of America.

God save the world from superintelligent assholes! I've seen the kinds of trouble wrought by that breed of arrogant jerks. Plenty of them hang out in the upper echelons of Seattle PD, but my concern about the kids at Olympia Prep was far more immediate. Somewhere among the superstraight kids who were "giving back" by doing their required "volunteer" work at Janie's House lurked a ruthless bastard—a smart and arrogant little weasel—whose sole mission in life was to destroy anything or anyone who dared to step too far away from the norm.

Josh Deeson had been different. Yes, he had taken his own life, but there were people in the background who had driven him to that level of desperation, and I wanted them held responsible. There were enough connections between the two cases that I felt certain that once we nailed Rachel Camber's killer, we'd be bringing down Josh's killer as well.

Up to that point I had been chasing

for answers about Josh Deeson's death because it was part of my job. Right then, though, it became personal—a quest more than a job. Why? Because I had been very much like Josh Deeson once—the poor kid; the outsider. Later on, I was like that at Seattle PD, too. I was the guy who kept his head down and did his job while the "smart" guys, especially the two-faced smart guys, made their way up through the ranks and into management.

I went to work as a cop because I was young and idealistic and thought I could save the world. When I made it to Homicide, I felt like I had come home. I knew by then that I couldn't save the whole world, but closing cases—one case at a time—was my personal contribution. Even after losing my family and while I was still drinking, closing cases consumed me, and far too often the victims turned out to be people who didn't quite conform to the norm.

Sitting there in the living room at the governor's mansion, I realized that was the case with Josh Deeson. He had been different, and the so-called normal people around him couldn't or wouldn't tolerate that. Their response to his being different had been to set out on a single-minded campaign to destroy him, and it had worked. He had finally given way under the pressure. The problem with suicide is that there's never a possibility of bringing someone to "justice." There is no justice.

Even though I didn't know the identity of the people who had driven Josh to kill himself, I did know something about them. In their worldview, they're the "nice" people—the "good" guys. There's nothing those turkeys hate worse than having their phony good-guy masks ripped away, and that's what I was determined to do—to unmask them and expose their culpability to the world.

I figured I owed one poor dead kid that much. So did the universe.

CHAPTER 21

We spent the next hour talking with Zoe Longmire, asking her for information about the kids from Olympia Prep who were connected to Janie's House. I started the interview thinking that Zoe might have been responsible for the destructive texting campaign against Josh. In the end, I came away doubting Zoe had been an active participant, but still I couldn't shake the suspicion that she knew more than she was saying about Josh's situation.

All during the interview, we let her believe that we were there primarily because we were looking into the causes behind Josh's suicide. For the time being we left Rachel Camber's murder off the table, our strategy being that Zoe would be more forthcoming without the red flag of a related murder investigation. We had mentioned Rachel's death to Meribeth Duncan and Greg Alexander, so word about what had happened was probably spreading through the Janie's House community, but so far nothing had hit the media.

Generally speaking, stories about murdered runaways from small towns in western Washington aren't thought to have "legs." As a consequence they don't get much media coverage. However, once some enterprising reporter made the connection between Josh's suicide (which was being covered in a very respectful fashion) and Rachel's death, it would take very little effort for Janie's House to be embroiled in the ensuing scandal.

It was also possible that the whole Janie's House enterprise might come to an end as a result. Their funding would dry up. Well-heeled contributors don't like having their names linked to places with problems. And once it started looking like having local students volunteering to help needy kids wasn't such a good idea, the schools around Olympia would withdraw their support as well.

As we conducted the interview with Zoe Longmire, it was clear that she was missing several other crucial pieces of the puzzle. Apparently Marsha Longmire and Gerry Willis hadn't breathed a word to anyone, and most especially to their daughters, about the existence of that ugly video clip. We didn't show it to her either. What we mostly did was give Zoe a chance to talk, to unburden herself to someone other than her grieving parents. Talking about her participation in Janie's House gave her something to discuss that wasn't Josh's suicide. As she spoke, I remembered Greg Alexander's remark about her blending in with the other kids and not lording it over anyone because she was the governor's daughter.

"We should probably interview your sister, too," Mel said when Zoe finally started to run out of things to say. "She's not here now, is she?"

There was the slightest moment of hesitation before Zoe shook her head.

"Do you know when she'll be home?"

"She's staying at Dad's place right now," Zoe said. "Gerry's sister is flying in from Michigan tonight, and she'll be staying in Gizzy's room. There are extra rooms on the third floor, but no one wants to stay there."

We didn't have to ask where Zoe's father's house might be because Ross Connors had already supplied us with a physical address for the governor's former husband and his new wife.

Mel and I were preparing to leave when Marsha and Gerry showed up.

"We just came from the mortuary," Marsha said. "The funeral will be Friday, the day after tomorrow."

I was a little surprised to hear that the body had already been released to a funeral home. Usually in a case like this there are several days between the death and the time of release. I guess with the governor's family involved, some effort had been made to streamline the process. Nevertheless, the strain of visiting the mortuary and making final arrangements had taken its toll on Josh's grandfather. Gerry Willis looked like he needed to lie down in the worst way. Marsha asked Zoe to help him to his room. When they had left the room, Marsha turned on us.

"What are you doing here?" she demanded angrily. "They've done the autopsy. Josh's death has been ruled a suicide. What more do you need to know?"

What a difference a day makes. Whatever welcome mat Marsha Longmire had put out for us a day earlier had evidently been rescinded.

My mother used to talk about the importance of telling the "unvarnished truth." As a little kid that was something I wondered about. If you were going to paint the truth, how would you do it and what kind of brushes would you use? Now I know the best way to varnish truth is to cover whatever's in question with a bright and shiny coat of pure BS.

"It has come to our attention that Josh was the target of numerous ugly text messages—harassing text messages. It's possible those had something to do with Josh's suicide, and we thought Zoe might have heard something about them."

"Did she?" Marsha asked.

"No," I answered. "Zoe had no idea about that."

A part of me wondered if that was completely true. I had a feeling in my gut that Zoe knew more than she was saying, but right then we didn't dare bring on the kind of tough questioning that would have given us a straight answer. That was the truth, but it wasn't the whole truth, and it was most definitely varnished. It was smooth enough to explain our presence and our need to talk to Zoe. It was even smooth enough to get us out of the house.

As we were leaving, Zoe came back into the room. We thanked her for her help, with Marsha hanging on our every word.

"Whew," Mel said, once we were back in the Mercedes. "There's been a change in the weather as far as Marsha is concerned."

"I noticed," I said. "So what say we go have a nice little chat with Gizzy before her mother has a chance to shut us down?"

"We were right not to mention the interview possibility to Marsha," Mel said. "Better to beg forgiveness later than to be told no in advance."

I got out my wallet and handed Mel the address Ross Connors had given me for Sid Longmire, the governor's ex. While I started the engine and fastened my seat belt, Mel fed the address information into the GPS. Eventually the GPS told us that our route was being calculated.

"What kind of a name is Gizzy?" I asked.

"It's probably what her little sister called her, or a babysitter. On the face of it, Giselle isn't such a bad name, and neither is Melissa. But the whole time I was growing up, kids called me Melly instead of Mel or Melissa. That's what the girls called me. The boys generally called me Smelly Melly."

"Jerks," I said.

"Yes," she agreed. "Most of them

were. I'd be willing to bet that Giselle hates the name Gizzy as much as I hated Melly."

The address was off Hawk's Prairie Road, north of Olympia. We drifted into a GPS-punctuated silence.

"I think Zoe knew more than she was willing to say about the texting," Mel said thoughtfully.

"I agree. The comments show too much knowledge about Josh's history for a passing acquaintance. The kid was a loner. There's no way he'd go around school talking up the fact that his mother died of an overdose or that he ended up in foster care. And who else besides Zoe or Gizzy would have a vested interest in telling him to go back where he came from?"

"My money's on Gizzy, with Zoe knowing exactly what was going on," Mel said grimly. "What a nice bunch of kids!"

"Did you find out anything about security cameras at Janie's House?" I asked.

"Yes, I did," Mel said. "According to Meribeth Duncan, there aren't any. On purpose—so they wouldn't 'infringe' on client privacy. That computer log system was evidently installed under the radar and without official sanction from the board of directors."

"Now that they know some of those kids might be engaging in criminal behavior, maybe they'll wise up," I suggested.

Mel shook her head in exasperation. "How do you spell 'Hear no evil; see no evil'? But Meribeth told me she'll try to reconstruct a list of the people who had keys—houseparents, tutors, and so forth—who could come and go as they pleased."

"Without any records that might be hard to do."

"Not as hard as you think," Mel said. "Don't forget Todd copied all those hard drives yesterday. I think he'll be able to dredge a whole lot of useful information out of those."

There had been a multiple-vehicle rush-hour accident in the northbound lanes of I-5, and traffic was at a standstill just north of Olympia. Originally the

GPS said we would arrive in twenty-two minutes. It ended up taking twice that.

"Did Todd manage to turn up any close friends on Josh's computer?" I asked.

Mel shook her head. "Not so far. He evidently played Internet chess with several people, but that's about it. I asked Katie Dunn to check last year's yearbook. 'Chess Club' was Josh's only listed activity. He's old enough to have a learner's permit, but there's no record that he ever applied for one. Most kids race to the nearest licensing office the moment they're eligible."

"Josh Deeson was a long way from being a 'most kids' kind of teenager," I said. "Maybe not bothering to get a driver's license was one way to thumb his nose at all the other kids by ignoring their usual rites of passage. He didn't care about them, and he didn't care who knew it. He was odd man out and he intended to stay that way."

"But why would Giselle be involved in this texting thing?" Mel asked. "What's her motivation?"

"Marsha Gray Longmire and I went to high school together," I said.

"Yes," Mel agreed with a laugh. "I gathered as much."

"Of all the girls in our class she was probably the coolest—she wore the best clothes; she drove the best car; she got the best grades. Did I mention she was valedictorian?"

"No," Mel said, "but it figures."

"She was cool; I was not cool."

"Maybe you weren't cool then and you aren't cool now," Mel said with a smile. "At least Marsha must have thought you were cool the day before yesterday. Why else did she ask for you?"

"Maybe because she thought she could call on old times' sake to help control the narrative."

"Which is?"

"As I said, Marsha was cool to the nth degree. Maybe Gizzy is just like her mother. DNA is like that. If she's one of the cool kids, the last thing she wants is to be irrevocably linked to someone who is not cool—someone who is the antithesis of coolness."

"Josh Deeson," Mel supplied. "But I still don't understand the point."

"Whoever sent the texts probably did so in the hope they'd succeed in sending Josh packing. That's what bullies do. They think that if they make things uncomfortable enough, the target will just fold and disappear. When Josh didn't bail, they upped the ante with the film clip. But Josh fooled them again. Instead of disappearing without a whimper, he committed suicide. Now cops are involved in what should have been a relatively harmless teenage prank. There's a real investigation. By now the kids involved have probably figured out that someone is going to come around asking uncomfortable questions. Maybe that meant the film star needed to disappear, too."

"Speaking of which, I wonder if the King County M.E. has done Rachel's autopsy yet?"

"Call 'em up and find out," I told her.

Mel pulled out her cell phone. After jumping through a few voice mail prompts, I heard her ask for Dr. Mellon.

I was relieved to hear that we had

lucked out and drawn Rosemary Mellon. She's a new addition to the King County M.E.'s office. She hasn't been around long enough to develop as many jurisdictional prejudices as some of the old guard. She's easy to work with—thorough but not terribly concerned with going through channels and across desks. I had an idea Ross Connors had handpicked her for the job.

Mel listened for several minutes, jotting down notes. When she got off the phone, she gave me a briefing.

"According to Rosemary, Rachel had been dead about eight to ten hours before being dumped in the water. There are clear signs of strangulation. She found some defensive wounds as well as tissue under her nails. She expects to be able to get a DNA profile, but there's no sign of sexual assault."

"I wonder if our enterprising filmmakers were looking for an encore performance—a real one this time."

Mel sighed. "Maybe," she said.

Sid Longmire's home was in what's called a "gated community," but on this summer evening no one was minding the gate. The guard shack was unoccupied, and we drove right up to the house.

I had given Mel a hard time about her objections to the age difference between Greg Alexander and his girlfriend, but that's what happens when you look askance at other people's foibles without taking your own into consideration. I had automatically expected Sid Longmire's wife to be of the trophy, arm-candy variety and hardly older than his daughters. When Monica Longmire answered the door, I knew at once that assumption was wrong. What the second Mrs. Longmire had going for her wasn't necessarily her looks or her age. Maybe Sid had tired of Marsha's power politics and excessive coolosity and had gone looking for stability instead. In contrast to Marsha's well-tailored good looks, Monica's face was plain and more than a little round. She had the ruddy complexion of someone who spends too much time in the sun, more likely gardening than golfing. And the smile lines on her face were exactly that—smile lines.

"Yes," Monica Longmire said, peering out past the security chain. "May I help you?"

Mel produced her badge. "We're looking for Giselle," she said. "We were told she'd be here with you and your husband. We need to ask her a few questions about Josh Deeson's circle of friends."

"I'm sorry. Gizzy isn't here right now," Monica said, opening the door. "She's out with her boyfriend. They were planning on seeing a movie and then she's going back home. That seemed like a bad idea to me—not the movie, going back home."

Monica motioned us inside the house and directed us to seating in the family room.

"Frankly, I thought she and Zoe would be better off being here for the next few nights so they could escape some of the drama," Monica continued. "It's hard for kids to hang around home when everyone is so upset. I'm pretty much an outsider when it comes to what goes on with Marsha and Gerry, but I know they're both really hurting.

As for Josh? That poor kid never had a chance. And poor Zoe, too," she added. "Finding Josh's body like that must have been a horrible shock."

Monica's apparently genuine concern for her stepdaughters didn't sound like part of the usual evil-stepmother tradition. But neither Mel nor I let on that as far as Governor Longmire knew, Giselle was still scheduled to stay with her father. Telling both sets of parents one thing and then doing something else is standard teenage behavior, even without a death in the family.

"We'd appreciate any insight you could give us," Mel said. "Did the two girls talk about Josh much?" she asked.

"When Josh first went to live with them, Zoe especially was all excited about it. Gizzy was less so. Zoe was under the impression that since they were so close in age they'd end up being great pals. I think it hurt her feelings when that didn't happen, but what do you expect when you start blending families? There are always a few bumps in the road. My boys are three and five years older than Giselle. The only thing they have in common with the girls is that they ostensibly belong to the same family. They share the occasional meal, usually on holidays, but they are not good friends, and they're never going to be. That's just the way it is. Sid and I are in love. The kids aren't in love. Deal with it."

"So Zoe was disappointed that she and Josh didn't bond," I said. "What was Giselle's reaction?"

"To having Josh parachuted into their lives?" Monica paused to consider for a moment before she answered. "Let's just say she wasn't thrilled. Gizzy isn't someone with the milk of human kindness running through her veins. We talked about the situation with Josh a few times. I tried to explain to her that there was nothing else Gerry and Marsha could do. Josh didn't have anywhere else to go or anyone to look after him. I think Gerry and Marsha both deserve credit for trying to do the right thing."

I had to admit to myself that Monica didn't come across as a conniving "other" woman who had broken up

Marsha's longtime marriage. Like Mel with Kenny Broward, I had come here expecting to find a marital "bad guy." So far there didn't appear to be any.

"What do you know about Janie's House?" Mel asked. "Did the girls ever talk about it?"

"Well, sure. The girls' school encourages involvement, even though I don't really approve," Monica said. "That whole noblesse oblige, us-and-them thing bothers me. Yes, I know the official Olympia Prep position is that student involvement with less fortunate kids is supposed to be great for everybody, but who are they kidding? I mean, poor kids already know they're poor without having the rich kids hanging around rubbing their noses in it."

"So you're not enamored of Janie's House?" I asked.

"Not at all, but that's just me," Monica said. "Both Zoe and Giselle were really caught up in helping out there last year. Zoe's the kind of kid who would break her neck trying to put a fallen bird back in its nest. As for Gizzy? I think her involvement with Janie's House was more of an ego thing than it was any-thing else. She's been back there again this summer, but only because Ron is still there."

"Ron?" I asked.

"Ron Miller is Giselle's boyfriend. He's a year younger than she is and gradu-ated from OP two weeks ago. I thought . . . no, make that I hoped that being apart for a year would be the end of their romance, but I was wrong. They're still as head over heels as ever. Next year could be a little tougher. He'll be going to Stanford, and she'll still be going to school in Tacoma. That will put a whole lot more distance between them. As my mother used to say, 'Dis-tance is to love as wind is to fire. Blows out the little ones and fans the big ones.'"

"Sounds like you're hoping for the first option."

Monica nodded. "And, at Sid's insis-tence, keeping my mouth shut about it, too," she said with a tight smile. "It's the voice of experience speaking when I tell you that first-boyfriend types don't always make the best husband material. Ron is certainly smart enough, but he has a mean streak. Sid takes the position that saying one bad word about him would just mean pushing Giselle in Ron's direction that much more. Sad to say, that's probably true."

"In other words, you don't like Ron much?" Mel suggested.

"Yes," Monica answered, "but I try not to show it."

"What does Ron do at Janie's House?"

"He's some kind of special assistant in the computer lab. He's into computers in a big way. I think he's planning on studying computer science in college. But didn't you say you wanted to talk to Gizzy about Josh's suicide? What does any of this have to do with that?"

I could have given her chapter and verse. Let's see. Some poor little rich kid with a mean streak who was romantically linked to Giselle and who was intimately involved with the Janie's House computer system sounded like exactly the kind of person we needed to find, not so much because of Josh's suicide but because of Rachel's murder. We didn't have to tell Monica Longmire that, and we didn't. It was time to back off from angling for more information about Ron Miller right then for fear of tipping our hand.

"We're just looking for background material," Mel said reassuringly. "Trying to understand what sent Josh over the edge."

"'Edge' is the right word," Monica said. "That must be how Josh felt—like he was walking on the edge of a cliff. From what the girls said, I'm sure there was a chasm between his old life and his new one. It doesn't surprise me that he couldn't bridge it. It's a tragedy, of course, but somewhat predictable."

"You have a nice place here," Mel said, abruptly changing the subject.

It was important to keep the interview on a cordial basis. Mel's comment was designed to maintain the smooth flow going with the added benefit that it was also true.

The house was stylish but more comfortable than your basic *House Beautiful* photo spread. We were in a great room that was part kitchen and part family room. The kitchen was all granite countertops and stainless steel appliances, and a huge flat-screen TV was situated over a gas-log fireplace in the family room area. Out through a set of sliding doors were a patio with a swimming pool and hot tub gleaming in the nearly setting sun. Beyond that I could see a golf-course fairway. Even in Washington's down real estate market I estimated the place was worth more than a million bucks, give or take.

Monica looked around and laughed. "Yes," she said. "Not nearly as grand as the governor's mansion, but a little more modern."

"If I had a choice, this is the one I'd pick any day of the week," Mel said. "But how do the girls get back and forth?"

"Zoe's still too young to drive, so either Sid picks her up and brings her out or I do. Of course, now that Giselle is home for the summer, she can do some of the driving. Marsha and Sid share custody. When school was in session, it used to be the girls stayed with their mother during the week and then we had them every other weekend, with the situation reversed during the summer. Now that they're older and especially with Giselle off at school, we're all a lot more flexible. They come and go at their own discretion. I think it's really important for everyone that we keep things as civilized as possible."

"Commendable," Mel said. "What kind of car does Giselle drive?"

"It's an Acura," Monica said. "A silver Acura. Sid bought it for her when she graduated from high school."

A car pulled into the driveway and I heard the sound of a garage door opening.

"That'll be Sid," Monica told us. "He's been out of town for several days."

It seemed likely that Sid Longmire's view of our visit would be far less cordial than Monica's, especially if the governor had managed to alert him as to what was going on. We decided it was time to beat a hasty retreat.

"We'll be going then," I said.

"You don't want to talk to him, too?"

"No, thanks," I assured her. "We appreciate your help."

We made a quick exit out the front

door and were gone before Sid Long-mire was able to unload his luggage from the car and come inside.

Sometimes the best way to win a confrontation is to avoid it in the first place.

CHAPTER 22

"She wasn't at all what I expected," I said as we walked back out to the car.

"Not what I expected, either," Mel agreed. "A lot older and a whole lot more squared away."

I was relieved to know that I wasn't the only one who had arrived at Sid and Monica's house with some erroneous preconceived notions.

During the interview with Monica Longmire, my cell phone had vibrated three different times in my pocket. Once in the car, Mel immediately got on the phone, checking with Records for li-

censing information on Giselle Longmire's Acura and for any vehicles owned
or driven by her boyfriend, Ron Miller,
or by other members of his family.

I have a Bluetooth earpiece for my
cell phone, but I'm not in love with it.
Even though Mel and I put it to good
use to save our bacon a few months
ago, I use it only under duress. Most of
the time it stays in my pocket until the
battery runs out of juice. Rather than
use a state-sanctioned "hands-free"
device, I pulled into a parking place beside the guard shack, pulled out my
phone, checked the missed calls, and
listened to my messages.

I recognized all three of the numbers.
Two were from Rebekah Ming, the manager at Tumwater Self-Storage. There
were two calls from her but only one
message. "Mr. Beaumont, I've had several customer complaints about garbage being hauled into the storage facility. You need to come by and empty
it *every* day. Please. We don't want to
attract vermin."

The other one was from Ralph Ames.
"I understand you're in Olympia at the

Red Lion for the next couple of days. I happen to be coming down there to-morrow. Hoping to have breakfast. I'll be there right around eight. Let me know if you can't make it."

From my door-to-door salesman days, I recognized that as an assumed close. When one asked for an appoint-ment, the standard question was al-ways: "Which would be better for you, mornings or afternoons?" The question is designed to leave the dreaded words "Not ever" out of the list of possible an-swers, with the underlying assumption being that of course you want to see me.

The idea of Ralph just "happening" to be in Olympia at that ungodly hour—a good ninety miles from Seattle—was also bogus. Ralph isn't a spontaneous kind of guy. He doesn't ever just "hap-pen" to go someplace. He has appoint-ments—deliberate appointments—and like it or not, Mel and I would be having breakfast with him in the morning. Evi-dently the governor's garbage, piling up in the storage unit, couldn't wait until then.

Mel was still on her phone and on hold. Here's an idea. Why don't cell phone companies discount the minutes people spend online without talking to anyone?

"Breakfast with Ralph tomorrow morning at the hotel at eight A.M.," I told her, putting the car in gear. "But right now we're on our way to Ross's storage unit. You dodged garbage detail yesterday, but not today."

"Dressed like this?" she asked.

"We'll be careful."

Moments later Mel was taking notes, holding the phone to her mouth with her shoulder and typing them into her laptop.

"Okay," she said when she ended the call "Here's the scoop on Ron Miller—Ronald Darrington Miller lives on North Cooper Point Road."

"Darrington is his middle name?" I asked. "Like the town along Highway 2? It sounds a little pretentious."

"Oh, right," Mel said with a laugh. "Look who's talking. Is being named after a town in Texas pretentious?"

She certainly had me there.

"Middle name notwithstanding, Ron is seventeen years old and already has two traffic stops to his credit—a Minor in Possession and a speeding ticket, reduced from reckless driving. The MIP charge was dropped for no apparent reason."

"No wonder Monica doesn't like him much. And how did the MIP get dropped? Political pull of some kind?"

"Maybe. Probably."

"What make and model car?"

"A brand-new Camaro with temporary plates. Probably a high school graduation present."

"I guess it was too much to hope that he would be driving a green pickup truck."

"I guess," Mel agreed.

With a detour by an all-night drugstore for a bottle of Febreze, we drove straight to Tumwater Self-Storage. As soon as we stepped into the hallway I understood why Rebekah had been so insistent. Foul garbage odors permeated the entire floor. We let ourselves into the storage unit and went to work. I took pity on Mel and gave her the recycling while I tackled the coffee-grounds-leaking garbage. She finished hers in a hurry and then she helped me with mine.

Later on someone told us that finding what we found that night was just "blind luck." I beg to differ. It wasn't luck; it was work. And it wasn't because we were slapdash about it either. Mel and I worked our way through the garbage slowly and methodically and—because of our clothing—carefully as well. There was nowhere to sit. We did it crouching or, in my case, bending over, because the tarp with the garbage on it was on the floor and my knees don't do "crouch" anymore. I was about to give it up when something shiny caught the light from the bottom of a pile of used coffee grounds.

I brushed away the grounds and there it was—a watch with a stainless steel watchband. "Hey," I said, "what do you know! Look what I found!"

I picked it up carefully in my gloved fingers and held it up to the light. I would have had to get out my reading glasses to read the front of the watch. Mel didn't.

"It says 'Seiko,'" she reported. "I could be wrong, but it looks exactly like the one we found on Josh Deeson's body. Which means we have two watches—two interchangeable watches. What does that mean?"

I blew off the remaining coffee grounds and slipped the watch into an evidence bag. Meanwhile, Mel came over and looked through the trash in the same general area where I had been searching. It stood to reason that if anything else of interest had been thrown away, it would be found in close proximity to the watch. We spent another half hour picking through the trash, but we found nothing more than broken eggshells, soggy mounds of dead melon balls, and rotting strawberries. When we had finished, we dragged the tarps to the Dumpster, where we emptied and folded them. After returning them to the storage unit, we left the key at the office and headed back to the car.

It was almost ten by then but not yet fully dark. We were on our way to the hotel. I was dead tired, but Mel had caught her second wind.

"Let's go take a look at Ron Miller's place before we call it a night," Mel suggested.

She fed the Millers' address into the GPS and off we went. By the time we reached North Cooper Point Road, it was full dark. Even so, it was possible to see that Ron Miller's family lived in a home that made Sid Longmire's place look like a slum and the governor's mansion look modest. This wasn't a gated community so much as a gated estate or a gated compound with several buildings looming into view. We drove past the driveway entrance slowly but without stopping.

Mel gave a whistle. "These people have moolah," she observed. "So maybe showing up unannounced in the middle of the night to talk to their fair-haired boy isn't such a good idea."

I had visions of a Garvin McCarthy look-alike riding to the rescue before Mel and I had a chance to open our mouths.

"How about this?" I asked. "It's been a long day. Let's call it a job for tonight. Ron Miller may be tied in pretty tight with Janie's House, but the place was closed all day today. If his conscience is bothering him, I'm willing to bet that he'll show up there bright and early tomorrow, trying to get the lay of the land and figure out if the closure had anything to do with him. If he's our guy, he'll want to make sure his tracks are properly covered. I think Meribeth Duncan is far more likely to give us a crack at talking to Ron Miller than his parents will."

"Agreed," Mel said. "Time to head for the barn."

Back at the hotel we stopped off at the coffee shop for a late supper. I had soup; Mel had salad. Once up in our room, I booted up my computer while Mel got first dibs on the bathroom. Hidden among all those penis enlargement spam messages was an e-mail from Todd Hatcher.

I checked on all the Web sites the person posing as Greg Alexander had visited. Surprise, surprise. Several of them feature snuff films. I think maybe we're on to someone who is making

and selling this crap. And there's a new one—one that appears to feature the same girl and most likely isn't faked. The strangulation was done barehanded and photographed with a stationary camera. If you can find the perpetrator, there should be defensive wounds on his hands and arms. I'm sending you a copy of the new clip. Warning: Don't log on to the sites yourself. If you do, your spam folder will fill up with this junk within a matter of minutes.

I sent Todd a thank-you note and said that we'd be in touch tomorrow, which, it turned out, was very close to being today. There was an e-mail from my daughter, Kelly, with a photo of Kayla, my granddaughter, missing her right front tooth. That one rocked me because it didn't seem possible that Kayla was already old enough to be losing her baby teeth.

Then, there at the bottom of the newmail list lurked the one from Sally

Mathers. I still didn't know how to answer it, but I didn't want her to think I was ignoring it, either.

Received your e-mail. Involved with a complicated investigation. I'll get back to you when I can.

All of which was the truth, with only the smallest possible amount of varnish.

Mel emerged from the bathroom with nothing on and slipped into bed. I told her about the message from Todd.

"That squares with what the M.E. told us, too," she said.

When she turned off her light, I got the message: Close the computer; step away from the chair; get in bed; turn out your light. I did all of the above.

Moments later I was snuggled up beside her in bed. I was drifting off to sleep when she awakened me with a snort of laughter.

"What's so funny?" I grumbled.

"You are," she said. "I can't get over the idea that you thought it was strange that Ron Miller's middle name came from an actual town. You don't have any room to talk."

"I didn't say it was strange," I corrected. "I said it was pretentious. And now that I've seen Ron Miller's parents' house, I'm not backing off on a single word of it. I'll give Ron Miller the benefit of the doubt. He may not be pretentious, but his parents definitely *are.*"

When Mel's cell phone alarm went off the next morning, it was time for our complicated single-bathroom tango. I stayed in bed snoozing while she did what she needed to do. Then, once she headed out the door for the elevator, I hit the bathroom. It was ten to eight by then, so I had to step on it. When I came down to the restaurant five minutes later, Mel and Ralph were seated together at a small table, both of them looking like they'd just stepped out of a store window. Compared to the two of them, I looked like a much-rumpled bed.

This is nothing new. Ralph Ames has always been a suave kind of guy. When I first met him, he was Anne Corley's attorney. After her death, he came my way as part of the deal right along with the money I inherited from her. Since then, he's been the one who has kept that inheritance not only intact but also growing. I believe that he's now close to having been my attorney longer than he was Anne's. And next to my former partner Ron Peters, Ralph is also my best friend.

In other words, I like the guy, but there are times when I also resent the hell out of him. I find it particularly provoking that, no matter the circumstances, he always manages to look like perfection itself. Even though I was wearing clothing fresh from the dry cleaner's plastic bag, I couldn't compete with Ralph's terminal dapperness. And there's no explaining Mel's ability to look great no matter what, either.

As a consequence I was feeling a bit grumpy when I joined them in the restaurant where they sat, heads ducked close together, studying something on the table in front of them. I took one of the two remaining empty chairs.

Once I was seated—next to Mel and

across from Ralph—I could see they were examining three eight-by-ten photos that lay on the table. Ralph glanced up at me and then pushed the photos in my direction.

"To what do we owe . . . ?" I began, pulling out my reading glasses and sticking them on my nose. When I saw the subject matter of the photos, my question dwindled away into shocked silence.

The first picture was one I recognized right off. It was my senior portrait from the *Shingle,* the Ballard High School yearbook. In it I wore my first-ever store-bought suit, purchased on layaway at JCPenney's. At first glance I thought the other two were pictures of me as well. Upon closer examination, however, I realized that although the young man in the photo certainly looked like me, he wasn't me. I didn't recognize either the pose or the clothing. The third picture was of the same guy, grinning my own familiar grin. He was obviously fresh from basic training and wearing a World War II–vintage U.S. Navy uniform.

Ralph tapped first that photo and

then the other lightly with his finger. "Meet Hank Mencken, Beau," he said. "I believe this gentleman was your father."

For a time I could barely breathe. Yes, I'd had a hint in Sally's e-mail that this was coming and that I might finally be able to put a name on my father's identity, but nothing had prepared me for the shock of that moment when I saw his photo for the first time. The world seemed to shift on its axis as I stared into the face of a complete stranger and discovered that it was almost a mirror image of my own.

Just as I had taken one look at Zoe Longmire and known at once that Marsha Gray Longmire was her mother, the same thing was true here. As I looked into the eyes in that photograph and studied the set of the jaw and the distinctive shape of the nose, I knew beyond a shade of doubt that I had found my family tree—my heritage and lineage.

"Mel told me about the e-mail," Ralph was saying. "She thought I should try to find out what I could in advance of your making contact with Sally Mathers in case she was somehow trying to scam you. As near as I can tell, she's not. She seems to be on the level."

I tried to pay attention to his words, but I couldn't. All I could do right then was stare in stunned silence at the face of someone who had been absent from my life for more than six decades, from before my birth. My mother and I never discussed my father when I was growing up. It was almost as though he was a ghost who hadn't ever existed in real life. And now the ghost was here, smiling back at me with a crooked grin and straight teeth. Those could have been my own, too.

For a moment, my eyes blurred with tears. How different all our lives would have been if my father hadn't died in that motorcycle wreck or if he and my mother had married before I was born. What if he had lived long enough to take us back to Texas with him, back to Beaumont? Would my mother and father have lived happily ever after? Would my mother have been able to make the transition from being a Seattle girl to living in the wilds of East Texas? Would there have been other kids besides me in the family, a sister or a brother, perhaps, or maybe even both?

And what would my life have been like if I had been raised as Jonas Piedmont Mencken, with part of my name coming from my mother's father and part of it from my father's father? What would it have been like to grow up as the son of a loving father, as opposed to being a cast-off grandson, disowned twice over by two hard-bitten, hidebound old men who had no truck with a "no-good" woman who had borne a child out of wedlock? How had they justified turning away from that mother and child? After all, I was the *result* of an "unholy" union, not the *cause* of it. Why had they chosen to punish me right along with her?

All the while I was growing up, every holiday had served as a bleak reminder of how different our lives were from everyone else's. Other kids came back to school after Thanksgiving and Christmas and Easter with stories of joyous holiday dinners and family celebrations complete with grandparents and cousins, aunts and uncles. For our little family it was always just the two of us—my mother and me and no one else.

I guess that's part of what was going through my mind right then as I looked at the photos—that whole catalog of what-ifs and might-have-beens as opposed to what was.

When I could talk again, I looked at Ralph. "Tell me about him," I said.

"Hank was a kid from a well-respected family. They had quite a lot of money— oil money, it turns out—but Hank wasn't especially studious and he wasn't drawn to the family business, either. He was a kid who liked to have fun, a little too much fun on occasion. Liked to walk on the wild side and all that. As Ms. Mathers told you in that e-mail, he got in some kind of hot water back home and was given a choice of joining the service or going to jail. He joined the navy. That's how he ended up in Washington State, where he met your mother.

"I believe that after he died and before you were born, your mother made an effort to contact the family. They

thought she was some kind of gold dig-
ger who was after the family money,
and refused all contact."

"Which explains why she made up a
last name for me rather than using hers
or his."

Ralph nodded. "When your father's
parents, your grandparents, subse-
quently died, your aunt, your father's
sister, became your grandparents' sole
heir."

"Sally Mathers's mother."

"Yes, Hannah. From what your cousin
said in that e-mail, I wouldn't be surprised if your aunt might want to name
you as a beneficiary in her will."

"That seems unlikely to me, doesn't it
to you?" I asked.

Ralph shrugged. "Stranger things
have happened."

"I sent Sally an e-mail when we got
back to the hotel last night," I said. "I
told her I was involved in a case and
that, as soon as it was resolved, I'd get
back to her. But I don't think I ever believed any of this was real. I thought it
was some kind of pipe dream."

"It's not a pipe dream," Ralph said.

"I've checked newspaper records both here in Washington and in Texas. Hank Mencken's military records show that he died in a motorcycle crash outside Bremerton in the last year of World War II. His body was transported back to Texas, where he was accorded a full military funeral and burial. Because of the family's status in the community, his death received a good deal of coverage in the local newspaper. The *Beaumont Daily Ledger* no longer exists, but its archives have been digitized and turned over to the Texas State Historical Association. That's where I found these two photos."

The waitress showed up with menus and a carafe of coffee. I picked up the photos and held them out of harm's way so no inadvertent drips from the pot would mar them.

Mel reached over and touched the back of my hand. "Are you all right?" she asked.

I shook my head. On the one hand, I wasn't all right. On the other hand, I was. For the first time in my entire life I was a whole person—one with both a mother and a father.

"It's a little much to take in all at once," I said.

Ralph nodded. "I've made some discreet inquiries," he said. "If you want to see your father's sister before she passes, you should probably go to Texas as soon as possible. She's a cancer patient who has decided to accept no additional treatment."

"You mean like hospice?" I asked.

Ralph nodded. "Pain meds only. If you use your jet card, you can be there in a matter of hours."

"I can't walk away from this case," I said. "Ross Connors is counting on us."

And so is Josh Deeson, I thought.

Like me, Josh had been a fatherless kid until Marsha Longmire and Gerry Willis had tried to take him under their wing. Unfortunately, Josh had turned away from everything they'd offered him—a new family, a place in their universe, life itself. He had rejected it all. I didn't want to make the same mistake.

But on the other hand . . .

"Let me pull together a few more

documents," Ralph continued, "so that when you go you'll have the benefit of the full story insofar as we know it. But don't go by yourself," he cautioned. "Take Mel with you."

"Are you kidding?" I said. "She's my partner. When it comes to family matters, she's got my back."

I looked at Mel. I expected her to be smiling; she wasn't.

"I was worried that I had overstepped by turning Ralph loose on this," she said. "I wasn't sure how you would react."

"I'm still not sure how I'm going to react," I said. "But I think I needed something to get me off dead center and help me overcome decades of inertia."

"So it's all right then?"

I nodded.

The waitress stalked up to our table. "What'll you have this morning?" she said. "And do you want separate checks?"

"No," I said. "One check only. This one's on me."

We ordered breakfast. I don't remember what I ate. I don't remember what was said. I sat there the whole time continuing to stare down at the pair of photographs of the man who had been my father.

It was an odd sensation. Seeing him made me happy and sad. Glad to see who he was and to know he had once existed. Sad to realize that I had never known him; would never know him. And sad, too, to realize that he never knew me or my kids, especially his grandson, Scott, whose face was stamped with the same indelible family features—the Mencken family's in Hank's world; the Beaumont family's in mine.

Hello and good-bye at the same time. It made me happy; it broke my heart.

Then Mel's phone rang. She answered. "No!" she said. "When?" And then, "Okay. We'll be right there."

She picked up her purse. "Sorry," she told Ralph. "Time to go to work."

"What?" I asked.

"That was Ross," she said. "There's been a fire at Janie's House overnight. He says the office building is a total loss."

CHAPTER 23

Ralph's cell phone rang just then, too. Answering, he waved at us while I gathered up the photos and took them along as we left the restaurant.

"Are you okay?" Mel asked as we got into the car.

"Okay," I said, "and more than a little amazed. Thanks for putting Ralph on the case."

"You're welcome," she said.

It took only a few minutes to drive from the Red Lion to what was left of Janie's House. Contrast is everything. The restaurant had been quiet and verging on sedate. At Janie's House, chaos reigned for several blocks in either direction on Seventeenth Avenue Southeast. As Ross had told Mel, the middle building in the three-house complex had burned to the ground. Sparks from that had ignited the roof on one of the other two buildings and had burned through the shingles and into the attic space. No doubt that one would have suffered both smoke and water damage. Only the charred back wall of the middle building was still standing when we arrived. Firemen swarmed around it, extinguishing hot spots.

Our Special Homicide badges were enough to get us through the police barricades. Officers there told us that the fire chief in charge of the incident was Alan Mulholland. Dressed in full firefighting gear, he stood at the center of the action waving his arms and shouting out orders, while a frantic Meribeth Duncan, wearing sweats and with her orange-and-purple hair in sleep-tossed disarray, dogged his every step.

"How is it possible that there's this much damage when the fire department is just down the street?" she demanded. "Couldn't you have done something sooner?"

"Look, lady," he said impatiently, "we were here less than four minutes after the call came in. You should have had hardwired smoke detectors in all the buildings. The one in the second building went off just fine when the roof caught fire," he said, pointing toward the house next door.

"All three buildings had the same kind of equipment," Meribeth insisted. "We had to install smoke detectors in order to bring them up to code. We have state-of-the-art intrusion detectors as well."

"Then maybe you should have a chat with the installer," Mulholland said. "This one didn't work at all."

Mel took Meribeth by the arm and led her away, giving me a clear shot at Mulholland.

"Is there a chance someone disabled the alarm?" I asked.

"That's a possibility, I suppose," Mulholland began, then he stopped answering my questions, glared at me, and fired back one of his own. "Who the hell are you?"

When I showed him my badge, he gave me an appraising look. "Special Homicide," he mused. "That's Ross Connors's outfit, isn't it?"

I nodded.

"What are you doing here? I haven't released any information about finding a body."

"Is there one?" I asked.

My question was met with a sharp "No comment."

Which told me that there was a body, but I didn't press him about it.

"We're here working another case," I told him.

"A case connected to what happened here?" he asked.

"Could be," I said.

When someone starts a game of non-cooperation, it's always pleasant to return the favor.

"So what are we talking about here," I asked, "arson?"

Mulholland gave me a long look. Then, because I seemed to have passed some kind of first-responder professional muster, he gave me a reasonable answer.

"Looks good for arson, but we don't know that for sure," Mulholland said. "It'll have to cool off before we can do any real investigating. It's too soon to send in the accelerant-sniffing dogs, but I'd say, yes, my best guess is arson. And, yes, there's at least one body in the rubble and maybe more. If it turns out that alarms and sprinkler systems were disabled, that would boost the likelihood of it being an inside job."

Mel came over and joined us at that point. "How tough is that to do?"

Mulholland looked at her and then at me. "We're together," I said.

"It might be tough, but for someone with a reasonable amount of tech savvy, it wouldn't be impossible."

"Who called in the fire?" I asked.

"Some guy out delivering newspapers on his morning route saw it first. The 911 call came in just after six A.M., but the fire had been burning for some time before that. It looks like the fire was started in one of the back rooms, so it wasn't visible from the front until

after it had a good burn going. My lieutenant over there has the delivery guy's
contact information. Other than the fire,
he didn't see anyone. At least that's
what he told us."

As Mel went to get the contact information, my phone rang. I hauled it out
of my pocket. Caller ID said it was a
restricted call. That usually means that
the caller is a member of some political
action committee bent on saving the
whales or opposing abortion. How so-
licitors at both ends of the political
spectrum ended up with my cell phone
number on their lists is more than I can
understand, and I didn't make it easy
for them. There was an unmistakable
hint of frost in my voice when I answered.

"Who's calling?"

"Captain Hoyt, with the Washington
State Patrol," Joan Hoyt said. "Dr.
Mowat just sent over the official copy of
his autopsy report on Josh Deeson. It
turns out there was one item in particular he failed to mention to me earlier."

"Anything we should know?" I asked.

"Apparently Josh was sexually active," Joan said, "and not in the boy-girl sense of the word, either. There's no way to tell if it was consensual or not, but there's evidence of a recent sexual encounter that included sodomy."

"What do you mean by 'recent'?" I asked.

"Within ten to twelve hours of his death," Jan answered.

"Is there enough for a DNA profile?"

"Mowat says not, but you and I know that's a load of crap. I know they can extract DNA profiles from tiny microscopic samples, but I also know DNA testing isn't cheap. I think that's the real reason Mowat is dragging his heels. For him it boils down to a budgetary issue. He doesn't want to squander his resources on something that's going to turn out to be a simple suicide. Don't worry, though," Joan added. "I may have figured out a way to bypass him on this. To do that, however, I'll need your help."

"What kind of help?" I asked.

"I seem to remember there were dirty clothes in the hamper in Josh Deeson's room."

"Right," I said. "I remember that, too."

"I want those clothes," Joan declared. "The room is still designated as a crime scene, so I'm hoping his family members have stayed out of it. I considered sending an officer over to the governor's mansion to collect any and all clothing from the hamper in his bedroom, but I'm not eager to have to explain why we're asking for it. You seem to have a good rapport with the governor and her husband. Do you think you and Ms. Soames could handle it?"

"Wait a minute. These people's kid committed suicide and now we're going to show up and drop the emotionally incendiary bomb that maybe he was gay, too?"

"Maybe he was and maybe he wasn't," Joan said. "But one thing I know for sure is that Josh Deeson was a juvenile. According to Washington State law, that would make anyone having a sexual encounter with him guilty of statutory rape. That also makes Josh Deeson a victim."

When I didn't respond immediately, Joan went right on making her case.

"Look," she said. "We've got a bunch of kids here who have been involved in some pretty unsavory behavior. If you toss your ordinary sexual offender into the mix, who knows? We might get lucky and find some answers in the DNA database."

Unfortunately, that premise made sense to me. A lot of sexual predators use volunteer work as a cover for searching out and stalking potential victims. It was possible that knowing Josh could have been the victim of a sexual predator might help overcome some if not all of his guardians' objections to handing over his soiled clothing.

"All right," I said, allowing myself to be convinced. "We can give it a try."

As I closed my phone I thought again about Josh's haunting suicide note: "I can't take it anymore."

Our initial assumption had been that "it" had something to do with the texting harassment he'd been subjected to. Now I wondered if being involved in a same-sex relationship might have proved to be more than he could handle. I remembered that some of the harassing text messages had taunted him about having homosexual tendencies. I had thought that was just teenage meanness and spite. Maybe, however, those comments had some truth to them. If so, that, too, might have fueled Josh's self-loathing and despair.

By then, Fire Chief Mulholland was busy with someone else. Without bothering to tell him good-bye, I went looking for Mel. I found her huddled with some homicide cops from Olympia PD who were making it blatantly clear that they weren't pleased to have us on the scene.

"So that's all you're going to tell us, that the attorney general asked you to stop by an arson fire here in Olympia?" the ranking detective asked. "That he just happened to know there might be a body here?"

"Pretty much," Mel replied, giving them one of her winning smiles. That managed to defuse the situation, but it didn't make it go away entirely. Eventually the city cops would connect the dots and come nosing around the governor's mansion. Before that happened, however, Mel and I wanted to have all our own dots connected.

Not that I blamed the locals, Dr. Bonnie Epstein included, for being pissed. After all, when I was at Seattle PD, I hated having someone from another agency land in one of my own investigations. As I recalled those instances when someone else was the interloper, I couldn't remember a single time when the willing sharing of information in either direction had been part of the program. Same thing here. We weren't talking to them and they weren't talking to us.

"Come on," I told Mel. "We've got to go."

"Where?" she asked.

"To pick up some laundry."

Which tweaked the locals that much more. "What laundry?"

"Just some dirty clothes," I said.

We left the guys from Olympia PD staring at us in disgusted silence as we headed back to the car. On the way I explained the situation. Mel didn't like the idea of having to broach such a touchy subject with Josh's grieving family any more than I did.

"What are we going to do," she asked, "draw straws to see who's stuck explaining this bad news to Gerry Willis and Governor Longmire?"

Why was it, whenever there was bad news to deliver, we had to resort to pulling straws?

We threaded our way back through the police barricades and found the Mercedes trapped in the middle of a crowd scene. There were kids everywhere, hanging on one another, weeping and wailing. At the closest intersection someone had set up a hand-lettered sign that said WE ❤ JANIE'S HOUSE. Around the base of it was a collection of flowers and a few teddy bears. I'm never sure why there have to be teddy bears at memorials like that, but there are. Always.

We were almost to the car when Mel's phone rang. I could tell from her part of the conversation that the call was from Rosemary Mellon in Seattle with a few more details from Rachel Camber's autopsy. Mel was still on the phone when

I caught my first glimpses of someone who had to be Giselle Longmire.

DNA is funny that way. In the midst of that crowd of distraught teenagers, and sobbing hysterically like the rest of them, Gizzy was her mother's daughter through and through. Slender, tanned, fit, and lovely, she had come to the scene in a pair of exceedingly short shorts, but she seemed genuinely dismayed by the fire's devastation. While I watched, a tall young man wearing a tracksuit made his way through the crowd. When he reached Gizzy, she looked up at him gratefully and then fell against his chest, weeping uncontrollably and craving comfort, while the kid I assumed to be Ronald Darrington Miller gazed off over her head toward the firefighters still dealing with the aftermath of the blaze.

It was an unguarded moment. Ron was standing in a crowd of people, all of whom seemed to be mesmerized by the chaos around them. He had no idea he was being observed. If he had known I was studying him, he might have managed to conceal the look of smug self-satisfaction that washed across his face. Everyone else seemed to be caught up in the emotions of the moment while Ron appeared to glide effortlessly above the fray. Then Gizzy looked up at him and said something to him. In that moment, his face was transformed. Before he replied, he donned a convincing expression of concern.

Of all the people around, I'm pretty sure I was the only one who caught that sudden change. All the other kids gathered there really were shocked and dismayed. Ron Miller was playing at being shocked and dismayed. Big difference.

The cloud cover overhead broke up briefly, illuminating the two of them—Giselle and Ron—in a shaft of sunlight. And that's when I saw them for what they were: two of the beautiful people whose sense of perfection would have been offended by the very existence of someone less than perfect—namely an interloper like Josh.

I remembered what Monica Longmire had said about Giselle resenting his being added to her family. It seemed reasonable enough to assume that someone with her intimate knowledge of Josh's background could easily have provided fodder for all those taunting e-mails, while Ron's connections to the Janie's House computer and communications systems could have provided the delivery system. If that was the case, the two of them might not have been legally responsible for kicking the chair out from under Josh and his homemade noose, but they were morally responsible for putting him on that chair in the first place.

As for the video clip? That seemed to be part of the general harassment program. Was it possible then that Giselle and Ron, in all their native superiority, were also responsible for that? Had they pretended to murder Rachel Camber and then found it necessary to kill her once the investigation started to get too close? Or had they done it just for kicks? And did they really believe they could murder someone and get away with it?

The brief splash of sunlight went away, taking with it that single telling moment of clarity. I was left with something that was little more than an unfounded hunch. If I was going to follow up on it—if I was even considering investigating the possibility that one or both of the governor's daughters might be involved in the harassment of Josh Deeson or in the death of Rachel Camber—I needed some evidence that was a hell of a lot more compelling than a bare-bones hunch. I was pretty sure that we were going to have DNA evidence to work with. What I wanted now was something to compare it with. Without probable cause we wouldn't be able to *demand* DNA samples, but if we just happened to have some on hand . . .

My mother loved *Columbo*. Had she lived long enough to see the advent of video recorders, she would have watched each and every episode over and over. She loved how Peter Falk, playing the bumbling detective, always got his man . . . or woman. It seemed to me that this was an occasion that called for a real-life bumbler.

When Mel is talking on the telephone, she doesn't like to be interrupted by anyone or anything, but that didn't keep me from pestering her while she was taking notes from Rosemary's phone call.

"I need some of your business cards," I said.

Mel glared at me in exasperation and shook her head as if to say, "Go away. Can't you see I'm busy?"

When I persisted, she finally let loose with an exaggerated sigh. Then she handed me her purse—her oversize, magic, man-eating purse. Under ordinary circumstances I wouldn't have ventured into the damned thing, but I was determined. I once saw a catalog photo of the ultimate Swiss Army knife with all of the Swiss Army tools loaded into one gargantuan assembly. The thing cost fourteen hundred bucks and looked huge, but I'm sure it would have disappeared into Mel's purse without a whimper.

I had to paw through any number of levels of stuff before I finally spotted what I was looking for—the little mother-of-pearl-covered card-shaped carrying case that holds Mel's business cards. I pulled some of them out of the case and slipped them into my right-hand pocket. Strictly speaking, for this kind of evidence gathering I should have been wearing gloves, but those would have given me away. For this to work I needed Giselle Longmire and Ron Miller to think of me as an incompetent idiot.

Leaving Mel standing there talking on the phone, I sauntered over to Giselle and Ron. "Gizzy?" I said.

The disapproving frown she leveled at me told me Mel was right. Giselle Longmire did *not* care for her nickname, and she most certainly didn't like being hailed by that name in public by someone who was, as far as she knew, a perfect stranger.

I held out my hand. "J. P. Beaumont," I said. "I'm a friend of your mother's. We went to Ballard High School together."

Her look softened, but only a little.

"I'm also a police officer," I continued, waving offhandedly back toward the fire scene and hoping they would assume that I was part of the fire investigation. "Are you involved with Janie's House?"

"I volunteer here," Gizzy said. "This is

my boyfriend, Ron Miller. He volunteers here, too."

I took Ron's hand and gave it a firm handshake. "At least we used to volunteer here," Ron said wryly.

It was summer. It was going to be a warm day. I noticed the long sleeves on Ron Miller's tracksuit and wondered if that was important.

"I work for the attorney general's office," I explained, keeping my tone both brisk and casual. I wanted them to think that whatever was going on here wasn't particularly important or critical. "We'll be working on this case with the Olympia PD."

"Oh," Ron said, equally casually. "Is it arson, do you think?"

Ah, yes. The old how-much-do-they-know routine. That's one of the interesting things about firebugs. They often want to be on the scene in person to assess the damage.

"Too soon to tell," I said, shrugging and waving his question aside. "By the time this is over, we'll probably be interviewing all of the people involved with Janie's House—employees, volunteers, and clients, but if you happen to hear any rumors about what went on, please don't hesitate to give me a call. By the way, when's the last time either of you was here?"

"Yesterday afternoon," Ron said.

"A couple of days," Gizzy replied.

Reaching into my right-hand pocket, I pulled out Mel's cards. I handed one to Ron and a second one to Gizzy. Involved in sizing me up, man-to-man, Ron didn't even glance at his card. Gizzy did.

"Funny," she said. "You don't look like a Melissa." She held up the card so I could see my mistake.

"So sorry," I apologized. "Let me have those back. They belong to my partner. I'd much rather you called me directly. Ms. Soames is a bit of a control freak, you see. She won't like it if she thinks I've been passing her cards out indiscriminately."

Shaking my head at my own stupidity, I quickly retrieved the two cards, dropped them into my right-hand jacket pocket, and pulled two of my own business cards out of the left. I handed those to Ron and Gizzy. Another boy approached us just then. I handed him one of my cards as well and gave him the same pep talk about calling me if he happened to hear anything about the origin of the Janie's House fire.

With that, and trying to conceal a smirk on my own face, I hurried back to Mel. She was sitting in the front seat of the car with her laptop open and the air card tuned up and running.

"What the hell was that all about?" she demanded. "Why did you need my business cards? Did you run out of yours?"

"DNA," I told her with a grin. "My DNA will be on the two business cards in my pocket, but with any kind of luck, we'll have DNA from Ron Miller and from Gizzy Longmire, too."

"You think she's involved in all this?" Mel asked.

"I'd bet money on it."

"In that case," Mel said, "good work. In fact, good for both of us. While you were playing sleight of hand with the business cards, I've had two phone calls. The first one was about Rachel Camber's autopsy. The second one was about the two watches. A friend who works at Macy's was able to give me the phone number for the company that serves as the national sales rep for Seiko. Maybe we can get one of Joan Hoyt's investigators to track that. With any kind of luck, they should be able to tell us which retailer sold each of our two watches and when. From that information, we may even be able to track back to the individual customer."

"Right," I said. "Good for both of us. In the meantime let's go see about collecting Josh's dirty clothes."

We pulled into the driveway to the governor's mansion and stopped just behind a bright red Audi. I was already dreading this encounter, and so was Mel. Having any kind of audience in attendance would make it that much worse.

The guard outside the front door nodded in recognition when we walked up to ring the doorbell. Before we could do so, however, Monica Longmire came striding out of the house. She stopped short in front of us.

"Are you here because she's missing?" Monica demanded.

There it was again—another case of faulty pronoun reference.

"Who's missing?" I asked. "What are we talking about?"

"Giselle," she said impatiently. "Gizzy. I came over here to have a word with Gerry and Marsha about it. Gizzy told her mother she was staying with us last night and she told us she was staying with her mother when in reality she didn't stay at either place. Now she isn't answering her phone. With everything that's going on around here, playing those kinds of games is utterly inexcusable, to say nothing of disrespectful. As if her parents weren't worried enough already, the idea that Gizzy could be dead in a ditch someplace . . ."

"She's not dead in a ditch," I replied reassuringly. "In fact, I spoke to Giselle just a few minutes ago. I can't imagine why she isn't answering her phone."

Monica's jaw dropped. "You saw her? You spoke to her? Where is she?"

"At the scene of the fire. Maybe the circuits are busy and that's why she isn't answering."

"What fire?" Monica demanded.

"There was a fire at Janie's House early this morning," I said. "A lot of kids who hang out there must have heard about it through the grapevine. A whole crowd of them showed up to survey the damage. That's where I saw Giselle last. She was there with a young man—"

"Ron Miller?" Monica frowned. "Was that little worm there, too?"

"Yes," I said. "He's not what I'd call little, but when she introduced us, that's the name she mentioned."

"All right then," Monica said. Spinning on her heel, she set out for the Audi. "I'm going to find that girl and give her a piece of my mind."

CHAPTER 24

Monica Longmire piled into the Audi, slammed it into gear, and took off. "That was a smooth way to get rid of her," Mel said. "I'm proud of you."

"Thanks," I said. "I think."

We rang the bell. I was surprised when it opened and Zoe was once again standing there. I hadn't seen her among the kids gathered at the scene of the fire, but she, too, looked as if she'd been crying.

"My mom's not here," she said, sniffling. "Our relatives are all flying in for the funeral. She had to go to the airport to pick someone up."

"Who is it?" Gerry called from somewhere inside the house, somewhere out of sight.

"Agents Beaumont and Soames," I called back. "We need to talk to you."

"Oh, for God's sake," Gerry Willis grumbled. "What now? Marsha isn't here. Gizzy has gone AWOL. Everything's falling apart. Let them in, Zoe."

A subdued Zoe led us into the living room. Gerry was seated on a sofa with a breakfast tray on the table in front of him. Good china. Good cups and saucers. Evidently the cook was still on duty.

"Can we get you something?" he offered.

I didn't want to have this awkward conversation with Zoe standing there hanging on my every word.

"I'd love some coffee," I said, nodding toward the pot. "Is that regular or decaf?"

"I'm only allowed decaf these days."

"I'd like some coffee, too," Mel chirped agreeably.

"Zoe," Gerry said, "would you please go ask the cook . . ."

Zoe set off. In one fluid motion, Mel fell into step beside her.

"I'll be glad to help carry," Mel said. It was a neat maneuver on Mel's part. It conveniently took Zoe out of the picture, but it also left me holding the bag.

"Well?" Gerry urged after a moment. "What's this about?"

"You don't need to worry about Gizzy," I said hurriedly. "We saw her just a few minutes ago."

"Where?"

"There was a fire at Janie's House last night. She was at the scene along with a bunch of other kids."

Gerry nodded. "Good," he said, reaching for his cell phone. "That's a relief. I need to call Monica and let her know—"

"Actually, we already did that," I said. "Mrs. Longmire was just leaving when we drove up. The last thing she said to us was that she was going to find Gizzy and give her a piece of her mind."

Gerry favored me with a rueful smile. "If anyone can pull that off, Monica can.

She's the best disciplinarian in the group."

In the annals of divorce-induced group-grope parenting, this struck me as being pretty civilized all the way around. It was good to see four grown-ups acting like grown-ups, putting aside their differences and doing what they could to care for the kids involved.

Gerry picked up his coffee cup, took a sip, and eyed me speculatively. "I have a feeling this isn't a social call," he said. "Why are you here?"

Direct questions merit direct answers.

"I'm sorry to have to bring this up," I said, "but the autopsy results have revealed that your grandson was sexually active."

"Sexually active," Gerry repeated. "Are you kidding? Josh was a kid—a shy, bumbling kid. I doubt he could even talk to a girl without falling all over himself."

"Not a girl," I said, meeting his eye. "I'm sorry to be the one giving you this difficult bit of news, but the evidence found by the medical examiner would be consistent with there being no female involvement."

Stunned, Gerry sat there for a moment saying nothing at all, then he shook his head. "This is unbelievable. Are you trying to tell me that Josh was caught up in some kind of homosexual relationship?"

I nodded.

There was another long period of silence. "That can't be," he said finally. "It just can't."

"Were there any boys he was especially close to?"

"No," Gerry said. "Not that I know of."

"Look," I said. "Josh was a minor. At his age, any kind of sexual encounter, consensual or not, would be regarded as sexual assault and as a criminal offense. That's why we're here today, sir, to see if we can find some justice for Josh."

"How?"

"I seem to remember there were dirty clothes in the hamper in Josh's room the other day. We're hoping we might be able to find DNA evidence that would point us in the direction of whoever did this."

"You want Josh's dirty clothes?"

"Yes."

"Then by all means go get them."

I went right then, while the getting was good. As soon as I started up the stairs, my knees went nuts. By the time I got to the top floor, I was sweating bullets and the pain was killing me. I stopped at the top of the stairs long enough to catch my breath and get my bearings. That's when I noticed the doors to a linen closet right there in the hallway. I opened them, and voilà! There were stacks of washed and ironed sheets and pillowcases. A clean pillowcase was exactly what I needed.

Grabbing one, I ducked under the crime scene tape and let myself into the room. The place was as we'd left it, with fingerprint powder marring every surface. The hamper, however, still full of dirty clothes, was untouched. I emptied the soiled clothing into the pillowcase and turned to make my escape in time to find a furious Governor Marsha Longmire blocking the doorway.

"What the hell do you think you're doing?" she demanded

I closed the pillowcase and tied it in a knot. "Collecting evidence," I said.

"What kind of evidence?" she wanted to know. "Josh is dead. His death has been ruled a suicide. What's the point of torturing my husband any further? Can't you just let it go?"

"No," I said. "I can't let it go. We've found evidence that Josh Deeson may have been the victim of a sexual assault."

"You mean you think he was raped?"

"Maybe," I said. "We also know that Josh was the target in a case of coordinated cyber bullying, with any number of kids sending him harassing text messages. The messages appear to have come primarily from cell phone accounts billed to Janie's House, although they seem to have been written by several different people."

"What kind of messages?" Marsha asked. "What are we talking about here?"

"Insulting, snide comments. In the old days when we were kids, the insults that were in fashion probably wouldn't have been much more damaging than 'Your mother wears G.I. boots.' The messages sent to Josh were far more destructive than that, and far more personal."

"But . . ." she began.

I dodged around her and started down the stairs.

"How did you find out about these supposed messages?" Marsha asked.

"They're not supposed messages or alleged messages or any other kind of weasel words. We know about them because Josh saved them," I said. "He downloaded them from his phone to a file on his computer."

"What does any of that have to do with Josh's dirty clothes?" Marsha demanded. "Besides, this is our home. Even if his room is still designated as a crime scene, you can't just come waltzing in here without a warrant."

"Your husband gave me permission," I said.

As I clambered down the long flights of stairs, I ached enough that I could barely walk and talk at the same time.

As I neared the ground floor, I heard the sound of assembled voices coming from the living room and could see a collection of suitcases that had been hastily deposited in the entryway.

Gerry must have heard Marsha and me arguing as we descended. He was waiting at the bottom of the stairs.

"I'm the one who gave Mr. Beaumont permission to collect Josh's clothes," Gerry said. "If you have a problem with that, Marsha, you need to discuss it with me." After telling his wife to back off, Gerry turned to me. "If you'll forgive me, Mr. Beaumont, I'm going to have to renege on that offer of coffee. We have people here now—out-of-town guests."

I nodded. "Of course," I said.

Zoe came past, headed for the stairs. Gerry stopped her. "Please go tell Ms. Soames that Mr. Beaumont is just leaving."

Nodding, Zoe went to do his bidding while Gerry walked me out to the car. When Mel emerged from the house, Marsha was still standing at the foot of the stairs.

"Do you think Josh was involved with

another boy?" Gerry asked in an undertone as I put the clothing-laden pillowcase in the trunk and pushed the button to close it. "With someone his own age?"

"I'm sorry, Mr. Willis," I said. "I really have no idea. It could be another kid. It could be an adult."

"Why don't you go see Mr. Dysart?" Gerry suggested quietly, speaking in what was almost a whisper.

"The guy who ran the chess club?"

Gerry nodded. "That's the one. I met him last May at the end-of-year dinner for the chess club. Josh thought the world of him, but I tell you true—the man gave me the willies."

"Gives him the willies?" Mel repeated as we drove away. "That's an expression I haven't heard in a long time."

Mel is younger than I am. There are times when we run head-on into a generation gap. It happens with jokes and music, and occasionally, as in this case, with vocabulary.

"Maybe not," I said, "but if he bothered Gerry that much, it's reason enough to stop by once more to see him. We should also have a chat with some of the other kids in the chess club. But before we talk to anyone, I want to go see Joan Hoyt. We'll give her what we have so she can get it to the crime lab."

Headquarters for the Washington State Patrol is on Linderson in Olympia. Once there, Mel went to have a chat with Records while I tracked down Captain Hoyt.

"How did it go at the governor's mansion?" Joan asked when I handed her the pillowcase filled with Josh Deeson's dirty clothes.

"About how you'd expect," I told her. "I don't think they'll be putting us on their Christmas card list."

I gave her the two business cards that I had briefly handed over to Gizzy Longmire and Ron Miller.

"What's this?" she asked.

"I'm hoping the crime lab will be able to lift prints and/or DNA off the cards."

"Related to Rachel Camber's murder?"

I nodded. Then I handed over Mel's and my garbage-sifting prize—Josh Deeson's extra Seiko watch.

"What's this?"

"Something Mel and I dug out of the governor's garbage. The watch looks a whole lot like a duplicate of the one Josh Deeson was wearing when he died, the one your crime scene team already took into evidence. Here's the number for the Seiko distributor. We need to find out when both watches were purchased, and, if we're lucky, find some trail to the individual purchasers."

Joan nodded. "I'll put someone on this right away."

By the time I was finished documenting the transfer of evidence, Mel was waiting for me in the car. Since she had her own key, she had been able to turn on the GPS.

"Take a look at this," she said. "I loaded in Sam Dysart's address. I wasn't paying that much attention to the relative distances last night when we stopped by there, but it's only a little over a mile from there back to the governor's mansion. That's well within walking distance for someone letting himself in and out of his third-floor bedroom with a pair of strategically placed rope ladders. And if you remember, when we asked Josh about who he had been with that night, he claimed he had been alone."

"It's all starting to make sense," I said. "If Josh was being sexually exploited by a coach-type adult from school, that would certainly explain his reluctance to discuss it."

"It might also explain where he went on that afternoon jog Gerry Willis thought was so unusual," Mel said. "But listen to this. Here's something interesting. Samuel D. Dysart, age fifty-seven, has no traffic citations, but he's been cited twice for loitering in Fort Defiance Park in Tacoma, late on two different Saturday nights. One occurrence happened two years ago and the other the year before that."

I allowed myself the luxury of an *aha* moment.

Loitering is a misdemeanor. Most civilians seem to place loitering citations on the same level of seriousness as littering violations. What loitering really means in the PC world of cop speak is that some unfortunate gay guy got caught wandering around in a public place in search of a casual sex hookup. Looking for love in all the wrong places constitutes risky behavior. In terms of potential danger, it's several steps down from Internet dating services. When two men end up "loitering" together and what goes on is between consenting adults, it's regarded as a relatively harm- less, victimless crime. Giving someone a citation for loitering is the civilian cop's version of "Don't ask, don't tell," and it's a charge that doesn't land the loi- terer on the list of registered sex offend- ers.

In this case, however, maybe it should have. Now there was a victim involved— a juvenile victim, since Josh Deeson had died several years shy of the age of consent.

"Dysart sounds like a hell of a nice guy," I muttered. "Just exactly the kind of person I'd want in charge of my son's high school chess club."

By that time, of course, Mel was al- ready on the phone with the high school principal's office, speaking to a secre- tary, and asking for the names of the kids who had signed up for the chess club to be e-mailed to her. After a question about how Samuel Dysart, a nonteacher, came to be in charge of the chess club, Mel listened for some time, typing on her computer the whole while.

"So here's the deal," Mel said once she was off the phone. "Twenty-some years ago, when Dysart was in his thirties, he was a nationally recognized championship chess player. Now he's a retired software engineer. Two years ago, when the school couldn't afford to pay one of its regular faculty members to be in charge of the chess club, they were delighted when Dysart showed up and volunteered his services."

"Sounds a lot like putting the fox in charge of the henhouse," I commented.

"Exactly," Mel agreed. "From then on, just like magic, there are no more loitering charges lodged against him. He doesn't have to go wandering around in parks in the middle of the night looking for connections, because the school is happy to send him a never-ending supply of potential victims."

The whole idea was anathema to me. By the time we stopped in front of Sam Dysart's house, I was half sick to my stomach. Child predators revolt me. That was one core value Anne Corley and I had had in common. Ditto for Mel Soames. Antipathy toward child abusers is evidently part of my first sort in picking potential mates.

When we drove up to Sam Dysart's house, everything looked pretty normal except for the fact that the curtains and blinds were still closed. The house was neat and clean like all the other houses on the block. A gardener's truck was parked at the curb, and a guy with a lawn mower was industriously mowing Dysart's small front yard.

Mel and I got out of the car and started up the sidewalk. When the gardener saw us, he turned off his mower.

"Nobody's home," he said without our asking. "I tried ringing the bell and knocking on the door because I was hoping to pick up a check. No such luck."

Mel turned around and marched back down the sidewalk. At first I thought she was leaving. Instead, she went to Dysart's mailbox. She opened it and pulled out a fistful of mail. After shuffling through it, she returned the stack of mail to the box. Then she came back to me.

"Considering the layers of junk mail and real mail, I'd say his mail hasn't been picked up since Tuesday."

Without having to discuss it, we fanned out and talked to the neighbors. Olympia isn't a small town, but it isn't a big city, either. People tend to know their neighbors. No one could remember seeing Sam Dysart for several days.

I spoke briefly to a woman who lived across the street.

"If there are three days' worth of mail in his mailbox," Agnes Jones said, "then something is definitely wrong. Whenever Sam goes out of town he always has me pick up his mail. He worries about identity theft. He'd never leave his mail in the box like that. Never."

"So when's the last time you saw him?"

"Let's see." She paused for a moment, frowning. "Now that you mention it, I don't think I've seen him since Monday. I was on my way back from the grocery store. He was driving out as I was driving in. We waved and that was it."

"You haven't seen him since then?"

"No, but that's not indicative of anything. Neither one of us keeps regular hours, so we come and go at odd times. It's not all that unusual for a week or so to pass without our ever laying eyes on each other."

"Does he have many visitors?" I asked.

Something about my question must have put her on edge. "Wait a minute," Agnes said. "Who are you? What's this all about again?"

I showed her my badge. "We're investigating a homicide." You'll notice I didn't say what homicide, but the answer seemed to satisfy her.

"I can't imagine Sam Dysart being mixed up in anything like that," she declared. "He's a perfectly nice man—a complete gentleman."

"And about his visitors?"

"Kids drop by from time to time," Agnes said. "Good kids," she added. "Clean-cut kids from the chess club at Olympia High. Did you know Sam was once a championship chess player?"

"Yes," I said. "So I heard."

When I crossed the street again, Mel had already finished with her share of the neighborhood canvassing and was waiting for me at the end of Sam Dysart's carefully edged driveway. By then the gardener had loaded up his tools and grass clippings and had left the premises.

"Anything?"

"The lady across the street claims that the last time she saw him was sometime around noon on Monday."

"What do you think?" Mel asked. "Is it possible a welfare check is in order?"

"I think so."

We stepped up onto the front porch. First we rang the bell. When there was no answer to that, we knocked. Again there was no response, so we walked around the side of the house to the backyard. The lot was far deeper than it was wide. In the far back of the property sat a small stand-alone cottage that looked like it had once been a single-car garage before being turned into either a storage shed or a tiny apartment. Ignoring that for the time being, we went to the back door of the main house and repeated the same knocking routine we had performed on the front porch—with similar results. No answer. When I tried the door, it was locked.

We were about to walk away when a telephone began to ring inside the house. I would have bet money it was Agnes from across the street calling to let Sam Dysart know that police officers had been nosing around his place. The phone rang several times and then went silent.

"Answering machine, most likely," Mel said.

Turning as one, Mel and I headed for the small building at the far end of the lot. On the side facing us there was a single curtained window and an old-fashioned door—an antique door that took an old-fashioned key, a skeleton key.

When I went to knock on the door, it fell open at my touch because it wasn't locked. It wasn't even closed all the way. As the door opened, a noxious odor exploded around us. We stood outside, covering our noses with our hands and peering into the stinky gloom of what was evidently a tiny apartment. My first thought was that we had stumbled across a blocked toilet and someone needed to call Roto-Rooter right away.

In the arcane world of Planning and Guessing, as opposed to Planning and Zoning, buildings like this are referred to as ADUs (accessory dwelling units). That's what bureaucrats call them. Ordinary, nonbureaucrat folks call those same structures mother-in-law apartments.

This one looked like a one-room cabin, complete with a small table— covered by a chessboard—a rumpled, unmade bed, a kitchen area with a sink, fridge, small stove, and microwave, and a closed door that most likely led into the bathroom with a plugged commode.

"Mr. Dysart," I called out. "Are you in there?"

Mel reached around the door frame

and located a light switch. Using a pen from her purse, she flipped on an overhead light. There was no sign of any kind of confrontation—no knocked-over furniture, no broken crockery. Fighting off the foul odor, I walked as far as the bathroom door and knocked on that as well.

"Mr. Dysart, police. Are you in there? Are you all right?"

In answer I heard an eerie croak uttering words that, loosely translated, sounded like "Help me." Instead of coming from inside the bathroom, the sound came from behind me on the far side of that unmade bed. As soon as I stepped closer, I realized that was where the odor came from as well. A man lay there on the floor, trapped between the wall he was facing and the side of the bed.

I've heard all those "I've fallen and I can't get up" jokes, and several of them ran through my mind as I wrenched the bed away from the wall. In the background, I heard Mel on the phone calling 911.

"Are you Mr. Dysart?" I asked.

He nodded emphatically. He had

been lying on his side, facing the wall. As soon as I moved the bed away from him, he flopped over onto his back with a wrenching groan. Initially I thought he was the victim of some kind of attack. When I reached out to help him, however, I realized that he had lost the use of his entire right side. Instead of dealing with a crime victim, Mel and I had encountered a serious medical emergency. Dysart appeared to have suffered a massive stroke. He had been stuck there on the floor, trapped between the wall and the bed and imprisoned in his own filth, for what must have been several days.

"Water," he croaked. "Please."

That much was understandable. I went to the kitchen cupboard, grabbed a glass, filled it, and came back.

"EMTs are on the way," Mel said.

I picked my way through the stinking mess, knelt at the man's head, and tried to raise him enough to offer him a sip of water. When I did so, the water ran back out one side of his mouth and dribbled down onto his chest.

Within a matter of minutes, units from

the Olympia Fire Department arrived on the scene. They bustled into the room in full firefighting regalia, bringing with them the chatter of radios and bags of equipment. While they worked, Mel stood studying the door to the building.

"What do you think are the chances that the skeleton key Josh was wearing opens this door?" she asked.

"Why don't we check?"

I plucked my phone out of my pocket and dialed Joan Hoyt.

"What about the key that was found on a chain around Josh's neck?" I asked her.

"My understanding is that Dr. Mowat has already released the body," Joan said. "That means his personal effects were sent either to the funeral home or else directly back to the governor's mansion."

Remembering the way Marsha Longmire had run me out of the house earlier, I knew which one I was hoping for.

My next call was to Larry Mowat at the Thurston County medical examiner's office. I was hoping to talk to a secretary or a receptionist—anyone but him—so of course he answered after the second ring.

"J. P. Beaumont here," I told him. "We need to know where you sent Josh Deeson's personal effects."

"'We' being you and that rabid dog you call a partner?" he asked.

"Mel Soames is my partner," I said. "She also happens to be my wife. Now answer the damned question!"

My response evidently surprised him. He swallowed whatever additional smart-assed comment he had intended to make.

"I did what I always do in cases like this. I sent the personal effects to the funeral home, along with the body."

"Which funeral home?"

"Nelson's mortuary on Pacific. Why?"

I hung up without answering and turned to Mel. "Let's go," I said.

"Where to?"

I knew generally where Pacific was, and I headed there without having to wait for Mel to work the GPS.

"To a funeral home," I told her. "Here's the deal. The key was released along with the body. I'm hoping we can get there and grab it before your friend Mowat can pull the plug on us. If we can pick it up without a hassle, fine. If we can't—if the personal effects have already been turned over to the family—then we're going to have to ask Ross for another court order."

This was one of the times when the gods were on our side. Larry Mowat is a top-down kind of guy. While he was consulting with Charles Nelson, the owner of the mortuary, Mel and I threw ourselves on the mercy of the minimum-wage-earning young woman who was running the Nelson Funeral Home's outer office. We showed her our badges. She handed over what we needed, and we gave her a receipt. We were out of there in five minutes flat with the phone ringing in the background as we hurried out the door.

We drove back to Sam Dysart's place. The ambulance was gone, although some fire department vehicles were still in attendance. As we walked through the side yard, the newly mowed grass was littered with medical debris. A young fireman was emerging from the cottage as we approached.

"Hey," he said. "You're not supposed to go inside here."

Mel showed him her badge while I walked up to the door and put the skeleton key in the old-fashioned lock. It turned home with a satisfying click.

"Bingo," I said. "Sam Dysart is our guy—Dysart and Josh." I pulled the door shut and locked it. "Now let's go see Ross Connors. We need a search warrant and some DNA evidence. We handle the evidence by the book. If Sam Dysart did this, I want him to go to jail for it for a very long time. I don't want there to be the smallest possibility that he's able to get off due to some mishandled piece of procedure or evidence."

"The man had a crippling stroke that went untreated for days," Mel pointed out. "If we lock him up, the taxpayers of Washington will end up footing his medical bills."

"Fine," I growled. "If paying a huge medical bill means the state treasurer has prevented one other kid from being victimized by this creep, it'll be worth it. Let's just say it will be taxpayer money well spent."

"Josh won't be there in court to testify against him."

"No," I said. "He won't, but we will be. Just as soon as we get the go-ahead on that search warrant. We'll be able to testify and so will the DNA from that glass of water I offered him a little while ago. Come on. Let's go."

CHAPTER 25

As we headed for the car, Mel's phone rang. I seem to remember that back in the old days we managed to get by without the constant use of cell phones, but I'm not sure how.

"No," she was saying. "As I told the officers on the scene, we had no idea there had been a fatality. We were there regarding another matter. If your officers want more information than that, they'll have to check with our boss, Ross Connors."

"What's going on?" I mouthed in her direction.

She shook her head and waved me off. And then my phone rang, too, with an unfamiliar number.

"Hello."

"Mr. Beaumont? Monica Longmire."

"Did you find Gizzy?"

"Yes, I did. She was right there where you said she'd be—in with that whole crowd of onlookers at Janie's House. The two of us had something of a set-to. I told her she was behaving badly to stay out all night and not answer her phone when things are at such sixes and sevens at home with what hap-pened to Josh. I told her she needed to stop being such a self-centered little twerp and start thinking about some-one else for a change. I said she should be home helping her mother and Gerry deal with their houseguests arriving for the funeral instead of being out running around. At which point she told me I wasn't her mother and needed to mind my own business. Ron stepped in then, called me a bitch, and told me to leave Gizzy alone.

"About that time a cop from Olympia PD showed up and started asking questions. I think that's when most of the kids there found out someone had died in the fire. It looked to me as though that's the first Gizzy knew about it, too. She turned pale as a ghost. I thought she was going to faint. Ron grabbed her by the arm and led her away. They got in his car and took off.

"Look," Monica continued. "I've tried to be a team player on this. I know the Millers were big supporters of Marsha's campaign. That's one of the reasons Sid asked me to keep my misgivings to myself where Ron and Gizzy are concerned, but I'm done with that.

"I spent twenty years of my life married to a man very much like Ron Miller. He had money to burn, and as far as the world was concerned, Dan Masterson was the greatest guy in the world. Butter wouldn't melt in his mouth. But at home and hidden underneath all that good-guy crap was a real snake. So I recognize the type. If the cops at the fire had bothered asking Ron any questions, I'm sure he could have lied his way out of it with no trouble at all. The problem is, I've known Gizzy since she was ten. She's not nearly as good a liar."

"Wait," I said. "Are you saying what I think you're saying—that you believe Ron Miller and Gizzy might have something to do with the fire at Janie's House?"

"That's exactly what I'm saying. Ron at least, and maybe Gizzy, too."

"Based on the expressions on their faces when the cop started asking questions?"

"That and the way they skipped out of there before the cops got around to talking to them."

Monica's words served to confirm my own private hunch, but two hunches don't make a case, and the fatality arson investigation itself wasn't Mel's and my deal. It belonged to Olympia PD.

"Look," I said. "Special Homicide operates under the direction and at the sole discretion of Attorney General Connors. Even with a death involved, the fire at Janie's House isn't our case. You'll need to speak to the guys here in Olympia."

"Have you looked at Ron's driving record?"

We had, but I didn't want to say so.

"Not really," I said.

"I know he has some points on his record," Monica said, "but not nearly as many as he ought to have."

We thought as much, too. "You're saying you think cops here in Olympia might give him a pass?" I asked.

"They have in the past."

"What do you mean?"

"There was a fire a few years ago at a boathouse out along Budd Inlet. It belonged to neighbors of the Millers'. It burned up the boathouse as well as the boat that was stored inside it. The fire ended up being declared an accident rather than arson. No charges were ever filed, but Ron's parents ended up paying for the damage. Does that sound like a pass to you?"

"How did you find out about this?" I asked.

"Gizzy told Zoe and Zoe told me."

"Well, you're right," I said. "It's sounding more and more like a pass all the time. I think Mel and I should have a chat with the charming young couple. Do you happen to know where they are right now?"

"At the governor's mansion," Monica answered. "They left the scene of the fire in Ron's Camaro. Gizzy's Acura was parked a few blocks away. That's where they said they were going once they picked up her car. They're there right now, probably having their asses chewed. Gerry was fit to be tied about the situation."

"We're only a mile or so away," I said. "We'll drop by and do a little piling on."

"I'll head home then," Monica said, "but please don't mention that I'm the one who raised this issue. If they find out I've been talking out of school, all hell is going to break loose. Gizzy will be furious, Sid will be furious, and so will the governor. Not Gerry, though. When it comes to Ron Miller, Gerry and I are pretty much on the same page, but we're the stepparents. You know how that goes. I have to live with these people."

Suspicions were all Gerry Willis had offered us about Sam Dysart, but those were looking a whole lot more viable now. In this case, Monica's suspicions about Ron Miller coincided with my own.

"Don't worry," I assured her. "You go on home. We won't give you away."

While I had been on the phone with Monica, Mel had been in touch with Ross's office. She had brought him up-to-date on the situation with Sam Dysart. We had been walking as we talked. By the time I got off the phone with Monica, Mel and I were buckled into the front seat of the S-550.

"Is Ross going to request search warrants?"

"Yes," Mel said. "And what about us? I take it we're headed for the governor's mansion?"

"That's the idea," I said. "It turns out Ron Miller may have had a previous firebug involvement that wasn't prosecuted. Try Googling Ronald Darrington Miller or a boathouse fire on Budd Inlet. The fire in question was declared accidental, but the bad boy's parents, who also happen to be among Governor

Longmire's big-time contributors, paid for the damages."

"And thus kept it off his record," Mel said, working her iPhone as I drove. "Tell me it doesn't pay to have friends in high places."

We both knew that wasn't true, because connections work to smooth out all kinds of little rough spots. Mel had just found an article about the fire when we pulled up at the end of the mansion's brick-paved driveway. The last two cars parked there were a silver Acura and a shiny new blue Camaro with a temporary paper plate affixed to the back window.

"Okay," she said. "The boathouse fire happened three years ago in July, allegedly from fireworks being shot off by an unnamed juvenile. Damage to the structure and contents was estimated to be in excess of seventy-five thousand dollars."

"Ron would have been fourteen back then," I said.

"He isn't a juvenile now," Mel said. "So what's the plan? Are we just going to blurt out something like, 'Hey, did you two have anything to do with the fire at Janie's House?'"

"No," I said. "We're going to tell them that we're interviewing everybody connected to Janie's House. Then we're going to divide and conquer. Most likely Ron and Gizzy cooked up some kind of story to tell their parents about where they were last night and what they did. I'll tackle Ron; you talk to Gizzy."

"If her mother lets me get anywhere near her," Mel said.

"Then we compare notes. If the stories don't stack up—and I'm willing to bet they won't—then we come back at them with lying to a police officer."

I parked directly behind the Camaro, close enough that I figured it wouldn't be easy for Ron to pull out without my moving first.

The same WSP guard nodded us through. We walked up to the front door and rang the bell. A woman in her forties, one I'd never seen before, opened the door. We didn't recognize her and she didn't recognize us

"May I help you?" she asked.

"We're here to see Giselle Longmire

and Ron Miller," Mel said. "I understand they're both here at the moment."

"You'd need to speak to the governor first, but she's completely occupied with a personal matter at the moment. I'm Liz Carnahan, her chief of staff. Can I help you?"

Over Liz's shoulder I could hear the sound of raised voices coming from somewhere nearby—probably the small study just off the front entryway. Marsha seemed to be doing most of the talking.

"Staying out all night is not okay! I expect both of you to show better sense than that. And how about a little respect for what's going on with Gerry? With all the people in town for the funeral tomorrow, the last thing we need is to have you behaving like this."

There were some mumbled replies— a male voice and a female one—but nothing that we could understand.

"I'm sorry," Liz Carnahan said. "This is a personal matter."

"If the governor is busy, perhaps we could have a word with Mr. Willis," I said, handing over a business card. "This concerns his grandson."

The chief of staff gave me the stink eye, but she took the card with her as she turned and disappeared into the house, leaving the door ajar behind her. A moment later, the door to the study slammed open. Ron Miller strode out into the foyer. Then he pushed his way past Mel and me without even acknowledging our presence while Giselle darted upstairs.

"I'll take him," I said, nodding after Ron. "You go tell Gerry Willis about Sam Dysart."

I left Mel standing on the front porch and hurried back to the driveway. Ron was in the Camaro, doing his best to get out of my deliberate automotive squeeze play. I walked up to the car and tapped on the driver's window, held up my badge, and waited until he rolled the window down.

"Got a minute?"

He looked at me and shook his head. I was a cop. He naturally assumed that made me dumb as a stump. I didn't want to do anything to disabuse him of that notion.

"I don't have to talk to you without one of my parents and/or my attorney in on the discussion," he said.

"Wait a minute," I said. "Are you invoking your Miranda rights when I haven't even said anything to you? I just wanted to talk to you about the Janie's House situation, but if you want to be Mirandized, then you must have reason to believe you're under suspicion in that incident."

"Aren't I?" He was an arrogant piece of work. He backed up again. This time his bumper dinged the one on the Mercedes.

"Hey," I said. "That's my car. You bump it again, there'll be trouble."

"Then move it out of the way so I can go."

He said it like he was accustomed to giving orders and having them obeyed. Mel, having made short work of talking to Gerry Willis, appeared at my side and took up a position just to the left of the Camaro's front bumper, holding up her iPhone. She didn't have to tell me that the video app was running. I already knew.

Ron wrenched on the steering wheel, slammed the Camaro into reverse, and stepped on the gas. This time he bumped the Mercedes hard enough to set off the alarm. Then he went forward enough to ram Gizzy's Acura too, setting off that alarm as well. In another time or two, he might have gotten loose, but by then Mel had joined me.

"If you do that again," I warned him, "I'm placing you under arrest for assault with a deadly weapon."

"You and who else, old man?" he demanded. Then he rammed the Mercedes one more time, just for good measure.

I reached in through the open window and tried to grab him. But the car sped back fast enough that all I got was a handful of tracksuit. He slipped out of the shirt like a snake shedding its skin. Then, leaving the Camaro still running, he slid across the seat and charged out through the door on the passenger side of the car.

As he took off, I saw him reach back

to pick up something from the passenger seat. For a sick moment, I thought it might be a weapon. He paused, as if considering his options, then ran off down the driveway, loping along at a speed that would have left me in the dust twenty years ago. But not Mel Soames. She runs every day—every single day—and she can run my socks off. I'm sure Ron Miller was counting on being able to outrun me, but he never anticipated that the suit-clad, high-heeled woman standing next to the front bumper of his car would kick off her pumps and take after him like a shot in her stocking feet.

Knowing my gimpy knees would make it impossible to keep pace, I switched off the ignition in the Camaro, grabbed the keys to that, and clambered into the Mercedes. I knew I couldn't keep up with either Mel or Ron, but I could sure as hell outdrive them. I turned off the alarm, pulled a U-turn, and went after them in hot pursuit.

At the end of the driveway, Ron paused long enough to throw something Frisbee-like up into the tall laurel hedge that lined both sides of the drive, then he darted off across the street and headed into the capitol campus.

Had it been a half hour later, people would have been streaming out of their office buildings. As it was, the path in front of him was relatively deserted. So was the path in front of Mel. And that slight pause was all she needed to close the gap between them to within that magic fifteen-foot margin.

"Police," she shouted. "Stop or I'll use my Taser."

I saw the jerky image of the bright red laser aiming light appear on Ron Miller's back. He didn't stop, but Mel had warned him once, and one warning is all punks like that get. She pressed the switch on her Taser, and Ron fell to the ground, flopping spastically to the concrete sidewalk and howling in outrage. By then Mel was on top of him, handcuffs in hand.

"Your arm," she ordered. "Give me your arm."

I slammed on the brakes, left the Mercedes sitting idling in the middle of the street, and ran to help. I could see that the spasm from the first Taser shock was starting to fade. By the time I reached them, Mel had one of Ron's hands in the cuffs and was struggling to grab the other while he tried desperately to buck her off. I reached into the melee, grabbed his free wrist with one paw, and handed it over to her. Then I grabbed Mel's Taser.

"Be still," I ordered, "or I'll Taser you again."

"Get off me, you crazy bitch!" he exclaimed. "You're hurting me. What's this all about? I wasn't really going to hit you with the car. Can't you guys take a joke?"

That's when I saw the scratches on his bare arms, scratches that were a couple of days old. That's when I knew for sure we had him.

"It's no joke," I said. "What did you throw up into the hedge back there?"

"Nothing," he said. "You made that up."

I could hear the sound of sirens. Someone had used their cell phone to report a disturbance. A squad car with a Capitol Police insignia was first on the scene. I was more than happy to have a local cop presence. I sure as hell didn't want to have to throw the guy into the backseat of my Mercedes.

A uniformed campus cop with a name badge that said OFFICER MARGARET WOOD leaped out of her squad car. "What's going on?" she demanded.

Mel stood up, straightened her rumpled suit, dusted her hands, and produced her ID wallet.

"Book Mr. Miller here on assault with a deadly weapon and resisting for starters," she said.

Seeing Mel standing there barefoot, wearing torn panty hose and with two bleeding knees, you'd have thought that she'd have a hard time commanding respect. She didn't.

"Help me haul him to his feet," she said.

"Yes, ma'am," Officer Wood said, and the two of them did just that.

"When you book him, be sure they get photos of those scratches on his arms," I said. "They could be important, because there are likely to be other charges to follow those."

Officer Wood looked at me, standing there with not a scratch on me. Then she looked at Mel—a one-raised-eyebrow look that was evidently an understandable question even though she said nothing aloud.

"My partner," Mel explained.

Officer Wood took charge of Ron Miller and loaded him into the backseat of her squad car. I followed them to the car in time to hear Ron muttering something about police brutality. His snide old-man comment to me still rankled. It sounded like something an immature seventh grader would say. It also sounded a lot like some of the text messages that had been sent to Josh Deeson.

"Too bad, tough guy," I said. "You were taken down by a girl, fair and square."

"What's this all about, anyway?" he wanted to know.

"It started out being about some text messages," I said. "But now it's turned into something else—like arson and murder. Just to let you know, you may have set fire to all the computers in

Janie's House, but it's too little, too late. We'd already copied everything on the hard drives just to be on the safe side."

He gave me a snarly stare and then turned away. I slammed the door shut and then walked back to the laurel hedges. They were flat on top, densely leafed and at least eight feet tall. Mel trailed after me as I attempted to peer up through the leaves.

"What are you looking for?" Mel asked.

"He threw something up there," I said. "Didn't you see it? He tossed something up into the hedge right here, just before he crossed the street."

Mel shook her head. "I stepped on a piece of gravel and looked down at my feet. When I looked back up, I had gained a lot of ground on him and I didn't know why."

I went back over to Officer Wood, who was on her radio and in the process of explaining to her sergeant that she was transporting someone to the Olympia city lockup. I waited until she finished.

"I need a ladder," I said. "Do you know where I could find one?"

"Someone from Physical Plant," she said. "How tall?"

"Tall enough to see the top of that laurel hedge."

She nodded and got back on her radio. An Econoline van with state license plates, a uniformed driver, and two kinds of ladders arrived within a matter of minutes, just after Officer Wood drove away in her squad car. By then, the interested crowd of onlookers had dissipated. Interestingly enough, among the people who had gathered around, I had seen no one I recognized from the governor's mansion. Given the proximity to all the excitement, that was a little surprising.

"Where do you want the ladder?" the guy from the van asked. I pointed, and he unfolded it where I thought it needed to be.

"Do you want me to do it?" Mel asked.

Ron's comment continued to play inside my head: "You and who else, old man?"

"No, I will," I said, speaking to Mel far

more harshly than she deserved. "You don't know what we're looking for."

I wasn't sure I did, either. I knew it was small and round and had flown through the air like a Frisbee. I went up and down the ladder three different times. Going up was bad enough. It hurt like hell, but it was doable. Coming down was a killer. Mel watched me go up and down the ladder the first time. As I wiped away tears, she shook her head and said nothing. Then, walking away and leaving me to it, she activated her iPhone and began making arrangements to have Ron's vehicle towed to the crime lab.

Finally my search paid off. It lay there on the carefully trimmed flat surface of the laurel hedge. At first glance it looked like a tiny coil of wire with a protuberance on one side. I grabbed it, slipped it into an evidence bag, and then climbed back down with my prize.

I handed the evidence bag over to Mel. "We need to document this," I said when I was finally able to speak again.

"What is it?" Mel asked, frowning as she peered at the bracelet through the glassine bag. "Why would Miller bother throwing away a useless coil of wire like this?"

That's when I realized Mel hadn't been with Ardith and Kenny Broward on the drive back to Packwood.

"It's not wire," I told her. "Unless I'm sadly mistaken, we've just found Rachel Camber's elephant-hair bracelet."

CHAPTER 26

While we waited for the tow truck to come collect Ron Miller's Camaro, I got on the phone with Ross Connors and asked for a time line on our requests for search warrants.

"Judge Reston tells me the one for Ron Miller's vehicle is not a problem since he tried to use it in the assault on Mel. Getting a warrant to search his home, which is actually his parents' home, however, is going to be a bit more challenging. You do know about Ron Miller's parents, don't you?" he asked.

"Let's just say I've seen the gates to their compound, and I know that a couple of years back they dropped a cool seventy-five thousand bucks to keep their fair-haired boy from facing arson charges."

"Yes," Ross said, "they certainly did. Ronald Miller, Senior, is a trial lawyer who specializes in beating up pharmaceutical companies for fun and profit. Mrs. Miller has recently decamped for what she hopes are greener pastures. I have a feeling Mr. Miller is going to take a dim view of having his son booked into a jail of any kind. By the time that happens, Daddy Miller will have one of his legal-beagle pals standing by to bail him out. If we're hoping to search Ron's room for additional evidence of any wrongdoing, we're going to need to have a very solid basis of probable cause, more than just a few scratches on his arms."

"We've got something more," I said. "While Ron was trying to outrun Mel, I saw him throw something up into the governor's laurel hedge. I just dragged it down from there. I'm pretty sure it's

Rachel Camber's elephant-hair bracelet."

"Rachel Camber," Ross said. "Of course, the dead girl from Packwood."

"Yes, I believe Ron was trying to smuggle the bracelet out of the governor's mansion just as we got there. Giselle Longmire, the governor's older daughter, is Ron Junior's girlfriend. There's a good chance that whatever Ron is mixed up with, Gizzy is, too."

"Oh, my," Ross said, shaking his head sadly. "What the hell's going on here? These are kids who should be growing up to be pillars of the community. I'm sure that's what their parents intended, but it sounds like they've turned out to be a bunch of delinquents."

"Thugs is more like it," I said. "And the worst kind of thugs—spoiled-brat thugs who are accustomed to having power and money and who expect to get their way no matter what."

"What's your plan?" Ross asked.

"First we're going to try talking to Giselle to see if we can get her to tell us what she knows, but I think it's a good bet that Governor Longmire won't let us anywhere near her."

Ross was quiet for a long time. For a moment I thought maybe he had hung up. "I'm not so sure about that," he said. "You and I know something about this kind of thing, Beau. We've both been betrayed by loved ones who made all the wrong choices. The fallout that came later almost destroyed us.

"When it comes to politics, Marsha Longmire and I are miles apart, but she's been a good governor, and I hate to see her torn apart by what's about to happen. Before you try to question Giselle, let me talk to Marsha and see what I can do. She may just surprise you. What exactly are we talking about here?"

I ticked off my suspicions one by one. "I believe Gizzy and Ron both played a part in the cyber bullying that went on with Josh Deeson before his suicide, including staging that film clip that we found on Josh's phone. The presence of Rachel Camber's bracelet, one her parents told me she wore every day, gives us a possible link between Ron

Miller and her murder. Last but not least is the fatal arson fire at Janie's House this morning. I think one or both of them burned down the building in hopes of frying whatever incriminating evidence was on the computers."

"Which Todd already has," Ross said.

"Yes, but Ron couldn't have known that. If Gizzy and Ron really were together all night—as they told her parents they were—then Gizzy was directly involved in the arson. If they weren't together, and she's providing an alibi for him, she's still rendering criminal assistance."

"Okay," Ross said. "Give me a couple of minutes. I'll get back to you."

I closed my phone and turned to Mel. I had heard her phone ring while Ross and I were talking.

"Thanks for letting me know," she said as she ended her call.

"For letting you know what?"

"That was Captain Hoyt," Mel said. "Sam Dysart didn't make it. He suffered another stroke in the ambulance on the way to the hospital, so he's out of the picture as far as any information or criminal charges are concerned. But WSP investigators managed to track down the serial number on the watch. Sam Dysart bought that replacement watch just last week, the one Josh was wearing when he died. The one Gerry Willis gave Josh was engraved with Josh's initials. The one found on Josh's body had no engraving. Dysart also paid for the watch to be gift wrapped. With any kind of luck, we will find some of the gift wrapping in the trash at Dysart's house."

"But why did he do it?" I asked. "Was the watch a thoughtful gift, a bribe, or what?"

"Since they're both dead, we'll probably never know," Mel said. "But as of right now, you and I are off the Dysart case. The Olympia PD Sex Crimes unit is on it. They'll search Dysart's house. They'll also interview the other kids in the chess club, past and present. Joan believes there's a good chance Sam Dysart used his position of authority to victimize more than just one kid."

"Me, too," I said grimly. "If that's the case, the school district is going to be liable big-time. But none of this is going to help Gerry Willis. His grandson is dead, and he isn't coming back. One way or another, Sam Dysart's relationship with Josh Deeson contributed to the despair that resulted in his suicide."

Mel nodded. "I agree, and that's exactly what I told Joan—that even if we don't end up having to prove all of this in a court of law, we need to have enough forensic evidence to be able to give Josh's family rock-solid answers about what really happened to him— with both the cyber bullying and the sexual exploitation. The truth may be uncomfortable, but it seems to me that knowing is better than not knowing."

My phone rang. It was Ross Connors calling back.

"All right," he said, "here's the deal. I've spoken to Governor Longmire and laid out the situation. I didn't make any specific promises about the benefits of Giselle turning state's evidence, but Marsha's a smart woman and she gets it. She understands that if Gizzy talks to you before you talk to Ron, her cooperation will be well received. I think she also believes that, given the opportunity, Ron would jump at taking a plea agreement in order to testify against Gizzy. She wants to talk to you first."

Those elusive pronouns again. "Gizzy wants to talk to us?"

"No, Governor Longmire and Mr. Willis want to talk to you. She says there's a patio out back by the kitchen at the governor's mansion. You're to meet them there."

"When?"

"Now. As soon as possible."

Mel and I went straight there. The patio outside the kitchen wasn't a patio so much as a covered arbor where whatever cook was on duty could step outside for a quick smoke and still be out of the rain. We found the governor and her husband sitting across from each other on the benches of a rough redwood picnic table. There was a large crystal ashtray on the table between them. Marsha was smoking; Gerry was not.

Marsha had been outraged earlier that morning when she had caught me in the act of lifting Josh's dirty clothes out of the hamper. Then she had been angered to the point of fury. Now she looked haggard and beaten down—defeated rather than angry. Marsha gestured for Mel and me to join them at the table, then she picked up her pack of cigarettes and held them in our direction.

I gave up smoking a long time before I gave up drinking. Cigarettes don't have much of a hold on me anymore. Mel stopped smoking a relatively short time ago, a matter of months rather than years. When the proffered pack came close to her, I saw Mel stiffen with temptation before she shook her head and murmured, "Thanks, but no thanks."

In her torn panty hose and dirt-smudged suit, Mel didn't look like someone ready to have a private audience with a sitting governor, but I don't believe Marsha paid the slightest bit of attention to anyone's looks. Her focus was elsewhere.

"Which one of you found the watch?" she asked.

I raised my hand. "I did," I said.

Marsha shook her head ruefully. "It

was smart of Ross to have you check through the trash. I guess we need to be more careful about what we toss in the garbage."

Since her comment didn't appear to be a question, I decided that no response was required.

"Show me what you found in the hedge," Marsha said.

That was an official command, and I complied immediately. I reached into my pocket and pulled out the evidence bag that contained Rachel Camber's bracelet. I handed it over to Marsha. She studied it briefly, then handed it back to me with an almost imperceptible shrug.

"I saw it earlier," she admitted. "It was there in Gizzy's underwear drawer along with the watch. At the time I had no idea what it was and didn't understand the significance. If I had, I might have tried to get rid of it, too, the same way I tried to get rid of the watch."

"You?" I stammered. "You're the one who tossed out the watch?"

Marsha looked me in the eye and nodded. "Yes," she said. "I willfully attempted to conceal evidence in an active homicide investigation. When I realized Josh had been coming and going without my knowledge, I wondered if my girls had been pulling the same stunt. One bad apple and all that. Zoe told Gerry just a little while ago that she and Gizzy have been letting themselves and their friends in and out that way for years, long before Josh ever came to live with us.

"On a hunch, I decided to stage an impromptu search-and-destroy mission of my own in both girls' rooms. I found that thing hidden in Gizzy's room," she said, nodding toward the bracelet, "along with a watch that seemed to be a duplicate of Josh's. By then we had already found Josh's body. I couldn't understand why there would be two watches instead of one, but it seemed to me that finding it in Gizzy's room meant that she was involved in what was going on, one way or the other."

Marsha paused and shrugged again. "What was I supposed to do? I'm a mother. I wanted to protect my child, so I tossed it. This morning, after Gizzy didn't come home last night, I mentioned to Monica that she might want to do the same thing—take a look in Gizzy's room at her father's house. This is what she found."

Marsha reached into her pocket, pulled out a thumb drive, and placed it in Mel's outstretched hand. "Monica dropped it off with Gerry while I was at the airport picking up my sister-in-law."

"The same clip?" I asked.

Marsha swallowed before she answered. "I wish," she said. "That one was faked. It's the same girl, but I believe this one is real. Gerry and I watched it together this afternoon. As soon as we saw what was on it, we knew we'd have to turn it in to the authorities. I was hoping to conceal Gizzy's involvement for a couple of days longer—long enough to get through Josh's funeral tomorrow afternoon. I wanted to give the out-of-town relatives a chance to go back home before we have our coming-to-God session with Gizzy about it. Obviously it's going to have to happen a whole lot sooner than that."

Marsha paused long enough to grind

out the remains of her cigarette in the ashtray and to draw a deep breath. Her hand lay limply next to the ashtray, as though she didn't have the physical strength to move it. Gerry Willis reached out, took her hand in both of his, and sat there looking at her, nodding encouragingly. They were in this mess together, and they would deal with it together.

"I'll be tendering my resignation as governor at a press conference immediately following Josh's funeral," Marsha continued. When no one made any comment to that announcement, she smiled wanly and continued.

"That's always the best time to come out with bad news—Friday afternoon, preferably after most of the news shows have put their evening newscasts to bed. I'll be saying that I'm resigning in the aftermath of a family tragedy to focus on my family. That will be true regardless of how deeply involved Gizzy was in everything that's happened. If you decide to lodge formal charges against me for tampering with evidence, that will be up to you and, of course, to the attorney general."

With that, Marsha plucked a cell phone out of her pocket and dialed a number.

"Hi, Liz," she said to her chief of staff. "I believe Giselle is upstairs in her room. Would you please tap on her bedroom door and ask her to join Gerry and me out on the kitchen patio? Thanks."

Mel waited until Governor Longmire closed her phone. "Is your daughter aware that Ron has been taken into custody?"

Marsha shrugged. "I'm not sure. If any of the other kids realize it, they might have sent her a message by now, but we haven't mentioned it to her or to anyone else."

"All right," Mel said.

We spent most of the next two minutes sitting there in uneasy silence. The birds that lived in the greenery around the governor's mansion were talking up a storm while the four of us had nothing to say. Eventually the kitchen door opened and Giselle Longmire stepped out onto the patio.

I had voted for Marsha Gray Longmire twice, both times she ran for governor, and both times she won. I had done it more for old times' sake—because she and I were both Ballard Beavers—than out of any particular party loyalty. I have to say, however, that I was never prouder of her conduct in the governor's office than in her decision to leave it. And the First Husband's behavior was amazing in its own right. To see him disregarding his own loss in favor of helping Marsha deal with hers is something I'll never forget and something I hope to emulate should I ever be called upon to do so. It offered mute testimony to the healing power of love between two people and how it can sustain us when everything else we hold dear is ripped away.

Gizzy appeared among us dressed a little more conservatively than she had been earlier at Janie's House. She approached the picnic table tossing her hair and smiling confidently, totally unaware that the damage she and Ron Miller had wreaked on others was about to come back and nail them both.

"You wanted to see me?" she asked cheerfully.

When Gizzy caught a glimpse of Mel and me sitting there at the picnic table with her parents, she hesitated. Her air of unquestioning confidence faltered a little.

"Mom," she protested. "These people are cops. What are they doing here?"

"They came to talk to you, Giselle," Marsha said.

It was June. Morning cloud cover had burned off during the course of the afternoon. Outside temperatures hovered in the low eighties, but Governor Longmire's voice was pure ice.

"I've spoken to both your father and to Monica," Marsha added. "They both agreed that due to the seriousness of the situation they would abide by my decision, and I have made it."

"What situation?" Gizzy asked, feigning innocence.

"Ron has been taken into custody," Marsha announced, making no effort to soften the blow. Gizzy's sudden sharp intake of breath showed it had landed.

"Initial charges have to do with assaulting a police officer and resisting arrest," Marsha continued, "but my understanding is that there are far more serious charges coming—something about the murder of a girl named Rachel Camber and about the fire at Janie's House last night."

"I don't know anyone named Rachel Camber," Gizzy protested. It was a half-hearted denial. I didn't buy it; neither did anyone else.

"She was from Packwood," Mel inserted quietly. "You may have known her as Amber Wilson."

Giselle Longmire suddenly looked stricken, but only because the seriousness of her situation was finally beginning to dawn on her. "You mean she's really dead?"

"Yes," Marsha replied coldly. "Like on the video clip I found hidden in your underwear drawer, as opposed to the pretend dead in the video we found on Josh's cell phone."

Gizzy stood very still and said nothing.

"Right this moment the authorities don't know what all is involved, who did what, or how much you participated," Marsha continued. "If we're lucky, you'll be considered an accessory after the fact. I'm telling you straight out that though you may be my daughter, you are not above the law. You could do yourself some good and speed the process considerably if you'd simply tell these investigators what you know."

Gizzy looked at her mother incredulously. "You think I should just talk to them? Shouldn't I, like, have a lawyer present or something?"

Marsha stood up.

"That's entirely up to you," she said. "If you want to ask for an attorney, that's certainly your prerogative, but if you want our support—Gerry's and my support, your father's and Monica's support—then you'll grow up and start taking responsibility for whatever part you played in all this.

"That means you need to come clean and to tell the truth. If you're not prepared to do that, you must understand that your father and I are fully prepared to cut you loose. Yes, we love you, but don't believe everything they tell you about unconditional love. There are conditions. We refuse to squander anything more on someone who has no respect for us or for our values.

"If you demand an attorney, fine, but be prepared to have one that is appointed for you by the courts. We won't be paying for it; neither will your father or Monica. Gerry and I took Josh into our home thinking we'd be able to give him a better life than what he'd had before. Your behavior and that of your friends took that chance away from him. Zoe has always looked up to you, but she's evidently known all along what you and Ron were doing to Josh. She finally told Gerry about that ugly texting nonsense this afternoon. She kept quiet about it out of misplaced loyalty to you, but the secret has been eating away at her for months, tearing her apart. So you've destroyed Josh, you've harmed your sister, and you've ruined me as well. As of tomorrow at this time, I will no longer be governor—all because of you."

"But . . ." Gizzy began.

"No buts!" Marsha mowed over her

daughter's attempted protest and stormed on. "You need to figure this out for yourself, Gizzy. You can cooperate with the cops in the feeble hope that your cooperation will buy you mercy from a judge or jury somewhere down the line. Or you can deny everything and trust that Ron Miller won't sell you down the river. If I were you, though, I don't think I'd count on that. We're all prepared to stick by you, but only if you do the right thing. If not? We're done."

Stunned with disbelief, Gizzy Longmire stared at her mother as Marsha stood up. Then Marsha reached down and helped her husband to his feet.

"Let's go," she said to him, pocketing her cigarettes. "We need to get back to our guests. We've left them alone long enough."

"But wait," Gizzy wailed as Marsha and Gerry started toward the house. "What's going to happen to me?"

Marsha stopped long enough to look at her.

"I have no idea," Governor Longmire said, shaking her head. "It's in your hands now. It seems to me you should have thought about that a long time ago."

On Gerry's way past his stepdaughter he paused long enough to lay a consoling hand on her shoulder. "Your mother's right, you know," he said softly. "If you want us to stick by you, we will, but you've crossed over the line, betrayed our trust. It's time for you to do the right thing."

With that, Governor Longmire and Gerry Willis disappeared into the kitchen, leaving Gizzy standing there dumbstruck watching them go.

CHAPTER 27

Once the kitchen door closed behind Gerry and Marsha, what followed was something my mother would have called "a pregnant pause." In all my years as a cop, I had never seen a suspect's parents step up the way Marsha and Gerry just had. And the fact that the other set of parental units was evidently on board and in total agreement with this unflinching bit of tough love was even more astonishing. In my experience, a crisis of this kind in divorced families usually devolves into a circular firing squad of finger-pointing.

As for Gizzy? I didn't know if she would go ahead and demand an attorney, as she had every right to do with or without parental approval, or if she would run for the hills.

"Is it true?" she asked finally. "Is Ron really under arrest?"

Mel nodded. "Yes, he's really under arrest. Usually, in these situations, the suspect who talks first is the one who gets the best deal. Not that Mr. Beaumont and I can make deals," Mel added, "because we can't."

"How bad will it be for me?" Gizzy asked.

Mel shrugged. "I have no idea," she answered. "That depends on what you've done, how much you know, and how much you can help us."

"Are you placing me under arrest?"

"Not right now. We're only taking you in for questioning."

"Will I have to walk through the house in handcuffs?"

Mel's handcuffs had disappeared much earlier in the afternoon when Ron Miller was locked in that capitol cop's squad car. I still had mine. We could have used those.

"We'll go around the outside of the house instead of through it so as not to disturb your parents' guests," Mel said. "But I don't think handcuffs are necessary at this time, do you?"

"No," Gizzy said. "They're not."

Mel took Gizzy's arm and started to lead her around the side of the house, back to the driveway. I was going to follow, but then thought better of it.

"I need to do one more thing," I said. "I'll meet you at the car."

I ducked back into the house through the kitchen.

When I stepped inside, the cook stopped what she was doing, placed both hands on her hips, glared at me, and shook her head.

"It's beginning to feel like Grand Central Station around here," she said.

"Sorry," I mumbled. "I need a word with Mr. Willis."

I found him by the bar in the living room, pouring himself a generous Scotch. With his recent surgery I wondered if that was wise, but that was his business, not mine.

"There's one more thing I need to tell you," I said. "I didn't want to bring it up in front of Marsha."

"What?" Gerry sounded bleak, as though he could hardly stand one more smidgeon of bad news.

"Sam Dysart is dead," I said.

Gerry's face brightened. "Hallelujah," he murmured. "How?"

"He had a stroke. The first one evidently happened several days ago. He had been lying alone on the floor in a cottage out behind his house ever since. Mel and I found him there when we went to his house to talk to him this afternoon. We called 911. He was in the ambulance and being transported when he suffered another stroke and died. We have reason to believe he purchased the watch Josh was wearing when he died.

"Mel and I have been ordered off the case. Joan Hoyt of the Washington State Patrol says the Olympia PD Sex Crimes unit will be taking over that aspect of the investigation. Once the DNA evidence is processed, we'll try to let you know the findings, but it won't be our responsibility to take it any further."

"If Dysart really did molest Josh, I hope he rots in hell," Gerry Willis said fervently. "But we're out of it, Mr. Beaumont. Yes, I want to know for sure, but beyond that, whatever he did or didn't do to Josh is over. I don't want to know anything more about it, and it's no one else's business."

"But the school district may be liable for bringing him on board," I objected.

"That's none of my concern. If there are other kids and other parents who want to make an issue of this, fine, but we're not bringing up his relationship with Josh with anyone. The poor boy is dead. Surely we can allow him that much privacy—that much respect."

"Yes, sir," I said. "I'll see to it."

And so will Ross Connors, I thought. *It's the least we can do.*

I let myself out the front door and joined Mel and Gizzy in the S-550. Gizzy was sitting in the backseat crying quietly when I got in behind the wheel. It didn't matter to me if her tears were due to fear or remorse. The fact that she was shaken enough to be crying seemed like a good sign.

I drove them to the Special Homicide Squad A office and stayed long enough to escort them into a tiny interview room. I turned on the room's video recording system and made sure it was up and running. I gave Mel an earpiece that allowed two-way communication from inside the interview room to anyone outside in the hallway. When I waved good-bye, Mel's parting words to me were simple.

"Bring back pizza and sodas."

Fair enough. We were conducting an updated version of the carrot-and-stick routine. In this case, Gizzy's parents were the stick and Mel—sweet-talking Mel—was going to be wielding the good cop's most effective carrot and the interview room's official secret weapon—pepperoni pizza. As I walked away, I heard Mel launch into the obligatory process of reading Giselle Longmire her rights.

There had been some necessary adjustments in our original plan, but we were also still on track with our general strategy. Mel would interview Gizzy while I tackled Ron Miller.

To that end, I drove straight to Olympia PD. When the guy at Olympia's lockup facility told me Ron Miller had lawyered up and wasn't speaking to anyone, I can't say I was surprised. Ron was accustomed to having his parents haul out their checkbooks and fix whatever mess he had gotten himself into. They had done it at least once before by paying for that burned-out boathouse. I was sure Ronald Darrington Miller was sitting in his cell right then, convinced that by tomorrow morning one or the other of his parents would come bail him out and everything would be fine. I, for one, was pretty sure that on this particular occasion, for the first time in Ron's highly privileged life, that strategy wasn't going to work. For one thing, I had firsthand knowledge of something Ron Miller and his parents didn't know—Marsha and Sid Longmire had had balls enough to throw their daughter under the bus. When they did that, they threw Ron there as well.

I couldn't interview Ron, but as long as I was at Olympia PD, I figured it wouldn't hurt to touch base with whoever was working the Janie's House arson case.

"They're not here," the desk sergeant told me when I showed him my badge and ID and asked my question. "They're out in the field doing a next-of-kin notification."

"For the victim from the fire?"

The sergeant hesitated for a moment before he nodded. "His name is Owen Wetmore, age thirty-five. Our investigators don't know if he's a victim, a participant, or both. When they recovered the body, his ID was in his back pocket, charred but still legible. His parents are off in Europe on some kind of a three-week cruise. The detectives went to Seattle to talk to the grandmother."

"At thirty-five, Owen is too old to be one of Janie's House's homeless clients," I said.

The sergeant nodded. "My understanding is that he's one of the house-parents."

Someone with keys, I thought.

I gave the sergeant a business card. "Have one of the detectives give me a call as soon as they get back," I said. "I may have some information for them."

"It could be late," he counseled. "It's a long way up to Seattle and back."

"Don't worry," I said. "It's going to be a long night for everyone concerned."

I stopped by the local Domino's franchise and picked up a large pizza and three Cokes before I headed back to the office. It was summer. The night was warm. The fragrance of pizza in the car reminded me of summertime parties I had attended long ago, back when I was Gizzy's age. It saddened me to think that this was most likely the last bite of freshly baked pizza Giselle Longmire would encounter for a very long time.

Back at headquarters, Ross Connors was standing outside the interview room watching through the glass. I was carrying the pizza in one hand and a cardboard multiple-cup container in the other. I set the load down on a nearby table and handed Ross a slice of pizza on a fistful of napkins.

"How's it going?" I asked.

"Mel's working her pretty good," Ross said, biting the tip off his piece of pizza. "What the hell were these kids thinking?"

"They weren't thinking," I said. Then I tapped on the door to the interview room, opened it, and held the door open with my toe long enough to let myself inside.

"Your pizza has arrived," I said with a flourish. After depositing the food on the interview table, I took my own drink and pizza and rejoined Ross outside in the hallway. Mel was clearly making progress with Gizzy. My hanging around and horning in on the discussion might have been enough of a distraction to mute her effectiveness.

"She said Ron and a pal of his came up with the idea of hiring Rachel to make videos," Ross said. "Gizzy was the one who thought it would be funny to send one of them to Josh."

"Videos—plural?" I asked. "As in more than one?"

Ross nodded. "A money-making venture. According to Gizzy, they did their filming in one of the outbuildings—an old caretaker's cottage—at Ron's family home out on North Cooper Point Road."

"She was in on it from the beginning?"

Ross nodded sadly. "They lured Rachel here over the weekend with the promise of making another four hundred bucks by reprising her phony death scenes."

"Would Ron Miller's film partner happen to be a guy named Owen Wetmore, by any chance?" I asked.

Ross shot me a look and nodded. He didn't ask me how I knew that, and I didn't tell him.

"Does Owen drive a green pickup truck?" I asked.

Ross nodded. "As a matter of fact, he does—a dark green Chevy Silverado."

Inside the room, Mel moved the pizza box aside and pushed a blue-lined notepad in front of Gizzy. "Write it all down," she said, handing her a pen. "When you're finished, sign it."

"All of it?" Gizzy asked faintly.

"All of it," Mel told her.

Mel stood up and stretched. Then she picked up another piece of pizza, came to the door, and knocked on it. We let her out.

Gizzy Longmire wrote her life-and-death essay for the better part of an hour. By the time she finally finished it, signed it, and handed it over to Mel, Joan Hoyt had already obtained a search warrant for the Ronald Miller residence on North Cooper Point Road. After dropping Giselle off at Olympia PD for booking, we went there, too, where officers from the Washington State Patrol, along with the arson detectives from Olympia, were already in the process of executing the search warrant. On the sidelines an outraged Ronald Miller, Senior, and his rudely awakened attorney ranted and raved to no effect. They might be able to run roughshod over any and all comers in a courtroom, but crime scenes are cops' turf, not theirs.

And that's what this was. As soon as we stepped into the caretaker's cottage

I knew we had found the place where Rachel Camber had played her fictional role as well as her real one. The soiled mattress on the narrow cot in one corner of the room told the story of her imprisonment and death, as did the very expensive video equipment that still stood in the center of the room.

Ron Miller may have staged more than one phony snuff video, but someone had failed to give him the memo that, in real life, death isn't a pretty picture. When a body stops working, there are consequences in terms of bodily functions. Nothing in Ron Miller's life experience had taught him the necessity of cleaning up his own crap, and he hadn't done so in this case, either.

It took hours to process the scene. The same Washington State Patrol crime scene team that had come to Josh Deeson's bedroom appeared for a return engagement. They took photos dogged by Mel, who took her own photos while I cataloged each and every shot. By the time we finally left there to return to the Red Lion, the sky was starting to lighten. It was only four-thirty, but morning comes early in the Pacific Northwest at the start of summer.

We went back to our room and stripped off our clothing. Mel removed her makeup, and we both fell into bed. Mel was asleep instantly—the sleep of the just, as we call it. It took two Aleves and the better part of forty-five minutes before I was able to fall asleep, still hearing Ron's words echoing in my head: "You and who else, old man?"

CHAPTER 28

Much later it was the sound of Mel's key in the lock that woke me. She came into the sun-filled room carrying a tray loaded with a coffeepot, two cups, two salad plates with silverware, a pair of napkins, and an enormous bowl of cut-up fresh fruit—several different kinds of melon, raspberries, strawberries, and blueberries.

"Ready to sit up and take nourishment?" she asked. She looked great.

"What time is it?"

"Twelve-thirty."

"I guess we missed checkout time."

"I guess so," she agreed. "But we don't have much time. Ross expects us at Josh Deeson's funeral, which starts at two. He wants us there for the funeral and for the press conference afterward."

Ross is our boss, and an order is an order. I took two Aleves. I drank coffee. I ate fruit. Then I crawled out of bed, limped into the bathroom, and took a long hot shower.

Josh's simple service was accompanied by mountains of floral arrangements and was conducted in the open air on the lawn outside the governor's mansion. It was pretty much a standard funeral service. When the minister opened the microphone for comments, I was surprised to see Zoe Longmire slip out of her spot next to her mother and make her way to the podium.

Her words were simple and heartfelt. "Josh lived with our family," she said. "I'm sorry I didn't know him better. I'll miss him."

It was graceful. It was charming. It set the tone, and I guess I shouldn't have been surprised because Zoe, like Gizzy, is her mother's daughter.

Once Zoe sat down, a pimply-faced kid who said his name was Chipper Lawson stood up and talked about how Josh Deeson had helped him learn to play chess and that he was grateful. It cheered me to know that Josh had had at least one friend at Olympia High, someone who wasn't Sam Dysart. And I made a note to myself to pass Chipper's name along to the Sex Crimes guys in Olympia. If Dysart had made a habit of targeting socially needy kids, Chipper would have been another likely target.

There were several kids present, some of whom I recognized as having been at the scene of the Janie's House fire. The only one of those that I knew by name was Greg Alexander. Dressed in a white shirt and tie, he stood to one side after the graveside service, talking quietly with Zoe.

Of all the kids we had met in the past few days, Greg seemed the most upright. Considering his troubled family background, I knew he was coming from a long way behind go, but somehow I sensed that he was going to make something of himself no matter what.

Giselle had been arrested the night before, but because she had not yet been formally charged, her name had not made it into the papers. I would assume that people at the service were puzzled by her absence, but no one mentioned it in my hearing.

It was late in the afternoon when we finally trooped back to the governor's mansion where, flanked by Gerry Willis, Ross Connors, and Lieutenant Governor Roger Sikes, Governor Marsha Longmire stood in the shade of the mansion's front portico and faced an army of microphones and cameras.

The press release announcing the briefing had given no indication of what was about to happen and didn't contain any advance notice of the governor's remarks. All it said was that she would be making an important announcement and that she would take no questions.

I watched Marsha Gray Longmire take her place behind the microphones with her customary grace and with her head held high. She waited for silence, then cleared her throat and began to speak.

"As you know, our family has been beset by tragedies this week, not only by the death of our ward, my husband's grandson, Josh Deeson, but also by learning that our daughter Giselle has been taken into custody here in Olympia due to her part in some illegal activities that went on without her parents' knowledge or approval. We are deeply saddened by the harm that her actions may have inflicted on other people and other families.

"In view of that, I can no longer function in this office. I thereby resign the post of governor, effective immediately. I have presented my letter of resignation to Attorney General Ross Connors and have notified Lieutenant Governor Sikes of my intention. My family will be moving out of the governor's mansion as soon as those details can be arranged. In the meantime, I hope you will respect our need for privacy as we deal with these appalling events. Thank you."

With that, she turned away. Then both she and Gerry Willis disappeared through the mansion's massive front doors, closing them firmly. By the time the group of stunned journalists rumbled to life, she was gone, and newly installed Governor Roger Sikes, with Ross Connors's capable help, was left to deal with the media fallout.

"Come on," Mel whispered in my ear. "Let's check out of the hotel and go home."

And we did.

"I asked Ross for next week off," Mel said as we rode the elevator up at Belltown Terrace. "We need to go to Texas. We can fly commercial or we can bite the bullet and take the jet. Which is it?"

I thought about the money the jet would burn, flying cross-country like that. Then I thought about my limping through airport concourses, getting on and off car-rental shuttles, and sitting for hours with my knees jammed up against the seat in front of me, while the guy seated there flew in full-recline mode.

Based on that, it wasn't a tough decision.

"We'll take the jet," I said.

We flew out of Boeing Field twenty-four hours later on a Citation X. On the flight Mel and I spent most of the time talking about what the rest of the state was just now learning—that a group of supposedly well-respected "good" kids, terminally bored "good" kids, had gone bad and transformed themselves into a bunch of hoodlums. Giselle Longmire and Ronald Darrington Miller weren't the only ones who would be facing charges.

Owen Wetmore, one of the Janie's House houseparents, had been a full partner in Ronald Miller's filming venture, and they had used Owen's keys and security code to come and go at will. According to Gizzy, as soon as Josh died, Ron realized that the subsequent investigation might lead back to him. He had decided on his own that Rachel had to go. And then, when Owen started freaking out afterward, Ron decided that both Owen and the Janie's House computers had to go as well.

Gizzy hadn't been present when Rachel died and she hadn't lit the match that started the Janie's House fire, but she had driven the getaway car. She had known about the planned fire in advance and had done nothing to stop it. I thought it was likely that she would face homicide charges of some kind in regard to Rachel Camber's death as well as Owen Wetmore's. She also had admitted stealing Josh's original watch—the one from Gerry Willis—just to bug him, just because she could. That day after the Janie's House fire, Ron had gone to the governor's mansion intent on retrieving what they both thought of as their trophies. They had been shocked to find the watch missing. He'd had the bracelet in hand and was on his way to Gizzy's father's house to pick up the thumb drive when Mel and I took him into custody.

It seemed to me that Gizzy and Ron deserved each other in every sense of the word—a twisted match made in hell rather than heaven. So far the judge had denied requests for bail from both defense attorneys. That had to come as a huge surprise, to Ron especially. For the first time in his life his parents' position in the community wasn't working for him. A denial of bail was only the first step in the process. Mel and I both knew that legal proceedings against the pair would take months.

We had obtained Giselle Longmire's confession without striking any kind of plea agreement. We had every reason to believe that her confession would withstand legal scrutiny and that they both would be going to prison for a very long time.

Between now and then, both families were living in an ongoing media nightmare. I wondered if Marsha and Gerry's marriage would survive all the strife. Gizzy's actions had torn holes in the fabric of their marriage that would probably never be mended.

As for Josh? The smoking gun had been found not in his cell phone records but in Sam Dysart's. A call from his phone to the governor's mansion landline had evidently summoned Josh on that out-of-character jog that had so puzzled his grandfather. Olympia police officers, executing a search warrant, had found the torn gift-wrapping paper and the box that had held the replacement watch we had found on Josh's wrist. Dysart had gone to great lengths to track down that particular model. I like to think Josh went to his death expecting that his grandfather would believe the ruse that the watch on his arm was the one he had given him.

Was the watch a bribe on Dysart's part in exchange for sex? Or was replacing Josh's missing Seiko a thoughtful gift? So far there was no clear answer to those questions. Regardless, Dysart's relationship with Josh had crossed the line. He had further victimized a kid who had already suffered far more than he should have. I was glad the man was dead. Dysart's death spared Gerry Willis at least one painful legal proceeding. And it probably kept Chipper Lawson, the pimply-faced chess player at Josh's funeral, from being Dysart's next victim.

"All of this makes me incredibly thankful that I don't have to be in high school anymore," I told Mel.

She nodded. "And it makes me grateful I never had kids," she said. "Kids today do stuff we never *considered* doing."

"Not all of them," I said, thinking about Greg Alexander, a kid who, despite a troubled home life, would one way or another make it where he was going.

A bell rang in the aircraft's cabin. We were starting our descent into Beaumont. It was time to raise our seats to their full upright position and fasten our seat belts.

When I had called my cousin in Texas to let her know our plans, I originally told her that we would rent a car. She wouldn't hear of it.

"Someone will be there to pick you up," she had said firmly.

Three and a half hours after leaving Seattle, when we landed at Southeast Texas Regional Airport, a shiny black Suburban limo was waiting for us next to the Fixed Base Operation. The Suburban drove out onto the tarmac to meet our plane. When the driver stepped out of the car next to the plane, he was wearing a gray suit with a starched white shirt, a bright blue tie, a gray felt Stetson, and a pair of highly polished black cowboy boots.

The pilot opened the hatch, letting an ungodly combination of the heat and humidity roar into the cabin.

"Welcome to Texas," he said.

I knew in that moment that I never wanted to live in Texas. If this was what Texas was like in June, I wasn't interested in seeing July or August.

The driver and our copilot took care of transferring our luggage from plane to vehicle while Mel and I settled into the backseat of the Suburban and reveled in air-conditioned comfort.

"I hope you know where you're going," I said jokingly to the driver when he got behind the wheel. "I have no idea."

"Yes, sir," he said. "I'm glad your plane was on time. Miss Hannah usually don't make it past seven o'clock or so. Sad to say, she's doing poorly. It's breaking Miss Sally's heart."

I had thought Sally would hire a local shuttle service to come to the airport to do the ferrying honors. Instead, she had sent someone who was clearly a long-time family retainer. When we pulled into the driveway on Shadow Bend Avenue, we saw that the house was huge. My first thought was that we were pulling up to a hotel rather than a private residence. The driver popped the back hatch and then hopped out onto the baking driveway.

Mel reached over and squeezed my hand. "Are you all right?" she asked.

"It's a little bigger than I anticipated," I said.

The driver opened the car door and helped us out. Once I was upright, I needed to stand still for a moment or two to let my knees straighten out. "Has Mrs. Mathers lived here long?" I asked.

"Long as I can remember, that's for sure," the driver said, handing Mel out of the vehicle as well.

While he was grappling with the luggage, a woman came flying out the door to greet us. She was blond with big hair and dressed like she was about to hit the roundup trail, complete with jeans and boots. This was someone who, like

Julie Hatcher, knew her way around horses.

"You must be Sally," I said.

"Oh my goodness!" she exclaimed, launching herself at me and grabbing hold of my neck. "Bless my soul if you don't look just like your daddy."

Of all the words I never expected to hear in my lifetime, those were at the very top of the list.

"This is my wife, Melissa Soames," I said.

"People call me Mel," Mel said, extending her hand. Sally Mathers ignored the proffered hand and wrapped Mel in a bear-hug embrace.

"Welcome, welcome, welcome!" Sally gushed. "I just can't believe you're really and truly here. Please, do come in."

She ushered us into a grand foyer that made the one in the Washington State governor's mansion look like a cheap reproduction.

"Bobby, please take their luggage up to their room," Sally said. "You've had a long trip. If you want to freshen up first, that would be fine, but I really want to take you to meet Mama. She usually has good spells late in the afternoons like this, but they don't last long. And I haven't told her you were coming. First I was afraid it might not happen, then I decided I wanted it to be a surprise."

"You're sure it won't be too much for her?" I asked.

"Oh, no," Sally said. "Mama's tough as nails."

Mel took her purse and ducked into a powder room just off the front entry. She came out with her lipstick refreshed and her hair combed, which, in my opinion, was more than she needed to do. Then Sally led us through the house. The artwork on the walls had names I recognized from my college humanities class. It made me smile to think that my first thought—and Ralph Ames's thought as well—was that Sally Mathers was running some kind of game in hopes of scamming me out of some money. Not.

Hallways fed off one another, as though the house had been enlarged over the years simply by adding another section. Finally, at the end of the last one, Sally opened the door on an enormous bedroom. It was unrelentingly pink. There were froths of pink curtains at the windows and a cloud of pink material crowning the four-poster bed. There seemed to be a whole houseful of furniture arranged in the spacious room: a flowered sofa along with several matching easy chairs and several pieces of high-gloss cherry furniture—coffee tables, end tables, and dressers.

A tiny white-haired woman lay in the middle of the bed, propped up by a mound of pillows and wearing a pair of amazingly thick glasses. She looked downright ancient.

"No company, Sally," Hannah Greenwald grumbled disapprovingly. "I told you very clearly that I was too tired for any more company today."

"He's come a long way to see you, Mama," Sally said respectfully. "This is Mr. Beaumont."

"Sure he is!" Hannah exclaimed. "Beaumont—that's not a fit name for a chicken. And if he's Mr. Beaumont, then I'm Miss Dallas."

Sally shot me a sympathetic glance, but I deserved it. After all, hadn't I made fun of Ronald Darrington Miller?

"Yes, ma'am," I said, suppressing a chuckle. "I suppose it is a silly name. Some might even call it pretentious."

That's all I said—those few words, but suddenly there was a sea change in that appallingly pink room.

"You come closer, young man," Hannah ordered. "Let me get a look at you."

I stepped forward. She reached out a bony hand and pulled me to her, peering up at me, her eyes huge behind those ungodly glasses. She studied me for a long time. Then she dropped my hand.

"There you have it," she said. "I guess I'm done."

"Mama . . ." Sally began.

"Yes, I'm dead already, and Saint Peter has sent Hank to take me through the Pearly Gates. Believe me, I'm ready."

"You're not dead," Sally scolded. "This is your brother's son, Jonas. He and his wife, Melissa, have come here all the way from Washington just to see you."

Hannah squinted at her daughter. "Are you sure? Are you just playing a trick on me?"

"I'm sure, Mama," Sally said. "It's no trick."

With that, Hannah Mencken Greenwald, the beloved aunt I never knew I had, broke down and sobbed like a baby. And I admit it—so did I.

Hannah stopped crying abruptly and looked at Sally. "All right then," she said. "Tomorrow first thing, you get Leroy over here. Tell him I need to change my will."

"Yes, Mama," Sally said. "I'll call him as soon as his office opens up in the morning."

Hannah frowned. "What year is it again?" she asked.

"It's 2009, Mama," Sally said. "June."

"All right then," Hannah said. "You-all had better hope I die this year or next. After that, the damned estate taxes are going to be sky-high, and I don't want you to give Uncle Sam one more nickel of my money than you have to."

I guess there wasn't much question about Hannah Mencken Greenwald being of sound mind.

CHAPTER 29

After that initial audience with Hannah, Sally took us to our room. It was upstairs. I had seen Bobby bounding up that carved double stair loaded down with our luggage, and I was dreading having to make that long climb under my own steam. To my immense relief, however, I discovered the house had a tiny elevator tucked invisibly into the wall behind the same stairway.

Our luggage had been taken to our room and unpacked. I was surprised to see my tux and one of Mel's silvery, shimmery gowns laid out on the bed.

"I thought so," Mel said. "We're expected to dress for dinner."

I spent the rest of the evening being very glad that I had turned the packing over to Mel instead of doing it myself.

Cocktails were served before dinner. Wine was served with dinner. After I had a word with the server, my glass of delightfully sweetened iced tea never made it below the halfway mark, and the food that was served easily outstripped anything we'd seen in the governor's mansion.

When dinner finally ended that night, somewhere on the far side of ten o'clock, I was glad to ride the elevator back upstairs and fall into bed.

We stayed for three days. When Hannah was up to it, I spent several hours of each day sitting in one of the flowery chairs in her room, chatting with Miss Dallas, as I teasingly called her. She wanted to know about my life, my kids, my work, my everything. In exchange, she told me stories about my father, her beloved Hank—her fun-loving, mischievous, sorely missed older brother. Hannah and I were like two parched travelers wandering in the desert. The stories we told back and forth slaked our thirst. And knowing my history—my family's history—made me feel whole.

While I talked to Hannah, Mel plied Sally for information. Each night, after dinner ended, we'd retreat to our room and compare notes. Painful as it is for me to admit it, that's pretty much all we did in that room—dress and talk and sleep.

Tuesday morning we packed our bags. Actually, Mel packed and I supervised. While we were in the breakfast room, Bobby brought the luggage downstairs. By ten o'clock we were ready to head for the airport.

Before we left, I made my way once more through the labyrinth of hallways to Hannah's gaily pink room. She was sitting up in bed, wearing a frothy pink robe that matched the decor. She was wearing powder and lipstick and a carefully combed wig.

"You've come to say good-bye," she said accusingly.

"Yes, Miss Dallas. I'm afraid I have."

Tears welled up in her eyes as she pulled me into a perfume-drenched hug. "I'm going to miss you," she declared. "But then I've missed you all your life. This way, though, I'm gonna die happy."

There was still a lump in my throat when I got back to the foyer.

Bobby took us to the airport and loaded our bags into the plane's luggage hold. It was hot as blue blazes. Even though they had a fan on in the plane while it waited on the ground, it was a huge relief when the engines came on and with them the real air-conditioning.

The plane took off, gaining altitude far faster than a lumbering commercial plane.

"Well," Mel said when we finally leveled off. "What do you think?"

"It was unbelievable," I said. "I can't think of anything that would make my life more complete."

"I can," she said.

"What?"

She picked up her purse—her amazing purse—and reached inside it. She fumbled around, found a business card, and handed it to me.

"Dr. Merritt Auld, Orthopedic Surgeon." Along with those words was a whole series of Seattle-area phone numbers.

"What's this?" I asked.

"Just what it says. Dr. Bliss tells me that when it comes to knee surgery, this guy is the best in the business. He already sent over your latest X rays. You have an appointment to see Dr. Auld tomorrow morning at ten o'clock for an initial consultation."

"Come on," I objected. "My knees aren't that bad."

"Yes, they are," she said.

"I don't need to have them fixed. I'm fine."

"Maybe you're fine, but I'm not. *I* need to have your knees in working order," Mel added forcefully. "If you won't have them fixed for you, then how about having them fixed for me?"

How could I argue with that?

"Right you are," I said. "Tomorrow morning, ten o'clock."